Contents

Foreword

by John Banville

Voyage au bout de la nuit, or *Journey to the End of the Night*, first published in 1932, is one of the greatest novels of the twentieth century. It is also the finest novel ever written by a far-right sympathizer, as its author was retrospectively labelled by critics after the War. Other examples of novels by political extremists of the right – *On the Marble Cliffs* by Ernst Jünger, or Curzio Malaparte's *Kaputt* – are at the least interesting, but Céline's exuberantly misanthropic masterpiece – which does not declare any political affiliation or entertain anti-Semitic ideas – is unique as a revolutionary work of art, and had a profound influence on writers as disparate as Samuel Beckett and William S. Burroughs, Jean Genet and Günter Grass. It could be said that without Céline there would have been no Henry Miller, no Jack Kerouac, no Charles Bukowski, no Beat poets.

Louis-Ferdinand Auguste Destouches – his grandmother's first name was Céline, hence the pseudonym – was born in 1894 in the Paris suburb of Courbevoie. His father worked as an insurance clerk and his mother was a lace-maker. In later years he liked to claim that he had spent a miserable childhood with his constantly warring parents, but this seems to have been another of his many exaggerations and embellishments, for a friend claimed that the couple lived together in comparative tranquillity. Ferdinand was barely into his teens when he went to work as a messenger boy, but his much-maligned parents must have had high ambitions for him, since they sent him to live for a year in Germany and another year in England, in order that he should learn a couple of useful languages. His early education was largely self-administered, and he seems from the start to have wanted to be a doctor.

First, however, at the age of eighteen, he enlisted in the French army, and two years later found himself fighting in the Great War. Within weeks of the opening of hostilities he was wounded in the arm while attempting to deliver a dispatch under heavy German fire, a piece of bravery – or stupidity, as the older and wiser Destouches would surely have said – for which he was awarded a military medal and which even brought him a brief moment of fame. The injury later led to his discharge from the army. He had a job for a while in London, where he got married – a union that was never registered with the French authorities – then went to Africa, to work for a French trading company in the Cameroons. Having returned to France, he was sent by, remarkably, the Rockefeller Foundation to Brittany to help in the fight against tuberculosis in the region.

By the early 1920s he was studying medicine in Rennes and was married, this time officially, to the daughter of the director of the medical school there. The couple had a daughter, Colette. However, in 1925 Céline abandoned his wife and child and got a job with the League of Nations and travelled extensively in Europe, Africa and America – his experiences studying working conditions at the Ford factory in Detroit left a lasting impression, and form the background to one of the most powerful sections in *Journey to the End of the Night*. Returning to France he opened a medical practice in a Paris suburb, specializing in obstetrics. Later he gave up the practice to work in a public dispensary, largely tending the poor.

These are the facts that were to be embellished, exaggerated and twisted into fantasy in his first and greatest novel. Céline was an autobiographical writer of a special kind. To say that he was cavalier with the facts would be an understatement. *Journey* is a dream version of his life. "Things as they are / Are changed upon the blue guitar," Wallace Stevens writes, and Céline's guitar was tuned to a mode that had not been heard since the days of Rabelais, François Villon and Jonathan Swift. He described himself as a comic lyricist, but while there is deep comedy and high lyricism in *Journey*, the savagery of its vision puts its author in the company of the Greek tragedians.

Journey is usually thought of as a First World War novel, but in fact the opening wartime sequence takes up only a fraction of the narrative. War for Céline is a kind of murderous circus performance. "Could I, I thought," says his protagonist, Bardamu, "be the last coward on earth? How terrifying!... All alone with two million stark-raving heroic madmen, armed to the eyeballs? […] You can be a virgin in horror the same as in sex." Caught up in this murderous roundabout, Bardamu quickly loses his innocence and learns the essential lesson: "Men are the thing to be afraid of, always, men and nothing else." And what is a man? "You know [...] the trick they play on tramps in the country? They stuff an old wallet with putrid chicken innards. Well, take it from me, a man is just like that, except that he's fatter and hungrier and can move around, and inside there's a dream."

The unexpected gleam of light at the end of that disgusted simile is typical of Céline's style. *Journey* may look like a rambunctious hotchpotch thrown together by a misanthrope in a hurry, but in fact the book is very carefully, indeed beautifully crafted. At intervals in Bardamu's fierce fight with the world the cannon smoke clears and we are given a glimpse of another landscape, where peace and beauty are possible:

> Between two lines of roses, the avenue, rising gently, led to the fountains. Outside the kiosk the soda-water lady seemed to be slowly gathering the evening shadows around her skirt. Further on, along the side paths, great cubes and rectangles of dark-coloured canvas were flapping, carnival booths, which the war had taken by surprise and suddenly filled with silence.

Bardamu's frenetic adventures take him from the battle front to a convalescent home for shattered psyches, on to a Conradian heart of darkness in colonial West Africa – "The natives, by and large, had to be driven to work with clubs – they preserved that much dignity – whereas the whites, perfected by public education, worked of their own free will" – where he is sold as a galley slave aboard a ship that takes him to New York, "a standing city", as he says in wonderment. He goes on to Detroit, where he is confronted with the horror of the assembly line – "We ourselves became machines, our flesh trembled in the furious din…" – until at last he escapes the New World nightmare and returns to France, finishes his medical studies and sets up as a doctor in the fictional suburb of Rancy, working among the poor, the maimed, the helpless and the hopeless.

Before and during the Second World War Céline disgraced himself by writing a series of rancidly anti-Semitic pamphlets. After the defeat of the Nazis in 1945 he fled first to Germany and then to Denmark. He was branded a collaborator and was sentenced to prison *in absentia*, although later he was granted amnesty and returned to live in France in

1951. He died of an aneurysm in 1961, broken in spirit and reputation, but still defiant. It was a sad and ugly end to the life of a great literary artist. His political enormities will not be forgotten, but neither will *Journey to the End of the Night*, his legacy and his masterpiece. It is a very great work, which opened an entirely new chapter in fiction-writing. Céline's personal and artistic honesty are of a piece. If he made mistakes, grievous mistakes, in his life, as a novelist he remained true to himself and to his art.

– John Banville, 2012

Introduction

by André Derval

The Heart of My Sensibility

In 1949, in exile in Denmark, Céline wrote in a preface to the first post-Second World War edition of *Journey to the End of the Night*: "It's for *Journey* that they're after me! Under the axe I'll bellow it! Between 'them' and me it's to the finish! To the guts! Too foul to talk about... pissed with Mystique! What a business! (...) The world of intentions amuses me... used to amuse me... not any more.

"If I weren't under such pressure, such duress, I'd suppress the whole lot... especially *Journey*... Of all my books it's the only really vicious one... That's right... The heart of my sensibility..." Perfectly aware that his reputation as an anti-Semitic writer is well established, Céline weighs the degree of provocation in his sentences. *Journey to the End of the Night* was an enormous commercial success in the early 1930s, widely acclaimed by critics, despite or because of its excesses. A novel which shook up political, social and literary convention, it was in fact co-opted by the left-wing intelligentsia, the very same one which condemned it after the publication of his political writings from 1936 onwards: *Mea culpa*, an anti-communist pamphlet written when he returned from the USSR, followed by texts openly in line with racist, far-right ideology, even pro-Hitlerian: *Trifles for a Massacre* (1937), *The School for Corpses* (1938) and *A Fine Mess* (1941). However, the 1949 preface is not only designed to play with paradox, to divert attention and opprobrium, in a grotesque manner, towards the work which brought him so much recognition and notoriety: there is undoubtedly genuine sincerity on the part of the author when he declares that they've been after him ever since *Journey*. And it is to this, to the novel's inveterate tendency to provoke countless scandals of varying degrees, that Céline is alluding.

A monumental fresco of the errings of the capitalist West at the start of the twentieth century, *Journey to the End of the Night* begins with the mass slaughter of the First World War, horrifying and absurd. This first part of the book, in which the libertarian inspiration is obvious, describes the various attempts of individuals, be they the "hero" Bardamu or his "negative double" Robinson, to escape from the mechanisms of destruction which have been triggered to destroy them. A continuation of *Under Fire* by Henri Barbusse and fitting in with the pacifist novels of the period, *Journey* goes beyond them in the implacable way it denounces war, the system that produces it and the psychologies which have made it possible and which it has inspired, paternalist or feminine, by the revelation of the underlying death instinct (a notion found in readings of Freud). Surrounded by horror, as much intellectual and moral as physical, the refractory individual has no way out apart from voluntary mutilation, execution for desertion or simulation, or insanity.

Second stage of the *Journey*, after a terrifying sea passage: Africa and colonial exploitation, which the narrator describes without concession, without compassion, although this section contains one of the rare passages that was dismissed as sentimental by the less agreeable critics: Alcide's account of the education of his niece in metropolitan France. Following that of the soldiers bogged down in senseless massacres, the description of the miserable condition of the natives, prey to the absurd inhumanity of the system, calls, by its very contiguity, for a general reflection on a world submitted to the laws of commerce and the arbitrary, a world resembling a universal prison. The conclusion of Bardamu's odyssey: the discovery of America, the model of a radiant future, of capitalist industrialization, which completes the grinding down of the individuals' last remaining strength and illusions. The "other world" having no hope to offer, best to return to "one's ghosts", with whom several scores still have to be settled: a career as a doctor to the poor awaits Bardamu, paving the way for some final explorations of the contemporary body and soul, in Paris, the outskirts, the suburbs and the provinces. Between despair and the social fantasy style used by writers such as Pierre Mac Orlan, the actors and settings of the underbelly of the Roaring Twenties march out, in a tragic, grotesque, obscene, sordid and grimy procession: patients, doctors, concierges, prostitutes, hoteliers, pensioners, outcasts and outsiders struggle and converge towards the final tragedy, giving a final touch to the denunciation of the sentimentality in which 1920s France was swimming, like a conjuration in response to the images of the recent worldwide carnage.

It can be easily understood why this book had the effect of a veritable boulder in the pond of convention which sought to cover up the realities of the experience of millions of men with a veil of modesty, a challenge to the official hypocrisies that were rewriting history to their own advantage. Hence an enormous success with readers, going beyond the usual scope for a literary best-seller to attain a political dimension – a reputedly non-reading public purchased the book and debated its ideas, assisted by the critics, who were not to be outdone by the author's bold declarations. In addition to these printed scandals, one should mention the fact that Céline did not win the Prix Goncourt that year, even though he was virtually guaranteed to do so. Press revelations of the covert details of the affair – the alleged pressure placed on the juries by Hachette, the distributor of the eventual winner's publishing company, Gallimard – even led to court cases and costly fines, which brought one newspaper to bankruptcy.

A first novel by an unknown author, writing under a pseudonym, who turned out to be a doctor from the Parisian suburbs, *Journey to the End of the Night* for a long time brought, with its commercial success, another scandal to bear on Céline: that of having escaped from the rule of the author of a single successful book, that status which some have for a number of years attempted to ascribe to him, with certain critics repeating after each new publication that his oeuvre was unreadable except for *Journey*, etc.

The overlap between the social position of the protagonist of *Journey* and that of Doctor Destouches naturally led to the question of how much autobiography one should read into it: clearly this *Journey* was not entirely *imaginary*, contrary to what was announced in the prefatory disclaimer. Various connections were immediately made with the episodes of the book: Louis Destouches was a First World War veteran, also injured and decorated; he spent time in Africa and the United States. This closeness between the autobiographical material and the fictional treatment was to be maintained and even increased throughout his subsequent works. As early as the second novel *Death on Credit*, the narrator takes care to mention that he is the author of *Journey*, that he practises medicine in the suburbs and that he will recreate the Belle Époque of his childhood in the heart of Paris. The mixed critical reception of *Death on Credit* – the completion of which had demanded considerable effort on Céline's part – was one of the reasons for his growing hostility towards journalists and intellectuals, and he adopted various prejudices common in far-right circles. Having left, according to his own claims, for Soviet Russia to spend his royalties, he was appalled on his return and published a short text, *Mea culpa*, lambasting the Communist regime, to which he added a revised version of his medical thesis on the tragic life of Semmelweis, who championed the use of antiseptic procedures in the field of obstetrics. The political pamphlets, mentioned above, would soon follow, of which the first, *Trifles for a Massacre*, helped him to find renewed commercial success. Close to collaborationist circles, without ever accepting any official duties or honours, he demonstrated his respect for the hardliners in various open letters to extremist newspapers. Shortly before the Liberation he published a novel set in London in 1916, *Guignol's Band*, on which he had been working since 1940 – it is interesting to note that it contains at least two Jewish characters whose portrayal, racial stereotyping notwithstanding, demonstrates some undeniable sympathy on the part of the narrator. Aware of the dangers surrounding him – members of the Resistance movement having explicitly named him as a traitor – Céline escaped to Germany in June 1944, along with his wife, the dancer Lucette Almanzor, and his cat Bébert, in the hope of reaching Denmark – they were soon joined by their friend the actor Robert Le Vigan, who was compromised by his work for Radio-Paris, which served German propaganda.

From this journey through Nazi Germany under Allied bombing, in places such as Baden-Baden, Berlin and Sigmaringen (to where the Pétain government had withdrawn), Céline would source the material for his final novels. Finding refuge in Denmark, he lived in hiding there for around nine months before being arrested following an extradition request by the French authorities: he would remain in captivity in prison and hospital until June 1947, then in exile until July 1951, when he benefited from an amnesty which applied to veterans with war injuries. On his return to France he published new works of fiction, stipulating his categorical opposition to any reissue of his political writings in his contract with his new publisher. *Fable for Another Time* and *Normance* appeared amid near-universal indifference: only marginal publications, anarchist or far-right, mentioned them. It must be said that Céline did everything to disorientate the reader (and insisted that his publisher generate no publicity for them): his style had been considerably transformed, becoming a complete breakdown of written form, by a narration which made use of a large palette of verbal resources, brutally and continually switching register, lexical field and subject. The latter of which in the second opus is principally and overwhelmingly (the duration of reading being considerably longer than that of the story being told) a night in Montmartre under English bombing. Returning to a more accessible writing style, Céline published, in 1957, the first volume describing the tribulations he encountered in the debris of the Third Reich, *Castle to Castle*, which related the Sigmaringen episode and did not fail to trouble the conscience of 1950s France, which was taking great care to maintain its image as the inheritor of Resistance values. A new series of scandals soon followed, with Céline being vociferously taken to task by former collaborators and replying by provocative one-upmanship which went as far as television studios. His works came out of the isolation they had been confined to for a decade; in 1960 *North* appeared, which retold the conditions of his supervised residence near Berlin (this book resulted in a lawsuit against his publisher, this time brought about by Germans). Céline died on 1st July 1961 of a stroke; he had just finished *Rigadoon*, a novel describing his train journeys through a Germany in flames, which would be published in 1969.

"Life then, I hold it back, in my two hands, with all that I know about it, all that can be guessed at, all that you should have seen, all that you have read, of the past, the present, not too much of the future (nothing makes you stray like the future), all that you should have known, the women you've kissed, all that you've exposed; people, what they didn't know you knew, what they've done to you; the failed health, spent pleasures, faint tunes dispersing, the tiny morsel of life they still conceal, and the secret of the cell buried deep in the kidney, the one that only wants to function for forty-eight hours, and no more, and will allow the first albumin to pass on its return to God... Yes... Yes... You understand me? You follow me? The deformed leg of the young cousin must also hold on to it, folded back, and the ship with sails so open to too many winds, which never ceases to circle the globe with its cargo in old dollars?... You must tie it to your dream..."

This extract from a postface to *Journey to the End of the Night*, 'Let Me Explain', published in 1933, reminds us of the first issues of Céline's foray into literature. Themes connected to biology irresistibly surface: they would lead their author to his racist stances at the end of the 1930s. The struggle against decomposition, against the intrinsic corruption of matter (the descriptions of mud are not miles away from those of the late-nineteenth-century decadent writers), is at the heart of the issues addressed by Céline's novels, a kind of redemption stemming from the effort of the flesh (or the meat, as the author would say) to free itself from gravity, in a graceful and poignant momentum, the emblematic figure of which is naturally the dancer. Obscenity, true obscenity, resides in the words plastered over the emotion. In an interview with the journalist Merry Bromberger published on 8th December 1932, Céline takes great care to point out, with this flair for the literary that he would never abandon: "Céline makes Bardamu rave, who says what he knows about Robinson. It shouldn't be seen as slices of life, but as a delirium... The content of the story? No one has understood it. Neither my publisher nor the critics, nor anyone. Neither have you! Here it is! It's the love we still dare to speak of in this hell, as if it were possible to compose quatrains in an abattoir!"

A meteorite partly originating in a "lyrical" tradition not widely represented in France, in which the author evokes François Villon, Shakespeare, André Chénier, sometimes Rabelais and Lamennais, Céline's literary project did however succeed in shaking up French literature, at the forefront of which he now features.

– André Derval, 2010

Author's Preface to the 1952 Gallimard Edition

Hey, they're putting *Journey* on the rails again.

What a feeling it gives me.

A lot of things have happened in fourteen years...

If I weren't under so much pressure, forced to earn my living, I can tell you right now, I'd suppress the whole thing, I wouldn't let a single line through.

Everything gets taken the wrong way. I've been the cause of too much evil.

Just think of all the deaths, the hatreds around me... the treachery... the sewer it adds up to... the monsters...

Oh, you've got to be blind and deaf!

You'll say: but it's not *Journey*! It's your crimes that are killing you, *Journey* has nothing to do with it. You yourself have been your ruin! Your *Bagatelles*! Your abominable lingo! Your imaging, clowning villainy! The law's clutching you, strangling you? Hell, what are you complaining about? You jerk!

Oh, many thanks! Many thanks! I'm raging! Fuming! Panting! With hatred! Hypocrites! Jugheads! You can't fool me! It's for *Journey* that they're after me! Under the axe I'll bellow it! Between "them" and me it's to the finish! To the guts! Too foul to talk about... pissed with Mystique! What a business!

If I weren't under pressure, forced to earn my living, I'm telling you right now, I'd suppress the whole lot. A homage I paid to jackals!... That's right!... A free gift... A tip... I threw my luck away... in '36... gave it to the executioners' wives! The prosecutors! The undertakers! One two three admirable books to cut my throat with! And listen to my groans! I made them a present! I was charitable, that's all!

The world of intentions amuses me... used to amuse me... not any more.

If I weren't under such pressure, such duress, I'd suppress the whole lot... especially *Journey*... Of all my books it's the only really vicious one... That's right... The heart of my sensibility...

It'll all start over again. The Sarabbath!* You'll hear a whistling from up above, from far away, from places without names: words, orders...

You'll get an eyeful of their machinations!... You'll come and tell me about it...

Oh, don't imagine that I'm playing! I've stopped playing... I've even stopped being amiable.

If I weren't under duress, as though standing with my back to something... I'd suppress the whole lot.

– Louis-Ferdinand Céline, 1952

*Journey to the End
of the Night*

To Elisabeth Craig

Our life is a journey
Through winter and night,
We look for our way
In a sky without light.

(*Song of the Swiss Guards*, 1793)

Travel is useful, it exercises the imagination. All the rest is disappointment and fatigue. Our journey is entirely imaginary. That is its strength.

It goes from life to death. People, animals, cities, things, all are imagined. It's a novel, just a fictitious narrative. Littré* says so, and he's never wrong.

And besides, in the first place, anyone can do as much. You just have to close your eyes.

It's on the other side of life.

Here's how it started. I'd never said a word. Not one word. It was Arthur Ganate* that made me speak up. Arthur was a friend from med school. So we meet on the Place Clichy. It was after breakfast. He wants to talk to me. I listen. "Not out here!" he says. "Let's go in!" We go in. And there we were. "This terrace," he says, "is for jerks! Come on over there!" Then we see that there's not a soul in the street, because of the heat; no cars, nothing. Same when it's very cold, not a soul in the street; I remember now, it was he who had said one time: "The people in Paris always look busy, when all they actually do is roam around from morning to night; it's obvious, because when the weather isn't right for walking around, when it's too cold or too hot, you don't see them any more; they're all indoors, drinking their *cafés crème* or their beers. And that's the truth! The century of speed, they call it! Where? Great changes, they say! For instance? In truth nothing has changed. They go on admiring themselves, that's all. And that's not new either. Words. Even the words haven't changed much! Two or three little ones, here and there..." Pleased at having proclaimed these useful truths, we sat looking at the ladies in the café.

After a while the conversation turned to President Poincaré,* who was due to inaugurate a small-dog show that same morning, and that led to *Le Temps*,* where I'd read about it. Arthur Ganate starts kidding me about *Le Temps*. "What a paper!" he says. "When it comes to defending the French race, it hasn't its equal!" And quick to show I'm well informed, I fire back: "The French race can do with some defending, seeing as it doesn't exist!"

"Oh yes, it does!" he says. "And a fine race it is! The finest in the world, and anybody who says different is a yellow dog!" And he starts slanging me. Naturally I stuck to my guns.

"It's not true! What you call a race is nothing but a collection of riff-raff like me, bleary-eyed, flea-bitten, chilled to the bone. They came from the four corners of the earth, driven by hunger, plague, tumours and the cold, and stopped here. They couldn't go any further because of the ocean. That's France, that's the French people."

"Bardamu," he says very gravely and a bit sadly, "our forefathers were as good as we are, don't speak ill of them!..."

"You're right, Arthur, there you're right! Hateful and spineless, raped and robbed, mangled and witless, they were as good as we are, you can say that again! We never change! Neither our socks nor our masters nor our opinions, or we're so slow about it that it's no use. We were born loyal, and that's what killed us! Soldiers free of charge, heroes for everyone else, talking monkeys, tortured words, we are the minions of King Misery. He's our lord and master! When we misbehave, he tightens his grip... his fingers are around our neck, that makes it hard to talk, got to be careful if we want to eat... For nothing at all he'll choke you... It's not a life..."

"There's love, Bardamu!"

"Arthur," I tell him, "love is the infinite placed within the reach of poodles. I have my dignity!"

"You do, do you? You're an anarchist, that's what you are!"

A wise guy, as you see, with only the most advanced opinions.

"That's right, you windbag, I'm an anarchist! And to prove it, I've written a kind of prayer of social vengeance, it'll bowl you over: *The Golden Wings*! That's the title!" And so I recite:

"A God who counts minutes and pennies, a desperate sensual God, who grunts like a pig. A pig with golden wings, who falls and falls, always belly side up, ready for caresses, that's him, our master. Come, kiss me!"

"Your little piece doesn't hold water," he says. "I'm for the established order, and I'm not interested in politics. What's more, the day my country asks me to shed my blood, it'll find me ready, and no slacker." That's what he said.

It so happened that the war was creeping up on us without our knowing it, and something was wrong with my wits. That short but animated discussion had tired me out. Besides, I was upset because the waiter had sort of called me a piker on account of the tip. Well, in the end Arthur and I made up. Completely. We agreed about almost everything.

"It's true," I said, trying to be conciliatory. "All in all, you're right. But the fact is we're all sitting in a big galley, pulling at the oars with all our might. You can't tell me different!... Sitting on nails and pulling like mad! And what do we get for it? Nothing! Thrashings and misery, hard words and hard knocks. We're workers, they say. Work, they call it! That's the crummiest part of the whole business. We're down in the hold, heaving and panting, stinking and sweating our balls off, and – meanwhile! – up on deck in the fresh air, what do you see? Our masters having a fine time with beautiful pink and perfumed women on their laps. They send for us, we're brought up on deck. They put on their top hats and give us a big spiel like as follows: 'You no-good swine! We're at war! Those stinkers in Country No. 2! We're going to board them and cut their livers out! Let's go! Let's go! We've got everything we need on board! All together now! Let's hear you shout so the deck trembles: "Long live Country No. 1!" So you'll be heard for miles around. The man that shouts the loudest will get a medal and a lollipop! Let's go! And if there's anybody that doesn't want to be killed on the sea, he can go and get killed on land, it's even quicker!'"

"That's the way it is exactly," said Arthur, suddenly willing to listen to reason.

But just then, who should come marching past the café where we're sitting but a regiment with the colonel up front on his horse, looking nice and friendly, a fine figure of a man! Enthusiasm lifted me to my feet.

"I'll just go see if that's the way it is!" I sing out to Arthur, and off I go to enlist, on the double.

"Ferdinand!" he yells back. "Don't be an arse!" I suppose he was nettled by the effect my heroism was having on the people all around us.

It kind of hurt my feelings the way he was taking it, but that didn't stop me. I fell right in. "Here I am!" I say to myself. "And here I stay!"

I just had time to call out to Arthur: "All right, you jerk, we'll see" – before we turned the corner. And there I was with the regiment, marching behind the colonel and his band. That's exactly how it happened.

We marched a long time. There were streets and more streets, and they were all crowded with civilians and their wives, cheering us on, bombarding us with flowers from café terraces, railway stations, crowded churches. You never saw so many patriots in all your life! And then there were fewer patriots... It started to rain, and then there were still fewer and fewer, and not a single cheer, not one.

Pretty soon there was nobody but us, we were all alone. Row after row. The music had stopped. "Come to think of it," I said to myself, when I saw what was what, "this is no fun any more! I'd better try something else!" I was about to clear out. Too late! They'd quietly shut the gate behind us civilians. We were caught like rats.

* * *

When you're in, you're in. They put us on horseback, and after we'd been on horseback for two months, they put us back on our feet. Maybe because of the expense. Anyway, one morning the colonel was looking for his horse, his orderly had made off with it, nobody knew where to, probably some quiet spot that bullets couldn't get to as easily as the middle of the road. Because that was exactly where the colonel and I had finally stationed ourselves, with me holding his orderly book while he wrote out his orders.

Down the road, way in the distance, as far as we could see, there were two black dots, plunk in the middle like us, but they were two Germans and they'd been busy shooting for the last fifteen or twenty minutes.

Maybe our colonel knew why they were shooting, maybe the Germans knew, but I, so help me, hadn't the vaguest idea. As far back as I could search my memory, I hadn't done a thing to the Germans, I'd always treated them friendly and polite. I knew the Germans pretty well, I'd even gone to school in their country when I was little, near Hanover. I'd spoken their language. A bunch of loud-mouthed little halfwits, that's what they were, with pale, furtive eyes like wolves; we'd go out to the woods together after school to feel the girls up, or we'd fire popguns or pistols you could buy for four marks. And we drank sugary beer together. But from that to shooting at us right in the middle of the road, without so much as a word of introduction, was a long way, a very long way. If you asked me, they were going too far.

This war, in fact, made no sense at all. It couldn't go on.

Had something weird got into these people? Something I didn't feel at all? I suppose I hadn't noticed it...

Anyway, my feelings towards them hadn't changed. In spite of everything, I'd have liked to understand their brutality, but what I wanted still more, enormously, with all my heart, was to get out of there, because suddenly the whole business looked to me like a great big mistake.

"In a mess like this," I said to myself, "there's nothing to be done, all you can do is clear out..."

Over our heads, two millimetres, maybe one millimetre from our temples, those long tempting lines of steel that bullets make when they're out to kill you were whistling through the hot summer air.

I'd never felt so useless as I did amid all those bullets in the sunlight. A vast and universal mockery.

I was only twenty at the time. Deserted farms in the distance, empty wide-open churches, as if the peasants had all gone out for the day to attend a fair at the other end of the county, leaving everything they owned with us for safekeeping, their countryside, their carts with the shafts pointing in the air, their fields, their barnyards, the road, the trees, even the cows, a chained dog, the works. Leaving us free to do as we pleased while they were gone. Nice of them, in a way. "Still," I said to myself, "if they hadn't gone somewhere else, if there were still somebody here, I'm sure we wouldn't be behaving so badly! So disgustingly! We wouldn't dare in front of them!" But there wasn't a soul to watch us! Nobody but us, like newly-weds that start messing around when all the people have gone home.

And another thought I had (behind a tree) was that I wished Déroulède* – the one I'd heard so much about – had been there to describe his reactions when a bullet tore open his guts.

Those Germans squatting on the road, shooting so obstinately, were rotten shots, but they seemed to have ammunition to burn, whole warehouses full, it looked to me. Nobody could say this war was over! I have to hand it to the colonel, his bravery was remarkable! He roamed around in the middle of the road, up and down and back and forth in the midst of the bullets as calmly as if he'd been waiting for a friend on a station platform, except just a tiny bit impatient.

One thing I'd better tell you right away, I've never been able to stomach the country, I've always found it dreary, those endless fields of mud, those houses where nobody's ever home, those roads that don't go anywhere. And if to all that you add a war, it's completely unbearable. A sudden wind had come up on both sides of the road, the clattering leaves of the poplars mingled with the sharp crackling sounds aimed at us from down the road. Those unknown soldiers missed us every time, but they spun a thousand deaths around us, so close they seemed to clothe us. I was afraid to move.

That colonel, I could see, was a monster! Now I knew it for sure, he was worse than a dog, he couldn't conceive of his own death. At the

11

same time I realized that there must be plenty of brave men like him in our army, and just as many no doubt in the army facing us. How many, I wondered. One or two million, say several millions in all? The thought turned my fear to panic. With such people this infernal lunacy could go on for ever... Why would they stop? Never had the world seemed so implacably doomed.

Could I, I thought, be the last coward on earth? How terrifying!... All alone with two million stark-raving heroic madmen, armed to the eyeballs? With and without helmets, without horses, on motorcycles, bellowing, in cars, screeching, shooting, plotting, flying, kneeling, digging, taking cover, bounding over trails, sputtering, shut up on earth as if it were a loony bin, ready to demolish everything on it, Germany, France, whole continents, everything that breathes, destroy, destroy, madder than mad dogs, worshipping their madness (which dogs don't), a hundred, a thousand times madder than a thousand dogs, and a lot more vicious! A pretty mess we were in! No doubt about it, this crusade I'd let myself in for was the apocalypse.

You can be a virgin in horror the same as in sex. How, when I left the Place Clichy, could I have imagined such horror? Who could have suspected, before getting really into the war, all the ingredients that go to make up the rotten, heroic, good-for-nothing soul of man? And there I was, caught up in a mass flight into collective murder, into the fiery furnace... Something had come up from the depths, and this is what happened.

The colonel was still as cool as a cucumber, I watched him as he stood on the embankment, taking little messages sent by the general, reading them without haste as the bullets flew all around him, and tearing them into little pieces. Did none of those messages include an order to put an immediate stop to this abomination? Did no top brass tell him there had been a misunderstanding? A horrible mistake? A misdeal? That somebody'd got it all wrong, that the plan had been for manoeuvres, a sham battle, not a massacre! Not at all! "Keep it up, colonel! You're doing fine!" That's what General des Entrayes,* the head of our division and commander over us all, must have written in those notes that were being brought every five minutes by a courier, who looked greener and more shitless each time. I could have palled up with that boy, we'd have been scared together! But we had no time to fraternize.

12

So there was no mistake? So there was no law against people shooting at people they couldn't even see! It was one of the things you could do without anybody reading you the riot act. In fact, it was recognized and probably encouraged by upstanding citizens, like the draft, or marriage, or hunting!… No two ways about it. I was suddenly on the most intimate terms with war. I'd lost my virginity. You've got to be pretty much alone with her as I was then to get a good look at her, the slut, full face and profile. A war had been switched on between us and the other side, and now it was burning! Like the current between the two carbons of an arc lamp. And this lamp was in no hurry to go out! It would get us all, the colonel and everyone else, he looked pretty spiffy now, but he wouldn't roast up any bigger than me when the current from the other side got him between the shoulders.

There are different ways of being condemned to death. Oh! What wouldn't I have given to be in jail instead of here! What a fool I'd been! If only I had had a little foresight and stolen something or other when it would have been so easy and there was still time. I never think of anything! You come out of jail alive, out of a war you don't. The rest is blarney.

If only I'd had time, but I didn't! There was nothing left to steal! How pleasant it would be in a cosy little jailhouse, I said to myself, where the bullets couldn't get in! Where they never got in! I knew of one that was ready and waiting, all sunny and warm! I saw it in my dreams, the jailhouse of Saint-Germain to be exact, right near the forest. I knew it well, I'd often passed that way. How a man changes! I was a child in those days, and that jail frightened me. Because I didn't know what men are like. Never again will I believe what they say or what they think. Men are the thing to be afraid of, always, men and nothing else.

How much longer would this madness have to go on before these monsters dropped with exhaustion? How long could a convulsion like this last? Months? Years? How many? Maybe till everyone's dead? All these lunatics? Every last one of them? And seeing as events were taking such a desperate turn, I decided to stake everything on one throw, to make one last try, to see if I couldn't stop the war, just me, all by myself! At least in this one spot where I happened to be.

The colonel was only two steps away from me, pacing. I'd talk to him. Something I'd never done. This was a time for daring. The way

13

things stood, there was practically nothing to lose. "What is it?" he'd ask me, startled, I imagined, at my bold interruption. Then I'd explain the situation as I saw it, and we'd see what he thought. The main thing is to talk things over. Two heads are better than one.

I was about to take that decisive step when, at that very moment, who should arrive on the double but a dismounted cavalryman (as we said in those days), exhausted, shaky in the joints, holding his helmet upside down in one hand like Belisarius,* trembling, all covered with mud, his face even greener than the courier I mentioned before. He stammered and gulped. You'd have thought he was struggling to climb out of a tomb, and it made him sick to his stomach. Could it be that this spook didn't like bullets any more than I did? That he saw them coming like me?

"What is it?" Disturbed, the Colonel stopped him short; the glance he flung at that ghost was of steel.

It made our colonel very angry to see that wretched cavalryman so incorrectly clad and shitting in his pants with fright. The colonel had no use for fear, that was a sure thing. And especially that helmet held in hand like a bowler was really too much in a combat regiment like ours that was just getting into the war. It was as if this dismounted cavalryman had seen the war and taken his hat off in greeting.

Under the colonel's withering look the wobbly messenger snapped to attention, pressing his little finger to the seam of his trousers as the occasion demanded. And so he stood on the embankment, stiff as a board, swaying, the sweat running down his chinstrap; his jaws were trembling so hard that little abortive cries kept coming out of him, like a puppy dreaming. You couldn't make out whether he wanted to speak to us or whether he was crying.

Our Germans squatting at the end of the road had just changed instruments. Now they were having their fun with a machine gun, sputtering like handfuls of matches, and all around us flew swarms of angry bullets, as hostile as wasps.

The man finally managed to articulate a few words:

"Colonel, sir, Sergeant Barousse has been killed."

"So what?"

"He was on his way to meet the bread wagon on the Étrapes road, sir."

"So what?"

14

"He was blown up by a shell!"

"So what, damn it!"

"That's what, colonel, sir."

"Is that all?"

"Yes, sir, that's all, colonel, sir."

"What about the bread?" the colonel asked.

That was the end of the dialogue, because, I remember distinctly, he barely had time to say "What about the bread?" That was all. After that there was nothing but flame and noise. The kind of noise you wouldn't have thought possible. Our eyes, ears, nose and mouth were so full of that noise I thought it was all over and I'd turned into noise and flame myself.

After a while the flame went away, the noise stayed in my head, and my arms and legs trembled as if somebody were shaking me from behind. My limbs seemed to be leaving me, but then in the end they stayed on. The smoke stung my eyes for a long time, and the prickly smell of powder and sulphur hung on, strong enough to kill all the fleas and bedbugs in the whole world.

I thought of Sergeant Barousse, who had just gone up in smoke like the man told us. That was good news. Great, I thought to myself. That makes one less stinker in the regiment! He wanted to have me court-martialled for a can of meat. "To each his own war!" I said to myself. In that respect, you can't deny it, the war seemed to serve a purpose now and then! I knew of three or four more in the regiment, real scum, that I'd have gladly helped to make the acquaintance of a shell, like Barousse.

As for the colonel, I didn't wish him any hard luck. But he was dead too. At first I didn't see him. The blast had carried him up the embankment and laid him down on his side, right in the arms of the dismounted cavalryman, the courier, who was finished too. They were embracing each other for the moment and for all eternity, but the cavalryman's head was gone, all he had was an opening at the top of the neck, with blood in it bubbling and glugging like jam in a kettle. The colonel's belly was wide open, and he was making a nasty face about it. It must have hurt when it happened. Tough shit for him! If he'd got out when the shooting started, it wouldn't have happened.

All that tangled meat was bleeding profusely.

Shells were still bursting to the right and left of the scene.

I'd had enough, I was glad to have such a good pretext for making myself scarce. I even hummed a tune, and reeled like when you've been rowing a long way and your legs are wobbly. "Just one shell!" I said to myself. "Amazing how quick just one shell can clean things up. Could you believe it?" I kept saying to myself. "Could you believe it!"

There was nobody left at the end of the road. The Germans were gone. But that little episode had taught me a quick lesson, to keep to the cover of the trees. I was in a hurry to get back to our command post, to see if anyone else in our regiment had been killed on reconnaissance. There must be some good dodges, I said to myself, for getting taken prisoner!... Here and there in the fields a few puffs of smoke still clung to the ground. "Maybe they're all dead," I thought. "Seeing how they refuse to understand anything whatsoever, the best solution would be for them all to get killed instantly... The war would be over, and we'd go home... Maybe we'd march across the Place Clichy in triumph... Just one or two survivors... In my dream... Strapping good fellows marching behind the general, all the rest would be dead like the colonel... Like Barousse... like Vanaille (another bastard)... etc. They'd shower us with decorations and flowers, we'd march through the Arc de Triomphe. We'd go to a restaurant, they'd serve us free of charge, we'd never pay for anything any more, never as long as we lived! 'We're heroes!' we'd say when they brought the bill... Defenders of the Fatherland! That would do it!... We'd pay with little French flags!... The lady at the till would refuse to take money from heroes, she'd even give us some, with kisses thrown in, as we filed out. Life would be worth living."

As I was running, I noticed my arm was bleeding, just a little though, a far from satisfactory wound, a scratch. I'd have to start all over.

It was raining again, the fields of Flanders oozed with dirty water. For a long time I didn't meet a soul, only the wind and a little later the sun. From time to time, I couldn't tell from where, a bullet would come flying merrily through the air and sunshine, looking for me, intent on killing me, there in the wilderness. Why? Never again, not if I lived another hundred years, would I go walking in the country. A solemn oath.

Walking along, I remembered the ceremony of the day before. It had taken place in a meadow, at the foot of a hill; the colonel had harangued the regiment in his booming voice: "Go to it, boys!" he had cried. "Go to it, boys! And long live France!" When you have no imagination, dying is small beer; when you do have an imagination, dying is too much. That's my opinion. My understanding has never taken in so many things at once.

The colonel had never had any imagination. That was the source of all his trouble, and of ours even more so. Was I the only man in that regiment with any imagination about death? I preferred my own kind of death, the kind that comes late... in twenty years... thirty... maybe more... to this death they were trying to deal me right away... eating Flanders mud, my whole mouth full of it, fuller than full, split to the ears by a shell fragment. A man's entitled to an opinion about his own death. But which way, if that was the case, should I go? Straight ahead? My back to the enemy. If the gendarmes were to catch me roaming around I knew my goose was cooked. They'd give me a slapdash trial that same afternoon in some deserted classroom... There were lots of empty classrooms wherever we went. They'd play court martial with me the way kids play when the teacher isn't there. The non-coms seated on the platform, me standing in handcuffs in front of the little desks. In the morning they'd shoot me: twelve bullets plus one. So what was the answer?

And I thought of the colonel again, such a brave man with his breastplate and his helmet and his moustache, if they had exhibited him in a music hall, walking as I saw him under the bullets and shellfire, he'd have filled the Alhambra, he'd have outshone Fragson,* and he was a big star at the time I'm telling you about. That's what I was thinking. My heart was down in the dumps.

After hours and hours of cautious, furtive walking, I finally caught sight of our men near a clump of farmhouses. That was one of our advance posts. It belonged to a squadron that was billeted nearby. Nobody killed, they told me. Every last one of them alive! I was the one with the big news: "The colonel's dead!" I shouted, as soon as I was near enough. "Plenty more colonels where he came from!" That was the snappy comeback of Corporal Pistil, who was on duty just then; what's more, he was organizing details.

"All right, you jerk, until they find a replacement for the colonel, you can be picking up meat with Empouille and Kerdoncuff here, take two sacks each. The distribution point is behind the church... the one you see over there... Don't let them give you a lot of bones like yesterday, and try and get back before nightfall, you lugs!"

So I hit the road again with the other two.

That pissed me off. "I'll never tell them anything after this," I said to myself. I could see it was no use talking to those people, a tragedy like what I'd just seen was wasted on such stinkers! It had happened too long ago to capture their interest. And to think that a week earlier they'd have given me four columns and my picture in the papers for the death of a colonel the way I'd seen it. A bunch of halfwits.

The meat for the whole regiment was being distributed in a summery field, shaded by cherry trees and parched by the August sun. On sacks and tent cloths spread out on the grass there were pounds and pounds of guts, chunks of white and yellow fat, disembowelled sheep with their organs every which way, oozing intricate little rivulets into the grass round about, a whole ox, split down the middle, hanging on a tree, and four regimental butchers all hacking away at it, cursing and swearing and pulling off choice morsels. The squadrons were fighting tooth and nail over the innards, especially the kidneys, and all around them swarms of flies such as one sees only on such occasions, as self-important and musical as little birds.

Blood and more blood, everywhere, all over the grass, in sluggish confluent puddles, looking for a congenial slope. A few steps further on, the last pig was being killed. Already four men and a butcher were fighting over some of the prospective cuts.

"You crook, you! You're the one that made off with the tenderloin yesterday!…"

Leaning against a tree, I had barely time enough to honour that alimentary dispute with two or three glances, before being overcome by an enormous urge to vomit, which I did so hard that I passed out.

They carried me back to the outfit on a stretcher. Naturally they swiped my two oilcloth sacks, the change was too good to miss.

I woke up to one of the Corporal's harangues. The war wasn't over.

* * *

Anything can happen, and I in my turn became a corporal at the end of that same month of August. Many a time I was sent to headquarters with five men for liaison duty under General des Entrayes. He was a little man, he didn't say much, and at first sight he seemed neither cruel nor heroic. But it was safer to suspend judgement… What he seemed to value most of all was his comfort. In fact he thought of his comfort

18

all the time, and even when we'd been busy retreating for more than a month, he'd chew everybody out in every new stopping place if his orderly hadn't found him a nice clean bed and a kitchen with all the modern appliances.

This love of comfort gave our chief of staff, with his four stripes, a lot of trouble. The General's domestic requirements got on his nerves. Especially since he himself, yellow, gastric in the extreme and constipated, wasn't the least bit interested in food. But he had to eat his soft-boiled eggs at the general's table all the same, and listen on that occasion to his complaints. Those are the things a soldier has to put up with. But I couldn't feel sorry for him, because as an officer he was a first-rate swine. Judge for yourself. After a whole day spent dragging ourselves up hill and down glade, through carrots and clover, we'd finally stop so the general could get to sleep somewhere. We'd find him a quiet, sheltered village, where no troops had been billeted yet, or if they had been, they'd have to move on in a hurry, we'd throw them out even if they'd already stacked their rifles, and they'd just have to spend the night in the open.

The village was reserved for the general staff, its horses, its mess, its luggage, and not least for that stinking major. The bastard's name was Pinçon, Major Pinçon. I hope they've killed him off by now (and not pleasantly). But at the time I'm talking about Pinçon was disgustingly alive. Every evening he'd send for us liaison men and give us a good chewing-out, to keep us on our toes and fire us with enthusiasm. Then he'd send us all over the place, after we'd run errands for the General all day. Dismount! Mount! Dismount again! And more of the same, carrying his orders in all directions. They might just as well have drowned us. It would have been more convenient for everybody.

"Dismissed!" he'd yell. "Get back to your regiments! And on the double!"

"Where is the regiment, sir?" we'd ask...

"At Barbagny?"*

"Where's Barbagny?"

"Over there!"

Over there, where he pointed, there'd be nothing but darkness, same as everywhere else, an enormous darkness that swallowed up the road two steps ahead of us, only a little sliver of road about the size of your tongue was spared by the darkness.

This Barbagny of his was at the end of the world. Try and find it! To find his Barbagny you'd have had to sacrifice at least a whole squadron! A squadron of brave men, what's more! And I wasn't brave at all, I couldn't see any reason to be brave, so obviously I had less desire than anyone else to find his Barbagny, the situation of which, incidentally, was pure guesswork as far as he was concerned. Maybe they thought they could make me go and commit suicide if they yelled loud enough. But either you have it in you or you don't.

I knew only one thing about that blackness, which was so dense you had the impression that if you stretched out your arm a little way from your shoulder you'd never see it again, but of that one thing I was absolutely certain – namely, that it was full of homicidal impulses.

As soon as night fell, that big-mouth major couldn't wait to send us to our deaths; it was something that came over him at sundown. We'd try a bit of passive resistance, we'd pretend not to understand, we'd try to take root in that cosy little billet, but when we finally couldn't see the trees, we had to resign ourselves to going away and dying a little; the General's dinner was ready.

From then on, it was all a matter of luck. Sometimes we'd find Barbagny and the regiment and sometimes we wouldn't. When we found it, it was mostly by mistake, because the squadron sentries would start shooting at us. So naturally we'd advance and be recognized, and usually spend the night doing all sorts of chores, carrying numberless bales of oats and buckets of water, and getting chewed out till our heads reeled, in addition to dropping with sleep.

In the morning, our liaison team, all five of us, would report back to General des Entrayes and get on with the war.

But most of the time we didn't find the regiment and we'd circle around villages on unknown trails, keeping away from evacuated hamlets and treacherous thickets – as much as possible we avoided those kinds of things because of German patrols. We had to be somewhere though while waiting, somewhere in the darkness. Some things couldn't be avoided. Ever since then I've known how wild rabbits must feel.

Pity comes in funny ways. If we'd told Major Pinçon that he was nothing but a cowardly stinking murderer, we'd only have given him pleasure, the pleasure of having us shot without delay by the MP captain, who was always following him around and who lived for nothing else. It wasn't the Germans that MP captain had it in for.

So for night after idiotic night we crept from ambush to ambush, sustained only by the decreasingly plausible hope of coming out alive, that and no other, and if we did come out alive one thing was sure: that we'd never, absolutely never, forget that we had discovered on earth a man shaped like you and me, but a thousand times more ferocious than the crocodiles and sharks with wide-open jaws that circle just below the surface around the shiploads of garbage and rotten meat that get chucked overboard in the Havana roadstead.

The biggest defeat in every department of life is to forget, especially the things that have done you in, and to die without realizing how far people can go in the way of crumminess. When the grave lies open before us, let's not try to be witty, but on the other hand, let's not forget, but make it our business to record the worst of the human viciousness we've seen without changing one word. When that's done, we can curl up our toes and sink into the pit. That's work enough for a lifetime.

I'd gladly have fed Major Pinçon to the sharks and his MP with him, to teach them how to live; my horse too while I was at it, so he wouldn't have to suffer any more; the poor fellow didn't have any back left it was so sore, only two plaques of raw flesh under the saddle, as big as my two hands, oozing rivers of pus that ran from the edges of his blanket down to his hocks. I had to ride him all the same, trot-trot... That trot-trot made him wriggle and writhe. But horses are even more patient than people. His trot was an undulation. I had to leave him out in the open. In a barn the smell of his open wounds would have been asphyxiating. When I mounted him, his back hurt him so badly that he arched it, oh, very politely, and his belly hung down to his knees. It felt like mounting a donkey. It was easier that way, I have to admit. We were tired enough ourselves with all the steel we had to carry on our heads and shoulders.

General des Entrayes was waiting for his dinner in his specially requisitioned house. The table had been set, the lamp was in its place.

"Beat it, Christ Almighty, the whole lot of you!" Pinçon yelled at us one more time, shaking his lantern under our noses. "We're sitting down to table! I'm telling you for the last time! Are those swine ever going to go!" he screamed. The passion of sending us to our death put a little colour into his diaphanous cheeks.

Sometimes the General's cook would slip us a bite before we left. The General had too much to eat, seeing the regulations allowed him forty rations all for himself! He wasn't a young man any more. In fact he must have been close to retirement age. His knees buckled when he walked and I'm pretty sure he dyed his moustache.

The veins in his temples, we could see in the lamplight as we were leaving, described meanders like the Seine on its way out of Paris. He had grown-up daughters, so it was said, unmarried and, like himself, not rich. Maybe those were the thoughts that made him so crotchety and cranky, like an old dog disturbed in his habits, who goes looking for his quilted basket whenever anyone opens the door for him.

He loved beautiful gardens and rosebushes. Wherever we went, he never passed up a rose garden. When it comes to loving roses, generals haven't their equal. It's a known fact.

Anyway, we finally set out. It was hard to get the plugs started. They were afraid to move because of their wounds, but in addition they were afraid of us and the darkness, afraid of everything, to tell the truth. So were we! A dozen times we went back to ask the major for directions! A dozen times he cursed us as cowards and filthy laggards. Finally, with the help of our spurs, we'd pass the last outpost, give the sentries the password, and plunge into our murky adventure, into the darkness of this no man's land.

After wandering a while from side to side of the darkness, we finally got part of our bearings, or so at least we thought... Whenever one cloud seemed lighter than another, we were convinced that we'd seen something... But up ahead of us there was nothing we could be sure of but the echo that came and went, the echo of our horses' hoof beats, a horrendous sound you wanted so bad not to hear that it stopped your breath. Those horses seemed to be trotting to high heaven, to be calling everybody on earth to come and massacre us. And they could have done it with one hand, just steady a rifle against a tree and wait for us. I kept thinking that the first light we'd see would be the flash of the shot that would end it all.

In the four weeks the war had been going on, we'd grown so tired, so miserable, that tiredness had taken away some of my fear. In the end the torture of being harassed night and day by those monsters, the non-coms, especially the low-ranking ones, who were even stupider, pettier and more hateful than usual, made even the most obstinate among us doubt the advisability of going on living.

Oh, how you long to get away! To sleep! That's the main thing! When it becomes really impossible to get away and sleep, then the will to live evaporates of its own accord. As long as we were still alive, we'd just have to look as if we were looking for our regiment.

Before a thought can start up in the brain of a numbskull, a lot of cruel things must happen to him. The man who had made me think for the first time in my life, really think, practical thoughts that were really my own, was undoubtedly Major Pinçon, that torture master. I therefore thought of him as hard as I could as I clanked along, crushed by the weight of my armour, an extra in this incredible international extravaganza, into which, I have to admit, I had leapt with enthusiasm.

Every yard of darkness ahead of us was a promise of death and destruction. But how would it come? The only element of uncertainty was the uniform of the killer. Would he be one of us? Or of them?

I hadn't done anything to Pinçon! No more than I had to the Germans!... With his face like a rotten peach, his four bands that glittered all over him from his head to his belly button, his scraggly moustache and his bony knees, with the field glasses dangling from his neck like a cowbell and his 1/1,000 map. I kept wondering why he was so intent on sending other people to their death. Other people who had no maps.

We four horsemen on the road were making as much noise as a battalion. They must have heard us coming ten miles away, or else they didn't want to hear us. That was always a possibility... Maybe the Germans were afraid of us? Why not?

A month of sleepiness on every eyelid, that's what we were carrying, and as much again in the backs of our heads, plus all those pounds of tin.

The men in my party didn't express themselves very well. Actually they hardly spoke at all. They'd come from the ends of Brittany, and what they knew they hadn't learnt at school but in the army. That night I tried to make a little conversation about the village of Barbagny with the one next to me, who was called Kersuzon.

"Kersuzon," I say. "We're in the Ardennes now... Do you see anything in the distance? I don't see a damn thing..."

"It's as black as an arsehole," Kersuzon says. That was enough...

"But," I suggest, "haven't you heard anyone mention Barbagny in the course of the day? Give you an idea where it is?"

"No."

That was that.

We never did find Barbagny. We went round in circles until morning and ended up in another village, where the man with the field glasses was waiting for us. The General was taking his black coffee in the arbour outside the mayor's house when we got there.

"Ah, Pinçon!" he says in a loud voice to his chief of staff as he sees us pass. "Youth is so wonderful!" After that he went out for a leak and then, stooped over, his hands behind his back, he took a little stroll. The General was very tired that morning, the orderly confided to me, he'd slept badly, some trouble with his bladder, so it seemed.

Kersuzon always gave me the same answer when I questioned him at night, as if I'd pressed a button, it kind of tickled me. Two or three times more he said the same thing about the arsehole and the darkness and a while after that he was killed, on his way out of some village we'd mistaken for some other village by some French soldiers who'd mistaken us for somebody else.

It was a few days, I remember now, after Kersuzon was killed that we dreamt up a little trick that suited us fine to keep from getting lost in the darkness.

So they were throwing us out of the billet. All right all right. We don't say a word. No griping, no comeback. "Clear out!" old wax face yelled as usual.

"Yes sir, very good sir!"

And off we'd go in the direction of the gunfire, we didn't wait to be asked twice, all five of us. You'd have thought we were going to pick cherries. It was rolling country around there, the Meuse with its vine-covered hills, grapes that weren't ripe yet, and autumn, wooden villages well dried by three months of summer, highly inflammable.

We'd noticed that one night when we couldn't figure out where to go. There was always a village burning in the direction of the gunfire. We didn't go too close, we gave that village a wide berth and just watched, like an audience, so to speak, from maybe ten or twelve kilometres away. And every night from then on all kinds of villages would burst into a blaze on the horizon, one after another, we'd be surrounded by them, dozens of burning villages in a circle, up ahead and on both sides, like a crazy carnival, sending up flames that licked the clouds.

We'd watch the flames as they swallowed up everything, churches and barns, one after another. The haystacks burned higher and livelier

24

than anything else, the beams reared up in the darkness, throwing off sparks, before crashing into a sea of light.

Even from twenty kilometres away you get a good view of a burning village. It was a merry sight. A tiny hamlet that you wouldn't even notice in the daytime, with ugly, uninteresting country around it, you can't imagine how impressive it can be when it's on fire at night! You'd think it was Notre-Dame! A village, even a small one, takes at least all night to burn, in the end it looks like an enormous flower, then there's only a bud, and after that nothing.

Smoke rises, and then it's morning.

We'd leave the horses saddled in a field close by, and they wouldn't move. We'd go and saw wood in the grass, all but one, naturally, who'd take his turn on guard. But when you've got fires to watch, the night passes a lot more pleasantly, it's not a hardship any more, you're not alone.

Unfortunately, the villages didn't last... After a month's time there wasn't a village left in that neck of the woods. The forests were shelled too. They didn't last a week. Forests make nice enough fires, but they don't last.

After that the roads were all clogged with artillery columns going in one direction and civilians running away in the other.

So naturally we couldn't go either way, we could only stay where we were.

We'd line up for the privilege of getting killed. Even the General couldn't find any billets with no soldiers in them. In the end we were sleeping in the fields, general or no general. Those who still had a bit of spirit lost it. That was when they started shooting men to bolster their morale, whole squadrons, and when our MP got a citation for the way in which he was carrying on his little private war, the real honest-to-goodness war.

* * *

They gave us a short rest, and a few weeks later we climbed back up on our horses and started north. The cold came with us. The gunfire was never far away. But we never came across any Germans except by accident, a hussar or a squad of riflemen here and there, in yellow and green, pretty colours. We seemed to be looking for them, but we moved on the moment we laid eyes on them. At every encounter two or three horsemen bit the dust, sometimes theirs, sometimes ours. And from far in the distance their riderless horses, with loose clanking stirrups, would come galloping towards us, we'd see their saddles with the peculiar cantles and all their leather as fresh and shiny as pocketbooks on New Year's Day. They were coming to see our horses, they made friends in no time. They were lucky! We couldn't have done that!

One morning when they rode in from a reconnaissance patrol, Lieutenant de Sainte-Engence* swore to the other officers that he hadn't made it up. "I carved 'em I tell you. Two of them!" he insisted, showing everybody his sabre, and true enough, the little groove was full of caked blood, that's what it's made for.

Captain Ortolan backed him up. "He was splendid! Bravo, Sainte-Engence!... Ah, Messieurs, if you'd only seen him! What a charge!"

Ortolan was in command of the squadron.

"I saw every bit of it! I wasn't far away! A thrust to the right... Zing! The first one drops!... A thrust full in the chest!... Left! Cross! Championship style!... Bravo again, Sainte-Engence! Two lancers! Less than a mile from here! Still lying there! In a ploughed field! The war's over for them, eh, Sainte-Engence?... A double thrust! Beautiful! I bet they spilt their guts like rabbits!"

Lieutenant de Sainte-Engence, whose horse had galloped a long way, received his comrades' compliments with modesty. Now that Ortolan had authenticated his exploit, his mind was at rest, so he rode off some distance and cooled off his mare by circling slowly round the assembled squadron as if he were just coming in from a steeplechase.

"We must send another patrol over there!" cried Captain Ortolan. "Immediately!" He was terribly excited. "Those two poor devils must have been lost to come this way, but there must be more behind them... Ah, Corporal Bardamu. Go take a look, you and your four men!"

The Captain was talking to me.

"And when they fire at you, try to make a note of their position and come right back and tell me where they are! They must be Brandenburgers!..."

The regular army men told me that in peacetime this Captain Ortolan hardly ever showed up for duty. Now that a war was on, he made up for it. He was indefatigable. His vigour and verve, even among all those other lunatics, were getting more unbelievable from day to day. It was rumoured that he sniffed cocaine. Pale, rings under his eyes, always dashing around on his fragile legs... Whenever he set foot on the ground, he'd stagger at first but then he'd get hold of himself and stride angrily over the furrowed fields in search of some new feat of daring. I wouldn't have been surprised if he'd sent us to get a light from the muzzles of the enemy's guns. He was in cahoots with death. I'd have sworn they had a contract, death and Captain Ortolan.

He'd spent the first part of his life (I had made it my business to find out) breaking his ribs in horse shows several times a year. And his legs, because of also being broken and not being used for walking, had lost their calves. When he walked, it was with nervous, pigeon-toed steps, as though walking on eggs. Seeing him in his enormous greatcoat, stooped over in the rain, you'd have taken him for the phantom hindquarters of a racehorse.

It needs to be said, though, that at the start of that monstrous enterprise, during the month of August and through September, certain hours, whole days now and then, certain stretches of road and parts of forest were still propitious to the doomed... In those places you could toy with the illusion that you were more or less safe, you could finish eating your bread and tinned meat without being too much plagued by the foreboding that this was the last time. But from October on there were no more of these little lulls, the hail fell thicker and sharper and faster, spiced with shot and shell. Soon we'd be at the heart of the storm, and the very thing we were trying not to see, our death, would be so close to our noses that we couldn't see anything else.

The night, which had terrified us at first, seemed almost pleasant by comparison. In the end we longed for the night and waited for it. It was harder for them to shoot at us then than in the daytime. That was the only difference that counted.

It's hard to face the facts, even in connection with war the imagination holds its own for a long time.

Cats who've been threatened by fire for too long end up by jumping in the water.

During the night we'd cadge a few minutes here and there that came pretty close to the blessed days of peace, those days that now seem too good to be true, when everything was benign, when nothing really mattered, when we did so many things that had come to seem so marvellously, superlatively delightful. Days of peace, days of living velvet…

But soon the nights as well were a merciless torment. Almost every night we'd have to keep our weary bones at work, put up with a little extra torture, just so as to eat or catch a little nap in the darkness. The food convoys moved up to the front lines at a disgraceful crawl, long limping lines of shaky wagons, bursting with meat, prisoners, wounded, oats, rice and MPs, and don't forget the wine in big, jiggling, pot-bellied jugs that reminded us of high old times.

Behind the rolling forge and the bread wagon men came dragging themselves on foot, prisoners in handcuffs, some of theirs and some of ours, condemned to this or that, lashed by the wrists to the MPs' stirrups, some due to be shot the next day and no more dispirited than the others. It didn't spoil their appetites either, they ate their ration of that tuna fish that's so indigestible (they wouldn't have time to digest it) while waiting by the side of the road for the convoy to shove off – and they ate their last chunk of bread too, with a civilian chained to them, who was said to be a spy but didn't know it. Neither did we.

The military torture continued in its nocturnal aspect, as we groped our way through the humpbacked streets of a village without light or face, bent under sacks that weighed more than a man, from one unknown barn to another, threatened and yelled at, haggard, with no better prospect than to end in a sea of liquid manure, sickened at the thought that we'd been tortured, duped to the entrails by a gang of vicious lunatics, who had suddenly become incapable of doing anything else than killing and spilling their guts without knowing why.

We'd flop down between two manure piles, but the non-coms would soon kick and bellow us to our feet, and send us to a different part of the convoy, to load or unload something else.

The village was gorged with food and soldiers, in the darkness bloated with fat, apples, oats, sugar, that we had to haul around and distribute to this squad and that squad. That convoy had brought everything except a ticket home.

Our detail was dead tired, we'd drop right next to our cart, and the Sergeant Major would come around and shine his lantern on the corpses. He was an ape with a double chin. Regardless of the chaos, he had to find a watering place for the horses! Oh yes, the horses had to drink! But I've seen four men, arse and all, drop with fatigue, and fall fast asleep with the water up to their necks.

After the watering we had to find the alley we'd come by and get back to the farm, where we thought we'd left the rest of our squad. If we didn't find it, we could always pass out at the foot of some wall and sleep for an hour, if there was an hour left. In this business of getting killed, it's no use being picky and choosy; you've got to act as if life were going on, and that lie is the hardest part of it.

The wagons started back to the rear. In flight from the dawn, they hit the road again. Squeaking in every crooked wheel, off they drove, and with them went my prayer that they'd be ambushed, cut to pieces, burnt that same day, the way you see in war pictures, supply column wiped out for ever and ever, with its escort of MP gorillas, horse soldiers, and lantern-swinging non-coms, with its work details, its sacks of lentils and flour that would never be cooked and never be seen again. Because there are many different ways of kicking in, of exhaustion or something else, but the worst is to do it while hauling enough sacks to fill the night with.

The day when those bastards would be shattered to the axles, they'd leave us alone, I thought, and even if only for one night, we'd be able to sleep with body and soul.

This food-supply business was just one more nightmare, a nasty little monster on top of the big one, the war. Brutes to the right of us, brutes to the left of us, they were all over the place. Condemned to a deferred death, the only thing that really mattered was an enormous longing for sleep, all the rest was torture, even the time and effort it took to eat. A bend in the brook, a familiar-looking wall... But mostly it was the smells that helped us find our farm, we'd reverted to dogs in the wartime night of the deserted villages. The smell of shit was the best guide of all.

The quartermaster was the guardian of the regiment's hatreds. He, until further notice, was master of the world. Anybody who talks about the future is a bastard, it's the present that counts. Invoking posterity is like making speeches to worms. There in the wartime village night the adjutant was corralling human cattle for the big slaughterhouses that had just opened. The adjutant was king. King of Death! Adjutant Cretelle! Absolutely! Nobody more powerful! And nobody as powerful, except one of their adjutants on the opposite side.

Nothing was left of the village, no living thing except terrified cats. First the furniture went, smashed up for firewood, chairs, tables, sideboards, from the lightest to the heaviest. And anything that the boys could carry, they made off with. Combs, lamps, cups, silly little things, even bridal wreaths, everything went. As if we'd had years of life ahead of us. They looted to take their minds off their troubles, to make it look as if they had years before them. Everybody likes that feeling.

As far as they were concerned, gunfire was nothing but noise. That's why wars can keep going. Even the people who make them, who fight in them, don't really get the picture. Even with a bullet in their gut, they'd go on picking up old shoes that "might come in handy". The way a sheep, lying on its side in a meadow, will keep on grazing with its dying breath. Most people don't die until the last moment; others start twenty years in advance, sometimes more. Those are the unfortunates.

I wasn't very bright myself, but at least I had sense enough to opt for cowardice once and for all. I imagine that's why people thought I was so uncommonly calm. Be that as it may, I inspired a paradoxical confidence in our Captain Ortolan, who decided that night to entrust me with a delicate mission. It consisted, he told me in confidence, of trotting before daylight to Noirceur-sur-la-Lys,* a city of weavers, situated some fourteen kilometres from the village where we'd camped. My job was to find out at first hand whether the enemy was there or not. All that day patrols had been contradicting one another, and General des Entrayes was good and sick of it. For that reconnaissance mission I was allowed to pick one of the less purulent horses in the platoon. I hadn't gone out alone in a long time. It made me feel as if I were starting on a trip. But my feeling of deliverance was illusory.

I was so tired when I set out that, hard as I tried, I couldn't properly visualize my own murder, I couldn't fill in the details. I moved from tree to tree, accompanied by the clanking of my hardware. All by itself my pretty sabre made as much noise as a piano. I don't know if I was deserving of sympathy, but in any case I was certainly grotesque.

What could General des Entrayes have been thinking, sending me out alone into that silence, all clothed in cymbals? Not about me, that's for sure.

The Aztecs, so the story goes, routinely disembowelled eighty thousand faithful a week in their temples of the sun, a sacrifice to the god of the clouds to make him send them rain. Such things are hard to believe until you get mixed up in a war. Once you're in a war, you see how it is: the Aztecs' contempt for other people's bodies was the same as my humble viscera must have inspired in our above-mentioned General Céladon des Entrayes, who, thanks to a series of promotions, had become a kind of god himself, an abominably demanding little sun.

The one tiny bit of hope I had left was of being taken prisoner. It didn't amount to much, a shred. A shred in the night, because the circumstances weren't conducive to polite preliminaries, far from it. The foe would shoot first and introduce himself afterwards. Besides, what would I say to this soldier, hostile by definition, who'd come from the other end of Europe for the express purpose of murdering me?... Suppose he hesitated for one second (that was all I'd need), what would I say to him?... And come to think of it, what would he be? A shop assistant? A professional soldier? A grave-digger? In civilian life? A cook?... Horses are lucky, they're stuck with the war same as us, but nobody expects them to be in favour of it, to pretend to believe in it. Unfortunate, yes, but free! Enthusiasm, the bastard, was reserved for us!

I could see the road clearly just then and, plunked down on the mud beside it, big squares and cubes of houses, their walls whitened by the moonlight, like big unequal blocks of ice, pale and silent. Would this be the end of it all? How much time would I spend in this desolation after they'd done for me? Before it was all over? In what ditch? Beside which one of these walls? Would they come and finish me off? With a knife? Sometimes they gouged out your eyes, cut off your hands, and so on... There were all sorts of rumours on the subject, and they were no joke! Who knows?... A hoof beat... Another... would be enough! This beast makes a noise like two men with iron boots fastened together, running with a jerky, uneven step...

My heart, a rabbit, warm in its little rib cage, fearful, cowering, bewildered.

You must feel pretty much the same way when you jump off the top of the Eiffel Tower. You'd like to stop yourself in mid-air.

That village kept its menace secret, but not entirely. In the centre of a square a tiny fountain gurgled just for me.

That night I had everything to myself. I was the owner of the moon, the village and an enormous fear. I was about to break into a trot with a good hour's ride ahead of me to Noirceur-sur-la-Lys, when I caught sight of a well-veiled light over a door. I headed straight for that light, surprised to detect inside myself a kind of daring, a deserter's daring to be sure, but more than I'd ever suspected. The light disappeared the next second, but I'd seen it all right. I knocked, I kept at it, I knocked again, I called out in a loud voice, half in German, half in French, to be on the safe side, to those strangers locked in the darkness.

The door finally opened by just a crack.

A voice asked: "Who are you?" I was saved.

"A dragoon…"

"French?" A woman speaking. I could see her now.

"Yes, French…"

"Some German dragoons were here this afternoon… They spoke French too…"

"Yes, but I'm really French…"

"I see!…"

She seemed to have her doubts.

"Where are they now?" I asked.

"They left at about eight o'clock, heading for Noirceur…" She pointed north.

A young girl, shawl and white apron, emerged from the shadow into the doorway.

"What did the Germans do to you?" I asked.

"They burned a house next to the town hall, and they killed my little brother, ran a lance through his belly… He was playing on the Red Bridge, watching them go by… Look!" She showed me. "There he is…"

She didn't cry. She relit the candle, that was the light I had seen. At the back of the room I saw – it was true – the little corpse lying on a mattress; it was dressed in a sailor suit with a big square collar, the face and throat were as livid as the candlelight. The child's arms and legs and back were bent, he was all doubled up. The lance had passed, like an axis of death, through the middle of his belly. His mother was on her knees beside him, crying her heart out. So was the father. Then they all started moaning at once. But my trouble was thirst.

"You wouldn't have a bottle of wine to sell me?" I asked.

"You'll have to ask my mother... She may know if there's any left... The Germans took a lot just now..."

Then the two women talked it over in an undertone.

The daughter came back and announced: "There's none left... the Germans took it all... We'd given them plenty without being asked, but even so..."

"Oh yes, they drank and they drank," said the mother, who'd suddenly stopped crying. "They're crazy about it..."

"Must have been more than a hundred bottles," said the father, still on his knees...

"And there's not a single one left?" I kept at it, still hoping, because of my terrible thirst, especially for white wine with a good bitter tang that wakes you up a little. "I don't mind paying..."

"There's nothing left but the best," the mother conceded. "It costs five francs a bottle..."

"That's fine!" I said, taking a big five-franc piece out of my pocket.

"Go and get one!" she said to the sister in a whisper.

The sister took the candle and a moment later brought up a bottle from the hiding place.

I had what I wanted, there was nothing more to stay for.

"Will they come back?" I asked, anxious again.

"Maybe," they all said together. "If they do, they'll burn everything in sight... They promised they would when they left..."

"I'll just go and see what they're up to."

"You're very brave... It's that way!" said the father, pointing in the direction of Noirceur-sur-la-Lys... He even stepped out on the road to see me on my way. The girl and her mother stayed behind, fearful, watching over the little corpse.

"Come back in!" they called out to him. "Joseph, come in. You've no business out there on the road..."

"You're very brave!" the father said to me again, shaking me by the hand.

I started off again, northward, at a trot.

"At least don't tell them we're still here!" the girl was shouting. She'd come out just for that.

"They'll see for themselves tomorrow whether you're here or not," I called back. I wasn't happy about giving them my five francs. There was five francs between us. Five francs is reason enough to hate people

33

and make you want them dead... There won't be any love to spare in this world as long as there's five francs.

"Tomorrow!" they repeated, fearing the worst...

Tomorrow, for them too, was far away, there wasn't much sense in that kind of tomorrow. The one thing any of us really cared about was living for one more hour, one more hour is a big deal in a world where everything has reduced itself to murder.

I didn't have far to go after that. I trotted from tree to tree, expecting to be challenged or shot from one minute to the next. Nothing happened.

It must have been about two in the morning, not much more, when I got to the top of a little hill, at a walk. Suddenly, looking down from there, I saw rows and rows of burning gas jets, and then in the foreground a station all lit up with its cars and its buffet, but not a sound came up to me... Nothing. Streets, avenues, street lamps, and more lights in parallel lines, whole neighbourhoods, and everything else a black voracious void, with this city plunked down as if it had been lost, lying there all lit up in the heart and centre of the darkness. I got down off my horse, made myself comfortable on a little hummock, and sat there looking at it for quite some time.

That didn't tell me if the Germans had moved into Noirceur, but since I knew that in a case like that they usually set fire to everything, I figured if they'd moved in and hadn't set fire to the place right away, they must have something very unusual up their sleeve.

No gunfire either. All very suspicious.

My horse wanted to lie down too. He tugged at his bridle and that made me turn round. When I turned back to the city, something about the look of the hummock in front of me had changed, not much, but enough to make me sing out: "Hey! Who goes there?..." That change in the layout of the darkness had taken place a few steps away... Must be somebody there...

"Don't shout too loud!" came a deep, hoarse voice, very French.

"You lost too?" he asked me. Now I could see him, an infantryman, the peak of his cap was cracked in "goodbye to the army" style. After all these years I remember that moment, his silhouette emerging from the grass the way targets used to in shooting galleries, soldier targets.

We came closer. I was holding my revolver, for two beans I'd have fired, don't ask why.

"Hey," he asks. "You seen them?"

"No, but I've come here to see them."

"You from the 145th Dragoons?"

"That's right. You?"

"I'm a reservist…"

"Oh!" I said. That amazed me. He was the first reservist I'd met in the war. We'd always been in with the Regular Army men. I couldn't see his face, but his voice was different from ours, sadder, which made him sound nicer. Because of that, I couldn't help trusting him a little. Which was something.

"I'm fed up," he said. "I'm going to get myself captured by the Boche…"

He wasn't keeping any secrets.

"How are you going about it?"

All of a sudden his plan interested me more than anything else. How was he fixing to get taken prisoner?

"I don't know yet…"

"How'd you manage to get away?… It's not easy to get taken prisoner!"

"To hell with that, I'll just surrender."

"What's wrong? You scared?"

"I'm scared, and besides, the war is stupid, if you ask me. I don't give a damn about the Germans, they never did anything to me…"

My feeling was that I should be polite to the Germans. I'd have liked this reservist to explain, while he was about it, why I had no stomach either to make war like everybody else… But he didn't explain a thing, he just kept saying he was fed up.

Then he told me how his regiment had been dispersed at dawn the day before, because some of our sharpshooters had fired on his company by mistake. They hadn't been expected just then, they'd arrived three hours ahead of schedule. So these sharpshooters, tired and taken by surprise, had fired across the fields and riddled them with bullets. I knew the story, I'd been through it myself.

"Never fear," he went on. "I saw my chance, and I took it! Robinson, I say to myself! – Robinson's my name, Léon Robinson – it's now or never, I says to myself. This is the time to get going… Right? So I started through a little clump of woods and pretty soon, what do you think, I run into our captain… he's leaning against a tree, in very bad shape!... Dying... He was holding his pants in both hands and vomiting... Bleeding all over and rolling his eyes... There was nobody with him. He was through... 'Mama! Mama!' he was snivelling, all the while dying and pissing blood...

"'Shut up!' I tell him. 'Mama! Mama! Fuck your mama!'... Just like that, on my way past, out of the corner of my mouth!... I bet that made him feel good, the bastard!... What do you think of that!... It's not every day you can tell the captain what you think... Too good to miss. A rare opportunity!... To get out of there faster I chucked my pack and gun... dropped 'em in a duck pond... You see, I don't take to killing people, I never learnt to... even in peacetime, I never cared for fights... I'd walk away... See what I mean?... In civilian life I tried to go to the factory regularly... I was kind of an engraver, but I didn't like it because of the arguments, I was happier selling the evening papers in a quiet neighbourhood where I was known, around the Bank of France... Place des Victoires, if you want to know... Rue des Petits-Champs... that was my territory... I never went beyond the Rue du Louvre and the Palais-Royal on one side, get the idea?... In the morning I'd run errands for shopkeepers... sometimes a delivery in the afternoon, odd jobs, see?... kind of unskilled... But one thing I don't want is weapons!... If the Germans see you with a weapon, you're cooked! But if you're dressed free and easy like I am now... nothing in your hands... nothing in your pockets... they get the idea that it won't be hard to take you prisoner, see? They know who they're dealing with... If you go up to the Germans mother-naked, that would be even better... Like a horse! They wouldn't know what army you belong to..."

"That's a fact!"

I caught on that being older is good for the mind. It puts sense into you.

"So you say they're down there?" We figured, we estimated our chances and looked for our future in the great luminous expanse of the silent city as though consulting the cards.

"Let's get started!"

First we'd have to cross the railway tracks. If there were sentries, they'd see us. Or maybe they wouldn't. We'd soon find out. Maybe there'd be an overpass, or maybe we'd take the tunnel.

"We'll have to hurry," said Robinson... "Gotta do these things at night, people aren't friendly in the daytime, everybody plays to the gallery in the daytime, even in the war, the daytime is a circus... You taking your horse?"

I took the horse. A precaution... to get away quicker if the reception was bad. We got to the level crossing, the big red-and-white arms were up. I'd never seen that kind of gate before. They weren't like that around Paris.

"Think they've moved in already?"

"Positive!..." he says. "Anyway, keep going!..."

Now we were forced to be as brave as the brave, because of the horse who was plodding slowly behind us and seemed to be pushing us with his noise; we couldn't hear anything else. Clop! Clop! – went his hooves. He'd put his foot down in the middle of the echo, as if he hadn't a care in the world.

So this Robinson was counting on the night to save us?... The two of us were walking down the middle of the street, with no attempt at concealment, in step what's more, we could have been drilling.

Robinson was right, the daytime was pitiless, from the earth to the sky. The way we were walking in the street, we must have looked perfectly harmless, as innocent as if we'd been coming back from leave. "Did you hear about the First Hussars, taken prisoner in Lille, every last one of them?... Marched right in, the way I heard it, they didn't know! The colonel in the lead... Down the main street, boy oh boy! And then the trap closed!... In front of them... behind them... Germans everywhere!... At the windows!... Everywhere... There they were... Caught like rats!... Like rats! Talk about luck!..."

"The bastards!..."

"Yeah, wasn't that something!..." We couldn't get over that marvellous capture, so neat, so conclusive... It really floored us. The shops had all their shutters closed, so did the houses, with their little gardens in front, all so neat and prim. But after the post office we saw a house, a little whiter than the rest, with all the lights on at all the windows, upstairs and down. We went and rang the doorbell, we still had our horse behind us. A thickset man with a beard opened. "I am the mayor of Noirceur," he told us right away without our asking, "and I am expecting the Germans!" This mayor steps out into the moonlight to look at us. When he saw we weren't Germans but still French, he wasn't so solemn any more. Friendly yes, but embarrassed. Obviously he hadn't been expecting us, we didn't quite fit in with the arrangements he must have made, the decisions he'd taken. The Germans were supposed to enter Noirceur that night, he'd been notified and he'd settled everything with the Préfecture, their colonel here, their field hospital there, etc. And what if they turned up now? With us there? There'd certainly be trouble! Dreadful complications... He didn't come out and say all that, but we could see what he was thinking.

So there in the darkness he starts talking to us about the interests of the public at large, in that enveloping silence. The public at large, that's all he would talk about... the material interests of the community... the artistic patrimony of Noirceur, entrusted to his care, a sacred trust if ever there was one... especially the fifteenth-century church... suppose they burned it down! Like the one in Condé-sur-Yser! Had we thought of that?... In a fit of temper... annoyed at finding us there... He impressed us with the full extent of our responsibility... Harebrained young soldiers that we were!... The Germans had no use for unsavoury towns with enemy soldiers still prowling around in them. That was common knowledge.

While he was lecturing us like that in an undertone, his wife and two daughters, luscious hefty blondes, put in a word here and there to back him up... The long and the short, they didn't want us there. In the air between us there hovered sentimental and archaeological considerations, suddenly sprung to life since there was no one in Noirceur that night to contest them... patriotic, ethical, word-propelled considerations, ghosts that the mayor tried to hold fast, but they faded away, undone by our fear and selfishness, and by the plain truth for that matter.

The mayor of Noirceur himself was knocking himself out with his touching effort to convince us that our duty was to clear out instantly. He wasn't as brutal about it as our Major Pinçon, but in his way he was every bit as determined.

The only argument we could have pitted against all those wielders of power was our contemptible little wish not to die and not to be burnt alive. Which didn't amount to much, especially when you consider that you can't come out with sentiments like that in the middle of a war. So we wandered off into other deserted streets. Everyone I'd met that night had bared his soul to me.

"Just my luck!" said Robinson as we were pushing off. "If only you'd been a German, you're an obliging sort, you'd have taken me prisoner and we'd be all set… It's hard for a man to get rid of himself in a war!"

"What about you?" said I. "Wouldn't you have taken me prisoner if you had been a German? Maybe they'd have given you the Médaille Militaire! Some funny word the Germans must have for their Médaille Militaire…"

Seeing as there was absolutely no demand for us as prisoners, we finally sat down on a bench in a little park and opened up the can of tuna fish Robinson had been warming in his pocket since morning. Now we could hear gunfire far in the distance, very far. If only both sides could have stayed in the distance where they were and left us alone!

Then we walked by the river, and alongside some half-unloaded barges we pissed long streams into the water. We were still leading the horse by the bridle, he tagged behind us like a great big dog. Near the bridge, in the ferryman's one-room house, there was a dead man stretched out on a mattress all alone, a Frenchman, a major of light cavalry, actually he looked something like Robinson.

"Ugly son of a bitch!" says Robinson. "I don't know about you, but I don't like dead people…"

"The funny part of it," I said, "is that he looks something like you. The same long nose, and you're not much older…"

"Well, you see, it's being so tired that makes us all look alike, but oh, if you'd seen me before!… In the days when I went bicycle-riding every Sunday!… I was really handsome! You should have seen the calves on me! You can't beat cycling! It develops the thighs too…"

We left the house, the match we'd lit to look at the stiff had gone out.

"You see, it's too late, you see!…"

Already, in the darkness at the end of the town, a long grey and green line marked the crest of the hill: day! One more! One less! We'd have to try and get through this one the same as the rest, the days had got to be like hoops, tighter and tighter to get through, and filled with bursts of shrapnel.

"Coming back this way tomorrow night?" he asked before we separated.

"Tomorrow night? There's no such thing!… What do you think you are, a general?"

"I don't think about anything..." he says, by way of conclusion. "No thoughts at all!... I think about not getting killed... that keeps me busy... One more day is one more day – that's what I think!"

"You're right... So long, pal, and good luck!..."

"Good luck to you too! Maybe we'll meet again!"

We each went back to the war. And then things happened, and a lot more things that it's not easy to tell about now, because people nowadays wouldn't understand them any more.

* * *

If you wanted to be respected and looked up to, you had to hurry up quick and pal up with the civilians, because they were becoming more and more vicious as the war went on. I saw that as soon as I got back to Paris. It also became clear to me that the women had ants in their pants and that the old men were talking big, and their fingers were all over the place, on arses, in pockets...

The civilians back home were infected with the idea of glory, they picked it up from the soldier boys and soon learnt how to bear up under it, bravely and painlessly.

Nurses and martyrs by turns, mothers were never without their long dark veils and those little diplomas the Ministry never failed to send by special messenger. In short, the home front was getting organized.

At a well-conducted funeral, you're sad too, but you think of other things, the will, your next holiday, the widow, who's a good-looker and said to be passionate, and your plans for continuing to live a great deal longer by contrast, and maybe never dying... You never can tell.

And as you follow the hearse, everybody lifts his hat to you. It's heart-warming. Then's the time to behave properly, to look dignified, not to laugh out loud, to gloat only internally. That's permissible. Everything's permissible internally.

During the war, instead of dancing on the mezzanine, you danced in the cellar. The boys had no objection, in fact they were all for it. They demanded it as soon as they got to town, and nobody thought it indecent. The one thing that's really indecent is bravery. You expect physical bravery? Then ask a worm to be brave, he's pink and pale and soft, just like us.

For my part, I had nothing to complain of. Actually, thanks to the Médaille Militaire I'd won and my wound and all, I was about to lose my innocence. They'd brought me the medal while I was in the hospital convalescing. And that same night I went to the theatre, to let the civilians see it during intermissions. A triumph. Those were the first medals seen in Paris. It floored them!

That was when I met little Lola from America in the lobby of the Opéra-Comique, and it was thanks to her that I really found out what was what.

There are certain dates that stand out after months and months when you might just as well have been dead. That evening at the Opéra-Comique with my medal was a turning point in my life.

Lola made me curious about the United States, because of the questions I started asking right away and that she hardly answered at all. When you launch into something that way, you never know when or how you'll get back...

At the time I'm speaking of, everybody in Paris wanted a uniform. Practically nobody was without one, except neutrals and spies, who to all intents and purposes were identical. Lola had a genuine official uniform, and it was really natty, decorated with little crosses all over, on the sleeves and on the tiny cap that she perched at a rakish angle on her wavy hair. She'd come to help us save France, as she told the hotel manager, to the best of her humble ability but with all her heart! We understood each other right away, but not completely, because the transports of the heart were beginning to give me a pain, I was more interested in the transports of the body. You can't trust the heart, not at all. I'd learnt that in the war – and how! – and I wasn't going to forget it in a hurry.

Lola's heart was tender, weak and enthusiastic. Her body was sweet, it was adorable, so what could I do but take her all together as she was? Lola was a good kid all right, but between us stood the war, the monstrous frenzy that was driving half of humanity, lovers or not, to send the other half to the slaughterhouse. Naturally this interfered with our relationship. For me, who was dragging out my convalescence as long as possible and wasn't the least bit eager to go back on duty in the flaming graveyards of battle, the absurdity of our massacre was glaringly obvious at every step I took in town. Whichever way I looked, I saw cynical, grasping cunning.

Still, I hadn't much chance of keeping out of it, I lacked the indispensable connections. The people I knew were all poor, people whose death is of no interest to anybody. And I could hardly count on Lola to keep me safe at home. Even if she was a nurse, I couldn't have conceived of anyone more bellicose than that sweet young thing – except maybe Ortolan. If I hadn't been through the muddy fricassee of heroism myself, her little Joan of Arc number might have stirred and converted me, but since my enlistment on the Place Clichy I had grown phobically allergic to heroism, verbal or real. I was cured. Radically cured.

For the convenience of the ladies of the American Expeditionary Force, the group of nurses Lola belonged to were quartered in the Hôtel Paritz* and, to make things even more delightful for her personally, she had been put in charge (she had connections) of a special service, whose mission it was to supply the Paris hospitals with apple fritters. Every morning tens of thousands of them were handed out. Lola performed this benign duty with a touching zeal, which, as it turned out, was later to have disastrous consequences.

Lola, it has to be admitted, had never made a fritter in all her life. She therefore hired a number of mercenary cooks, and after a few trials the fritters were ready for delivery, as juicy and sweet and golden as anyone could wish for. All Lola actually had to do was taste them before they were delivered to the various hospital wards. Every morning Lola got up at the stroke of ten, took her bath and went down to the kitchens, which were situated deep in the basement. This, I repeat, she did every morning, clad only in a black-and-yellow Japanese kimono that a boyfriend in San Francisco had given her the day before she left.

In short, everything was running smoothly, and we were happily winning the war, when one fine day at lunch I found her shattered, refusing to touch so much as a single dish. I was seized with foreboding: what misfortune or sudden illness had befallen her? I begged her to entrust herself to my watchful affection.

After conscientiously tasting fritters every day for a month Lola had put on two pounds! Her little belt bore witness to the disaster, she found herself obliged to move on to the next notch. She burst into tears. I did my best to comfort her. In a turmoil of emotion we repaired by taxi to several pharmacies, situated at a considerable distance from one another. The scales proved implacable. As ill luck would have it, they all confirmed that two pounds had indeed and undeniably been gained. I suggested that she turn her job over to a friend who, on the contrary, was eager to enlarge her allurements. Lola wouldn't hear of such a compromise, which she regarded as shameful, as a kind of desertion. That, I recall, is when she told me that her great-great uncle had been a member of the crew of the eternally glorious *Mayflower* which landed in Boston in 1677,* and that in view of such a past she couldn't dream of shirking her fritter duty, which may have been humble, but was nevertheless a sacred trust.

The fact remains that from that day on she barely touched her teeth – which, incidentally, were evenly set and very enticing – to the fritters. Her dread of putting on weight completely destroyed her enjoyment of life. She began to waste away. Soon she was as afraid of fritters as I was of shellfire. Because of the fritters we spent most of our time taking long healthy walks on the river banks and boulevards, and we stopped going to the Napolitain, because ice cream is another thing that makes ladies put on weight.

I had never dreamt of a place so comfortable to live in as her room, all pale blue with a bathroom adjoining. Photographs of her friends were all over, with dedications, not many women, lots of men, handsome, dark with curly hair, that was her type, she'd talk to me about the colour of their eyes and read me the dedications, which were tender, solemn, and every last one of them absolutely irrevocable. At first those effigies embarrassed me, I felt I was being rude, but then I got used to it.

The moment I stopped kissing her, I was in for it, she'd start on the war and her fritters. France figured prominently in our conversation. To Lola's way of thinking, France was some sort of chivalric being, not very clearly defined in space or time, but at the moment dangerously wounded and for that very reason very exciting. When anybody mentioned France to me, I instantly thought of my guts, so I wasn't nearly so open to patriotic ardour. Each man to his fears. Nevertheless, since she was sexually accommodating, I listened and never contradicted her. But when it came to my soul, she wasn't at all satisfied with me. She'd have liked to see me bubbling and bursting with enthusiasm, whereas I couldn't see a single reason for adopting that sublime state of mind; in fact I could see a thousand, all equally irrefutable, for persevering in the exact opposite disposition.

Obviously Lola was bursting with happiness and optimism, like all people on the good side of life, the ones with privilege, health, security, who still have a long time to live.

She kept bothering me with the soul, she was always going on about it. The soul is the body's vanity and pleasure as long as the body's in good health, but it's also the urge to escape from the body as soon as the body is sick or things are going badly. Of the two poses, you take the one that suits you best at the moment, and that's all there is to it! As long as you can choose between the two, you're all right. But I couldn't choose any more, my die was cast! I was up to my neck in the truth; death dogged my every step, so to speak. It was very hard for me to think of anything but my suspended sentence to be murdered, a fate which everyone else regarded as just the right thing for me.

In this kind of deferred death agony that hits you when you're lucid and in good health, the mind is open to nothing but absolute truths. Once you've been through it, you'll know what you're talking about till the end of your days.

My conclusion was that if the Germans were to come and pillage, massacre and burn everything in sight, the hotel, the fritters, Lola, the Tuileries, the cabinet ministers, their little boyfriends, the Coupole, the Louvre, the department stores, if they were to swoop down on the city and unleash the wrath of God and the fires of hell on this putrid carnival, to which nothing in the way of sordidness could possibly be added, I would have nothing to lose and everything to gain.

You don't lose much when the landlord's house burns down. Another landlord will always turn up, unless it's the same one, German or French, English or Chinese, to collect the rent... In marks or francs? What difference does it make, seeing as you've got to pay...

In short, my morale was damn low. If I'd told Lola what I thought of the war, she'd have taken me for a monster and banished me from the ultimate joys of her boudoir. So I was careful to keep my sentiments to myself. Besides, I had outside difficulties and rivalries to worry about. Quite a few officers were trying to filch her away from me. Their competition was redoubtable, armed as they were with the seduction of their Legions of Honour. And just then the American papers were beginning to be full of this damned Legion of Honour. She cuckolded me two or three times, and I'd go so far as to say that our relationship would have been in serious danger on those occasions, if it hadn't dawned on her that I could be put to a higher use, namely, made to taste the fritters every morning in her stead.

This last-minute specialization saved me. She could accept me as a substitute, for I was a valiant comrade-in-arms, hence worthy of so sacred a mission. From that moment on we were more than lovers, we were partners as well. The modern age had dawned.

To me her body was a joy without end. I never wearied of exploring that American body. I have to admit that I was a terrible lecher. I still am.

And I formed the pleasant and fortifying conviction that a country capable of producing bodies so daringly graceful, so tempting in their spiritual flights, must have countless other vital revelations to offer, of a biological nature, it goes without saying.

I made up my mind, while feeling and fondling Lola, that sooner or later I'd take a trip, or call it a pilgrimage, to the United States, the sooner the better. And the fact is that I knew neither peace nor rest (in an implacably adverse and harassed life) until I managed to go through with that profound and mystically anatomical adventure.

So it was in the immediate vicinity of Lola's rear end that I received the message of a new world. Of course Lola wasn't all body, she also had a wee little face that was adorable and just a bit cruel because of her grey-blue eyes that slanted slightly upwards at the corners like a wildcat's.

Just looking at her made my mouth water, like a sip of dry wine, that flinty taste. There was a hardness in her eyes, unrelieved by the amiably commercial oriental-Fragonard vivacity you find in nearly all the eyes in these parts.

We usually met in a café nearby. There were more and more wounded men hobbling through the streets, many of them very bedraggled. Collections were taken for their benefit, "days" for this group and "days" for that group, especially for the organizers of the "days". Lying, fucking, dying. A law had just been passed prohibiting all other activity. The lies that were being told surpassed the imagination, far exceeded the limits of the absurd and preposterous – in the newspapers, on posters, on foot, on horseback, on pleasure boats. Everybody was doing it. In competition, to see who could lie the most outrageously. Soon there wasn't a bit of truth in the city.

The little that had been left in 1914, people were ashamed of now. Everything you touched was phoney, the sugar, the aeroplanes, the shoes, the jam, the photographs; everything you read, swallowed, sucked, admired, proclaimed, refuted, defended was made up of hate-ridden myths and grinning masquerades, phoney to the hilt. The mania for telling lies and believing them is as contagious as the itch. Little Lola's French consisted of only a few phrases, but they were all patriotic: "*On les aura!...*", "*Madelon, viens!...*"* It was enough to make you cry.

Stubbornly, shamelessly, she harped on the deaths of those doomed to die, actually all the women did, as soon as it became fashionable to be brave for other people.

Just as I was looking within and discovering such an extraordinary taste for everything that took me away from the war! I often asked Lola questions about America, but her answers were vague, pretentious and manifestly unreliable, calculated to make a brilliant impression on me.

But by that time I distrusted impressions. I'd been taken in once by an impression, and nobody was going to hoodwink me again. Nobody.

I believed in her body, I didn't believe in her soul. I thought of Lola as a charming goldbrick, miles away from the war, miles away from life.

She flitted across my nightmare with the mentality of the patriotic press: pompons, fanfare, our own Lorraine, the cadets in their white gloves... In the meantime I made love to her more and more, I'd convinced her it was a good way to lose weight. But she set more store by our long walks. I hated long walks. But she insisted.

So we spent several hours every afternoon being athletic in the Bois de Boulogne, walking round the lakes and back.

Nature is a frightening thing, and even when it's solidly domesticated as in the Bois, it gives real city dwellers an eerie, anxious feeling. And that puts them in a confiding mood. The Bois de Boulogne may be damp, fenced in, greasy and trampled, but there's nothing like it for sending memories rushing irresistibly to the minds of city dwellers strolling under the trees. Lola was not immune to that melancholy, confidential anxiety. As we walked along she told me, more or less truthfully, a thousand things about her life in New York and her little girl friends over there.

I couldn't quite make out how much of the pot-pourri of dollars, engagements, divorces, dresses and jewellery that seemed to have made up her existence was worth trying to believe.

That day we headed for the racetrack. In those days and that neck of the woods you still saw lots of horse-drawn carriages, children on donkeys, other children kicking up dust and cars full of soldiers on furlough, always in desperate haste, between two trains, to track down the women strolling on the side paths, raising more dust in their hurry to go to dinner and make love, jumpy, oily, peering this way and that, tormented by the implacable clock and the lust for life. They sweated with passion, but also with the heat.

The Bois wasn't as well cared for as usual, it was neglected, in a state of administrative suspense.

"It must have been pretty here before the war…" Lola observed. "So chic!… Oh, tell me about it, Ferdinand!… Your races here… Were they like ours in New York?"

To tell the truth, I'd never been to the races before the war, but to amuse her I instantly made up dozens of colourful details, drawing on stories various people had told me. The toilettes… The ladies of fashion… The gleaming carriages… The start… The joyous, imperious horns… The water jump… The President of the Republic… The undulant betting fever, etc.

My idealized account was so much to her liking that it brought us together. At that moment Lola seemed to discover that we had at least one taste in common, well concealed in my case, namely, a taste for social functions. She went so far as to kiss me in a burst of spontaneous emotion, something, I have to admit, that she seldom did. And then she was touched by the sadness of bygone fashions. Everyone has his own way of mourning the passage of time. It was through dead fashions that Lola perceived the flight of the years.

"Ferdinand," she asked, "do you think there will be races here again?"

"When the war is over, Lola, I should think…"

"We can't be sure, can we?…"

"No, we can't be sure…"

The possibility that there would never again be races at Longchamp overwhelmed her. The sadness of the world has different ways of getting to people, but it seems to succeed almost every time.

"Suppose, Ferdinand, suppose the war goes on a long time, maybe for years... Then it'll be too late for me... to come back here... Do you understand, Ferdinand?... You know how I love beautiful places like this... so grand, so chic... It'll be too late... For ever too late... Maybe... Maybe I'll be old, Ferdinand. When the races start up again... I'll be old... You'll see, Ferdinand, it will be too late... I can feel it will be too late..."

She was as desolate as if she'd put on two more pounds. I said everything I could think of to comfort her and give her hope... She was only twenty-three after all... The war would be over soon, oh very soon... Good times would come again... as good as before, even better... For her at least... being so adorable... the lost years she'd catch up with no harm done!... She wouldn't run short of admirers... so soon... To please me she pretended she wasn't sad any more.

"Do we have to keep walking?" she asked.

"Your weight!"

"Oh, that's right, I'd forgotten..."

We left Longchamp, the children had gone. Nothing left but dust. The furlough boys were still chasing Happiness, but no longer in the copses, the pursuit of Happiness had moved to the café terraces around the Porte Maillot.

We headed for Saint-Cloud along the river bank, shrouded in a dancing halo of autumn mists. As we approached the bridge, some barges loaded to the gunwales with coal and lying low in the water were thrusting their noses under the arches.

Above the fences the park deployed a great fan of greenery. Those trees are as vast and gentle and strong as dreams. But trees were something else I distrusted, ever since I'd been ambushed. Behind every tree a dead man. Between two lines of roses, the avenue, rising gently, led to the fountains. Outside the kiosk the soda-water lady seemed to be slowly gathering the evening shadows around her skirt. Further on, along the side paths, great cubes and rectangles of dark-coloured canvas were flapping, carnival booths, which the war had taken by surprise and suddenly filled with silence.

"It's been a whole year since they went away!" the soda-water lady told us. "You won't see two people here in a whole day now... I come out of habit... There used to be so many people!..."

That was all the old lady knew, the rest of what had happened was a blank to her. Lola wanted to go and look at the empty tents, one of those funny sad impulses.

We counted about twenty of them, a long one full of mirrors and a lot of small ones, sweet stands, lotteries, even a small theatre traversed with draughts. There was a tent in every space between the trees; one of them, near the Grand Avenue, had lost its flaps, it was as well aired out as an old mystery.

These tents were leaning close to the mud and fallen leaves. We stopped near the last, the one that was bent lowest, it was pitching on its poles like a ship in the wind, with wildly flapping sails ready to snap the last of its cables. It swayed in the rising wind, a sheet of canvas flew up above the roof and flapped and flapped. The old name of the stand was written on the front in green and red letters; it had been a shooting gallery, the Gallery of the Nations.

There was no one to take care of it now. Maybe the owner had gone shooting with the rest of them, with his customers.

What a lot of bullets the little targets in the stand had taken! All of them riddled with little white dots! A wedding, that always got a laugh out of them: tin figures in the first row, the bride with her flowers, the cousin, the soldier, the groom with a big red face, and in the second row the guests, who must have been killed a good many times when the carnival was still operating.

"I bet you're a good shot, aren't you, Ferdinand? If the carnival were still running, I'd challenge you!... You are a good shot, aren't you, Ferdinand?"

"No, I'm not a very good shot..."

In the last row behind the wedding, another row was daubed in, the town hall with its flag. People must have shot at the town hall, too, when the gallery was working, at the windows, they'd open and a bell would clang, and they even shot at the little tin flag. And they'd shot at the regiment marching on an incline nearby, like mine on the Place Clichy, this one was between the pipes and the little balloons. People had shot at those things for all they were worth, and now they were shooting at me, yesterday and tomorrow.

"They're shooting at me, too, Lola!" I cried. It slipped out of me.

"Let's be going!" she said... "You're talking nonsense, Ferdinand, and we'll catch cold."

We descended the main avenue, the Avenue Royale, towards Saint-Cloud, avoiding the mud. She held me by the hand, hers was tiny, but I couldn't think of anything but the tin wedding at the shooting gallery up there, which we had left behind us in the shadow of the trees. I even forgot to kiss Lola, something had come over me, I felt very funny. I think it was then that my head became so agitated, with all the ideas going around in it.

It was dark when we got to the Pont de Saint-Cloud.

"Ferdinand, would you like to have dinner at Duval's? You like Duval's, don't you... It would cheer you up... There's always such a big crowd... Unless you'd rather eat in my room?" She was being very considerate that evening.

We finally decided on Duval's. But we'd hardly sat down when the place struck me as monstrous. I got the idea that these people sitting in rows around us were waiting for bullets to be fired at them from all sides while they were eating.

"Get out!" I warned them. "Beat it! They're going to shoot! They're going to kill you! The whole lot of you!"

I was hurried back to Lola's hotel. Everywhere I saw the same thing. The people in the hallways of the Paritz all seemed to be on their way to be shot and so did the clerks behind the big desk, all of them just ripe for it, and the character down at the door with his uniform as blue as the sky and as golden as the sun, the doorman, and the officers and generals walking this way and that, not nearly so gorgeous of course, but in uniform all the same, all ripe to be shot, there'd be shooting from every side, no one would escape, not this one, not that or the other. The time for joking was past.

"They're going to shoot!" I yelled at the top of my lungs in the middle of the lobby. "They're going to shoot! Beat it, all of you!..." I went to the window and shouted some more. What a disturbance! "Poor soldier boy!" the people said. The concierge led me gently to the bar, by suasion. He gave me something to drink and I drank quite a lot, and then the MPs came and took me away, not so gently. There'd been MPs at the Gallery of the Nations too. I'd seen them. Lola kissed me and helped them to take me away with their handcuffs.

Then I fell sick, I was delirious, driven mad by fear, they said at the hospital. Maybe so. The best thing to do when you're in this world, don't you agree, is to get out of it. Crazy or not, scared or not.

* * *

There was quite a commotion. Some people said: "That young fellow's an anarchist, they'll shoot him, the sooner the better... Can't let the grass grow under our feet with a war on!..." But there were others, more patient, who thought I was just syphilitic and sincerely insane, they consequently wanted me to be locked up until the war was over or at least for several months, because they, who claimed to be sane and in their right minds, wanted to take care of me while they carried on the war all by themselves. Which proves that if you want people to think you're normal there's nothing like having a lot of nerve. If you've got plenty of nerve, you're all set, because then you're entitled to do practically anything at all, you've got the majority on your side, and it's the majority who decide what's crazy and what isn't.

Even so my diagnosis was very doubtful. So the authorities decided to put me under observation for a while. My little friend Lola had permission to visit me now and then, and so did my mother. That was all.

We, the befogged wounded, were lodged in a secondary school at Issy-les-Moulineaux, especially rigged to take in soldiers like me, whose patriotism was either impaired or dangerously sick, and get us by cajolery or force to confess. The treatment wasn't really bad, but we felt we were being watched every minute of the day by the staff of silent male nurses endowed with enormous ears.

After a varying period of observation, we'd be quietly sent away and assigned to an insane asylum, the front or, not infrequently, the firing squad.

Among the comrades assembled in that suspect institution, I always wondered while listening to them talking in whispers in the mess hall, which ones might be on the point of becoming ghosts.

In her little cottage near the gate dwelt the concierge, who sold us barley sugar and oranges as well as the wherewithal for sewing on buttons. She also sold us pleasure. For non-coms the price of pleasure was ten francs. Everybody could have it. But watch your step, because men tend to get too confiding on such occasions. An expansive moment could cost you dearly. Whatever was confided to her she repeated in detail to the Chief Medical Officer, and it went into your court-martial record. It seemed reliably established that she'd had a corporal of

Spahis, a youngster still in his teens, shot for his confidences, as well as a reservist in the corps of engineers, who had swallowed nails to put his stomach out of commission, and a hysteric, who had described his method of staging a paralytic seizure at the front... One evening, to sound me out, she offered me the identification papers of a father of six, who was dead, so she told me, saying they might help me to a rear-echelon assignment. In short, she was a snake. In bed, though, she was superb, we came back again and again, and the pleasure she purveyed was real. She may have been a slut, but at least she was a real one. To give royal pleasure they've got to be. In the kitchens of love, after all, vice is like the pepper in a good sauce; it brings out the flavour, it's indispensable.

The school buildings opened out on a big terrace, golden in summer, surrounded by trees, with a magnificent panoramic view of Paris. It was there that our visitors waited for us on Thursdays, including Lola, as regular as clockwork, bringing cakes, advice and cigarettes.

We saw our doctors every morning. They questioned us amiably enough, but we never knew exactly what they were thinking. Under their affable smiles as they walked among us, they carried our death sentences.

The mealy-mouthed atmosphere reduced some of the patients under observation, more emotional than the rest, to such a state of exasperation that at night, instead of sleeping, they paced the ward from end to end, loudly protesting against their own anguish, convulsed between hope and despair, as on a dangerous mountain spur. For days and days they suffered, and then suddenly one night they'd go to pieces, run to the Chief Medical Officer, and confess everything. They'd never be seen again. I wasn't easy in my mind myself. But when you're weak, the best way to fortify yourself is to strip the people you fear of the last bit of prestige you're still inclined to give them. Learn to consider them as they are, worse than they are in fact and from every point of view. That will release you, set you free, protect you more than you can possibly imagine. It will give you another self. There will be two of you.

That will strip their words and deeds of the obscene mystical fascination that weakens you and makes you waste your time. From then on you'll find their act no more amusing, no more relevant to your inner progress than that of the lowliest pig.

Beside me, in the next bed, there was a corporal, a volunteer like me. Up until August he had been a teacher at a secondary school in Touraine, teaching history and geography, so he told me. After a few months on the front lines this teacher had turned out to be a champion thief. Nothing could stop him from stealing canned goods from the regimental supply train, the quartermaster trucks, the company stores and anywhere else he could find them.

So he'd landed there with the rest of us, while presumably awaiting court martial. But since his family persisted in trying to prove that he had been stupefied and demoralized by shell shock, the prosecution deferred his trial from month to month. He didn't talk to me very much. He spent hours combing his beard, but when he spoke to me it was almost always about the same thing, about the method he had discovered for not getting his wife with any more children. Was he really insane? At a time when the world is upside down and it's thought insane to ask why you're being murdered, it obviously requires no great effort to pass for a lunatic. Of course your act has got to be convincing, but when it comes to keeping out of the big slaughterhouse some people's imaginations become magnificently fertile.

Everything that's important goes on in the darkness, no doubt about it. We never know anyone's real inside story.

This teacher's name was Princhard. What can the man have dreamt up to save his carotids, lungs and optic nerves? That was the crucial question, the question we men should have asked one another if we'd wanted to be strictly human and rational. Far from it, we staggered along in a world of idealistic absurdities, hemmed in by insane, bellicose platitudes. Like smoke-maddened rats we tried to escape from the burning ship, but we had no general plan, no faith in one another. Dazed by the war, we had developed a different kind of madness: fear. The heads and tails of the war.

In the midst of the general delirium, this Princhard took a certain liking to me, though he distrusted me of course.

In the place and situation we were in, friendship and trust were out of the question. No one revealed any more than he thought useful for his survival, since everything or practically everything was sure to be repeated by some attentive stool pigeon.

From time to time one of us would disappear. That meant the case against him was ready and the court martial would send him to a military tribunal, the penal colonies, the front or, if he was very lucky, the insane asylum in Clamart.

More dubious warriors kept arriving, from every branch of service, some very young, some almost old, some terrified, some ranting and swaggering. Their wives and parents came to see them, and their children too, staring wide-eyed, on Thursdays.

They all wept buckets in the visiting room, especially in the evening. All the helplessness of a world at war wept when the visits were over and the women and children left, dragging their feet in the bleak, gas-lit corridor. A herd of snivelling riff-raff – that's what they were – disgusting.

To Lola it was still an adventure, coming to see me in that prison, as you might have called it. We two didn't cry. Where would we have got our tears from?

"Is it true that you've gone mad, Ferdinand?" she asked me one Thursday.

"It's true!" I admitted.

"But they'll treat you here?"

"There's no treatment for fear, Lola."

"Is it as bad as all that?"

"It's worse, Lola. My fear is so bad that if I die a natural death later on, I especially don't want to be cremated! I want them to leave me in the ground, quietly rotting in the graveyard, ready to come back to life... Maybe... how do we know? But if they burned me to ashes, Lola, don't you see, it would be over, really over... A skeleton, after all, is still something like a man... It's more likely to come back to life than ashes... Reduced to ashes, you're finished!... What do you think?... Naturally the war..."

"Oh, Ferdinand! Then you're an absolute coward! You're as loathsome as a rat..."

"Yes, an absolute coward, Lola, I reject the war and everything in it... I don't deplore it... I don't resign myself to it... I don't weep about it... I just plain reject it and all its fighting men, I don't want anything to do with them or it. Even if there were nine hundred and ninety-five million of them and I were all alone, they'd still be wrong and I'd be right. Because I'm the one who knows what I want: I don't want to die."

"But it's not possible to reject the war, Ferdinand! Only crazy people and cowards reject the war when their country is in danger..."

"If that's the case, hurrah for the crazy people! Look, Lola, do you remember a single name, for instance, of any of the soldiers killed in the Hundred Years War?... Did you ever try to find out who any of them were?... No! You see? You never tried. As far as you're concerned they're as anonymous, as indifferent, as the last atom of that paperweight, as your morning bowel movement... Get it into your head, Lola, that they died for nothing! For absolutely nothing, the idiots! I say it and I'll say it again! I've proved it! The one thing that counts is life! In ten thousand years, I'll bet you, this war, remarkable as it may seem to us at present, will be utterly forgotten... Maybe here and there in the world a handful of scholars will argue about its causes or the dates of the principal hecatombs that made it famous... Up until now those are the only things about men that other men have thought worth remembering after a few centuries, a few years, or even a few hours... I don't believe in the future, Lola..."

When she heard me flaunting my shameful state like that, she lost all sympathy for me... Once and for all she put me down as contemptible.

She decided to leave me without further ado. It was too much. When I left her that evening at the hospital gate, she didn't kiss me.

Evidently the thought that a condemned man might have no vocation for death was too much for her. When I asked her how our fritters were doing, she did not reply.

On my return to the dormitory, I found Princhard at the window with a crowd of soldiers around him. He was trying out a pair of dark glasses in the gaslight. The idea, he explained, had come to him last summer at the seashore, and since it was summer now, he was planning to wear them next day in the park. That park was enormous and exceedingly well policed by squads of vigilant orderlies. The next day Princhard insisted on my going for a walk on the terrace with him to try out his beautiful glasses. A blazing afternoon beat down on him, defended by his opaque lenses. I noticed that his nose was almost transparent at the nostrils and that he was breathing hard.

"My friend," he confided, "time is passing and it's not on my side... My conscience is immune to remorse, I have been relieved, thank God, of those fears... It's not crimes that count in this world... people stopped counting them long ago... What counts is blunders... And I believe I've made one... that's absolutely irremediable..."

"Stealing canned goods?"

"Yes, just imagine, I thought I was being so clever! My idea was to abstract myself from the battle and return, disgraced but still alive, to peace, as one returns, exhausted, to the surface of the sea after a long dive... I almost succeeded... but this war, undoubtedly, has been going on too long... So long that cannon fodder disgusting enough to disgust the Nation is no longer conceivable... She has begun to accept every offering, regardless of where it comes from, every variety of meat... The Nation has become infinitely indulgent in its choice of martyrs! Today there's no such thing as a soldier unworthy to bear arms and, above all, to die under arms and by arms... They're going, latest news, to make a hero out of me!... How imperious the homicidal madness must have become if they're willing to pardon – no, to forget! – the theft of a tin of meat! True, we have got into the habit of admiring colossal bandits, whose opulence is revered by the entire world, yet whose existence, once we stop to examine it, proves to be one long crime repeated ad infinitum, but those same bandits are heaped with glory, honours and power, their crimes are hallowed by the law of the land, whereas, as far back in history as the eye can see – and history, as you know, is my business – everything conspires to show that a venial theft, especially of inglorious foodstuffs, such as bread crusts, ham or cheese, unfailingly subjects its perpetrator to irreparable opprobrium, the categorical condemnation of the community, major punishment, automatic dishonour and inexpiable shame, and this for two reasons, first because the perpetrator of such an offence is usually poor, which in itself connotes basic unworthiness, and secondly because his act implies, as it were, a tacit reproach to the community. A poor man's theft is seen as a malicious attempt at individual redress, you understand?... Where would we be? Note accordingly that in all countries the penalties for petty theft are extremely severe, not only as a means of defending society, but also as a stern admonition to the unfortunate to know their place, stick to their caste, and behave themselves, joyfully resigned to go on dying of hunger and misery down through the centuries for ever and ever... Until today, however, petty thieves enjoyed one advantage in the Republic: they were denied the honour of bearing patriotic arms. But that's all over now, tomorrow I, a thief, will resume my place in the army... Such are the orders... It has been decided in high places to forgive and forget what they call my 'momentary madness', and this, listen carefully, in consideration of what they call 'the honour of my family'. What solicitude! I ask you, comrade, is it my family that's going to serve as a strainer and sorting house for mixed French and German bullets?... It'll just be me, won't it? And when I'm dead, is the honour of my family going to bring me back to life?... I can see how it will be with my family when these warlike scenes have passed... as everything passes... I can see my family on fine Sundays... joyfully gambolling on the lawns of a new summer... while three feet under papa, that's me, dripping with worms and infinitely more disgusting than a kilo of turds on Bastille Day, will be rotting stupendously with all my deluded flesh... To fertilize the fields of the anonymous ploughman – that is the true future of the true soldier! Ah, comrade! This world, I assure you, is only a vast device for kidding the world! You are young. Let these minutes of wisdom be as years to you! Listen well, comrade, and don't fail to recognize and understand the telltale sign, which glares from all the murderous hypocrisies of our society: 'Compassion with the fate, the condition of the poor...' I tell you, little men, life's mugs, beaten, fleeced to the bone, sweated from time immemorial, I warn you that when the princes of this world start loving you, it means they're going to grind you up into battle sausage... That's the sign... It's infallible. It starts with affection. Louis XIV at least, and don't forget it, didn't give a hoot in hell about his beloved people. Louis XV ditto. He wiped his arsehole with them. True, we didn't live well in those days, the poor have never lived well, but the kings didn't flay them with the obstinacy, the persistence you meet with in today's tyrants. There's no rest, I tell you, for the little man, except in the contempt of the great, whose only motive for thinking of the common people is self-interest, when it isn't sadism... It's the philosophers, another point to look out for while we're at it, who first started giving the people ideas... when all they'd known up until then was the catechism! They began, so they proclaimed, to educate the people... Ah! What truths they had to reveal! Beautiful! Brilliant! Unprecedented truths! And the people were dazzled! 'That's it!' they said. 'That's the stuff! Let's go and die for it!' The people are always dying to die! That's the way they are! 'Long live Diderot!' they yelled. And 'Long live Voltaire!' They, at least, were first-class philosophers! And long live Carnot,* too, who was so good at organizing victories! And long live everybody! Those guys at least don't let the beloved people moulder in ignorance and fetishism! They show the people the roads of Freedom! Emancipation! Things went fast after that! First teach everybody to read the papers! That's the way to salvation! Hurry hurry! No more illiterates! We don't need them any more! Nothing but citizen-soldiers! Who vote! Who read! And who fight! And who march! And send kisses from the front! In no time the people were good and ripe. The enthusiasm of the liberated has to be good for something, doesn't it? Danton wasn't eloquent for the hell of it. With a few phrases, so rousing that we can still hear them today, he had the people mobilized before you could say fiddlesticks! That was when the first battalions of emancipated maniacs marched off! The first voting, flag-waving suckers that Dumouriez* led away to get themselves drilled full of holes in Flanders! As for Dumouriez himself, who had come too late to these new-fangled idealistic pastimes, he discovered that he was more interested in money and deserted. He was our last mercenary... The gratis soldier was something really new... So new that when Goethe* arrived in Valmy, Goethe or not, he was flabbergasted. At the sight of those ragged, impassioned cohorts, who had come of their own free will to get themselves disembowelled by the King of Prussia in defence of a patriotic fiction no one had ever heard of, Goethe realized that he still had much to learn. 'This day,' he declaimed grandiloquently as befitted the habits of his genius, 'marks the beginning of a new era!' He could say that again! The system proved successful and pretty soon they were mass-producing heroes, and in the end, the system was so well perfected that they cost practically nothing. Everyone was delighted. Bismarck, the two Napoleons, Barrès,* Elsa the Horsewoman.* The religion of the flag promptly replaced the cult of heaven, an old cloud which had already been deflated by the Reformation and reduced to a network of episcopal money boxes. In olden times the fanatical fashion was: 'Long live Jesus! Burn the heretics!' But heretics, after all, were few and voluntary... Whereas today vast hordes of men are fired with aim and purpose by cries of: 'Hang the limp turnips! The juiceless lemons! The innocent readers! By the millions, eyes right!' If anybody doesn't want to fight or murder, stinking pacifists, grab 'em, tear 'em to pieces! Kill them in thirteen juicy ways! For a starter, to teach them how to live, rip their guts out of their bodies, their eyes out of their sockets, and the years out of their filthy slobbering lives! Let whole legions of them perish, turn into smidgens, bleed, smoulder in acid – and all that to make the Nation more beloved, more fair, and more joyful! And if in their midst there are any foul creatures who refuse to understand these sublime truths, they can just go and bury themselves right with the others, no, not quite, their place will be at the far end of the cemetery, under the shameful epitaphs of cowards without an ideal, for those contemptible slugs will have forfeited the glorious right to a small patch of the shadow of the municipal monument erected by the lowest bidder in the central avenue to commemorate the reputable dead, and also the right to hear so much as a distant echo of the Minister's speech next Sunday, when he comes around to urinate at the Prefecture and sound off over the graves after lunch…"

But from the end of the garden someone was calling Princhard. The head physician had sent his orderly to get him on the double.

"Coming," Princhard cried. He had barely time enough to hand me the draft of the speech he had been trying out on me. A ham if there ever was one.

I never saw Princhard again. He had the same trouble as all intellectuals – he was ineffectual. He knew too many things, and they confused him. He needed all sorts of gimmicks to steam him up, help him make up his mind.

It's been a long time since that night when he went away, when I think about it. But I remember it well. Suddenly the houses at the end of our park stood out sharply, as things do before the night takes hold of them. The trees grew larger in the twilight and shot up to the sky to meet the night.

I never made any attempt to get in touch with Princhard, to find out if he had really "disappeared", as they kept saying. But it's best if he disappeared.

* * *

While the war was still on, the seeds of our hateful peace were being sown.

A hysterical bitch, you could see what she'd be like just by watching her cavorting in the dance hall of the Olympia. In that long cellar room, you could see her squinting out of a hundred mirrors, stamping her feet in the dust and despair to the music of a Negro-Judaeo-Saxon band. Britons and blacks, Levantines and Russians were everywhere, smoking and bellowing, military melancholics lined up on the red plush sofas. Those uniforms that people are beginning to find it hard to remember were the seeds of the present day, of something that is still growing and that won't become total shit for a while yet, but will in the long run.

Every week, after spending a few hours at the Olympia, warming up our desires, a few of us would go calling on our friend Madame Herote,* who kept a lingerie, glove and book shop in the Impasse des Bérésinas* behind the Folies-Bergère, a covered passage that isn't there any more, where little girls brought little dogs on leashes to do their business.

We went there to grope for our happiness, which all the world was threatening with the utmost ferocity. We were ashamed of wanting what we wanted, but something had to be done about it all the same! Love is harder to give up than life. In this world we spend our time killing or adoring, or both together. "I hate you! I adore you!" We keep going, we fuel and refuel, we pass on our life to a biped of the next century, with frenzy, at any cost, as if it were the greatest of pleasures to perpetuate ourselves, as if, when all's said and done, it would make us immortal. One way or another, kissing is as indispensable as scratching.

My mental state had improved, but my military situation was still uncertain. I had leave to go out now and then. Anyway, the name of our lingerie lady was Madame Herote. Her forehead was low and so narrow that at first you felt uneasy in her presence, but her lips were so smiling and voluptuous that after a while you didn't see how you could get away from her. Under a surface of staggering volubility and unforgettable ardour, she concealed a set of simple, rapacious and piously mercantile aims.

In a few months she piled up a fortune, thanks to the Allies and thanks above all to her womb. Her ovaries, it has to be said, had been removed, she had been operated for salpingitis the year before. That liberating castration had made her fortune. Gonorrhoea in a woman can be providential. A woman who spends her time worrying about pregnancy is a virtual cripple, she'll never go very far.

Old men and young men thought, and so did I, that love was easily and cheaply available in the back rooms of certain lingerie-bookshops. That was still true some twenty years ago, but today a lot of things aren't done any more, especially some of the most agreeable. Every month Anglo-Saxon puritanism is drying us up a little more, it has already reduced those impromptu backroom carousals to practically nothing. Now marriage and respectability are the thing.

In those days, for the last time, there was still freedom to fuck standing up and cheap, and Madame Herote put it to good use. One Sunday an auction room appraiser with time on his hands sighted her shop and went in; he's still there. He was slightly gaga, and gaga he remained, but nothing more. Their happiness aroused no interest in the neighbourhood. In the shadow of the newspapers, with their delirious appeals for ultimate patriotic sacrifices, life went on, strictly rationed, larded with precautions and more trickily resourceful than ever before. Those are the heads and tails, the light and shade, of the same coin.

Madame Herote's appraiser invested money in Holland for his better-informed friends, and for Madame Herote as well, once they became intimate. Her stock of neckties and brassieres and negligees attracted customers of both sexes and brought them back time and time again.

Any number of national and international encounters took place in the pink shadow of those curtains, amid the incessant loquacity of Madame Herote, whose substantial, talkative and overwhelmingly perfumed person would have put the most bilious of males in a lecherous mood. Far from losing her head in these miscellaneous gatherings, Madame Herote turned them to her advantage, first in terms of money, since she levied a tithe on all sentimental transactions, but also through her enjoyment of all the lovemaking that went on around her. She took pleasure in bringing couples together and as much or more in breaking them up by means of tale-telling, insinuations and out-and-out treachery.

She never wearied of fomenting happiness and tragedy. She stoked the life of the passions, and her business prospered.

Proust, who was half ghost, immersed himself with extraordinary tenacity in the infinitely watery futility of the rites and procedures that entwine the members of high society, those denizens of the void, those phantoms of desire, those irresolute daisy-chainers still waiting for their Watteau, those listless seekers after implausible Cythereas. Whereas Madame Herote, with her sturdy popular origins, was firmly fastened to the earth by her crude, stupid and very specific appetites.

Maybe, if people are so wicked, it's only because they suffer, but years can elapse between the time when they stop suffering and the time when their characters take a turn for the better. Madame Herote's impressive material and amatory success hadn't had time yet to soften her rapacious instincts.

She was no more hateful than most of the shopkeeping ladies about, but she took so much trouble convincing people of the contrary that one doesn't tend to forget her. Her shop was more than a meeting place, it was a kind of secret gateway to a world of wealth and luxury, in which, much as I had wanted to, I had never set foot until then, and from which I was promptly and embarrassingly ejected after one furtive incursion, my first and last.

In Paris the rich live together. Their neighbourhoods adjoin and coalesce, so as to form a wedge of urban cake, the tip of which touches the Louvre and the rounded outer edge is bounded by the trees between the Pont d'Auteuil and the Porte des Ternes.* That's the good slice of the city. All the rest is shit and misery.

At first glance the rich neighbourhoods don't look so very different from the rest of the city, except that the streets are a little cleaner. But if you want to go deeper in your excursion, to get inside the people who live there, you'll have to rely on chance or on intimate connections.

Madame Herote's shop could give you some little access to this preserve, through the Argentines who came in from the privileged neighbourhoods to buy shirts and underwear and flirt with the unusual selection of ambitious, theatrical, musical and well-built young friends whom Madame Herote deliberately gathered around her.

I, who, as they say, had nothing to offer but my youth, became much too interested in one of them. Little Musyne they called her in her crowd.

In the Passage des Bérésinas, the shopkeepers all knew one another, it was like a provincial village wedged for years between two Paris streets, in other words everybody slandered and spied on everybody else as much as was humanly and deliriously possible.

What the shopkeepers mostly talked and complained about before the war was the petty, desperately thrifty life they all led. Among other sordid hardships, the chronic complaint of those shopkeepers was being obliged by the prevailing gloom to light their gas at four in the afternoon because of their showcases. But inside the shops, the selfsame twilight made for an atmosphere conducive to off-colour propositions.

Nevertheless, a good many of the shops were being ruined by the war, while Madame Herote's, thanks to the young Argentines, to officers with per-diem allowances, and to the advice of her friend the appraiser, enjoyed a prosperity on which, as you can easily imagine, the whole neighbourhood commented in the most vitriolic terms.

It was just about then, for instance, that the famous pastry shop at No. 112 lost its best customers. The latest mobilization was to blame. So many horses had been requisitioned that the ladies with the long gloves, who had dropped in regularly at teatime, would have been obliged to walk. They stopped coming, and they never came back. Sambanet, the music binder, was suddenly unable to resist the urge, which had long tormented him, to sodomize a soldier. A bungled attempt one night did him irreparable harm with certain patriotic gentlemen, who accused him forthwith of being a spy. He was obliged to close up shop.

Then Mademoiselle Hermance, at No. 26, who had hitherto specialized in the sale of a certain mentionable or unmentionable item made of rubber, would have been doing all right under the prevailing circumstances if she hadn't found it so unconscionably difficult to procure her "merry widows", which were made in Germany.

In short, it was only Madame Herote who, on the threshold of a new era of lighter-than-air democratic lingerie, found an easy way to prosperity.

Plenty of anonymous letters were written from shop to shop, and they didn't mince words. Madame Herote preferred for her entertainment to write to highly placed persons, so demonstrating that a virulent ambition was the cornerstone of her character. She wrote several to the President, for instance, just to convince him that he was a cuckold, and some to Marshal Pétain* in English, with the help of a dictionary, to drive him crazy. But what's an anonymous letter? Water off a duck's back! Every day Madame Herote received a whole packet of these unsigned letters, which didn't smell good, I assure you. She'd be pensive, upset, for about ten minutes, but then she'd recover her composure, she didn't care how or by what means, but she got it back good and solid, for there was no place for doubt in her inner life, and still less for truth.

Among her customers and protégées, there were several young ladies from the entertainment world – actresses and musicians – who came with more debts than clothes. Madame Herote gave them advice, and it helped them no end. One of them was Musyne, the most attractive of the lot for my money. Musyne was a musician, she played the violin, a very shrewd little angel, as I was soon to learn. Implacable in her determination to succeed here on earth and not in heaven, she was doing all right at the time of our first meeting in an adorable, exceedingly Parisian and now completely forgotten little act at the Variétés.*

She'd appear with her violin in a kind of impromptu prologue in melody and verse. A charming, complicated genre.

Smitten as I was, my days became a frenzy, dashing from the hospital to the back door of her theatre. I was seldom alone in waiting for her. The ground forces would snatch her away in a twinkling, the flyers had an even easier time of it, but undoubtedly the seduction prize went to the Argentines. As more and more soldiers swarmed to the colours, their cold-storage meat business assumed the proportions of a tidal wave. Little Musyne made a good thing of those profiteering days; she knew what she was doing, since then the Argentines have gone out of existence.

I didn't understand. I was being cheated by everything and everybody, women, money and ideas. I was a sucker and I didn't like it. I still run into Musyne now and then, every two years or so she crosses my path, as people one has known well tend to. Two years is the time it takes to perceive at one glance, a glance as sure as instinct, the ugliness that can come over a face, even one that was delicious in its day.

For a moment you hesitate, then you accept the face as it has become, with its repugnant cumulative disharmony. What can you do but acquiesce in this slow, painstaking caricature which two years have etched, but accept the passage of time, that portrait of ourselves? Then we can say that we've really recognized each other (like some foreign banknote that one hesitates to accept at first sight), that we hadn't taken a wrong turn, that each on his own we'd travelled the right road, the inevitable road to decay, for another two years. That's all there is to it.

When she bumped into me like that, I frightened her so with my big head it looked as if she wanted to run away, to avoid me, to turn aside, anything… Obviously, as far as she was concerned, I stank of a whole past. But I've known her age for too long, and try as she will she absolutely can't escape me. She stands there, evidently put off by my existence, as if I were a monster. She, so sensitive, feels obliged to ask me crude, stupid questions, the kind that a housemaid caught stealing sugar might ask. All women are domestics at heart. But possibly she imagines this revulsion more than she feels it; that's the only consolation I can find. Maybe I'm not really repulsive, but only give her the illusion that I am. Maybe I'm an artist in that line. After all, why wouldn't there be an art of ugliness as well as beauty? Maybe it's a gift that needs to be cultivated.

For a long time I thought little Musyne was stupid, but that was only because I was vain and she had run out on me. Before the war, you know, we were all a lot more ignorant and conceited than today. A little nobody like me was much more likely to take rubbish for rainbows than he would be today. I thought being in love with somebody as adorable as Musyne would give me every kind of strength and virtue, especially the courage I lacked, just because she was so pretty and such a gifted musician! Love is like liquor, the drunker and more impotent you are, the stronger and smarter you think yourself and the surer you are of your rights.

Dozens of Madame Herote's cousins had made the supreme sacrifice, so she never left her passage except in deep mourning. To tell the truth, she seldom went out, because her appraiser boyfriend was pretty jealous. We gathered in the dining room behind the shop, which with the coming of prosperity had taken on the appearance of a little salon. There we would chat and pass the time in a pleasant, well-behaved kind of way under the gas jet. Little Musyne at the piano would charm us with classical pieces, only classical music was thought fitting in those sorrowful times. We'd sit there for whole afternoons, side by side, the appraiser in the middle, musing over our secrets, our fears and hopes.

Madame Herote's maid, whom she had hired only a short time before, was always bursting with impatience to find out when this one would finally make up his mind to marry that one. In her village free love was unheard of. All those Argentines and officers and slippery-fingered customers filled her with an almost animal terror.

More and more often Musyne was monopolized by the South American customers. What with waiting for my angel, I soon got to know the caballeros' kitchens and servants very well. Naturally the valets took me for a pimp. In the end everybody took me for a pimp, including Musyne and, I'm pretty sure, the regulars at Madame Herote's shop. There was nothing I could do about it. Sooner or later people are bound to classify you as something.

I wangled another two months' convalescent leave, and there was even some talk of a medical discharge. Musyne and I decided to go and live together in Billancourt. This was actually a subterfuge to ditch me, because she took advantage of its being so far away to come home less and less frequently. She was always finding some pretext for spending the night in Paris.

The nights in Billancourt were soft and sweet, enlivened now and then by those childish air-raid or Zeppelin alarms which provided the civilian population with thrills and self-justification. While waiting for Musyne, I'd walk as far as the Pont de Grenelle,* where the darkness rises from the river to the overhead Métro tracks, with their strings of lights traversing the darkness and their enormous metallic hulks hurling themselves like thunder at the flanks of the big buildings on the Quai de Passy.

There are neighbourhoods like that in big cities, so stupidly ugly that you're almost always alone there.

In the end Musyne was showing up at our so-called home only once a week. More and more often she'd spend the evening accompanying some lady singer at the house of some Argentine. She could have made a living playing at the movies, and it would have been a lot easier for me to call for her, but the Argentines were lively and paid well, while the movie houses were dismal and the pay was wretched. Life is made up of those little preferences.

To complete my misery, the Theatre of the Armies came along. In no time Musyne got to know dozens of people at the Ministry. More and more often she went off to entertain our soldier boys at the front and stayed away for weeks on end, serving up sonatas and adagios to the troops. The front seats in the orchestra would be occupied by top brass, well-placed to admire her legs, while the soldiers, seated on wooden stands behind their commanders, had to make do with melodious echoes. After the performance, of course, she would spend exceedingly complicated nights in the hotels of the army area. One day she came home as happy as a lark, brandishing a certificate of heroism, signed if you please by one of our glorious generals. With that diploma she became a real success.

It made her ever so popular with the Argentine colony. They fêted her, they were mad about my Musyne, oh, what an adorable little front-line violinist! So rosy-cheeked and curly-headed, and a heroine to boot. Those Argentines knew which side their bread was buttered on, their admiration for our glorious generals knew no bounds, and when my Musyne came back to them with her authentic document, her pretty phiz and her nimble, heroic little fingers, each tried to love her more than the next, they tried to outbid each other, so to speak. The poetry of heroism holds an irresistible appeal for people who aren't involved in a war, especially when they're making piles of money out of one. It's only natural.

Ah, jaunty heroism! Strong men have swooned away! The shipbuilders of Rio offered their names and their shares to the adorable young thing who feminized the warlike valour of the French so charmingly for their benefit. Musyne, I have to admit, had managed to outfit herself with a delightful little repertory of war adventures, they were wonderfully becoming, like a jaunty little cap. Sometimes she amazed me with her skilful touch, and listening to her I had to own that when it came to tall stories I was a clumsy faker compared to her. She had a gift for locating her fantasies in a dramatic faraway setting that gave everything a lasting glow. It often struck me that when we combatants spin yarns they tend to be crudely chronometric and precise. Her medium was eternity. Claude Lorrain* was right in saying that the foreground of a picture is always repugnant and that the interest of an artwork must be seen in the distance, in that unfathomable realm which is the refuge of lies, of those dreams caught in the act, which are the only thing men love. The woman who can turn our despicable nature to account has no difficulty in becoming our darling, our indispensable and supreme hope. We expect her to preserve our illusory raison d'être, but on the other hand she can make a very good living while performing this magic function. Instinctively, Musyne did just that.

The Argentines lived in the Ternes area and on the fringes of the Bois, in small private houses, resplendent and well-fenced-in, which were kept so delightfully warm in that wintry weather that when you came in from the street your thoughts suddenly took an optimistic turn, you couldn't help it.

In my jittery despair, I had taken to waiting for Musyne in the butler's pantry as often as possible, a stupid thing to do. Sometimes I waited until morning, I was sleepy, but jealousy kept me awake, and so did the vast amounts of white wine the servants poured out for me. I seldom saw the Argentine masters of the house, I heard their songs and their blustering Spanish and the piano which never stopped but was usually being played by other hands than those of my Musyne. What, meanwhile, was she doing with her hands, the slut?

When she saw me at the door in the morning, she made a face. I was still as natural as an animal in those days. I was like a dog with a bone, I wouldn't let go.

People waste a large part of their youth in stupid mistakes. It was obvious that my darling was going to leave me, flat and soon. I hadn't found out yet that mankind consists of two very different races, the rich and the poor. It took me, and plenty of other people, twenty years and the war to learn to stick to my class and ask the price of things before touching them, let alone setting my heart on them.

So as I warmed myself in the pantry with the servants, I was unaware that the people dancing over my head were Argentine gods – they could have been German, French or Chinese, that didn't mean a thing, the point was that they were gods, rich people, that's what I should have realized. Them upstairs with Musyne, me downstairs with nothing. Musyne was thinking seriously of her future, and naturally she preferred to do that kind of thinking with a god. I too was thinking of my future, but in a kind of delirium, because my constant companion was a muted fear of being killed in the war or of starving when peace came. I had a death sentence hanging over me, and I was in love. A nightmare, to put it mildly. Not far away, less than a hundred kilometres, millions of brave, well-armed, well-trained men were waiting to settle my hash, and plenty of Frenchmen were waiting, too, to pump me full of lead if I declined to be cut into bleeding ribbons by the opposite side.

A poor man in this world can be done to death in two main ways, by the absolute indifference of his fellows in peacetime or by their homicidal mania when there's a war. When other people start thinking about you, it's figure out how to torture you, that and nothing else. The bastards want to see you bleeding, otherwise they're not interested! Princhard was dead right. In the shadow of the slaughterhouse, you don't speculate very much about your future, you think about loving in the days you have left, because there's no other way of forgetting your body that's about to be skinned alive.

Since Musyne was slipping away from me, I took myself for an idealist, which is the name we give to our little instincts clothed in high-sounding words. My leave was drawing to an end. The newspapers were summoning every conceivable combatant to the colours, first of all, it goes without saying, the ones without connections. An official order had gone out that no one should think of anything but winning the war.

Musyne, like Lola, was extremely eager to have me get back to the front on the double and stay there, and since I seemed to be dragging my feet, she decided to expedite matters, which was unusual for her.

One night, when for a change we went home to Billancourt together, the fire brigade came by blowing bugles, and everybody in our house went scrambling down to the cellar in honour of some Zeppelin.

Those petty panics, when a whole neighbourhood in pyjamas would pick up candles and vanish, cackling and clucking, into the bowels of the earth to escape a peril that was almost entirely imaginary, showed up the terrifying futility of those people, who behaved by turns like frightened hens and vain and obedient sheep. These preposterous inconsistencies ought to disgust the most patient, the most tenacious of sociophiles for good and all.

At the first blast of the bugle, Musyne forgot every bit of the heroism for which she had been cited at the Theatre of the Armies. She insisted on rushing into some hole and dragging me with her, into the Métro, the sewers, anywhere, as long as it was sheltered and deep enough underground! After a while the sight of all those people, our fellow tenants, fat and thin, jovial and majestic, descending four by four, into the salutary pit, armed even me with indifference. Brave or cowardly – there's not much difference. A poltroon in one situation, a hero in another – it's the same man, and he doesn't think any more in one circumstance than in the other. Everything unrelated to making money is infinitely beyond him. The question of life and death escapes him completely. Even on the subject of his own death his cogitations are feeble and oblique. He understands money and theatricals, nothing else.

Musyne whined when I resisted. Other tenants urged us to come along, and in the end I gave in. There were several cellar compartments to choose from, and various suggestions were made. The majority finally favoured the butcher's storage cellar: it was deeper down, so they said, than any of the others. On the stairs I caught a whiff of an acrid odour that I knew only too well and which I absolutely couldn't bear.

"Musyne," I said, "are you really going down there? With all that meat hanging on hooks?"

The question surprised her. "Why not?"

"Well," I said, "I have certain memories. I'd rather go back upstairs…"

"You mean you're leaving me?"

"You'll join me as soon as it's over!"

"But it may go on for a long time…"

"I'd rather wait for you upstairs," I said. "I don't like meat, and it'll be over soon."

During the alert, sheltered in their dens, the tenants exchanged sprightly comments. Some ladies in dressing gowns, the last to arrive, swept with elegance and grace into that odoriferous chasm, where the butcher and his wife bade them welcome, at the same time apologizing for the artificial cold, indispensable for the conservation of their merchandise.

Musyne vanished with the rest. I waited in our apartment, a night, a whole day, a year… She never came back to me.

From that time on I became harder and harder to please. I had only two thoughts in my head: to save my skin and go to America. But getting away from the war was a first step which kept me busy and breathless for months and months.

The patriots kept clamouring: "Guns! Men! Ammunition!" They never seemed to get tired. It looked as if they wouldn't be able to sleep until poor Belgium and innocent little Alsace were wrested from the German yoke. It was an obsession which, so we were told, prevented the best of our fellow citizens from breathing, eating or copulating. But it didn't seem to prevent the survivors from swinging business deals. Morale was doing all right on the home front.

There was every reason to ship us back to our regiments in a hurry. But when the medics looked me over, they still found me subnormal, barely good enough to be sent to another hospital, this one for the bones and nervous system. One morning six of us, three artillerymen and three dragoons, all of us sick and wounded, left the depot in search of this institution where shattered courage, demolished reflexes and broken arms were repaired. First, like all wounded soldiers at the time, we stopped for a check-up at the Val-de-Grâce,* that noble pot-bellied citadel, with its beard of trees. The corridors smelt like a third-class railway carriage – a smell that's gone today, for ever no doubt, compounded of feet, straw and oil lamps. We didn't last long at the Val, they'd barely caught sight of us when two bedandruffed and overworked administrative officers chewed us out good and proper, threatened us with a court martial, and projected us via other administrators into the street. They had no room for us, so they said, and directed us, very vaguely, to a bastion situated somewhere in the outskirts.

From bistro to bastion, from white wine to *café crème*, the six of us wandered about, at the mercy of every misdirector, in search of this new refuge which seemed to specialize in the treatment of incompetent heroes like us.

Only one of us had even the most rudimentary personal property, and that fitted nicely into a little tin box marked "Biscuits Pernot", a well-known brand at the time, though I never hear it mentioned any more. In that box our comrade kept a few cigarettes and a toothbrush. Come to think of it, we used to kid him about the care he took of his teeth, which was most unusual at the time. "Homosexual" we used to call him!

Finally, in the middle of the night, we approached the outworks, swollen with darkness, of the Bicêtre bastion. No. 43 it was called. That was the place.

It had just been renovated to serve as a home for elderly cripples. They hadn't even finished laying out the garden.

When we got there, there wasn't a soul in the military section, only the concierge. The rain was coming down in buckets. The concierge was terrified when she heard us, but we made her laugh by touching her in the right place. "I thought it was the Germans," she said. "They're miles away!" we told her. "Where are you wounded?" she asked with concern. "All over, but not in the cock!" said one of the artillerymen. That, I don't mind telling you, was real wit, just the kind the concierge liked.

Later on some old men on public welfare were lodged in that bastion with us. New buildings with miles and miles of window glass had been thrown up for them in a hurry, and there they were kept like insects until the end of the war. On the surrounding hills a rash of skimpy housing lots vied for possession of the seas of mud inadequately contained by rows of precarious shacks, in the shadow of which one would occasionally see a head of lettuce and three radishes, of which, it is hard to say why, the nauseated slugs were making the house owner a present.

Our hospital was clean. You have to hurry to see that kind of thing, move in at the beginning, the first few weeks, because maintenance isn't a French virtue, we have no taste for it, in fact, we're downright disgusting in that respect. We flopped on six metal beds, at random and by moonlight, the building was so new the electricity hadn't been put in yet.

Early next morning the doctor came and introduced himself, he seemed delighted to see us and exuded cordiality. He had reasons for being pleased, he'd just been promoted to major, and in addition he had the most beautiful eyes you ever saw, velvety and unreal, he made use of them to flutter the hearts of several volunteer nurses, who surrounded him with attentions and sympathetic mimicry and feasted on every word and move of their dear doctor. At the very first meeting he took our morale in hand and told us as much. Taking one of us by the shoulders and shaking him with paternal familiarity, he explained the regulations in a comforting tone and indicated the quickest and surest way of getting ourselves sent back to the front to get clobbered some more.

Wherever they came from, no two ways about it, that was their only thought. It seemed to give them a kick. It was the new vice. "France, my friends," he proclaimed, "has put her trust in you. France is a woman, the most beautiful of all women! She is counting on your heroism! She has been a victim of the most cowardly, the most abominable aggression. She has a right to expect her sons to avenge her to the hilt! To restore, even at the cost of the extreme sacrifice, every square inch of her territory! All of us here in the hospital, my friends, will do our duty, and we expect you to do yours! Our science is at your disposal! It is yours! All its resources will be devoted to curing you! Help us with your good will! I know we can count on your good will! We hope, we trust, that each one of you will soon resume his place side by side with his dear comrades in the trenches! Your sacred place! Defending your beloved soil! *Vive la France!* Forward to battle!" He knew how to talk to soldiers.

We were all standing at attention at the foot of our beds. Behind him a brunette, one of his group of pretty nurses, was having a hard time controlling her feelings, which were made visible by three or four tears. The other nurses, her friends, tried to comfort her: "Don't worry, sweetie, he'll be back... I'm sure he will!..."

Her cousin, a plumpish blonde, was consoling her the most. As she passed us, holding her up with both arms, the plump one told me this weakness had overcome her pretty cousin because her fiancé had just gone off to the navy. Our impassioned medical authority tried to soothe the tragic and beautiful emotion aroused by his short, vibrant speech. He was embarrassed and grieved. The apprehension he had awakened in this profound and noble heart, all sensibility and tenderness, was too painful. "If we had only known, Doctor," the blonde cousin whispered, "we'd have warned you... They love each other so dearly, you can't imagine!..." The group of nurses and the Master went their way. Chattering and swishing they receded down the corridor. They had finished with us.

I tried to recollect and to fathom the meaning of the speech the man with the beautiful eyes had just made, but far from depressing me, when I thought it over, his words struck me as just what was needed to disgust me with the whole idea of dying. My comrades were of the same opinion, but they did not, like me, see a kind of challenge or insult in them. They made no attempt to understand what was going on around us; all they saw, and that unclearly, was that the usual delirium of the world had so increased in the last few months that there was nothing stable left for a man to build his existence on.

Here in the hospital, just as in the Flanders night, death stalked us. Here, to be sure, it threatened from a distance, but just as implacably, once the Administration set it in pursuit of your trembling carcass.

Here, it was true, they didn't bawl us out, in fact they spoke gently, and they never talked about death, but our death sentence showed up distinctly in the corner of every paper they asked us to sign and in all the precautions they surrounded us with: those tags around our necks... and wrists... whenever they let us out for a few hours. And all the advice they gave us... We felt counted, watched, serial-numbered, enrolled in the vast multitude that would soon be leaving for the front. So naturally all the civilian and medical personnel around us seemed more cheerful than we were. The nurses, the bitches, weren't in the same boat, their only thought was to go on living, to live longer and longer, to live and love, to stroll in the park and to copulate thousands and thousands of times. Every one of those angelic creatures had a plan all worked out in her perineum, like a convict, a little plan for love later on, when all of us soldier boys should have perished in God knows what mud and God knows how!

Then they would sigh with a very special commemorative tenderness that would make them more attractive than ever; interspersed with heartbreaking silences, they would evoke the tragic days of the war, the ghosts... "Do you remember little Bardamu?" they would say in the gathering dusk, thinking of me, the lad who had coughed so much and given them such a time to make him stop... "Poor boy, his morale was way down... I wonder what became of him?"

A few poetic regrets, if adroitly placed, are as becoming to a woman as gossamer hair in the moonlight.

What I couldn't help hearing under their spoken words and expressions of sympathy was this: "Nice little soldier boy, you're going to die... You're going to die... This is war... Everyone has his own life... his role... his death... We seem to share your distress... But no one can share anyone else's death... A person sound in body and soul should take everything that happens as entertainment, neither more nor less, and we are wholesome young women, beautiful, respected, healthy and well bred... For us the automatism of biology transforms the whole world into a joyous spectacle, into pure joy! Our health demands it! We can't afford the ugly dissipations of sorrow... We need stimulants and more stimulants... You'll soon be forgotten, dear little soldier boys... Be nice, die quickly... and let's hope the war will be over soon, so we can marry one of your charming officers... preferably one with dark hair!... And long live the Nation that Papa's always talking about!... How wonderful love must be when Johnny comes marching home!... Our little husband will be decorated!... Cited for bravery... You can shine his lovely boots on our happy wedding day if you like... if you're still in existence, soldier boy... Won't you be happy about our happiness, soldier boy?..."

Every morning we saw our doctor, time and again we saw him surrounded by his nurses. He was a scientific luminary, we were told. The old men from the charity hospital next door would come jerking past our rooms, making useless, disjointed leaps. They'd go from room to room, spitting out gossip between their decayed teeth, purveying scraps of malignant, worn-out slander. Cloistered in their official misery as in an oozing dungeon, those aged workers ruminated the layer of shit that long years of servitude deposit on men's souls. Impotent hatreds grown rancid in the pissy idleness of dormitories. They employed their last quavering energies in hurting each other a little more, in destroying what little pleasure and life they had left.

Their last remaining pleasure! Their shrivelled carcasses contained not one solitary atom that was not absolutely vicious.

As soon as it was settled that we soldiers were going to share the relative comfort of the bastion with those old men, they began to detest us in unison, but that didn't stop them from begging for the crumbs of tobacco on our window sills and the bits of stale bread that had fallen under our benches. At mealtimes they pressed their parchment-skinned faces against the windows of our mess hall. Over their crinkled rheumy noses, they peered in at us like covetous rats. One of those invalids seemed smarter and wickeder than the rest, he'd come and entertain us with the songs of his day, Old Man Birouette* he was called. He'd do anything we asked provided we gave him tobacco, anything except walk past the hospital morgue, which incidentally was never idle. One of our jokes was to make him go that way, while supposedly taking him for a little stroll. "Won't you come in?" we'd say when we got to the door. He'd run away, griping for all he was worth, so fast and so far we wouldn't see him again for at least two days. Old Man Birouette had caught a glimpse of death.

Professor Bestombes, our medical major with the beautiful eyes, had installed a complicated assortment of gleaming electrical contraptions which periodically pumped us full of shocks. He claimed they had a tonic effect, and we had to put up with them on pain of banishment. It seems that Bestombes was very rich; he must have been to be able to buy all those expensive electrocution machines. He could afford to throw money around because his father-in-law, a political bigwig, had done some heavy finagling while purchasing land for the government.

Naturally the doctor exploited his advantages. Crime and punishment, it all adds up. We took him as he was, and we didn't hate him. He examined our nervous systems with meticulous care and questioned us in a tone of polite familiarity. This sedulously cultivated good nature enchanted the nurses in his section, who all came from excellent families.

Every morning these cuties looked forward to his displays of affability, which were just so yummy. In short, we were all actors in a play – he, Bestombes, had chosen the role of a benevolent, profoundly human and humane scientist. We pulled together, that was the essential.

In this new hospital I shared a room with Sergeant Branledore,* a re-enlisted man. He was an old hospital hand. He'd been dragging his perforated intestines around for months and had been in four different hospitals.

He had learnt in the process how to attract and to hold the active sympathy of the nurses. He vomited, pissed and shat blood with astonishing frequency; he also had a lot of trouble breathing, but none of that would have sufficed to win him the special good graces of the nurses, who had seen worse. So between two choking fits, if a doctor or nurse was passing, Branledore would sing out: "Victory! Victory! Victory will be ours!" Or he'd murmur those same words with one corner or the whole of his lungs, as the circumstances required. Thus attuned to the ardently aggressive literature of the day by a well-calculated bit of histrionics, he enjoyed the highest moral standing. That man knew his stuff.

Since all the world was a stage, acting was the thing. Branledore knew what he was doing. And indeed nothing looks more idiotic, nothing is more irritating than a sluggish spectator who turns up on stage by mistake. When you're up there, you've got to join in, come to life, act a part, take the plunge or clear out. Especially the women demanded a show, the bitches had no use at all for clumsy amateurs. Unquestionably war went straight to their ovaries, they demanded heroes, and if you weren't a hero you had to pretend to be one or be prepared for the most ignominious fate.

After a week in this new hospital we realized that we would absolutely have to change our image, and thanks to Branledore (a lace salesman in civilian life) the selfsame men, who on our arrival had been terror-stricken, shunning the light, haunted by disgraceful memories of slaughterhouses, metamorphosed into an incredible gang of swashbucklers, determined to conquer or die and, take my word for it, armed with derring-do and the most outrageous language. Our speech had indeed become vigorous and so obscene that the ladies sometimes blushed, but they never complained, because it is generally agreed that a soldier is as brave as he is wild and cruder than there is any need to be, so much so that his bravery can be measured by the crudeness of his language.

At first, though we copied Branledore to the best of our ability, our patriotic act wasn't quite right, it wasn't really convincing. It took a good week, two in fact, of intensive rehearsing before we had fully caught on.

As soon as that scientific luminary, our Professor Doctor Bestombes, noticed the striking improvement in our moral attitudes, he decided to encourage us by admitting a few visitors, our parents to begin with.

To judge by stories I had heard, certain soldiers, really gifted types, experienced a kind of intoxication, you might even speak of a voluptuous thrill, in combat. Whenever I tried to imagine this particular brand of pleasure, just trying laid me low for at least a week. I felt so incapable of killing anyone that I thought I might just as well give it up right away and abandon the whole idea. Not that I lacked experience, they'd done everything possible to inculcate a taste for killing, but I simply had no talent in that direction. Maybe my initiation should have been more gradual.

One day I decided to tell Professor Bestombes how hard I was finding it, body and soul, to become as brave as I should have liked to be and as the undoubtedly sublime circumstances required. I was uneasy, afraid he would think I was being insolent and talking out of turn. Not at all! The great man said he was delighted that I'd come to him and bared my troubled soul so fully and frankly.

"You're better, friend Bardamu!" he concluded. "You're better, that's all there is to it! Yes, Bardamu, I regard your coming to me like this, absolutely of your own free will, as a most encouraging sign of a marked improvement in your mental state... Vaudesquin,* that modest but infinitely wise observer of moral breakdown in the soldiers of the Empire, summed up his findings, back in 1802, in a memoir that is quite unjustly neglected by students of the present day, but must nevertheless be regarded as a classic. In it he describes, with remarkable insight and precision, the so-called 'confessional crises' met with in moral convalescents, and terms them the most encouraging of all symptoms... Almost a century later our great Dupré* established his now celebrated nomenclature of the same symptom and characterized the identical crisis as a 'recollection of memories'; according to the same author, this crisis, if the cure is properly administered, should soon be followed by a massive breakup of anxiety percepts and the definitive liberation of the area of consciousness, this being the second stage in the process of psychic recovery. Elsewhere, employing the bold terminology that was his special gift, Dupré devises the formula 'disencumbering cogitative diarrhoea' for this crisis, which is accompanied by intense euphoria, a marked resumption of relational activity, a sudden and striking restoration, among other things, of sleep, which in some cases has been known to go on for days at a time, and lastly, at a more advanced stage, by conspicuous hyperactivity of the genital functions, amounting, sometimes in patients who were previously frigid, to a positive sexual frenzy: 'The patient recovers not by easy stages, but at a gallop.' Such was the magnificently descriptive metaphor by which another of our great French psychiatrists of the last century, Philibert Margeton,* characterized this recuperative triumph, this sudden resurgence of normal functions in a patient recovering from the fear syndrome... As for you, Bardamu, I already, at the present moment, regard you as a true convalescent... Would it interest you, Bardamu, since we have arrived at this gratifying conclusion, to know that I shall be reading a paper on the fundamental characteristics of the human mind at the Society for Military Psychology tomorrow?... It is not without its merits, I venture to believe."

"Oh yes, Professor, I take a passionate interest in these questions..."

"Well then, Bardamu, to make a long story short, the thesis I put forward is that before the war man was an unknown quantity for the psychiatrist and the resources of his psyche an enigma..."

"That is also my humble opinion, Professor..."

"You see, Bardamu, the war, by providing us with such unprecedented means of trying men's nervous systems, has been a miraculous revealer of the human mind! Recent pathological disclosures have given us matter for centuries of meditation and fascinating study... Let's face it... Up until now we hardly suspected the richness of man's emotional and spiritual resources! Today, thanks to the war, all that has changed... By a process of breaking and entering, painful to be sure, but decisive, nay providential for science, we have penetrated his innermost depths! Ever since the first revelations came to my attention, the duty of the modern psychologist and moralist has been clear to me, Bestombes, beyond any possible doubt! Our psychological conceptions are in need of total revision!"

I, Bardamu, was of exactly the same opinion.

"Yes indeed, Professor, I am convinced that…"

"Ah, you think so too, Bardamu, you say so yourself! In man, you see, there is a balance between good and evil, between egoism on the one hand and altruism on the other… In elite subjects more altruism than egoism. Am I right? Don't you agree?"

"Exactly, Professor, you've hit the nail on the head…"

"And what, Bardamu, I ask you, what is the highest-known concept, the concept best-suited to arousing the altruism of the elite subject and compelling it to manifest itself unequivocally?"

"Patriotism, Professor!"

"Ah, you see? The word is yours, not mine! You understand… Bardamu! Patriotism and glory, which is its corollary and proof!"

"How true!"

"Ah! Our soldier boys… at their first baptism of fire they spontaneously cast off all sophisms and subsidiary concepts, in particular the sophism of self-preservation. Instinctively and immediately they merge with our true raison d'être, the Nation. For the attainment of truth, Bardamu, intelligence is not only superfluous, it is in the way! Like all essential truths, the Nation is a truth of the heart! The common people understand that… and that is where the inept scientist goes wrong…"

"It's beautiful, Professor! Too beautiful! I am reminded of the Ancients!"

Bestombes pressed both my hands almost affectionately.

And in a fatherly tone he added for my special benefit: "That, Bardamu, is how I mean to treat my patients, electricity for the body, and for the mind massive doses of patriotic ethics, injections as it were of invigorating morality!"

"I understand, Professor!"

I was indeed beginning to understand more and more.

On leaving him I joined my invigorated companions at Mass in the brand-new chapel. I caught sight of Branledore in a corner, demonstrating his moral vigour by giving the concierge's little girl lessons in enthusiasm. He beckoned me to join him, and I did.

That afternoon some of our parents came from Paris for the first time since we'd been there, and from then on they came every week.

I had finally written to my mother. She was glad to see me again and whimpered like a bitch whose puppy has been given back to her.

She thought she was doing me a lot of good by kissing me, but she was miles behind the bitch, because she believed what they said when they took me away from her. A dog only believes what it can smell. One afternoon my mother and I took a long walk through the streets around the hospital, dawdling down half-finished byways, with lamp-posts that hadn't been painted yet, between long, oozing house fronts with their windows full of gaudy dangling rags, the shirts of the poor. We listened to the crackling song of the frying pans, a tempest of rancid fat. In the great shapeless desert surrounding the city, the rot in which its false luxury ends, the city shows everyone who wants to look the garbage piles of its enormous posterior. There are factories one avoids when out for a stroll, which emit smells of all sorts, some of them hardly believable. The air around us couldn't possibly stink any worse. Nearby a little street carnival moulders between two chimneys of unequal height, the wooden horses cost too much for the rickety dribbling children with nosefuls of fingers, who long for them and stand spellbound, sometimes for weeks on end, attracted and repelled by their forlorn rundown look and the music.

What efforts are made to keep the truth away from these places, but it comes back again and again, to grieve for everybody. Drinking is no help, red wine as thick as ink, nothing helps, the sky in those places never changes, it's a vast lake of suburban smoke, shutting them in.

Underfoot the mud drags you down with fatigue, and the sides of existence are also closed, shut off by hotels and more factories. Even the walls in that section are coffins. With Lola gone for good and Musyne too, I had nobody left. That's why I finally wrote to my mother, just to see somebody. I was only twenty, and all I had was a past. The two of us together, my mother and I, walked through dozens of Sunday streets. She told me little things about her business, what the people around her were saying about the war, that it was sad, "horrible" in fact, but that with plenty of courage we'd all come through in the end, the ones that got killed were an accident, like in the races, if you kept your seat properly you wouldn't fall. To her the war was just one more affliction, she tried not to think about it too much, because it frightened her in a way; it was full of terrifying things she didn't understand. She had no doubt that poor people like her were born to suffer in every way, that that was their role on earth, and that if things had been going so badly of late, the cumulative faults of the poor must have a good deal to do with it... They must have been very naughty – of course they hadn't meant to be, but they were guilty all the same, and giving them a chance to expiate their transgressions by suffering was a great kindness... My mother was an "untouchable".

That resigned, tragic optimism was her only faith and the foundation of her character.

The two of us, in the rain, went down streets of vacant lots. The pavements in that part of the world sink and evade your step, in winter the branches of the little ash trees at the edge hold the raindrops a long time, a tenuous fairyland trembling in the breeze. Our way back to the hospital led past a number of newly built hotels, some had names, others hadn't even gone to that much trouble. "Rooms by the week" was all they had to say for themselves. The war had suddenly emptied them of all the workers and wage slaves who had lived there. They wouldn't even come back to die. Dying is work too, but they'd do it somewhere else.

My mother was tearful as she took me back to the hospital. She accepted the accident of my death, and not content to acquiesce, she wondered if I was as resigned to it as she was. She believed in fate as implicitly as she did in the beautiful standard metre at the Conservatoire des Arts et Métiers, which she had always spoken of with respect, because she had learnt in her youth that the one she used in her notions shop was a scrupulous copy of that superb official original.

Between the housing lots in that degraded countryside there were still a few fields and gardens here and there and, attached to those scraps of land, a few aged peasants wedged in between the new buildings. When there was time left before I had to be back, my mother and I went to watch them, those comical peasants obstinately poking iron into the earth, that soft grainy substance, where the dead are laid to rot but which gives us our bread all the same. "The ground must be terribly hard," my mother said every time she saw them. She was puzzled. You see, she only understood miseries that resembled her own, city miseries, and she tried to figure out what the country kind could be like. That was the only curiosity I ever saw in my mother. It was all the diversion she needed for a Sunday, and she took it back to the city with her.

I never heard from Lola, or from Musyne either. Those sluts were on the good side of the situation, from which we, the flesh earmarked for sacrifice, were barred by smiling but implacable orders. Twice I'd been sent back to the places where the hostages were corralled. My future was all settled.

* * *

As I've told you, Branledore, my neighbour at the hospital, enjoyed permanent popularity with the nurses. He was swathed in bandages and dripping with optimism. All the other patients envied him and copied his manner. Once we'd become presentable and ceased to be moral lepers, we all began to get visits from socialites and political bigwigs. People started telling each other in the drawing rooms that Professor Bestombes's Neuro-Medical Centre had become a temple and home, as it were, of the most intense patriotic fervour. Our visiting days came to be patronized not only by bishops, but also by an Italian duchess, a big munitions magnate, and before long by the personnel of the Opéra and the Comédie-Française. A beautiful young actress from the Comédie, who recited poetry like nobody's business, came to my personal bedside and declaimed some superlatively heroic lines for my special benefit. As she spoke, her perverse red hair (she had the complexion that went with it) was tossed by extraordinary waves that sent vibrations straight to my perineum. When this divine creature questioned me about my feats of arms, I gave her so many poignant details that she began to devour me with her eyes. Deeply moved, she asked leave to have the most intense passages in my narrative framed in verse by a poet who happened to be one of her admirers. I consented without hesitation. Informed of this project, Professor Bestombes expressed his special approval. He even granted an interview on the subject to an "illustrated national weekly", whose photographer took our picture all together on the hospital steps with the beautiful actress beside us. "In these tragic days," cried Professor Bestombes, who never missed a trick, "it is the poet's highest duty to revive our taste for the epic! This is no time for trivial artifice! Down with emasculated literature! A new soul has been born to us in the great and noble tumult of battle! The great patriotic renewal demands this! The lofty summits to which our glory is destined!... We demand the sustaining grandeur of the epic!... For my part, I find it admirable that this sublime, creative and never to be forgotten collaboration between a poet and one of our heroes should have taken place under our very eyes in this hospital which I direct!"

Branledore, my room-mate, whose imagination had been rather outdistanced by mine and who didn't figure in the photograph, was seized with a keen, tenacious jealousy. He became my embittered rival for the palms of heroism. He made up new stories, he surpassed himself, no one could stop him, his exploits verged on delirium.

It was difficult for me to get the jump on him, to improve on his extravagances, yet none of us at the hospital resigned himself to defeat; in a fever of emulation we all vied with one another in composing brilliant pages of "military history" in which to figure sublimely. In those heroic romances we wore the skins of phantasmagoric characters, but deep within them our ludicrous selves trembled body and soul. I'd like to have seen people's faces if they had found out what we were really like. The war had been going on too long.

Our great friend Bestombes received the visits of innumerable foreign celebrities, neutrals, sceptics and scientists of all persuasions. Spruce, besabred inspectors from the War Ministry passed through our wards, their military careers had been extended, they had been rejuvenated and revitalized with pay increases. So naturally they were generous with praise and citations. Everything was perfect. Bestombes and his wounded heroes were the pride of the medical profession.

My fair admirer from the Comédie came back and paid me a private visit, while her pet poet was completing the rhymed narrative of my exploits. One day I finally ran into this pale, anxious young man in one of the corridors. The doctors, he told me, had assured him that the fragility of his heart strings was well-nigh miraculous. Consequently these same doctors, always concerned with the protection of the frail, had kept him out of the army. To make up for which our young bard had undertaken, at the risk of his health and last spiritual energies, to forge *The Moral Cannon of Our Victory*. A magnificent – and it goes without saying – unforgettable weapon. Practically everything was unforgettable in those days.

I wasn't going to complain, since he had picked me from among so many undeniably brave men as his hero! And, I have to admit, they honoured me royally. It was magnificent. The recitation was given at the Comédie-Française itself, as part of a so-called poetic afternoon. The whole hospital was invited. When my vibrant redhead appeared on the stage, striding grandly, her figure draped in the for once voluptuous folds of the tricolour, the whole audience, flushed with desire, rose to its feet and gave her one of those ovations that never seem to end. Naturally I had known what to expect, but my amazement was real all the same. I could not conceal my stupefaction from my neighbours at hearing her, my magnificent friend, thrill and throb and sigh in such a way as to make the dramatic effect of the episode I had dreamt up for her more vivid and more moving. Her poet was miles beyond me for fantasy, he had monstrously magnified mine, enhanced it with flamboyant rhymes and high-sounding adjectives, which fell with a solemn reverberation on the breathless, admiring silence. Coming to the climax of a period, the most impassioned of the lot, the actress turned towards the box where Branledore and I and a few other wounded men were sitting, and held out her two magnificent arms as though offering herself to the most heroic among us. At that particular moment the poet was faithfully rendering a deed of awe-inspiring bravery that I had attributed to myself. I don't remember exactly what it was, but I'm sure it was something pretty good. Luckily, when it comes to heroism, people are willing to believe anything. The audience caught the meaning of her symbolic offering, turned in our direction, ecstatic, stamping, bellowing with joy, and clamoured for the hero.

Branledore took up the whole front row of the box and blotted out the rest of us. He hid us almost completely with his bandages. He did it on purpose, the bastard.

But two of our comrades climbed up on chairs behind him so the crowd could admire them over his head and shoulders. They brought the house down.

I came close to crying out: "But it's all about me! Me and nobody else!" I knew my Branledore, we'd have exchanged insults in front of all those people, we might even have used our fists. So in the end he was the winner, he triumphed. Just as he'd planned, he had the whole storm of applause to himself. Defeated, we took refuge backstage, where fortunately we were fêted again. That was some comfort. But our actress and inspiration wasn't alone in her dressing room. The poet, her poet, our poet was with her. He had the same weakness for young soldier boys as she did. They made it clear to me very artistically. A handsome offer. They repeated it, but I ignored their kind suggestions. I was the loser, because they had influence and things might have worked out very well. I left them abruptly, I was nettled. Silly of me, I was young.

To recapitulate: the aviators had snatched Lola away from me, the Argentines had taken Musyne, and now this harmonious invert had filched my magnificent actress. Sadly I left the Comédie as the last torches were being extinguished in the corridors and returned alone, without recourse to the tram, to our hospital, that mantrap plunked down in the tenacious mud of the rebellious suburbs.

* * *

The plain truth, I may as well admit it, is that I've never really been right in the head. But just then such fits of dizziness would come over me for no reason at all that I could easily have been run over. The war had given me the staggers. When it came to pocket money, all I could count on during my stay at the hospital were the few francs my mother managed to scrape up for me each week. So as soon as I could I went looking for little extras here and there, wherever I could find them. One of my old bosses looked like a likely prospect, and I went right over to see him.

I remembered opportunely that in a certain obscure period of my life shortly before the war I had worked as a helper for this Roger Puta* who owned a jewellery shop near the Madeleine. My work for that loathsome jeweller consisted of menial jobs, such as polishing the silverware in the shop. There was lots of it, every shape and size, and it was hard to take care of in the gift-giving holiday season because it was always being handled.

As soon as my classes were out at medical school, where I was engaged in exacting and (because I kept flunking the exams) interminable studies, I hightailed it to the backroom of Monsieur Puta's shop, where I laboured for two or three hours, until dinner time, applying whiting to his *chocolatières*.

In return for my work, I was fed, copiously I have to admit, in the kitchen. Then in the morning before school, I had to take the watchdogs out for a piss. All that for forty francs a month. Puta's jewellery shop on the corner of the Rue Vignon sparkled with thousands of diamonds, each one of which cost several decades of my salary. They're still sparkling in the exact same place, by the way.

When everybody was mobilized, this Puta got himself assigned to the auxiliaries and put under the special orders of a certain cabinet minister, whose car he drove from time to time. But he also made himself useful, unofficially of course, by supplying the ministry with jewels. The higher officials speculated, with gratifying results, on present and future transactions, and the longer the war went on, the more jewels were needed. Monsieur Puta got so many orders that he sometimes had trouble filling them.

When he was overworked, Monsieur Puta managed to look slightly intelligent, because of the fatigue that tormented him, but only then. When rested, his face, in spite of his undeniably fine features, became so harmonious in its idiotic placidity that it would be hard not to carry a despairing memory of it with one to the grave.

His wife, Madame Puta, seldom left the cashier's desk, in a manner of speaking she and the desk were one. She had been brought up to be a jeweller's wife. That had been her parents' ambition. She knew her duty inside and out. The prosperity of the cash drawer brought happiness to husband and wife. Not that Madame Puta was bad-looking, not at all, she could even, like so many others, have been rather pretty, but she was so careful, so distrustful, that she stopped short of beauty just as she stopped short of life – her hair was a little too well dressed, her smile a little too facile and sudden, and her gestures a bit too abrupt or too furtive. You racked your brains trying to figure out what was too calculated about her and why, you always felt uneasy when she came near you. This instinctive revulsion that shopkeepers inspire in anyone who goes near them and who knows what's what is one of the few consolations for being as down at heel as people who don't sell anything to anybody tend to be.

The petty cares of business were everything to Madame Puta. In this she resembled Madame Herote, but with a difference: in her case, they possessed her body and soul, just as God possesses his nuns.

And yet from time to time she would give a thought to the world around her. For instance, she might indulge in some little expression of sympathy for parents with sons at the front. "How dreadful this war must be for people with grown-up children!"

"Think before you shoot your mouth off!" her husband responded without delay. Such mawkishness found him ready and resolute. "I suppose there's no need of defending France?"

Good as gold, but first and foremost good patriots, stoics in short, they went to sleep every night of the war directly above their shop with its millions, a French fortune.

In the brothels that he visited now and then, Monsieur Puta, though demanding, refused to be taken for a spendthrift. He'd set them straight at the outset. "I'm no Englishman, dearie, and I know the score! I'm just a little French soldier, and I'm not in a hurry!" That was his opening statement. The girls respected him for his well-regulated way of taking his pleasure. He liked to enjoy himself, but couldn't be taken in, a real man. He knew human nature and took advantage of his knowledge to sell a few jewels to the assistant madam, who had no faith in stocks and bonds. As for his military career, Monsieur Puta was making impressive progress, from temporary discharges to permanent deferments. After God knows how many providential medical examinations, he was finally exempted for good. One of the highest joys of his existence was to contemplate and if possible to handle a shapely thigh. In this one pleasure at least he got the better of his wife, who took no interest in anything but the business. Take a man and woman with otherwise equal qualities, you always seem to find a little more uneasiness in a man, however stagnant and narrow-minded. This Puta had just a dash of the artist in him. Lots of men are like that, their artistic leanings never go beyond a weakness for shapely thighs. Madame Puta was glad she had no children. She voiced her pleasure in being sterile so often that one day Monsieur Puta spoke of their satisfaction to the assistant madam. "Yes," said the assistant madam. "But after all somebody's children have to go. It's a duty!" That was true, the war involved duties.

The cabinet minister whose car Puta drove had no children either. Cabinet ministers never have children.

Around 1913, at the same time as me, there was another helper doing menial jobs in the shop; his name was Jean Voireuse.* At night he was some kind of extra in the little theatres, and in the afternoon he delivered parcels for Puta. The pay was small, but he didn't mind. He managed to make ends meet thanks to the Métro. He delivered his parcels on foot almost as quickly as if he'd taken the Métro, and kept the price of the ticket. All velvet. True, his feet smelt a little, quite a lot in fact, but he knew it and asked me to let him know when there were no customers in the shop so he could safely go in and settle his accounts

87

with Madame Puta. As soon as she had the money, she'd send him out to the back room with me. During the war again his feet stood him in good stead. He was reputed to be the fastest courier in his regiment. While on convalescent leave, he came to see me at the Bicêtre fort; in fact it was then we decided to get in touch with our old boss. We didn't let the grass grow under our feet. When we got to the Boulevard de la Madeleine they had just finished dressing the shop window...

"Well, well! Who'd have expected!" Monsieur Puta was rather surprised to see us. "But I'm glad to see you all the same. Come right in! You're looking well, Voireuse! Fine and dandy! But you, Bardamu, you look sick, my boy! Oh well, you're young! You'll recover! You youngsters are in luck when all's said and done! Great days, great experience for you! Up there! And out in the open too! This is history, my boys! Make no mistake! And what history!"

We didn't answer, we thought we'd let Monsieur Puta go on a while before touching him... And on he went:

"It's rough in the trenches, I won't deny that!... But it's no bed of roses here either, you know!... You boys have been wounded? All right, but I'm absolutely tired out! For two years now I've been on night duty! Do you know what that means? Imagine! Exhausted! Worn to a frazzle! Oh my God! The streets of Paris at night! No lights, my friends... Driving a car, as often as not with the Minister in it! In a hurry! You simply can't imagine!... I could get killed a dozen times every night!..."

"Oh yes," Madame Puta put in, "and sometimes he drives the Minister's wife too..."

"Oh yes, and it's not over yet..."

"Dreadful!" we said in unison.

"What about the dogs?" Voireuse asked to be polite. "What's become of them? Does somebody still take them out in the Tuileries?"

"I've had them put away! They were bad for business!... German shepherds! The customers, you see!..."

"A pity!" said his wife. "But the new dogs we have now are very nice, they're Scotch... they smell a little... not like our German shepherds, do you remember, Voireuse?... They hardly smelt at all. We could shut them up in the shop even after the rain..."

"That's right!" said Monsieur Puta. "Not like old Voireuse here with his feet! Do your feet still smell, Jean? You young scamp!"

"They still smell a little, I think," said Voireuse.

At that moment some customers came in.

"I won't keep you any longer, my boys," said Monsieur Puta, intent on getting Jean out of the shop as quickly as possible. "Keep well, that's the main thing! I won't ask you where you've come from! Certainly not! Security first is my motto!"

At the word "security" Puta made a very serious face, like when giving back change... So that was the end of our visit. As we were leaving, Madame Puta gave us each twenty francs. The shop was polished as spick and span as a yacht, we were afraid to walk through because of our boots, which looked monstrous on the fine carpet.

"Oh, Roger! Look at them!" Madame Puta cried out. "Aren't they comical!... They're not in the habit any more! They walk as if they'd stepped in something!"

"The habit will come back!" said Monsieur Puta amiably, glad to be rid of us so quickly and cheaply.

Out in the street we realized we wouldn't go far with our twenty francs each, but Voireuse had another idea.

"Come on," he says, "we'll go and see a lady I know, her son was a buddy of mine, killed on the Meuse. I go and see his parents every week and tell them how their son was killed... They're rich... The mother gives me a hundred francs or so every time... They say it makes them happy... So..."

"But what'll I do? What'll I say to this lady?"

"Well, you'll tell her that you were there too... She'll give you another hundred francs... They're the right kind of rich! Take it from me! Not like that stinking Puta... They don't count their pennies..."

"All right," I said. "But are you sure she won't ask me for details?... Because I didn't know her son, see?... I'll be flummoxed if she asks for..."

"No, no, don't worry... Say the same as me... Just nod your head and say yes... Nothing to worry about! The woman is broken-hearted, so if someone comes and talks about her son it makes her happy... That's all she wants... Anything at all... It's easy..."

I wasn't very enthusiastic, but I badly wanted the hundred francs, which struck me as providential and unusually easy to come by.

"All right," I said finally. "But don't expect me to make anything up, I'm warning you! Promise? I'll say the same as you, not a word more... How did he get killed anyway?"

"A shell hit him smack in the face, a pretty big one, at Garance the place was called, on the Meuse front, on the bank of some river... Boy, they didn't find 'this much' of him! Absolutely nothing left, a memory... And you know, he was a big man, strong and husky and athletic, but what would you expect? Nobody can stand up against a shell!"

"That's a fact!"

"Wiped off the face of the earth!... His mother still finds it hard to believe! I've told her over and over again... She insists that he's just missing... Crazy idea... Missing!... It's not her fault, she never saw a shell, she doesn't see how a man can vanish into thin air, like a fart, and that it's all over, especially when the man is her son..."

"It's only natural!"

"By the way, I haven't been to see her for two weeks... But you'll see how it is when I go in... The mother receives me right away in the drawing room... It's a beautiful house... You'll see... so many curtains and carpets and mirrors you'd think you were in a theatre... A hundred francs is nothing to them, they'll hardly miss it... About five francs to me... Today she'll be good for two hundred... because she hasn't seen me for two weeks... You'll see, the servants with gilded buttons..."

At the Avenue Henri-Martin we turned left and went on a little way, then we came to a gate surrounded by trees in a little private road.

"See?" said Voireuse, when we were standing in front of it. "It's practically a chateau... What did I tell you?... The father's supposed to be high up in the railways... a big shot..."

"You sure he's not a stationmaster?" I said, making a joke.

"Don't be stupid!... There he is now. He's coming to meet us..."

But the old man didn't come out right away. He was walking around the lawn, stooped over, talking to a soldier. We went nearer. I recognized the soldier, it was the reservist I had met that night at Noirceur-sur-la-Lys, when I was on reconnaissance. I even remembered the name he'd given me: Robinson.

"Do you know that footslogger?" Voireuse asked me.

"Yes, I know him."

"Maybe he's a friend of theirs... They must be talking about the mother. I hope they don't prevent us from going to see her... Because she's the one that mostly forks over the money..."

The old gentleman came over to us.

"My dear friend," he said to Voireuse in a quavering voice. "It grieves me to tell you that since your last visit my poor wife has succumbed to our great sorrow… Last Thursday we left her alone for a moment, she had asked us to… She was in tears…"

He couldn't finish his sentence. Suddenly he turned away and left us.

"I know you," I said to Robinson, as soon as the old gentleman was far enough away.

"And I know you…"

"What happened to the old lady?" I asked him.

"Well," he informed us, "she hanged herself the day before yesterday, that's all!" He added: "Of all the lousy luck! She was my army godmother!… Such things only happen to me! A calamity!… My first leave!… For six months I'd been looking forward to this day!…"

Voireuse and I couldn't help laughing at Robinson's discomfiture. A nasty surprise if there ever was one, but her being dead didn't give us our two hundred smackers, and we'd made up a new story specially for the occasion. So none of us was very happy.

"You and your big mealy mouth, you bastard!" We were ragging Robinson, trying to get a rise out of him. "You thought you had a good thing, didn't you? A sweet little feed with the old folks? Or maybe you thought you'd screw your fairy godmother?… Serves you goddamn right!…"

We couldn't stay there all day looking at the grass and laughing, so we all three together started off in the direction of Grenelle. We all counted our money, it didn't come to much. Seeing as we had to get back to our respective hospitals and barracks that same evening, there was just enough for dinner at a bistro, and maybe there'd be a little something left over, but not enough to go upstairs at the whorehouse. We went in anyway, but we only had a drink at the bar.

"Say," said Robinson, "it's good to see you again. But what do you think of that kid's mother? The bitch, hanging herself just when I'm due to arrive!… I won't forget her in a hurry!… Do you see me hanging myself?… Unhappy, you say?… I'd hang myself every day!… What about you?"

"Rich people are more sensitive…" said Voireuse.

Voireuse had a good heart. "If I had six francs," he went on, "I'd go upstairs with the brunette over there by the slot machine…"

"Go ahead," we told him, "you'll tell us if she knows how to suck…"

We rummaged in our pockets, but counting the tip there wasn't enough to give him his piece. Just enough for another coffee each and a cassis. When we'd finished, we went out and roamed around some more.

We broke up on the Place Vendôme and went our separate ways. Saying goodbye, we couldn't see one another, and we spoke softly because of the echoes. No light, it wasn't allowed.

I never saw Voireuse again. I've often run into Robinson. As for Jean Voireuse, it was the gas that got him on the Somme. He died two years later by the sea, in Brittany, in a navy sanatorium. He wrote to me twice when he first got there, but no more after that. He'd never seen the ocean. "You can't imagine how beautiful it is," he wrote to me. "I bathe a little, it's good for my feet, but I think my voice is gone for good." That made him unhappy, because his big ambition was to get into a theatre chorus some day.

A chorus is better paid and more artistic than being an ordinary extra.

* * *

The army finally dropped me. I'd saved my guts, but my brains were scrambled for good. Undeniably. "Beat it!…" they said. "You're no good for anything any more!…"

"To Africa!" I said to myself. "The further the better!" The ship that took me on board was a ship like any other, Consolidated Corsairs, that was the line. It was bound for the tropics with a cargo of cotton goods, officers and civil servants.

That boat was so old that the copper plate with its birth date had been removed from the upper deck; the date was such ancient history it had inspired the passengers with fear and witticisms.

So they shoved me on board in the hope that I'd recuperate in the colonies. My well-wishers were dead set on me making my fortune. Personally I just wanted to get away, but a man should always try to look useful if he's not rich, it didn't look as if my studies would ever end and I couldn't go on for ever. I didn't have enough money to go to America. "So Africa it is!" I said, and let myself be steered to the tropics where, I was told, you were sure to get ahead fast, provided you behaved and were reasonably temperate.

Those prognostics gave me food for thought. There wasn't much to be said for me, but my manners were all right, and I was self-effacing. Deference came easy to me, I lived in constant fear of not being on time, but took good care never to get ahead of anybody. In short, I had delicacy...

After all, if you manage to escape alive from an international slaughterhouse run rampant, it's a sign of tact and discretion. But let's get back to our trip. It looked fairly promising as long as we were in European waters. In small, adenoidal, mutually suspicious groups, the passengers lolled and lounged in the shade between decks, in the toilets and in the smoking room. From morning to night they steeped themselves in Picon and gossip. They belched, they dozed, they shouted, and never expressed the least regret for anything they had left behind in Europe.

Our ship's name was the *Admiral Bragueton*.* If it kept afloat on those tepid seas, it was only thanks to its paint. Any number of coats laid on, layer after layer, had given the *Admiral Bragueton* a kind of second hull, in the manner of an onion. We were heading for Africa, the real, grandiose Africa of impenetrable forests, fetid swamps, inviolate wildernesses, where black tyrants wallowed in sloth and cruelty on the banks of never-ending rivers. I would barter a pack of "Pilett"* razor blades for big long elephant's tusks, gaudy-coloured birds and young slaves. Guaranteed. That would be the life! Nothing in common with the emasculated Africa of travel agencies and monuments, of railways and candy bars. Certainly not! We'd be seeing Africa in the raw, the real Africa! We the boozing passengers of the *Admiral Bragueton*.

But as soon as we'd passed the coast of Portugal, things started going bad. One morning we woke up in the midst of a steam bath, pervasive and alarming. The water in our glasses, the sea, the air, our sheets, our sweat, everything was hot, sultry. From then on, by night and day, it was impossible to have anything cool in your hands, under your arse or in your throat, except the ice from the bar in your whisky. A dull despair descended on the passengers of the *Admiral Bragueton*, condemned to sit permanently in the bar, held fast by little pieces of ice, exchanging threats and incoherent apologies after their card games.

It didn't take long. In that despondent, changeless heat the entire human content of the ship congealed into massive drunkenness. People moved flabbily about like squid in a tank of tepid, smelly water. From that moment on we saw, rising to the surface, the terrifying nature of white men, exasperated, freed from constraint, absolutely unbuttoned, their true nature, same as in the war. That tropical steam bath called forth instincts as August breeds toads and snakes on the fissured walls of prisons. In the European cold, under grey, puritanical northern skies, we seldom get to see our brothers' festering cruelty except in times of carnage, but when roused by the foul fevers of the tropics, their rottenness rises to the surface. That's when the frantic unbuttoning sets in, when filth triumphs and covers us entirely. It's a biological confession. Once work and cold weather cease to constrain us, once they relax their grip, the white man shows you the same spectacle as a beautiful beach when the tide goes out: the truth, fetid pools, crabs, carrion and turds.

Once we had passed Portugal, everybody on board started unleashing his instincts, ferociously; alcohol helped and so did the blissful feeling conferred, especially on soldiers and civil servants, by the knowledge that the trip was absolutely free of charge. The knowledge that for four consecutive weeks their bed, board and liquor won't cost a thing is in itself enough to make most people delirious with thrift. Consequently, when it became known that, alone of all the ship's passengers, I had paid my own fare, I was looked upon as a shameless and intolerable swine.

If on leaving Marseille I had had some experience of colonial society, I would have gone down on my knees and begged the pardon and indulgence of the colonial infantry officer I kept running into, the highest in rank of those on board, for my unworthiness, and perhaps, for safety's sake, I'd also have humbled myself before the senior civil servant. Then those phantasmagorical passengers might have tolerated my presence in their midst and nothing would have happened. But I was ignorant, and my foolhardiness in supposing that I was entitled to breathe the same air as they almost cost me my life.

One can never be too anxious. Thanks to a certain ingenuity, I lost nothing but what self-respect I had left. This is what happened. Some time after the Canary Islands, I learnt from one of the stewards that my fellow passengers, by common accord, thought me affected, not to say insolent... that they suspected me of being a pimp and a pederast... even something of a cocaine addict... but only on the side... Then the suspicion made its way around that I must have left France to escape the consequences of certain heinous crimes. But I was only at the beginning of my troubles. At that point I learnt that on this line it was customary to treat paying passengers with extreme caution, accompanied by bullying; I'm speaking of those who were not travelling free, either on military-transportation orders or on the basis of some bureaucratic arrangement, for as everyone knows, the colonies belong to the upper reaches of the administration.

After all there are few plausible reasons for an unknown civilian to venture into those parts... A spy, a suspicious character... they found a thousand reasons for giving me sinister looks, the officers straight in the eye, the ladies with a knowing smile. After a while, even the deck hands and stewards, encouraged by the passengers, took to exchanging heavily caustic remarks behind my back. In the end no one doubted that I was the biggest and most intolerable, in fact the only out-and-out blackguard on board. A promising outlook.

My neighbours at table were four toothless and bilious postal officials from Gabon. They had been friendly to me, chummy in fact, at the start of the voyage; now they never said a word to me. They had tacitly agreed that I was a man to be watched. I seldom left my cabin, and then only with infinite precautions. The air was so hot it weighed on our skins like a solid. Behind my bolted door I lay naked, trying to imagine what plan those diabolical passengers had cooked up to destroy me. I didn't know anyone on board, yet they all seemed to know me. An exact description of me must have taken instant form in their minds, like that of a famous criminal published in the newspapers.

Through no fault of mine, I had been cast in the indispensable role of the "foul and loathsome villain", shame of the human race, whose presence has been recorded down through the centuries, who is as well known to everyone as God and the Devil, but who during his passage on this earth is so changeable and evasive as to elude everyone's grasp. For this "villain" to be at last isolated, identified and cornered, exceptional circumstances had been needed, such as were to be met with only in the narrow confines of this ship.

A great moral carnival was in the offing aboard the *Admiral Bragueton*. The "unclean beast" would not escape his fate. That was me.

This in itself made the trip worthwhile. Isolated among these spontaneous enemies, I laboured to identify them without their noticing. Especially in the morning, I was able to watch them with impunity through the porthole of my cabin. Before breakfast, covered with hair from pelvis to eyebrows and from their rectums to the soles of their feet, they would emerge to take the air in pyjamas that were transparent in the sunlight; or, glass in hand, sprawled against the rail, they would belch and retch, especially the captain with the bulging bloodshot eyes, whose liver started plaguing him at daybreak. Regularly at dawn he would ask his cronies about me, curious to know if I hadn't been "tossed overboard" yet, "like a gob of spit"! And he'd illustrate his remark by spitting into the frothing sea. Boy oh boy!

The *Admiral* wasn't getting ahead very fast, just groaning along from roll to roll. It was more like a sickness than a voyage. As I examined the members of the morning council from my porthole, they all seemed rather seriously ill – malarial, alcoholic, syphilitic in all likelihood – at a distance of ten metres, their visible decay was some consolation for my own troubles. These bigmouths, after all, were just as defeated as I was!... Still bragging, nothing more! That was the only difference! The mosquitoes had worked them over, sucking their blood and pumping their veins full of poisons that would never go away... Treponemas were filing away their arteries... Alcohol was corroding their livers... The sun was cracking their kidneys... Crab lice were clinging to their pubic hair and eczema to the skin of their bellies... The searing light would scorch their retinas!... In not so long a time what would be left of them? A bit of brain... To do what with, I ask you, where they were going! To commit suicide? Where they were going a brain wouldn't do them a bit of good... No two ways... it's no joke growing old in a place where there's nothing to do... but look at yourself in a mirror with verdigris for silvering, and see yourself getting seedier and seedier, more and more decrepit... Rot sets in quickly in the jungle, especially when it's atrociously hot.

The north at least preserves your flesh; northerners are pale once and for all. Between a dead Swede and a young man who has had a bad night there's not much to choose. But the day after a colonial lands, he's already full of maggots. Those infinitely laborious little worms have been waiting for him personally, and they'll stay with him a lot longer than life will. He's a bag of worms, that's all.

We had another week at sea before putting in to Bragamance, the first of the promised lands. I felt as if I were living in a case of dynamite. I had just about given up eating for fear of sitting down at their table or crossing the deck in the daytime. I'd stopped talking altogether. I was never seen taking the air. It would have been hard to be as little in evidence on that ship as I was and yet stay on board.

My cabin steward, a family man, was kind enough to inform me that those dashing colonial officers had lifted their glasses and sworn a solemn oath to slap my face at the first opportunity and then chuck me overboard. When I asked him why, he didn't know and asked me in turn what I had done to warrant so much hard feeling. We were left with our perplexity. It was unlikely to be cleared up. They didn't like my face, that's all.

You won't catch me taking another trip with people so hard to please. In addition, they had so much time on their hands, sequestered with themselves for thirty whole days, that it didn't take much to stir them up. And besides, when you stop to think about it, at least a hundred people must want you dead in the course of an average day, the ones in line behind you at the ticket window in the Métro, the ones who look up at your apartment when they haven't got one themselves, the ones who wish you'd finish pissing and give them a chance, your children and a lot more. It happens all the time, and you get used to it. On a boat this same impatience is more noticeable, which makes it more upsetting.

In that bubbling cauldron, the suint of those scalded beings is concentrated, the presentiment of the vast colonial solitude that will soon bury them and their destinies and make them groan like the dying. They cling, they bite, they rend, they froth at the mouth. My importance on the ship increased prodigiously from day to day. My rare appearances at table, silent and stealthy as I tried to make them, took on the magnitude of significant events. The moment I entered the dining room, the hundred and twenty passengers gave a start and began to whisper...

Advancing from malignant suppositions to slanderous conclusions, the colonial officers at the captain's table, fortified with aperitif after aperitif, the tax collectors and especially the lady schoolteachers on their way back to the Congo (of these there was quite an assortment on board the *Admiral Bragueton*) puffed me up to infernal proportions.

On boarding the ship in Marseille, I had been nothing, just a dreamy sort of nobody, but now, thanks to the concentrated attention of all those alcoholics and frustrated vaginas, I found myself changed beyond recognition, endowed with alarming prestige.

The captain of the ship, a shady, breezy, racketeering type, had gone out of his way to shake hands with me at the start. When he crossed my path now, he didn't even seem to know me, it was as if I'd been wanted for some sordid crime, guilty from the start... Guilty of what? When men can hate without risk, their stupidity is easily convinced, the motives supply themselves.

From what I seemed to discern of the compact malevolence that held me in its vice, the female section of the conspiracy was masterminded by one of the schoolteachers. She was going back to the Congo to die, or so at least I hoped, the bitch. Almost always she was trailing around after the officers, so handsome in their resplendent tight-fitting tunics and further embellished by the oath they had sworn to crush me like a noisome slug well before the next port of call. They wondered out loud whether I would be as repulsive flattened out as I was erect. In short, they were having a fine time. The schoolteacher whetted their fury, called down thunders on the deck of the *Admiral Bragueton*, resolved to know no rest until I had been picked up gasping, punished for ever for my imaginary impertinence, chastised for daring to exist, brutally beaten, bruised and bleeding, imploring pity under the boot and fist of one of those heroes, whose muscular prowess and spectacular rage she was burning to admire. A scene of high carnage, from which her weary ovaries promised themselves an awakening. As good as being raped by a gorilla. Time was passing, and it's dangerous to keep the aficionados waiting too long. I was the bull. The whole ship was clamouring, quivering from port to starboard.

The sea enclosed us in that boiler-plated circus. Even the engine-room crew knew what was going on. And since we only had three days ahead of us before putting into port, three decisive days, several matadors volunteered. The more I avoided the showdown, the more aggressive, the more threatening they became. The executioners began to rehearse. They cornered me between two cabins, at a bend in the corridor. I escaped by the skin of my teeth, but going to the toilet was getting downright dangerous. With only three days to go, I decided to forgo the needs of nature. The portholes were all I needed.

Crushing hatred and boredom were all around me. It can't be denied, the boredom on ships is something unbelievable; to tell the truth, it's cosmic. It fills the sea, the ship, the heavens. It's enough to unhinge the soundest of minds, so what would you expect of those chimerical deadheads?

A sacrifice! And I was the victim. Things came to a head one evening after dinner, at which, ravaged by hunger, I had put in an appearance. I bent over my plate and didn't budge, I didn't even dare to take out my handkerchief to wipe the sweat off my brow. Nobody had ever eaten his dinner more discreetly. From the engines a faint, continuous vibration rose up under my behind. My table companions must have known what sentence had been passed on me, for to my surprise they started talking to me freely and amiably about duels and stabbings, and asking me questions... Just then the schoolteacher from the Congo, the one whose breath was so strong, appeared in the lounge. I had barely time to notice that she was wearing a sumptuous lace evening dress. With nervous haste she sat down at the piano and played, if you can call it playing, a number of pieces, always skipping the finale. The atmosphere became intensely furtive and strained.

I jumped up and ran, hoping to take refuge in my cabin. I had almost reached it when one of the colonial officers, the chestiest and most muscular of the lot, barred my way, without violence but firmly. "Suppose we go up on deck!" he enjoined me. We had only a few steps to go. For the occasion he was wearing his cap, the one with the most gold braid, and he had fastened his buttons from collar to fly, something he hadn't done since our departure. So this was to be a full-dress dramatic ceremony! A tight spot for me, my heart was pounding on a level with my belly button.

This preamble, this abnormal full dress made me foresee a slow and painful execution. That officer looked to me like a chunk of the war, obstinate, inexorable, murderous, which someone had suddenly plunked down in front of me.

Behind him, blocking the doorway, appeared four junior officers, vigilant in the extreme, the escort of doom.

Flight was impossible. The speech that followed must have been carefully rehearsed. "Sir, you have before you Captain Frémizon* of the colonial army! In the name of my comrades in arms and of the passengers on this ship, who are justly indignant at your unspeakable behaviour,

I have the honour to demand an explanation!... Certain remarks you have made about us since we left Marseille are intolerable!... If you have any grievances, sir, the time has come to state them out loud!... to proclaim audibly what you have been saying in a shameful undertone for the last twenty-one days! To tell us at last what you think..."

On hearing these words I was very much relieved. I had feared some sudden death blow impossible to parry, but in talking, the Major was offering me a way out. Any possibility of cowardice becomes a glowing hope if you're not a fool. That's my opinion. Never be picky and choosy about the means of escaping disembowelment, or waste your time trying to find reasons for the persecution you're a victim of. Escape is good enough for the wise.

"Captain!" I replied, putting into my voice all the conviction of which I was capable under the circumstances. "What an extraordinary mistake you are in danger of making! You! Me! How can you think me capable of such ignominious sentiments? How monstrously unjust! Indeed it is more than I can bear! When only yesterday I was fighting for our beloved country! When over the years my blood has mingled with yours in innumerable battles! Oh, Captain, sir, how could you think of crushing me beneath such an injustice?"

Then, addressing the whole group:

"What abominable slander has abused you, gentlemen? Leading you to imagine that I, to all intents and purposes your brother, would dream of spreading foul calumnies about heroic officers! This is too much! Really too much!" And I went on: "Oh, for such a thing to happen at the very moment when these heroes, these incomparable heroes, are preparing to resume, with what courage I need not say, their sacred duty of safeguarding our immortal colonial empire! Where the most glorious soldiers of our race have covered themselves with eternal glory. The Mangins! The Faidherbes! The Gallienis!*... Oh, Captain! To suspect me! Of this!"

At that point I pulled up short. I hoped my silence would impress them. Luckily it did for a moment. Thereupon, without delay, taking advantage of the mumbling armistice, I went straight up to the Captain and, in an access of emotion, gripped both his hands.

With his hands enclosed in mine I felt fairly safe. Still clasping them, I continued, as volubly as ever, and while assuring him that he was right, a thousand times right, suggested that we make a fresh start, but get our signals straight this time! This unbelievable misunderstanding, I assured him, had been brought about by my stupid though natural timidity! I admitted that my behaviour could reasonably have been interpreted as unconscionable disdain by the ladies and gentlemen present, these "heroes and charmers... this providential conclave of astounding characters and talents... Not forgetting the incomparably musical ladies, the ornaments of our good ship!..." After making this profuse and elaborate apology, I implored them to admit me without delay or restriction to their joyous patriotic brotherhood... in which I hoped, now and for ever, to cut an admirable figure. And of course without releasing the Major's hands, I redoubled my eloquence.

As long as a soldier isn't killing, he's a child and easily amused. Since he is not in the habit of thinking, it costs him a crushing effort to understand when spoken to. Captain Frémizon wasn't killing me, he wasn't drinking and he wasn't doing anything with his hands or feet. He was only trying to think. For him that was much too much. In short, I'd caught him by the head.

Gradually, during this ordeal by humiliation, I felt my self-respect weakening, weakening a little more, seeping away, and finally abandoning me completely – officially as it were. Say what you please, that's a beautiful moment. After that incident I became infinitely light and free, morally speaking of course. Fear is probably, more often than not, the best means of getting you out of a tight spot. Since that day I've never felt the need of any other weapons, or virtues for that matter.

The captain couldn't make up his mind, and his friends, who had come there expressly to wipe up my blood and play knucklebones with my dispersed teeth, had to content themselves with catching words in mid-air. The civilians who had come rushing, tingling with eagerness at the news of an impending corrida, were looking very dangerous. Since I didn't know exactly what I was talking about, but only that I'd better keep it lyrical at all costs, I held on to the captain's hands and stared at an imaginary point in the cottony fog through which the *Admiral Bragueton* was making its way, puffing and spitting from one turn of the propeller to the next. Finally, to wind up my harangue, I ventured to raise one arm above my head, releasing one of the Captain's hands, but only one, and flung myself into my peroration: "Gentlemen, aren't we all agreed that brave men will always come to an understanding in the end? So damn it all, *vive la France*! *Vive la France!*" That was Sergeant

Branledore's gimmick. And once again it worked. That was the only time France ever saved my life, otherwise the opposite has been closer to the truth. I observed a moment's hesitation in my audience – after all, it's hard for an officer, however ill-disposed, to strike a civilian who has just shouted "*Vive la France!*" as loud as I had. That hesitation saved me.

I reached into the group of officers, grabbed two arms at random, and invited everybody to come to the bar and drink to my health and our reconciliation. The heroes resisted for barely a minute, and then we drank for two hours. But the females, silent and increasingly disappointed, kept their eyes on us. Through the portholes of the bar I saw the obstinate schoolteacher-pianist prowling like a hyena, surrounded by other females. The bitches had a strong suspicion that I'd conned myself out of the trap, and were determined to nab me at the next turn. Meanwhile, men among men, we went on drinking under the useless but stultifying electric fan, which since the Canaries had been wearing itself out churning the tepid, cottony atmosphere. Still, I had to keep up my verve and spout the kind of talk, nothing too difficult, that would appeal to my new friends. For fear of putting my foot in it, I overflowed with patriotic admiration, and kept asking those heroes, one after another, for stories and more stories of colonial feats of arms. War stories, like dirty stories, appeal to the military of all countries. The best way to make a sort of peace, a fragile armistice to be sure, but precious all the same, with men, officers or not, is to let them bask and wallow in childish self-glorification. There's no such thing as intelligent vanity. It's an instinct. And you'll never find a man who is not first and foremost vain. The role of admiring doormat is about the only one that one man is glad to tolerate in another. With these soldiers I had no need to tax my imagination. It was enough to appear impressed. It's easy to ask for more and more war stories. Those boys were crammed full of them. It was like the good old hospital days. After each story I made sure to express my approbation, as Branledore had taught me, with a glowing phrase: "Splendid! Why, that deserves to go down in history!" There's a formula that can't be beat! Little by little, the group I had wormed my way into decided that I was all right. They started telling the same kind of cock-and-bull war stories as I had heard in the old days and later dished out myself in imagination contests with my pals in the hospital. Except their setting was different: their fairy tales happened in the jungles of the Congo instead of the Vosges or Flanders.

Once Captain Frémizon, the one who a moment before had volunteered to purge the ship of my putrid presence, perceived that I listened more attentively than anyone else, he began to give me credit for no end of delightful qualities. His arterial flux seemed attenuated by the effect of my original praises, his vision cleared, his bloodshot, alcoholic eyes even began to sparkle despite his besotted state, and the sprinkling of doubts about his own worth, which he had somehow conceived deep within him and which assailed him in times of extreme depression, were for a time adorably dissipated by the miraculous effect of my intelligent and pertinent comments.

No doubt about it, I was a creator of euphoria! I had them slapping their thighs for all they were worth! I alone knew how to make life worth living in spite of the agonizing humidity! Wasn't I the most inspired of listeners?

As we were thus shooting the shit, the *Admiral Bragueton* began to slow down, she seemed to be making hardly any headway; not an atom of breeze around us, we must have been skirting the coast, moving as sluggishly as if the sea had been molasses.

The sky above us was molasses too, a black, viscous mass that I eyed hungrily. I'd have liked best to get back into the night, even sweating and groaning, no matter how! Frémizon went on and on with his stories. I had the impression that land was near, but my plan for escape filled me with alarm… Gradually our conversation ceased to be military and became first ribald, then frankly filthy, and in the end so incoherent that it was hard to keep it going. One after another of the company gave up and fell asleep, crushed under the weight of their snores, a nasty kind of sleep that scraped the caverns of their noses. That was the time to get away. One must never miss up on those remissions of cruelty that nature manages to impose on the most vicious and aggressive of this world's organisms.

By then we were anchored a short distance from the coast. All we could see of the shore was some lanterns moving back and forth.

Very quickly a hundred bobbing canoes full of screeching black men came crowding around the ship. There were black men all over the decks, offering their services. In a few seconds I carried the few bundles I had done up in secret to the gangway and slipped down it behind one of the boatmen, whose features and movements were almost entirely hidden from me by the darkness. At the bottom of the

103

steps, on a level with the splashing water, I wondered anxiously where we were going.

"Where are we?" I asked.

"At Bambola-Fort-Gono!"* the shadow answered.

We pushed off and paddled hard. To make us go faster I helped him.

I had time to get one last look at my menacing fellow passengers. In the light of the cabin lamps, laid low by apathy and gastritis, they grunted and fermented in their sleep. Bloated and sprawling, they all looked alike now, officers, civil servants, engineers and traders, pimply, potbellied and swarthy, intermingled and more or less identical. Dogs look like wolves when they're asleep.

A few moments later I was back on land. Under the trees the night was thicker than ever, and behind the night lay all the complicities of silence.

* * *

In this colony of Bambola-Bragamance the Governor reigned triumphant over everybody. His soldiers and civil servants hardly dared breathe when he deigned to let his eyes fall on them.

Far below these notables, the resident traders seemed to thieve and thrive more easily than in Europe. Not one coconut, not one peanut in the entire colony evaded their brigandage. As fatigue and ill health overcame the civil servants, it began to dawn on them that they'd been had, that all they had gained by being sent out here was stripes and forms to fill out and very little pay. So naturally they looked at the traders with a envious eye. The military faction, even more dull-witted than the other two, subsisted on a diet of colonial glory, washed down by quantities of quinine and miles of red tape.

Understandably, a life spent waiting for the thermometer to go down made everybody more and more cantankerous. The consequence was private and collective quarrels, preposterous and interminable, between the military and the administration, between the administration and the traders, between these two in temporary alliance and the military, between the whole lot of them and the black population, and finally between blacks and blacks. The little energy that hadn't been sapped by malaria, thirst and the heat was consumed by hatred so fierce and deep-seated that it wasn't uncommon for these colonials to drop dead on the spot, poisoned by themselves like scorpions.

Nevertheless, this virulent anarchy was held in check, like crabs in a basket, by a hermetic police structure. The civil servants griped in vain, for the Governor, to keep his colony in subjection, was able to recruit all the moth-eaten mercenaries he needed, impoverished blacks driven to the coast by debts, defeated by the law of supply and demand, and needful of something to eat. These recruits were taught the law and how to admire the Governor. The Governor seemed to wear all the gold in his treasury on his uniform... in the blazing sunshine, it surpassed belief, even without the plumes.

He went to Vichy for the baths every year, and he never read anything but the *Official Gazette*. A number of the civil servants cherished the hope that he'd sleep with their wives some day, but the Governor didn't care for women. He didn't care for anything. He survived each new epidemic of yellow fever like a charm, while so many of the men who'd have liked to bury him died like flies at the first whiff of fever.

There was a story that one 14th July, as he was reviewing the troops of the Residency, caracoling up ahead of his Spahi guards who were carrying a flag as big as a house, some sergeant, delirious with fever no doubt, rushed out in front of him, shouting: "Get back, you jerk!" It seems the Governor was very much upset by this outrage which, as it happened, was never satisfactorily explained.

It is hard to get a faithful look at people and things in the tropics, because of the colours that emanate from them. In the tropics colours and things are in a turmoil. To the eye, the various reflections projected by a small sardine can lying upon the road at midday can take on the dimensions of an accident. You've got to watch out. It's not just the people who are hysterical down there, objects are the same way. Life only becomes tolerable at nightfall, but then almost immediately the darkness is taken over by swarms of mosquitoes. Not one or two or a hundred, but billions of them. Survival under those conditions is quite an achievement. A carnival by day, a colander by night, a quiet war.

When the hut you sleep in has filled at last with silence and the air is almost fit to breathe, the termites, those loathsome beasts eternally engaged in eating away the uprights of your cabin, get to work. The day a tornado hits this treacherous filigree, whole streets will go up in dust.

The town of Fort-Gono where I'd landed, the capital of Bragamance, was perched precariously between sea and jungle, but supplied – adorned, so to speak – with enough banks, brothels, cafés, café terraces, and even a recruiting office, to make it a small metropolis. There was even a Place Faidherbe and a Boulevard Bugeaud,* in case you wanted to take a walk. The whole was a clump of gleaming edifices surrounded by jagged rocks, riddled with larvae, trampled by successive soldiers and officials.

At about five o'clock the military element would grouse and gripe over their aperitifs – the price of which, as it happened, had just gone up when I arrived. A delegation of consumers was about to petition the Governor to issue a decree enjoining the café owners from playing fast and loose with the prices of absinthe and cassis. If some of the regulars were to be believed, the very foundations of colonization were threatened by ice. Indeed it cannot be denied that the introduction of ice into the colonies has sparked off a process of emasculation. Riveted by force of habit to his iced aperitif, the colonial could no longer hope to dominate the climate by stoicism alone. The Faidherbes, the Stanleys, the Marchands,* be it noted in passing, had nothing but good things to say of the tepid, muddy beer, wine and water they drank for years without complaining. There you have it. That's how colonies are lost.

I learnt plenty more in the shade of the palm trees which, all along those avenues of precarious dwellings, throve in provocative contrast. It was only that garish raw greenery which prevented the place from looking exactly like La Garenne-Bezons.

At nightfall the native hookers came out in strength, wending their way between clouds of hungry mosquitoes armed with yellow fever. There were Sudanese girls as well, offering the passer-by the treasures under their loincloths. For extremely moderate prices you could treat yourself to a whole family for an hour or two. I'd have liked to flit from cunt to cunt, but necessity obliged me to look for work.

The Director of the Compagnie Pordurière* du Petit Congo, so I heard, was looking for an inexperienced man to take charge of one of the trading posts in the bush. I went without delay to offer my incompetent but enthusiastic services. The Director's reception of me was not exactly friendly. That lunatic – I may as well call a spade a spade – lived not far from the Government House in a spacious straw bungalow built on piles. Before even looking at me, he fired several questions about my past; then, somewhat appeased by my naive answers, his contempt took a more indulgent turn. Still, he did not yet see fit to offer me a seat.

"To judge by your papers, you know something about medicine?" he observed.

I replied that I had indeed studied for a time in that field.

"It'll come in handy," he said. "How about some whisky?"

I told him I didn't drink. "Smoke?" Again I declined. Such abstinence surprised him. In fact he scowled.

"I'm suspicious of employees who don't smoke and drink... Are you a pederast by any chance?... No? Too bad!... They don't steal as much... That's been my experience... They get attached... Well," he was kind enough to hedge. "By and large I seem to have noticed that quality, that advantage, in pederasts... Maybe you'll prove me wrong..." And changing the subject: "You're hot, aren't you? You'll get used to it! You'll have to! How was your trip?"

"Uncomfortable!" I said.

"Well, my friend, you haven't seen a thing. Come and tell me what you think of this country when you've spent a year in Bikomimbo, the place where I'm sending you to replace that joker..."

His Negress, squatting beside the table, was fiddling with her feet and scraping them with a little piece of wood.

"Beat it, you slut!" her master flung at her. "Go and call the house boy! And get me some ice while you're at it!"

The boy took his time coming. Infuriated, the Director sprang to his feet and received him with two brutal slaps in the face and the same number of resounding kicks in the gut.

"These people will be the death of me!" the Director predicted with a sigh, slumping back into his armchair, which was covered with dirty, rumpled, yellow canvas.

"Look, old man," he said, suddenly grown friendly, as though liberated for a while by his access of brutality, "would you mind handing me my whip and my quinine... there on the table... I oughtn't to get so excited... It's stupid to fly off the handle like that..."

From his house we overlooked the river port, which shimmered through dust so dense, so compact, that we heard the clanking and thumping more clearly than we could see what was going on. On the shore files of black men were busy, encouraged by whips and curses, unloading hold after hold of ships that were never empty, climbing up flimsy, teetering gangplanks with big baskets balanced on their heads – like vertical ants.

Through a scarlet haze I saw them coming and going in jerky lines. Some of these working shapes carried an extra black spot on their backs: those were mothers toting their babies along as additional burdens with their sacks of palm cabbage. I wonder if ants can do that.

"Doesn't it always seem like Sunday here?..." the Director joked. "So jolly! So colourful! And the females always naked. You've noticed? Good-lookers too, don't you agree? Of course it seems strange when you've just arrived from Paris, I won't deny it. And look at us! Always in white ducks! Like at the seashore! Aren't we a sight for sore eyes? All dressed up for First Communion! It's always a holiday here, take it from me! Day in and day out, just one glorious Assumption Day! And it's like this all the way to the Sahara! Think of it!"

He stopped talking, sighed, grunted, said "Shit!" two or three times, mopped his forehead, and started up again.

"Out where the Company's sending you, it's deep in the bush. Very damp!... Ten days' trip from here... First by sea... Then up the river. The river's all red, you'll see... And on the other side it's the Spaniards... The man you're replacing at the post up there is a rotter... just between you and me... I tell you... He simply won't send us his accounts, that bastard! Nothing we can do! We've sent him letter after letter!... A man doesn't stay honest long when he's alone! You'll see!... You'll see that as well!... He's written, says he's sick... Big deal! Sick! I'm sick too! What does he mean sick? We're all sick! You'll be sick yourself before you know it! That's no excuse! What do we care if he's sick!... The Company comes first! When you get there, take an inventory, that's the essential!... There's food enough for three months and merchandise for at least a year... You won't run short!... Don't start at night, whatever you do!... Be on your guard! He's got his own Negroes, he'll send them down the river to pick you up, maybe they'll chuck you overboard. I bet he's trained them! They're as rascally as he is! Fact! He's probably dropped a hint to those Negroes about you!... That's the kind of thing they do around here! And be sure to take your quinine with you, your own, get it before you leave... He might doctor his, I wouldn't put it past him!"

The Director thought he'd given me enough advice and stood up to say goodbye. The tin roof over our heads seemed to weigh at least two thousand tons, it absorbed all the heat of the day and sent it down on us. We were both making faces with the heat. We could just as well have dropped dead.

"Perhaps," he added, "there's no point in our meeting again before you leave, Bardamu! Everything wears out so down here! Well, no, maybe I'll run down to the warehouses before you go and see how you're making out!... You'll hear from us when you get there... There's a mail every month... The mail goes out from here... Well, good luck!..."

And he vanished into the shadow between his helmet and his jacket. I could clearly see the tendons in the back of his neck, curved like two fingers pressing against his head. He turned round again:

"Don't forget to tell that loafer to come back here in a hurry!... I've got a few things to say to him!... And not to waste time on the way! Oh, the rat! I only hope he doesn't croak before he gets here!... That would be a shame! A bleeding shame! Oh, the bugger!"

One of his blacks went ahead of me with a big lantern and took me to the place where I was to live before leaving for the Bikomimbo of my dreams.

We passed through avenues full of people who seemed to have come out for a stroll after dark. The night, hammered by gongs, was all around us, interspersed by brief snatches of song as incoherent as sobs, the big black night of the hot countries, with its brutal tom-tom heart that always beats too fast.

My young guide glided along easily on bare feet. There must have been Europeans in the bushes, you could hear them wandering about, their easily recognizable white men's voices, aggressive and hypocritical. The bats came whirling and weaving through the swarms of insects attracted by our light. Under every leaf of the trees there must have been at least one cricket, to judge by the deafening din they made together.

Halfway up a hill we were stopped at a crossroads by a group of native riflemen arguing around a coffin draped in a big, undulating French flag.

It was somebody who had died in the hospital, and they didn't know exactly where to bury him. Their orders were vague. Some wanted to put him in one of the fields down below, some insisted on a garden at the top of the hill. The question had to be decided one way or the other, so the boy and I joined in the discussion.

In the end the pall-bearers decided for the lower rather than the upper burial ground, because it was easier to walk downhill. Then we met three young white boys, the kind that in Europe go to rugby matches on Sunday, enthusiastic, noisy, pale-faced spectators. Like myself they were employed by the Compagnie Pordurière and were kind enough to show me the way to the unfinished shanty where my portable folding bed was temporarily situated.

The edifice, when we got there, was absolutely empty except for a few utensils and my so-called bed. As soon as I lay down on that wobbly filiform object, two dozen bats emerged from the corners and took to whishing back and forth like a volley of fans over my apprehensive repose.

The young black, my guide, came back to offer me his intimate services. Then, disappointed when I told him I wasn't in the mood that evening, he offered to introduce me to his sister. I'd have been curious to know how he expected to find his sister in such darkness.

Not far away the village tom-tom chopped my patience into little bits. Thousands of hard-working mosquitoes took possession of my legs, but I didn't dare set foot on the ground because of the scorpions and snakes which, I assumed, had started on their abominable hunting expeditions. The snakes had plenty of rats to choose from, rats were gnawing away at everything that can be gnawed, I heard them on the wall, on the floor, and quivering, ready to drop, on the ceiling.

Finally the moon rose, and things were a little quieter in the shanty. All things considered, life in the colonies was no great shakes.

Nevertheless, the next day came, a steaming cauldron. An enormous desire to go back to Europe took hold of me body and soul. Only one thing prevented me from clearing out – lack of money. That was enough. Anyway, I only had another week to spend in Fort-Gono before going to my job in Bikomimbo, which I'd heard described so delightfully.

The biggest building in Fort-Gono after the Governor's Palace was the hospital. I ran into it wherever I went; I couldn't walk a hundred metres in the town without coming across one of its pavilions, smelling faintly of carbolic acid. From time to time I ventured down to the docks to watch my anaemic young colleagues – whom the Compagnie Pordurière recruited in France by emptying whole settlement houses –

at work. They seemed possessed by a bellicose haste to unload freighter after freighter without stopping. "Harbour fees are so dreadfully costly!" they kept saying, sincerely distressed, as if it had been their own money.

They belaboured the black porters with a will. They were conscientious, you couldn't deny it, and they were also flabby, heartless sons of bitches. In other words, they were well chosen, as mindlessly enthusiastic as any employer could dream of. Sons that would have delighted my mother, worshipping their bosses, if only she could have had one all to herself, a son she could have been proud of in the eyes of the world, a real legitimate son.

Those half-baked little specimens had come to tropical Africa to offer their flesh, their blood, their lives, their youth to their bosses, martyrs for twenty-two francs a day (minus deductions), and they were happy, yes, happy down to their last red corpuscle, for which ten million mosquitoes were lying in wait.

The colonies make these little clerks fat or make them thin; either way they hold them fast; there are only two ways to die under the sun, the fat way and the thin way. There's no other. You may have a preference, but it's your constitution that decides whether you get fat or whether the bones jab at your skin.

The Director up there on the red cliff, cavorting diabolically with his Negress under the tin roof with the ten thousand kilos of sunshine on it would be no better off when his time was up. He was the skinny kind. Sure, he was putting up a fight. It looked as if he could beat the climate. Looked! In reality he was crumbling even faster than the others.

The story was that he'd thought up a beautiful scheme that would make him a fortune in two years... But he'd never have time to carry it out, even if he applied himself to defrauding the company day and night. Twenty-two directors before him had tried to make a fortune, each with his own system, like at roulette. All this was well known to the stockholders, who were keeping an eye on him from up above, still higher up, from the Rue Moncey in Paris. The Director made them laugh. How childish! The stockholders were the biggest bandits of all; they knew their Director was syphilitic and much too horny for the tropics, they knew he downed enough quinine and bismuth to burst his eardrums and enough arsenic to make his gums drop out.

In the Company's bookkeeping the Director's months were numbered, numbered like the months of a pig's life.

My little colleagues never exchanged ideas. Only set formulas, baked and rebaked like dry crusts of thought. "Worry won't get us anywhere!" they said. "Never say die!…" "The Director's a jerk!…" "Negro skin is good for tanning!" etc.

In the evening after work we'd meet for aperitifs with an "assistant manager", a Monsieur Tandernot from La Rochelle. If Tandernot hobnobbed with the traders, it was only because they'd pay for his drinks. He was a pitiful case, stone-broke. His position in the colonial hierarchy was the lowest possible, overseeing road construction in the middle of the jungle. His militiamen had clubs, and naturally the natives worked. But since no white man ever used the new roads that Tandernot built, and since the blacks preferred their own tracks through the jungle where it was harder to lay hands on them for tax purposes, and since Tandernot's government roads didn't actually go anywhere, they soon vanished under a dense growth of vegetation, from month to month if the truth be known.

"Believe it or not!…" that astonishing pioneer would say. "Last year I lost a hundred and twenty-two kilometres of them!"

During my stay, I only heard Tandernot boast about one thing, the one achievement he was humbly vain about: he was the only European capable of catching cold in Bragamance with the thermometer at forty-four degrees in the shade… That one distinction consoled him for many sorrows… "I've caught another rotten cold!" he'd announce proudly over his aperitif. "You don't see that happening to anyone else!" And other members of our sickly group would cry out: "Good old Tandernot! What a man!" This little satisfaction was better than nothing. Where vanity is at stake, anything is better than nothing.

Another way the Company's petty clerks amused themselves was putting on fever contests. It wasn't difficult. These matches could go on for days, and they whiled away the time. When evening came and, almost always, the fever with it, they'd take their temperatures. "Hey, I've got thirty-nine!…" "Hell, that's nothing. I can work up forty any time I feel like it!"

These readings were absolutely accurate and above board. By the light of hurricane lamps they'd compare thermometers. The winner would tremble and gloat. "I'm sweating so much I can't piss!" said the most emaciated of the lot, a skinny young fellow from the Pyrenees, a champion of febrility who had come to Bragamance, so he told me, to get away from a seminary where he "hadn't enough freedom". But time was passing, and none of my companions could tell me exactly what species of freak the man I was replacing in Bikomimbo belonged to.

"He's funny!" they told me, and that was all.

"When you start out in the colonies," said the little Pyrenean with the high fever, "you've got to show what you're good for! It's all one way or the other! As far as the Director's concerned, you'll either be solid gold or solid shit! And another thing: he'll judge you right away!"

I was very much afraid of being put down as "solid shit" or worse.

These young slave-drivers, my friends, took me to see another employee of the Pordurière, who deserves special mention. He operated a store in the European quarter. Mouldering with fatigue, oily and decrepit, he dreaded the slightest ray of light because of his eyes, which two years of uninterrupted baking under a tin roof had dried out atrociously. It took him a good half-hour every morning to open them, so he told me, and another half-hour before he could see more or less clearly. Every ray of light was torture. A big mangy mole.

Suffocation and suffering had become second nature with him, and so had thieving. If he'd suddenly woken up healthy and honest, it would really have thrown him off balance. Even today, at this distance, I'd call his hatred for the Director General one of the most violent passions it has ever been given me to observe. At the thought of the Director, a violent rage would make him forget the pain he was in, and on the slightest pretext he'd rant and rave, all the while scratching himself from top to toe.

He never stopped scratching, in ellipses so to speak, from the lower end of his spinal column to the top of his neck. He dug furrows into his epidermis and dermis with his bloody fingernails, while continuing to wait on his numerous customers, most of them virtually naked blacks.

With his free hand he would plunge busily into various repositories to the right and left of him in the dark shop. Without ever making a mistake, deft and admirably quick, he would take out exactly what the customer wanted, stinking leaf tobacco, damp matches, cans of sardines, a ladleful of molasses, super-alcoholic beer in phoney bottles, which he'd suddenly drop if overcome by the desire to scratch in the cavernous depths of his trousers. Then he would thrust in his whole arm, and it would emerge through the fly, which he always left partly open as a precaution.

He referred to the ailment that was eating away his skin by its local name, "corocoro". "This miserable corocoro!... When I think that the stinking Director hasn't caught it yet, it makes me itch a hundred times worse!... The corocoro can't get a hold on him!... He's too rotten already. That pimp isn't a man, he's an infection!... Pure unadulterated shit!..."

When he said that, we'd all burst out laughing, the black customers too, in emulation. He frightened us a little. But he had one friend, a wheezing, greying little fellow who drove a truck for the Pordurière. He used to bring us ice that he'd evidently stolen here and there from ships tied up at the wharf.

We'd drink his health at the bar, surrounded by the black customers, who looked on enviously. These customers were the more sophisticated blacks, who'd lost their fear of doing business with white men, a kind of elite so to speak. The other blacks, not so smart, preferred to keep their distance. Matter of instinct. But the most enterprising, the most contaminated of the blacks got taken on as clerks in the store. You could recognize the black clerks by the way they cursed and yelled at other blacks. My colleague with the corocoro traded in crude rubber, which came in sticky balls that the natives would bring in from the bush in big sacks.

While we were in the store, listening to him by the hour, a family of rubber gatherers came to the door and froze with timidity, the father in the lead, wrinkled, girt in a skimpy orange loincloth and holding his long machete.

The savage was afraid to come in despite the encouragements of one of the native clerks: "C'mon in, nigger! Come look see! We no eat savages!" Won over by these kind words, they stepped into the sweltering shack, at the back of which our corocoro man was ranting.

Apparently that native had never seen a store or possibly even a white man before. One of the women, with a big basket of crude rubber balanced on her head, followed him with downcast eyes.

Quickly the recruiting clerks grabbed her basket and put the contents on the scales. The savage didn't know what the scales were about or anything else. His wife was still afraid to raise her head. The rest of the family waited outside, staring wide-eyed. The clerk told them to come in, so that they wouldn't miss the show.

That was the first time they had all trekked in from the bush to the white man's town. It must have taken them a good long time to collect all that rubber. So naturally they were interested in the outcome. You hang little cups on the trunks of the trees, and the rubber oozes into them very very slowly. Sometimes you don't get so much as a small glassful in two months.

After the weighing, our scratcher dragged the bewildered native behind the counter, did a little reckoning with a pencil stub, and shoved a few coins into the man's hand. Then he said: "Beat it! That's it!…"

All his little white friends were convulsed to see how cleverly he had handled the transaction. The black man stood there by the counter, looking lost in his skimpy orange underdrawers.

One of the black clerks yelled at him to wake him up: "You no savvy money? You savage?" This clerk knew his onions, he was used to these peremptory transactions, he had probably been trained. "You no speaky French?" he went on. "You missing link, eh?… What you speakum anyway? Couscous? Mabillia? Jackass! Bushman! You heap big jackass!"

The savage just stood there with his hand closed on his coins. He would have run away if he had dared, but he didn't dare.

"What you buy with dough?" the scratcher put in. "I haven't seen such an idiot in a long time! He must have come a long way. What you wait for? Gimme that dough!"

He grabbed the money, and in place of the coins gave the black man a bright green handkerchief that he had deftly spirited from some secret hiding place under the counter.

When the black man hesitated to leave with the handkerchief, the scratcher went a step further. He certainly knew all the tricks of the conqueror's trade. Shaking the big square of muslin before the eyes of a wee black child, he said: "Ain't it pretty, you little turd? Did you ever see one like it, little sweetie, little stinkpot, little fart?" And with a one-two-three he tied it around the child's neck. Now the child was dressed.

The whole family stared at the child, decked out in the green cotton object… There was nothing more they could do, because the handkerchief had come into the family. They could only accept it, take it, and go.

They all backed slowly out. They crossed the threshold. When the father, who was last, turned around to say something, the sharpest of the clerks, who was wearing shoes, helped him leave with a swift kick in the arse.

The entire little tribe stood silently on the other side of the Avenue Faidherbe, under the magnolia tree, watching us finish our aperitifs. It looked as if they were trying to understand what had happened to them.

The corocoro man was treating us. He even played his gramophone for us. You could find anything in his store. It made me think of the supply depots in the war.

* * *

As I've told you, there were lots of blacks and small whites like myself working in the warehouses and plantations of the Compagnie Pordurière du Petit Togo at the same time as me. The natives, by and large, had to be driven to work with clubs – they preserved that much dignity – whereas the whites, perfected by public education, worked of their own free will.

Wielding a club is tiring in the long run. The white men's hearts and minds, on the other hand, have been crammed full of the hope of becoming rich and powerful, and that costs nothing, absolutely nothing. We've heard enough about Egypt and the Tartar tyrants! In the art of squeezing the last ounce of labour out of a two-legged animal, those primitive ancients were pretentious incompetents! Did they ever think of calling their slave "Monsieur" or letting him vote now and then, or giving him his newspaper? And especially had they thought of sending him to war to work off his passions? After twenty centuries of Christianity (as I personally can bear witness) your modern man simply can't control himself when a regiment passes before his eyes. It puts too many ideas into his head.

Accordingly, I decided to keep a close watch on myself from then on and learn to keep my mouth scrupulously shut, to conceal my longing to get away – in short, to prosper if possible and come what may, in the service of the Compagnie Pordurière. Not a moment to lose.

Alongside our warehouses, on the muddy river banks, whole nests of crocodiles, insidious and unmoving, lurked in wait. Built of metal, they enjoyed the delirious heat, and so apparently did the blacks.

At midday you couldn't help wondering if all this bustle of toiling masses, this hubbub of screeching, overexcited blacks on the docks was possible.

To learn the secret of numbering sacks before taking to the bush, I had to submit to gradual asphyxiation in the Company's main warehouse along with the other clerks, between two scales wedged into the alkaline crowd of ragged, pustular, singing black men. Each one of them drew a little cloud behind him and shook it in cadence. The dull thuds of the overseers' clubs descended on their magnificent backs without provoking the least complaint or protest. Dazed and passive, they suffered pain as unquestioningly as the torrid air of that dusty furnace.

The Director came by from time to time, always aggressive, to make sure I was mastering the techniques of numbering sacks and falsifying weights.

With sweeping blows of his club he cleared his path to the scales through the press of natives. "Bardamu," he said to me one morning when he was in high spirits. "You see these Negroes all around us?... Well, when I came to Little Togo almost thirty years ago, those loafers still lived by hunting, fishing and intertribal massacres!... I was a small trader then... Well, as true as I'm standing here, I'd seen them coming home to their village after a victory, loaded with more than a hundred baskets of bleeding human flesh to stuff their bellies with!... Hear that, Bardamu?... Bleeding!... Their enemies! A feast!... Today, no more victories! We've accomplished that much! No more tribes! No more flimflam and foolishness! Today we've got a labour force and peanuts! Good hard work! No more hunting! No more guns! Peanuts and rubber!... To pay taxes with! Taxes to get us more rubber and peanuts! This is life, Bardamu! Peanuts! Peanuts and rubber!... And say... well, I'll be damned. There's General Tombat."*

True enough, he was coming our way, an old man crumpling under the enormous weight of the sun.

The general wasn't exactly a soldier any more, but he wasn't exactly a civilian either. Confidential agent of the Pordurière, he took care of liaison between the Administration and the business community, an

117

indispensable function, although the two lived in a state of permanent competition and hostility. But the General was a shrewd manoeuvrer. For instance, he had disentangled a shady deal in enemy holdings, which had been judged inextricable in high places.

At the beginning of the war General Tombat's ear had been split, not very badly, just enough to get him honourably retired after Charleroi.* He had immediately offered his services to "Greater France". But long after Verdun,* that epic battle was still on his mind. He was always shuffling a handful of telegrams. "Our little *poilus* will hold on! They are holding on!..." It was so hot in the warehouse and France was so far away that we could have done without General Tombat's predictions. But just to be polite we all, and the Director with us, declared in chorus: "They're marvellous!" On these words Tombat left us.

A few moments later the Director opened up another violent path through the tightly packed torsos and vanished in his turn into the peppery dust.

The Director had eyes like glowing coals, he was consumed with a passion to control the Company. He frightened me a little, and I had difficulty in getting used to his presence. I found it hard to believe that in all the world there could be a human carcass capable of such maximum-tension greed. He seldom said anything to us straight out, he spoke only in muffled hints, and he seemed to live and breathe for the sole purpose of conspiring, spying and betraying. I was told that he stole, swindled and peculated incomparably more than all the other officials put together, and they were no slouches, I assure you. But I can easily believe it.

During my stay in Fort-Gono, I had a little leisure in which to roam around. The only really desirable spot I came across in the whole town was the hospital.

Whenever you get to a new place, certain ambitions turn up inside you. My ambition was to be sick, just plain sick. Every man to his taste. I walked around those promising hospital pavilions, so doleful, withdrawn and unmolested, and I never relinquished their antiseptic charm without regret. The lawns around them were brightened by furtive little birds and anxious multicoloured lizards. An earthly Paradise in its way.

As for the blacks, one soon gets used to them, their sluggish good nature, their slow gestures and the protuberant bellies of their women.

Those blacks stink of their misery, their interminable vanities and their repugnant resignation; actually, they're just like our poor people, except they have more children, less dirty washing and less red wine.

When I'd finished inhaling and sniffing at the hospital, I followed the native crowd and stopped for a while outside the pagoda-like edifice near the fort that a restaurant owner had built for the entertainment of the sexy young jokers of the colony.

The prosperous whites of Fort-Gono went there at night and gambled doggedly, meanwhile drinking and yawning and belching with a will. For two hundred francs you could lay the luscious *patronne*. The young jokers had a lot of trouble with their trousers when they wanted to scratch, because their suspenders kept sliding off.

At night big crowds poured out of the native huts and collected around the pagoda, never weary of seeing and hearing the whites jigging around the mechanical piano as off-key waltzes wheezed from its moth-eaten strings. When she heard the music, a blissful look came over the *patronne*, meaning that she felt like dancing.

After trying in vain for several days, I managed to have a few talks with her in private. Her periods, she confided, lasted no less than three weeks. Fault of the tropics. In addition, her customers wore her out. Not that they made love very often, but since drinks at the pagoda were on the expensive side, they tried to get their money's worth by pinching her arse something terrible before leaving. That was what wore her out mostly.

As a businesswoman, the *patronne* knew all the gossip of the colony, all the desperate love affairs that transpired between the fever-harried officers and the handful of civil servants' wives, they too menstruating interminably and languishing for days on end in the deep reclining chairs of their verandas.

The streets, offices and shops of Fort-Gono were awash with mutilated desires. To do everything people did in Europe, despite the abominable temperature and their own progressive, insurmountable decay, seemed to be the prime obsession and grimacing satisfaction of those maniacs.

The fences could hardly contain the swollen, wildly aggressive vegetation of the gardens; the rampant foliage moulded delirious lettuces around the houses, those chunks of dried-out egg white, in which some jaundiced European was rotting away. All along the Avenue

Fachoda,* the liveliest and most fashionable street in Fort-Gono, there were as many overflowing salad bowls as Government officials.

Every night I went back to my shack, which would no doubt never be finished, where my skeleton of a bed had been put up by my depraved boy. He set traps for me, he was as sensual as a cat, he wanted to become part of my family. I, however, was haunted by other, far more pressing preoccupations, especially by my plan to take refuge for a while in the hospital, the only respite within my reach in that torrid carnival.

In peace as in war, I took no interest at all in futile pastimes. Even the sincerely and eminently obscene offers that came to me through the boss's cook struck me as colourless.

For the last time I made the rounds of my young friends at the Pordurière, trying to garner some information about that disloyal employee, the one I had orders to replace at all costs in the bush. Empty chit-chat.

Nor did I learn anything substantial in the Café Faidherbe at the end of the Avenue Fachoda, abuzz at the twilight hour with hundreds of slanders, rumours and calumnies. Nothing but impressions. Whole dustbins full of impressions were overturned in that half-light encrusted with multicoloured lamps. Shaking the lace of the giant palm trees, the wind blew clouds of mosquitoes into the customers' saucers. The Governor, thanks to his exalted rank, figured prominently in the discourse round about. His inexpiable crumminess was the mainstay of the aperitif conversation in which the nauseated colonial liver seeks relief before dinner.

At that hour all the cars in Fort-Gono, ten in all, drove back and forth past the café. They never seemed to go very far. The Place Faidherbe had the characteristic atmosphere, the overdone decor, the floral and verbal excess of a subprefecture in southern France gone mad. The ten cars left the Place Faidherbe only to come back five minutes later, having once more completed the same circuit with their cargo of anaemic Europeans, dressed in unbleached linen, fragile creatures as wobbly as melting sorbet.

For weeks and years these colonials passed the same forms and faces until they were so sick of hating them that they didn't even look at one another. The officers now and then would take their families for a walk, paying close attention to military salutes and civilian greetings, the wives swaddled in their special sanitary napkins, the children, unbearably plump European maggots, wilted by the heat and constant diarrhoea.

To command you need more than a kepi; you also need troops. In the climate of Fort-Gono the European cadres melted faster than butter. A battalion was like a lump of sugar in your coffee; the longer you looked the less you saw. Most of the white conscripts were permanently in the hospital, sleeping off their malaria, riddled with parasites made to order for every nook and cranny in the body, whole squads stretched out flat between cigarettes and flies, masturbating under mouldy sheets, spinning endless yarns between fits of painstakingly provoked and coddled fever. Poor bastards, they were having a rough time, a pitiful crew in the soft half-light of the green shutters, re-enlisted men soon fallen from celebrity, side by side – the hospital was mixed – with civilians, all hunted men in flight from the bosses and the bush.

In the apathy of those long malarial siestas, the heat is such that the flies also rest. From bloodless, hairy arms on both sides of the beds dangle grimy books, all in tatters. Half the pages are missing because of the dysentery cases, who never have enough paper, and also because of the sourpuss nuns, who have their own way of censoring books in which God is not treated with enough respect. The military crabs victimize the nuns as much as everybody else. When they want a good scratch, they lift up their habits behind the screen where this morning's stiff is still so hot that he hasn't yet managed to grow cold.

Depressing as the hospital was, it was the only place in the whole colony where you could feel forgotten, safe from the people outside, the bosses. A vacation from slavery, that was the main thing, anyway the only happiness within my reach.

I made enquiries about the requirements for admission, the habits and idiosyncrasies of the doctors. By that time the prospect of leaving for the bush filled me with despair and thoughts of revolt; already I was planning to contract every available fever as soon as possible, to return to Fort-Gono desperately ill and so emaciated, so repulsive that they'd not only have to take me, but also to ship me back to France. I already knew some wonderful tricks for getting sick, and I was learning special new ones for the colonies.

I prepared to overcome a thousand difficulties, for neither the directors of the Compagnie Pordurière nor the military authorities were easily discouraged from tracking their chill-racked, cadaverous prey and pouncing on them as they played cards between the pissy beds.

They would find me resolved to rot with whatever disease proved necessary. Unfortunately you didn't usually stay in the hospital for long, unless you wrote finis there to your colonial career once and for all. Sometimes the toughest and smartest of the fever patients, those with the greatest strength of character, managed to slip aboard a transport bound for France. That was a happy miracle. Most of the hospital patients gave up, recognized that the regulations had defeated them, and went back to the bush to lose what weight they had left. If the quinine relinquished them to their maggots while they were still in the hospital, the chaplain would simply close their eyes at about six in the evening, and four Senegalese would carry the bloodless husks to the plot of red clay beside the church in Fort-Gono. That church, incidentally, was so hot under its tin roof that you never went there twice, more tropical than the tropics. To stand up in that church you'd have to pant like a dog.

That's the way it goes. You can't deny it, men have a hard time doing all that's demanded of them: butterflies in their youth, maggots at the end.

I tried here and there to get a little more information, a few facts to go by. Because what the Director had told me about Bikomimbo seemed incredible. Apparently the place was an experimental trading post, an attempt to penetrate the bush, at least ten days' journey from the coast, isolated in the midst of the natives and their jungle, which had been described to me as an enormous reservation crawling with animals and diseases.

I wondered if my young friends at the Pordurière, who oscillated between aggressiveness and extreme depression, weren't simply jealous of me. Their idiocy (which is all they could call their own) varied with the amount of liquor they had ingested, the letters they had received and the amount of hope they had lost during the day. As a general rule, the more moribund they felt, the more they swaggered and strutted. If they'd been ghosts (like Ortolan at the front) their gall would have known no bounds.

Our aperitifs went on for three whole hours. We always talked about the Governor, the focus of all our conversations; then we talked about possible and impossible swindles, and lastly about sex: the three colours of the colonial flag. The civil servants present made no bones about accusing the military of wallowing in peculation and abuse of authority, but the military paid them back in kind. The traders, for their part, regarded all these prebendaries as hypocritical impostors and bandits. A rumour that the Governor was being recalled had been in circulation every morning for the past ten years, yet the delightful telegram announcing his disgrace never arrived, and this in spite of at least two anonymous letters mailed to the Minister for the Colonies each week, imputing a thousand meticulously described atrocities to that local tyrant.

The blacks are lucky with their onion skins; the white man, encased between his acid sweat and his tropical shirt, poisons himself. It's not safe to go near him, I'd learnt my lesson on board the *Admiral Bragueton*.

In only a few days I heard some sweet stories about my Director! His past was as full of low dodges as a prison in a seaport town. His past had just about everything in it, including, I imagine, some magnificent miscarriages of justice. True, his looks were against him, his face had the terrifying look of an undeniable murderer, or rather, to be fair, the look of a reckless man in a terrible hurry to get ahead – which amounts to the same thing.

If you passed by at siesta time, you might see, sprawled in the shade of their houses on the Boulevard Faidherbe, a few white women, the wives of officers or settlers, who were even more devastated by the climate than the men, frail creatures with pleasingly hesitant voices, infinitely indulgent smiles, their pallor coated with rouge, as though happy on their deathbeds. These transplanted middle-class women showed less courage and pride of bearing than the *patronne* of the pagoda, who had no one but herself to lean on. The Compagnie Pordurière consumed quantities of small clerks like me, every year it lost dozens of these subhumans in the jungle trading posts not far from the swamps. Pioneers!

Every morning the Army and Business came to the office of the hospital, whimpering and begging for their men. Not a day went by but some captain came threatening and calling down God's thunders on the Head Physician to make him send those three malarial card-playing sergeants and two syphilitic corporals back to their units on the double, because how could he put a company together without non-coms? If told that his slackers were dead, he'd stop bothering the hospital management and go back to the Pagoda for a few more drinks.

Men, days, things – they passed before you knew it in this hotbed of vegetation, heat, humidity and mosquitoes. Everything passed, disgustingly, in little pieces, in phrases, particles of flesh and bone, in regrets and corpuscles; demolished by the sun, they melted away in a torrent of light and colours, and taste and time went with them, everything went. Nothing remained but shimmering dread.

At last the freighter, which was to take me along the coast to the vicinity of my trading post, anchored within sight of Fort-Gono. The *Papaoutah* was her name. A small ship, wood-burning and flat-bottomed, built for estuaries. I was the only white on board, and they assigned me a small space between the kitchen and the toilet. We moved so slowly that at first I thought we were being cautious in getting out of the roadstead. But we never went any faster. This *Papaoutah* was incredibly short on power. We edged along within sight of the coast, an endless grey line tufted with small trees in the dancing heat mists. What a trip! The *Papaoutah* ploughed through the water as slowly and painfully as if she herself had sweated it all. She would undo one little wave after another as cautiously as if they'd been bandages. The pilot, it seemed to me from a distance, must have been a mulatto; I say "seemed" because I never summoned up the energy to go up on the bridge and see for myself. Until about five o'clock I stayed in the shaded gangway, wedged in among the blacks, who were the only passengers. If you don't want the sun to burn your brains through your eyes, you have to blink like a rat. After five you can indulge in a look around – the good life. That grey fringe, that tufted country at the water's edge, looked like flattened dress shields and didn't appeal to me at all. The air was unbreathable, even at night it was hot, sultry and salty. Everything was so cloying it raised my bile, what with the smell of the engine and in the daytime the water that was too brown on one side and too blue on the other. This was even worse than the *Admiral Bragueton*, except of course for the murderous officers.

At last we approached the port of my destination. Its name, I was told, was Topo. After coughing, spitting and quaking on the surface of that oily dishwater for three times as long as it takes to eat four canned meals, the *Papaoutah* finally pulled up at the landing.

Three enormous thatched huts stood out from the shaggy banks. From a distance and at first glance the place was rather attractive. This, I was told, was the mouth of a big sandy river, which I was to mount by canoe on my way to the heart of the jungle. I was scheduled to spend only a few days here at Topo by the sea, just time enough to frame my last colonial resolutions.

We headed for a flimsy dock, and before reaching it the *Papaoutah* scraped a sand bar with its fat belly. Well I remember that dock, it was made of bamboo, a story in itself. They told me it had to be rebuilt every month, because of the tricky, nimble little molluscs that came by the thousands and ate it up. This endless rebuilding, in fact, was one of the heartbreaking occupations that weighed on Lieutenant Grappa, Commander of the Topo station and the surrounding territory. The *Papaoutah* called only once a month, but a month was all the molluscs needed to eat up her dock.

As soon as I landed, Lieutenant Grappa took possession of my papers, checked them for authenticity, copied them into a blank register, and invited me in for an aperitif. I was the first traveller, he informed me, to come to Topo in two years. Nobody came to Topo. There was no reason to come to Topo. Sergeant Alcide was Lieutenant Grappa's second in command. In their isolation there was no love lost between them. "I always have to watch that subordinate of mine," said Lieutenant Grappa at our first meeting, "or he tends to get too familiar!"

Since any happenings they might have imagined in that wilderness would have been too implausible (for what could happen in such a place?), Sergeant Alcide prepared in advance a whole sheaf of "Nothing to report" reports, which Grappa signed without delay, and the *Papaoutah* carried them away to the Governor General.

Among the lagoons round about and in the depths of the jungle several moth-eaten tribes lived in misery and stagnation, decimated and befuddled by trypanosoma and chronic poverty; even so, these tribes paid a small tax, collected of course with clubs. From among their younger set a few militiamen were recruited to wield these same clubs. The militia consisted of twelve men.

I know what I'm talking about. I knew them well. Lieutenant Grappa equipped the lucky bastards in his own way and fed them regulation rice. One rifle for all twelve, but each had his own little flag. No shoes.

But, since all things are relative and comparative in this world, the native recruits thought Grappa was treating them splendidly. Every day, in fact, he turned away volunteers and enthusiasts, young men who had had their fill of the bush.

The hunt in these parts didn't yield much, and at least one grandmother a week was eaten for want of gazelles. At seven o'clock every morning Alcide's militiamen reported for drill. Since I lived in one corner of his hut, where he had made room for me, I had a ringside seat for the fantasia. Never has any army in the world had more willing soldiers. In response to Alcide's commands, those primitives would wear themselves out pacing the sand in columns of four, eight and finally twelve, imagining they had packs, shoes and even bayonets, and better still, going through the motions of using them. Barely emerged from a nature so vigorous and so close at hand, they wore nothing but an apology for khaki shorts. They had to imagine all the rest, and did. At Alcide's peremptory command, these ingenious warriors deposited their imaginary packs on the ground and lunged into empty space to disembowel illusory enemies with illusory bayonets. Then, after simulating the unbuttoning of jackets, they would stack invisible rifles and, in response to another sign, fling themselves with unfeigned passion into an abstraction of rifle drill. To see them disperse, gesticulating with studied precision, and lose themselves in intricate, epileptic and insanely useless movements was deeply depressing. Especially when you remember that in Topo the raw, stifling heat, so perfectly concentrated in that sandpit between the combined polished mirrors of the sea and the river, would have made you swear by your bleeding buttocks that you were being forced to sit on a chunk of sun that had just fallen off.

But these implacable conditions didn't stop Alcide from sounding off. Not at all. Passing over the heads of his incredible drill squad, his roars mounted to the tops of the venerable cedars at the edge of the jungle. And the thunder of his "Ten-shun!" reverberated still further.

Meanwhile Lieutenant Grappa was administering justice. We'll have more to say about that. Or from a distance, from the shade of his hut, he'd be supervising the ephemeral construction of his ill-fated dock. He had ordered complete uniforms and equipment for his recruits, and every time the *Papaoutah* showed up, he went down to the dock with sceptical optimism to take delivery. For two years he'd been clamouring for those uniforms. It may have been especially humiliating for Grappa as a Corsican to see that his militiamen were still stark naked.

In our hut, Alcide's I mean, a small, semi-clandestine trade was carried on in small objects and miscellaneous odds and ends. As a matter of fact, all the commerce of Topo passed through Alcide's hands, for he and he alone possessed a small stock of tobacco, both packaged and in the leaf, several litres of brandy and a few bolts of cotton goods.

It was plain that the twelve militiamen felt a real liking for Alcide, though he bawled them out interminably and kicked their rear ends rather unjustly. But those nudist soldiers had discerned in Alcide the unquestionable signs of kinship, of fellow membership in the great family of the innately, incurably poor. Black or not, tobacco created a tie, it always does. I had brought a few newspapers with me from Europe. Alcide looked through them, trying to take an interest in the news, but though he tried three times to fix his attention on those ill-assorted columns, he couldn't get through them. "You know," he confessed to me after his vain effort, "I don't really give a shit about the news any more! I've been here for three years now!" It shouldn't be thought that Alcide was trying to impress me by playing the hermit. Actually, the ruthlessness, the manifest indifference of the whole world where he was concerned, had driven him, in his capacity as a re-enlisted sergeant, to regard the whole world outside of Topo as a distant planet.

Alcide was a good sort, obliging, generous and all. I realized that later, a little too late. He was crushed by his enormous resignation, that basic quality that makes it as easy to kill poor bastards in and out of the army as to let them live. Poor people never, or hardly ever, ask for an explanation of all they have to put up with. They hate one another, and content themselves with that.

Around our hut, scattered over the lagoon of torrid, pitiless sand, there were strange little flowers, fresh and short-lived, green, pink or purple, the kind that in Europe you only see painted on certain pieces of porcelain, a kind of primitive no-nonsense morning glory. Closed on their stems, they endured the long abominable days, then opened in the evening and trembled in the first balmy breezes.

One day when Alcide saw me picking a little bunch of them, he warned me: "Pick them if you want to, but don't water the little bitches, it kills them... They're delicate, not at all like the sunflowers we used to grow for the army kids in Rambouillet!... You could piss on them!... They'd drink anything!... If you ask me, flowers are like men... The bigger the dumber!" That was an obvious dig at Lieutenant Grappa, whose body was bulky and ramshackle, his hands short, purple and terrifying. The kind of hands that would never understand anything. And indeed, Grappa made no attempt to understand.

I stayed in Topo for two weeks, during which I shared not only Alcide's existence and food, his bed fleas and sand fleas (two species), but also his quinine and the inexorably tepid and diarrhoeic water of the nearby well.

One day when Lieutenant Grappa was feeling convivial he invited me to his house for coffee. Grappa was jealous, he never let anyone see his native concubine. Consequently, he picked a day when his Negress was visiting her parents in their village. It was also the day when his court of justice convened, and he wanted to impress me.

The motley mass of complainants and screeching witnesses had arrived early in the morning. In bright-coloured loincloths they crowded round the hut. Defendants and mere public stood mixed helter-skelter, all smelling strongly of garlic, sandalwood, rancid butter and saffron-scented sweat. Like Alcide's militiamen, all these people seemed intent first and foremost on frenzied illusory motion; in transports of imaginary argument, they spewed castanets language and shook their clenched fists.

Deep in his creaking, groaning cane chair, Lieutenant Grappa smiled at all this assembled incoherence. He trusted for guidance in the post interpreter, who in a loud and barely intelligible mumbo-jumbo communicated unbelievable complaints.

Take, for instance, the one-eyed sheep that a certain girl's parents refused to return despite the fact that their daughter, though married in due form, had never been delivered to her husband, because in the meantime the bride's brother had somehow seen fit to murder the bridegroom's sister, who had been guarding the sheep at the time. And many similar but even more complicated grievances.

Around us a hundred faces, impassioned by these questions of custom and interest, bared their teeth with little clicking or big gurgling sounds, Negro words.

The heat was nearing its height. I looked up past the edge of the roof to see if some disaster was approaching in the sky. Not even a storm.

"I'm going to straighten this whole thing out immediately!" Grappa finally declared; the heat and interminable palavers had driven him to a decision. "Where's the bride's father?... Bring him here!"

"Here he is!" cried a dozen natives, pushing an elderly, decrepit-looking black man swathed with great dignity in a yellow loincloth – Roman style – to the front. With one clenched fist the old man beat time to everything that was being said around him. He didn't look as if he'd come to make a complaint, more likely he hoped for a bit of entertainment long after he'd given up expecting any tangible results from his lawsuit.

"All right!" said Grappa. "Twenty strokes! Let's get this over with! Give this old pimp twenty strokes!... That'll teach him to pester me every Thursday for the last two months with his batty sheep story!"

The old man saw four husky militiamen coming towards him. At first he didn't understand what they wanted with him, but then he began to roll his eyes, which were bloodshot like the eyes of a terrified old animal that has never been beaten before. He made no real attempt to resist, but neither did he know what position to take so the scourge of justice would inflict the least pain.

The militiamen pulled him by the toga. Two of them wanted him to kneel, but the other two told him to lie prone. In the end, they just laid him out on the ground any which way, lifted up his toga, and subjected his back and buttocks to a score of blows with a flexible rod that would have made a healthy mule bellow for a week. He wriggled and writhed, the fine sand spurted all round him mixed with blood, he spat sand as he howled, he made me think of an enormous pregnant basset bitch being tortured.

The public was silent while this was going on. All you could hear was the sound of the beating. When it was over, the old man, though half-unconscious, tried to get up and cover himself with his Roman loincloth. His mouth and nose and most of all his back were bleeding profusely. Droning their comments and chit-chat in funereal tones, the crowd led him away.

Lieutenant Grappa relit his cigar. In my presence, he affected an air of aloofness from these things. I don't believe he was more Neronian than anyone else, but he disliked being obliged to think. That infuriated him. What exasperated him when performing his judicial functions was the questions he was asked.

The same day we witnessed another two memorable thrashings pursuant to further disconcerting reports of dowries taken back, poisonings threatened... promises unfulfilled... children of uncertain origin...

"Oh!" Grappa cried. "If they only knew how completely cold their bickerings leave me, they'd stay in their jungle where they belong instead of chewing my ear off with their cock-and-bull stories!... Do I bother them with my troubles?" But then he started on a different idea: "You know, I'm almost beginning to think those apes are developing a taste for my justice!... For two years I've been trying to get them disgusted with it, but every Thursday they come back for more... Believe it or not, young man, it's almost always the same ones who keep coming!... A bunch of perverts if you ask me!..."

Then the conversation turned to Toulouse, where he spent all his leaves and where he was planning to settle in six years when he retired. It was all right with me! We had pleasantly arrived at the Calvados stage when we were disturbed again by a native who'd been sentenced the week before but was late in having his sentence carried out. Now, two hours after everyone else, he'd come of his own free will to get his thrashing. He'd been on the trail for two days and two nights, and he had no intention of going back to his village with his business undone. But he was late, and in matters of penal punctuality Grappa was uncompromising: "He asked for it! Why didn't he wait his turn last time?... I sentenced the bastard to those fifty strokes last Thursday, not today!"

Still, the client protested, for he had a good excuse; he'd had to hurry back to his village to bury his mother. He had three or four mothers all to himself. Excellent arguments...

"It will have to wait till the next session!"

But our client would barely have time for the trip to his village and back before the following Thursday. He went on protesting, he wouldn't budge. It took several violent kicks in the arse to get that masochist out of the camp. They gave him some pleasure, but not enough... In the end he went to Alcide, who took advantage of the situation to sell him a whole assortment of tobacco, in the leaf, in packages, and in the form of snuff.

Well entertained by these various incidents, I took my leave of Grappa. It was time for his siesta, and he withdrew to the interior of his hut, where his native housekeeper, who had just come back from her village, was already reclining. That black woman had a magnificent pair of tits, and she had been well schooled by the Sisters in Gabon. Not only did the young lady speak French (with a lisp), she also knew how to administer quinine in jam and to dig chiggers out of the soles of one's feet. She knew a hundred ways of making herself agreeable to a white man without tiring him or by tiring him, whichever he preferred.

Alcide was waiting for me. He was rather miffed. It was probably the invitation with which Grappa had honoured me that prompted him to confide in me. What he told me was pretty strong stuff. Unasked, he modelled Grappa's portrait in steaming cow shit. I replied that he had taken the words out of my mouth. Alcide's vulnerable point was that, in defiance of army regulations, which strictly forbade it, he was trading with the natives in the jungle round about and with his twelve militiamen as well. He mercilessly sold those people tobacco on credit. When payday came around, there was no pay for the militiamen to collect: they had smoked it all up. They smoked up advances. This petty irregularity, what with the rarity of cash in the region, hampered the collection of taxes.

Lieutenant Grappa was too cautious a man to provoke a scandal in Topo while he was in command, but he was definitely pissed off, maybe he was jealous. Understandably enough, he felt that whatever negligible sums of money the natives called their own should remain available to the tax collector. Each man to his taste and humble ambitions.

At first this system of credit against their pay had seemed rather strange and even outrageous to the riflemen, whose sole purpose in working was to smoke Alcide's tobacco, but he had got them used to it by kicking them in the arse. By that time, they'd given up trying to collect their pay, they calmly smoked it up in advance, among the bright-coloured flowers outside Alcide's hut, between two stints of imaginary drill.

In short, there was room in Topo, small as it was, for two systems of civilization: Grappa's, which you might call Roman and which consisted of flogging your subjects for the sole purpose of extracting tribute – of which, if Alcide was to be believed, Grappa retained a disgraceful percentage for his own strictly personal use; and the more elaborate Alcide system bearing witness to a higher stage of civilization, in which every soldier becomes a customer. This military-commercial complex is much more modern and hypocritical, the basis of our own system.

Lieutenant Grappa was no great shakes at geography. For his knowledge of the vast territories committed to his charge, he relied on a few rudimentary maps that he had at the post. He was none too eager to know more about those territories. After all, we know what trees and the jungle are, we can see them very nicely from a distance.

Tucked away in the fronds and hollows of that immense steam bath, a few thinly disseminated tribes stagnated amid their fleas and flies, stultified by their totems and unflaggingly gorging themselves with putrid manioc... Utterly naive, frankly cannibalistic, maddened by poverty and ravaged by a thousand plagues. No earthly reason to go near them. Nothing to justify troublesome administrative incursions, which could yield no results whatsoever. When Grappa had finished meting out justice, he preferred to turn towards the sea and contemplate the horizon from which he had come one day and across which he would sail one day, if all went well...

Familiar and all in all agreeable as the place had become to me, the time came when I had to think of leaving Topo for the post that was to be my dwelling place and occupation after several days of fluvial navigation and sylvan peregrinations.

Alcide and I were getting on fine together. We tried to fish for sawfish, a variety of shark that infested the waters in front of our hut. He was just as clumsy as I was. We never caught anything.

The only furnishings in his hut were his folding bed, mine and a few crates, some empty, some full. I had the impression that what with his little business he must be putting quite a lot of money aside.

"Where do you keep it?..." I asked him several times. "Where do you hide your filthy lucre?" Just to get his goat. "Planning a big spree when you get back?" I was only teasing him. Twenty times at least, as we dug into the inevitable canned tomatoes, I'd entertain him with amazing episodes of the heroic joyride from whorehouse to whorehouse that would celebrate his return to Bordeaux. He never said anything. He'd only laugh, as though my little stories amused him.

Apart from the drill and the court sessions, nothing happened in Topo, nothing whatever, so naturally, for want of other subjects, I'd take up the same old joke as often as possible.

Once, towards the end of my stay, I thought of writing to Monsieur Puta to touch him for some money. Alcide promised to mail my letter the next time the *Papaoutah* called. Alcide kept his writing materials in a small biscuit tin, just like the one Branledore had had, exactly the same. All re-enlisted sergeants seemed to have them. When he saw me start opening the box, Alcide made a movement to stop me. I was surprised and embarrassed. I had no idea why he wouldn't let me open it, but I put it down on the table. "Oh, all right, open it!" he said finally. "Hell, it doesn't matter!" The photograph of a little girl was pasted to the inside of the lid. Just the head, a sweet little face with long curls, the way they wore them in those days. I took out pen and paper and quickly closed the lid. I was embarrassed at my indiscretion, but I also wondered why it had upset him so.

First I figured that the child must be his and he hadn't wanted to talk about her. I asked no questions, but then I heard him behind my back, trying to tell me something in a strange bumbling voice I'd never heard. I felt very uncomfortable. I knew I ought to help him tell me his story, but I didn't know how to go about it. I knew it would be a painful story to listen to, and I wasn't looking forward to it.

"It's nothing!" I finally heard him say. "It's my brother's daughter... They're both dead..."

"Her parents?..."

"Yes, her parents..."

"Then who's bringing her up? Your mother?" I asked him that to show I was taking an interest.

"My mother's dead too..."

"Who then?"

"Well, me!"

He grinned and blushed crimson, as if he'd done something absolutely indecent. Then he hastened to rectify:

"All right, I'll explain... I'm having her brought up in Bordeaux by the Sisters... But don't get me wrong, they're no Sisters of Charity!... High-class Sisters... She's my responsibility and you needn't worry. She'll want for nothing! Her name is Ginette... Sweet little girl... Like her mother... She writes to me, she's making good progress, but you know, those schools are expensive... Especially now that she's ten... I want her to have piano lessons at the same time... What do you think of the piano?... Well, in my opinion the piano is the right thing for girls... Don't you agree?... And what about English? English can come in handy... Do you know English?..."

As Alcide confessed his failing – not being generous enough – I began to look at him more closely, with his little cosmetic moustache, his eccentric eyebrows and his burnt-black skin. The delicacy of the man! And how he must have scrimped and saved on his meagre wages... his pitiful allowances and tiny clandestine business... for months and years in this infernal Topo!... I didn't know what to say, I had no experience, but his heart was so much superior to mine that I went red in the face... Next to Alcide I was an impotent slob, boorish and vain... No two ways. Plain as day.

I didn't dare speak to him any more. Suddenly I felt unworthy to say a word to him. I, who only yesterday had kept him at a distance and even looked down on him a little.

"I haven't been lucky," he went on, unaware that he was embarrassing me with his confidences. "Imagine, two years ago she had infantile paralysis... Imagine that... You know what infantile paralysis is?"

He went on to explain that the child's left leg was atrophied and that a specialist in Bordeaux was treating her with electricity.

"You think she'll get it back?..." he asked me.

I assured him that she would recover completely with time and electricity. He spoke very circumspectly of his dead mother and of the child's infirmity. He was afraid, even at a distance, of harming her.

"Have you been to see her since her illness?"

"No... I've been here the whole time."

"Will you go and see her soon?"

"I don't think I'll be able to go for another three years... You see, I do a little business here... That's a big help to her... If I went on leave now, my place here would be taken before I got back... Especially with that bastard..."

So Alcide had asked to do a double hitch, to stay in Topo for six consecutive years instead of three, for the sake of his little niece, of whom he had nothing but a few letters and that little photograph. "What bothers me," he said after we'd gone to bed, "is that she hasn't anybody for the holidays... That's hard on a little girl..."

Obviously Alcide was perfectly at ease, at home so to speak, in the higher regions, on terms of familiarity with the angels. You wouldn't have known it to look at him. With hardly a thought of what he was doing, he had consented to years of torture, to the crushing of his life in this torrid monotony for the sake of a little girl to whom he was vaguely related. Motivated by nothing but his good heart, he had set no conditions and asked nothing in return. To that little girl far away he was giving enough tenderness to make the whole world over, and he never showed it.

Suddenly he fell asleep in the candlelight. After a while I got up to look at his face. He slept like everybody else. He looked quite ordinary. There ought to be some mark by which to distinguish good people from bad.

* * *

There are two ways of getting into the jungle. One is to cut a tunnel through it, the way rats do in a bale of hay. That's the stifling way. I jibbed at that. Or you can endure the misery of sitting huddled in a hollow tree trunk, while they paddle you up the winding river from copse to snag, waiting for the endless days to pass and laying yourself open without defence to the deadly glare. And finally, dazed by the yapping of the black men, you reach your destination in some sort of condition.

At first your paddlers always need time to catch the cadence. Arguments. A paddle strikes the water, two or three rhythmic howls, the jungle sends back an answer, eddies, she's gliding, two paddles, three, still groping for the rhythm, waves, inarticulate burblings, a backwards glance at the sea, flattening out as it recedes, and up ahead the long smooth expanse into which you're toiling. And for a while yet, far away on his dock, almost swallowed up by the sea mists, Alcide under his enormous bell-shaped pith helmet, a chunk of head, the face a small cheese, and below it the rest of him, floating in his tunic, lost in a strange white-trousered memory.

That's all I have left of the place, of Topo.

Have they managed to defend that scorching hamlet against the insidious scythe of the yellowish-brown river? Are its flea-bitten huts still standing? Are new Grappas and unknown Alcides still training new recruits in imaginary combat? Is the same plain-dealing brand of justice still being meted out? Is the drinking water still so rancid? So tepid? So bad that whenever you try to drink it, it leaves you disgusted for days on end?... Is there still no refrigeration? And what of those acoustic battles in your ears between the flies and the everlasting hum of the quinine... Sulphate? Chloride?... But most of all: are there still black people sweltering and pustulating in that cauldron? Who knows? Maybe not...

Maybe none of all that is there any more, maybe a tornado broke loose one night, maybe the Little Congo, just in passing, gave Topo one good lick with its muddy tongue and it was all over. Maybe the whole place is dead and gone, the very name wiped off the maps, and nobody left to remember Alcide... Maybe his little niece has forgotten him too. Maybe Lieutenant Grappa never saw his Toulouse again... Maybe the jungle, which has always, year after year when the rainy season sets in, had designs on the dune, has recaptured the whole settlement, crushed it beneath the shade of its giant mahogany trees, even those unexpected little sand flowers that Alcide didn't want me to water... Maybe it's all gone.

I'll long remember those ten days going up the river... Huddled in the bottom of the canoe, watching out for muddy whirlpools, picking furtive passages between enormous drifting branches, nimbly avoided. A labour for convicts on the lam.

After every sundown we'd camp on a rocky promontory. Finally one morning we left that filthy native canoe and slipped into the forest by a hidden path that twined through the moist green gloom, lit only here and there by a ray of sunlight falling from the roof of that vast cathedral of leaves. Monstrous felled trees forced us to make frequent detours. Whole Métro trains could have manoeuvred with ease in the hollows left by their roots.

Suddenly the full light was on us again, we had come to a clearing and had to climb, an additional effort. The rise we had come to overlooked the endless forest, rolling over red, yellow and green peaks, modelling and smoothing hill and dale, as monstrously spacious as the sea and the sky. I was given to understand by signs that the man whose habitation we were looking for lived just a little further on... in another valley. And there he was waiting for us.

He had built a sort of hut between two big boulders, sheltered, as he informed me, from the eastern tornadoes, which were the worst, the most furious. That, I was willing to admit, was an advantage, but the hut itself definitely belonged to the lowest, most ramshackle category, an almost theoretical edifice, coming apart at every seam. I had foreseen something of the sort, but this surpassed all my expectations.

The man must have thought I looked downcast, because he addressed me rather brusquely, to shake me out of my thoughts. "Come off it, you'll be better off here than in the trenches! Here at least you can worry along! The food is rotten, I can't deny it, and there's nothing to drink but pure mud, but you can sleep as much as you like... There's no big guns here and no bullets! All in all, it's a good deal!" He talked something like the Director General, but he had pale eyes like Alcide's.

He must have been close to thirty, with a beard... I hadn't taken a good look at him on arriving, because on arriving I'd been thrown off by the dilapidation of the set-up he was supposed to bequeath me and which might possibly be my home for years... But observing him later on, I found a distinctly adventurous face with sharply accentuated angles, one of those rebellious faces that plunge into life head-on instead of rolling with the waves, with a big round nose, and cheeks like coal barges, plashing against destiny with a soft babbling sound. That was an unhappy man.

"It's true," I said. "There's nothing worse than war!"

I thought we'd said enough for the moment. I had no desire to say any more. It was he who went on:

"Especially now that they make them so long... Well anyway, friend, you'll see that it's no joke here! There's nothing to do... It's a sort of holiday... Except who'd want to spend a holiday in a place like this?... Well, maybe it's a matter of temperament. I wouldn't know..."

"How about the water?" I asked. The water I saw in the cup I had poured myself had me worried, it was yellowish. I drank some, it was sickening and as warm as in Topo. A three-day sediment of mud.

"Is this the water?" The water torture was starting all over again.

"Yes, that's all there is, except rainwater... But when it starts raining, the shack won't last long. You see the condition it's in?" I saw.

"The food," he went on, "is all tinned. That's what I've been eating for a whole year... It hasn't killed me!... Convenient in a way, but it doesn't stick to the ribs... The natives eat putrid manioc, that's their business, they like it... For the last three months it's been running through me... Diarrhoea. Maybe it's fever too, I've got both... Around five o'clock I'm more lucid... That's how I know I've got fever, because it's hard to feel hotter than you do already in this climate!... Actually, it's probably the chills that tell you you've got a fever... And not being quite so bored, maybe that's another sign... but that's a matter of temperament too... maybe a few drinks would cheer us up... but I don't go for drink... it doesn't agree with me..."

He seemed to think very highly of what he called "temperament".

Then, while he was at it, he gave me a little more of his delightful information: "By day it's the heat, at night it's the noise that's hard to bear... It's unbelievable... The animals go chasing round and round, to fuck or to kill each other, how do I know?... Either way, you never heard such a hullabaloo!... The loudest are the hyenas!... They come up close to the shack... You'll hear them!... You won't have any doubts... It's nothing like the quinine music... Sometimes you can mistake birds or big flies for quinine... It's conceivable... But hyenas, the enormous way they laugh... They're smelling your flesh... That's what makes them laugh!... They're in a hurry to see you pass on!... You can even see their eyes shining, so I'm told... They feed on dead bodies... I've never looked into their eyes... I'm sorry in a way..."

"Sounds delightful!" I said.

But he hadn't finished with the night life.

"Then there's the village," he went on... "There aren't a hundred Negros in it, but they make enough rumpus for ten thousand, those bastards!... You'll tell me what you think of it! And man! If it's tom-toms you're after, you've come to the right place!... If they're not beating them because the moon is out, they're beating them because the moon has gone by... There's always some reason!... The sons of bitches seem to be in cahoots with the animals to drive us crazy! So help me, I'd shoot the whole lot of them if I weren't so tired... As it is, I put cotton in my ears... That's even better... As long as I had Vaseline in my medicine chest, I greased the cotton with it, now I use banana oil... Banana oil does the trick... That way they can gargle with thunderstorms if it makes them happy! It's no skin off my arse with my ears full of greased cotton! I don't hear a damned thing! These Negros are sick, they're perverts! You'll see!... All day long they squat on the ground, you wouldn't think them capable of moving as far as the nearest tree to piss against, but the minute it's dark, surprise! Vice! Nerves! Hysteria! Chunks of the night gone hysterical! That's Negros for you, take it from me! Degenerate scum!..."

"Do they often come and buy from you?"

"Buy? You're out of your mind! The trick is to rob them before they rob you! That's business! At night of course they do as they please, with greased cotton in both ears!... They'd be fools to stand on ceremony!... Besides, as you see, my shack has no door... so naturally they help themselves... for them it's the good life..."

"But what about your inventory?" I asked, utterly dismayed at what he had told me. "The Director General told me very clearly to draw up a meticulous inventory the moment I got here!"

"I have the honour," he replied with perfect calm, "of telling you that the Director can kiss my arse..."

"But won't you have to see him on your way through Fort-Gono?"

"I will never see either Fort-Gono or the Director again... It's a big forest, my young friend..."

"But where will you go?"

"If anyone asks you, tell them you don't know! But since you seem eager to learn, let me give you some very good advice before it's too late! Don't worry about the Company any more than the Company worries about you! If you can run as fast as the Company screws its employees, I can tell you right now that you're due to win the Grand Prix!... So be thankful that I'm leaving you a little cash and ask no more!... As for the stock, if it's true that the Director told you to take charge of it... tell him there isn't any left, and that's that!... If he won't believe you, who cares?... They take us all for thieves anyway! So it won't make any difference to public opinion if for once we get a little something out of it... And besides, don't worry, the Director knows more about financial scams than anybody, so why contradict him? That's my opinion! What's yours? Everybody knows that for a man to come here he has to be prepared to kill his father and mother! Am I right?..."

I wasn't so sure all he'd been telling me was true, but either way this predecessor of mine struck me as an out-and-out bandit.

I wasn't at all easy in my mind. "Another mess I've fallen into!" I said to myself with increasing conviction. I stopped talking with that thug. In one corner, stowed every which way, I found the merchandise he was leaving me, a few scraps of cotton goods... But loincloths and shoes by the dozen, some boxes of pepper, several lamps, a douche can, a staggering quantity of canned "*cassoulet à la Bordelaise*", and lastly a picture postcard of the Place Clichy.

"Next to the ridgepole you'll find the rubber and ivory I've bought from the Negros… I worked hard at first… And oh yes, here are three hundred francs… That's what's coming to you."

Coming to me for what? I had no idea, but I didn't bother to ask him.

"You may still be able to manage a bit of barter," he said. "Because, you know, you'll have no use for money out here, only when you want to clear out…"

He started laughing. Not wanting to cross him at the moment, I did likewise, I chimed in as if everything were hunky-dory.

In spite of the extreme destitution in which he'd been living for many months, he had surrounded himself with an elaborate domestic staff, consisting mostly of young boys, who fell all over themselves in their eagerness to bring him the household's one and only spoon or the matchless cup, or to extract with consummate skill the classical and inevitable burrowing chiggers from the soles of his feet. In return, he would often oblige them with a kindly hand between their thighs. The only work I ever saw him do was scratching himself, but that, like the shopkeeper at Fort-Gono, he did with the marvellous agility that can be observed only in the colonies.

The chairs and tables he bequeathed me showed me what ingenuity can do with crushed soapboxes. That sinister individual also taught me how it is possible, for want of anything better to do, to propel those ungainly, caparisoned caterpillars which, quivering and foaming at the mouth, kept assailing our forest cabin, far into the distance with a short swift kick. God help you if you are clumsy enough to crush one! You'll be punished with an entire week of intense stench, which rises slowly from that unforgettable mash. He had read somewhere that those horrible monsters were the oldest animals in the world, dating, so he claimed, back to the second geological period! "When we've come as far as they have, my boy, won't we stink too?" His exact words.

The sunsets in that African hell proved to be fabulous. They never missed. As tragic every time as a monumental murder of the sun! But the marvel was too great for one man alone. For a whole hour the sky paraded in great delirious spurts of scarlet from end to end; after that the green of the trees exploded and rose up in quivering trails to meet the first stars. Then the whole horizon turned grey again and then red, but this time a tired red that didn't last long. That was the end. All the colours fell back down on the forest in tatters, like streamers after the hundredth performance. It happened every day at exactly six o'clock.

Then the night set in with all its monsters and its thousands and thousands of croaking toads.

The forest is only waiting for their signal to start trembling, hissing and roaring from its depths. An enormous, love-maddened, unlit railway station, full to bursting. Whole trees bristling with living noisemakers, mutilated erections, horror. After a while we couldn't hear each other talk in the hut. I had to hoot across the table like a barn owl for my companion to understand me. I was getting my money's worth. And remember, I didn't like the country.

"What's your name?" I asked him. "Did you say Robinson?"

He had just been telling me that the natives in those parts suffered horribly from every conceivable disease and that the poor bastards were in no condition to engage in any kind of trade. While we were talking about the natives, so many flies and insects, so large and in such great numbers, dashed against the lamp in such dense squalls that we finally had to put it out.

Before dousing the lamp, I caught a glimpse of Robinson's face, veiled by a curtain of insects. That may be why his features impressed themselves more sharply on my memory, whereas before that they hadn't reminded me of anything in particular. He went on talking to me in the darkness, while I retraced the steps of my past with the sound of his voice as a charm with which to open the doors of the years and months and finally of my days, wondering where I could have run into this man. But I found nothing. No answer. You can lose your way groping among the shadows of the past. It's frightening how many people and things there are in a man's past that have stopped moving. The living people we've lost in the crypts of time sleep so soundly side by side with the dead that the same darkness envelops them all.

As we grow older, we no longer know whom to awaken, the living or the dead.

I was trying to identify this Robinson when gales of hideously exaggerated laughter, not far away in the night, made me jump. Then they fell silent. It must have been the hyenas he'd told me about.

And then there was nothing but the villagers and their tom-toms, those crazy drums made of hollow wood, termites of the wind.

The name Robinson gnawed at me more and more insistently. In the darkness we talked about Europe and the meals you can order if you've got the money, not to mention the drinks! So deliciously cool! Not a word about the next day, when I was to be left alone, for years perhaps, with all those tins of cassoulet... Would war have been better? No, worse! Definitely worse!... He thought so too... He'd been in the war himself... And nevertheless he was getting out of here... He was fed up with the forest, and that was that... I tried to bring him back to the war. But he wouldn't oblige.

Finally, as we were getting ready for bed, each in his corner of that shambles of leaves and partitions, he came right out with it: he preferred the risk of being haled into court for theft to living on cassoulet as he'd been doing for almost a year. Then I saw the lie of the land.

"Haven't you any cotton for your ears?" he asked me... "If not, you'd better make some with the nap of a blanket and a drop of banana oil. You can make very nice little plugs that way... I for my part refuse to put up with the bellowing of those baboons!..."

Actually that concert had everything in it but baboons, but he clung to his inept, generic term.

It suddenly occurred to me that this business with the cotton must be a cloak for some fiendish trick. I was seized with fear that he'd murder me there on my folding bed and make off with what was left in the money box... The idea paralysed me. But what could I do? Call for help? Call who? The village cannibals?... I thought of myself as missing. Even in Paris a man without money, without debts, without hope of an inheritance, hardly exists, he's missing to all intents and purposes... So what could I expect here? Who'd bother to come to Bikomimbo and even honour my memory by spitting in the water? Nobody of course.

Hours of intermittent terror. He didn't snore. All those sounds, those calls from the forest made it hard for me to hear him breathe. No need of cotton. I kept puzzling, and finally the name Robinson revealed a body, a posture, a voice I had known... And just as I was giving in to sleep, the whole man stood before my bed, I held him fast, not him of course, but the memory of this Robinson, the man at Noirceur-sur-la-Lys in Flanders, who'd been with me on the fringes of that night when we went looking for a hole through which to escape from the war, and then the same man later in Paris... It all came back to me.

Years passed in a few moments. I'd been unhappy, sick in the head... Now that I knew, now that I'd placed him, I couldn't help it, I was thoroughly scared. Had he recognized me? In any case he could count on my silence and complicity.

"Robinson! Robinson!" I cried out cheerfully, as if I had good news for him. "Hey, old man! Hey, Robinson!..." No answer.

With pounding heart I got up, expecting a mean jab in the gut... Nothing. Then, rather bravely, I groped my way to the other end of the shack, where I'd seen him go to bed. He was gone.

Striking a match now and then, I waited for daybreak. The day came in a burst of light and so did the black servants, laughing and offering me their enormous uselessness. At least they were cheerful, I'll admit that. From the first, they tried to teach me the art of not giving a damn. I did my best to explain with a series of carefully studied gestures how terribly Robinson's disappearance had me worried. No use. It was all the same to them. True, it's senseless to worry about anything that isn't right in front of your nose. What bothered me most about all this was the money box. But when someone walks off with a money box, you seldom see him again... I therefore decided that Robinson was most unlikely to come back and murder me. Which was that much gained.

So the whole landscape was mine! I'd have all the time I needed, I thought, to study the surface and the depths of this leafy immensity, this ocean of red, of mottled yellow, of flamboyant hams and head cheeses, magnificent no doubt for people who love nature. I definitely didn't. The poetry of the tropics turned my stomach. The thought of all those vistas repeated on me like tuna fish. Say what you like, it will never be anything but a country for mosquitoes and panthers. And not for me.

I preferred to go back to my shack and fix it up in anticipation of the tornado that could not be long in coming. But I was soon obliged to abandon my attempts at reinforcement. The standard parts of the structure were amenable to further disintegration but defied repair, the vermin-infested thatch was coming apart, you couldn't have made a decent urinal out of my home.

After I had described a few listless circles in the bush, the sun forced me to go back in and silently collapse. The same old sun! At the noon hour everything falls silent, everything is afraid of burning up. And it wouldn't take much, grass, animals and people are heated through. Meridian apoplexy.

My one and only chicken, bequeathed to me by Robinson, dreaded the noon hour the same as I did, it would go back in with me. For three weeks the chicken lived with me like that, following me like a dog, clucking constantly, seeing snakes wherever it went. One day of extreme boredom, I ate it. It had no taste at all, its flesh had been bleached by the sun like an awning. Maybe that was what made me so sick. Be that as it may, the morning after that meal I couldn't get up. Around noon, completely groggy, I dragged myself to the medicine chest. There was nothing in it but some iodine and a map of the Nord-Sud Métro.* I hadn't seen a single customer in the store, only a few villagers who came to look-see, interminably gesticulating and chewing cola, ridden with sex and malaria. They gathered in a circle around me and seemed to be discussing my ugly mug. I was completely sick, I felt as if I had no further use for my legs, they just hung over the edge of my bed like unimportant and rather ridiculous objects.

All the runners brought me from the Director in Fort-Gono was letters stinking with insults and idiocy – and, what's more, threatening. Businessmen all think of themselves as big or little professional wizards, but in practice they usually turn out to be hopeless incompetents. My mother, writing from France, admonished me to take care of my health, as she had during the war. My head could be all set for the guillotine, and still my mother would scold me for forgetting my muffler. She never missed an opportunity to try and convince me that the world is a kindly place and that she'd done a good job in conceiving me. This alleged Providence was the great subterfuge of maternal thoughtlessness. It was easy for me, I have to admit, to leave all my boss's and mother's hogwash unanswered, and the fact is I never did answer their letters. Only it didn't improve my situation.

Robinson had made off with almost everything that fragile edifice had contained, but who'd believe me if I said so? Write letters? What for? To whom? At about five every afternoon I shook with a violent fever, my bed jiggled and rattled as if I'd been vigorously jerking off. A bunch of blacks from the village had come to wait on me and taken possession of the hut; I hadn't sent for them, but to send them away would have been too much of an effort. They squabbled over the remains of the stock, rummaged through the kegs of tobacco, tried on the last of the loincloths, felt the material, and took them off, adding, if that was possible, to the general disorder of my establishment. The

144

rubber was all over the ground, mingling its juice with the bush melons and those sickly-sweet papayas that taste like pissy pears. I ate so many of them in place of beans that now, fifteen years later, the memory of them still turns my stomach.

I tried to gauge the degree of hopelessness to which I had fallen. I couldn't. "Everybody steals!" Robinson had said to me three times before disappearing. The Director was of the same opinion. In my fever those words ran through me like shooting pains. "You've got to get by!..." He'd said that too. I tried to get up, I couldn't make it. He'd been right about the water we had to drink, it was worse than mud, it was concentrated muck. Little black boys brought me bananas, big ones, little ones, red ones and more and more papayas, but I was so sick of all that and everything else! I'd have vomited up the whole globe.

As soon as I felt a tiny bit better and not quite so dazed, I was seized again with a horrible fear, the fear that the Company would call me to account. What would I say to those devils? How would I get them to believe me? They'd have me arrested for sure! And who would try me? A bunch of special judges, something like a court martial, armed with terrible laws they had gotten from God knows where, who never tell their real intentions and who for the sheer fun of it make you drag your bleeding steps up the steep path overlooking hell, the path that leads poor bastards to their death. The law is a big Luna Park of suffering. When a poor man lets himself get caught in it, you'll hear him screaming for centuries on end.

I preferred to lie there in a stupor, trembling and foaming at the mouth with a forty-degree fever, than to be lucid and forced to think of what would happen to me in Fort-Gono. I even stopped taking my quinine, because I figured the fever would keep life away from me. You get drunk on what you've got. While I lay there sweltering, I ran out of matches. They'd been in short supply. Robinson hadn't left me a thing, only "*cassoulet à la Bordelaise*". But plenty of that, I assure you. I threw up whole tins of it. And even to arrive at that result, you had to heat them.

The shortage of matches provided me with one little amusement, watching my cook light his fire with two pieces of flint and some dry grass. It was while I was watching him that the idea came to me. With plenty of fever added, my idea became wonderfully vivid. Though clumsy by nature, I was able after applying myself for a month to light a fire with two sharp stones like a savage. In short, I was learning how to make do under primitive conditions. Fire is the first thing; then there's hunting, but I wasn't interested in that. My flame was all I needed, and I practised conscientiously. Day after day I had nothing else to do. I never got nearly as good at the sport of propelling the caterpillars of the "secondary". I didn't quite get the knack. I squashed a lot of them, and then I lost interest. I gave them the run of the house – like old friends. There were two big storms, the second went on for three days and, worse, for three nights. At last I had drinking water in the bucket, tepid to be sure, but even so... In the deluge the scraps of goods in my little stock began to run and intermingle, a disgusting mess.

Some of the natives obligingly brought me lianas from the forest to anchor my shack to the ground, but in vain; at the slightest wind, the leafy walls would flap wildly against the roof like wounded wings. There was nothing I could do about it. Never a dull moment.

Blacks big and small decided to join me in my downfall, they got more and more familiar. And they were so very happy. What fun. They came and went as they pleased in my so-called home. Freedom. As a sign of perfect understanding we exchanged signs. If I hadn't had fever, I might have started learning their language. There wasn't time enough. I made very good progress in fire-making, but I hadn't yet mastered their best manner. I wasn't very quick about it. Showers of sparks still flew into my eyes, which gave my black friends a good laugh.

When I wasn't mouldering with fever on my folding bed or working my primitive tinderbox, I thought of the Company's accounts. It's funny how hard it is to throw off one's dread of irregular accounts. I'd undoubtedly inherited that from my mother, she'd contaminated me with her "He who steals a pin will steal a pound... and end up murdering his mother." We all find it hard to throw off those ideas. We pick them up in childhood, and they come back to terrify us later on, in every crisis. What weaknesses! Our only hope of getting rid of them is the force of circumstances! Luckily the force of circumstances is enormous. Meanwhile the store and I were sinking. One of these days we'd be swallowed up by the mud, which got thicker and more viscous with every downpour. The rainy season. What looked like a boulder yesterday was oozy molasses today. Tepid water fell in cascades from dangling branches and followed one everywhere, it invaded the hut and spread round about as in an old abandoned riverbed. The rain made a porridge of my merchandise, my hopes and my accounts, and so did my fever, which was also very moist. The rain was so compact that when it hit you it stopped your mouth like a lukewarm gag. But the flood didn't stop the animals from getting together, the nightingales started making as much noise as jackals. Anarchy all over the ark, and I a doddering Noah. This, I thought, had been going on long enough.

All my mother's adages weren't about honesty. As I remembered opportunely, she used to say when burning old bandages: "Nothing purifies like fire!" A mother leaves you something for every turn of Fate. You just have to take your pick.

The time had come. My pieces of flint were not very well chosen, not sharp enough, most of the sparks struck my hands. In the end, however, some of my merchandise took fire in spite of the dampness: a parcel of sopping-wet socks. It happened after sundown. The flames rose impetuously. Wildly jabbering, the villagers gathered round the blaze. The crude rubber that Robinson had bought was sizzling in the middle, and the smell reminded me invincibly of the famous Telephone Company fire on the Quai de Grenelle that I'd gone to see with my Uncle Charles, who sang sentimental ballads so well. That was the year before the big Exposition, when I was very young. Nothing brings memories to the surface like smells and flames. My shack smelt exactly that way. Though drenched, it burned very thoroughly to the ground, merchandise and all... No more accounts. The owls and leopards, toads and parrots must have been flabbergasted. It takes something to impress that crowd. Like war with us. Now the forest could come back and cover the wreckage with its thundering leaves. I hadn't saved anything but my personal belongings, my folding bed, the three hundred francs and naturally, sad to say, a few cans of cassoulet for the road.

When the fire had been burning for an hour, hardly anything was left of the shack. A few tongues of flame in the rain and a few jabbering black men poking about in the ashes with the tips of their spears amid gusts of the smell that clings to all catastrophes, emanates from all the defeats of this world, the smell of smoking gunpowder.

Now was the time to make quick tracks. Back to Fort-Gono, retrace my steps? Try to explain my conduct and the circumstances of the present disaster? I hesitated... Not for long. Nothing can be explained. The world only knows how to do one thing, to roll over and kill you,

147

as a sleeper kills his fleas. That would be a stupid way to die, I said to myself, to let myself be crushed like everybody else. To put your trust in men is to get yourself killed a little.

In spite of the condition I was in, I decided to head straight into the bush in the direction taken by that devil Robinson.

* * *

Often on my way I heard the beasts of the jungle with their plaints and calls and tremolos, but I hardly ever saw them. I don't count the little wild pig I almost stepped on one day not far from my shelter. Hearing those torrents of calls and screams and roars, you had the impression that they were close by, hundreds and thousands of them. And yet, when you got to the place where the hubbub came from, there was nobody there, except for those big blue guinea fowl, all trussed up in their plumage as if they were going to a wedding and so clumsy when they jumped coughing from branch to branch that you thought they must have had an accident.

Lower down, in the musty undergrowth, big heavy butterflies, bordered like death notices, quivered with the effort of opening their wings, and lower still it was us, sloshing through the yellow mud. We had trouble getting ahead, especially because the blacks were carrying me in a litter made of sacks sewn end to end. They could easily have tossed me in the drink while we were crossing a stream. Why didn't they? I found out later. Or they could have eaten me, since that was one of their customs.

Now and then I'd question them with my thick tongue, and every time they answered: "Yes, yes." Always glad to oblige. Good fellows. Whenever my diarrhoea let me go for a while, the fever took hold. You wouldn't believe how sick I was.

I couldn't see things clearly any more, or rather, everything was beginning to look green. After nightfall all the animals of creation surrounded our camp. We'd make a fire. But here and there, even so, a cry would pierce the great black awning that stifled us. Despite its horror of men and fire, a wounded, dying animal would manage to complain to us, seeing we were right there.

After the fourth day I stopped even trying to distinguish reality from the absurd fever images that went chasing one another through my head along with fragments of people and endless tatters of resolutions and disappointments.

Even so, I tell myself today when I think about it that the bearded white man we met one morning on a stony promontory near the meeting of two rivers must have been real. A cataract nearby was making a hellish din. He was a sergeant, something like Alcide, except this one was Spanish. Worrying along from trail to trail, we'd ended up in the colony of Rio del Rio, an ancient possession of the Crown of Castile. That poor Spanish soldier also had a shack. I seem to remember that he laughed when I told him about my misadventures and what I'd done with my shack! His, I have to admit, looked a little better, but not much. His special cross was the red ants. On their annual migration those little bastards had elected to pass straight through his shack, and they'd been at it for going on two months.

They took up practically all the space; you could hardly turn round, and if you got in their way, they pinched you hard.

He was overjoyed when I gave him some of my cassoulet, because he'd been living on tomatoes for the last three years. I couldn't better that. All by himself, he told me, he had downed more than three thousand cans. Tired of preparing the tomatoes in different ways, he had taken to sucking the cans like eggs, through two little holes in the lid.

When the red ants discovered that a new variety of canned goods had arrived, they mounted guard around the cassoulet. It wouldn't have been advisable to leave a freshly opened can standing; they'd have summoned the whole nation of red ants to the shack. There are no bigger communists anywhere. And they'd have eaten up the Spaniard too.

My host informed me that the capital of Rio del Rio was called San Tapeta,* a seaport famous all along the coast for its transoceanic galleys.

It so happened that the track we were on ended there; we would just have to go straight ahead for three days and three nights. I was good and sick of my delirium, so I asked the Spaniard if he knew of some good native medicine that would straighten me out. My head was acting up something terrible. But he wouldn't hear of any such mumbo-jumbo. For a Spanish colonial he was strangely Africanophobic, so much so that when he went to the toilet he refused to use banana leaves and kept a whole sheaf of the *Boletín de Asturias*, cut up in little pieces for that express purpose. And he didn't read the paper, same as Alcide.

For three years he'd been living there alone with the ants, a few little kinks, and his old newspapers. What with his awful Spanish accent, which was so strong it was like having somebody else in the room, it was hard to get him stirred up about anything. When he bawled out his natives, it was like a tempest. For loudness of mouth, Alcide couldn't hold a candle to him. I took such a liking to that Spaniard that in the end I gave him all my cassoulet. Out of gratitude he made me a lovely passport on grainy paper stamped with the arms of Castile, with a signature so elaborate, so finicky, that it took him at least ten minutes to get it right.

He'd told the truth, you couldn't miss the road to San Tapeta, you only had to follow your nose. I don't remember the trip, but of one thing I'm sure, that as soon as we got there they handed me over to a priest who was so gaga that having him beside me gave me a kind of comparative self-confidence. But not for long.

The town of San Tapeta was plunked down on the side of a rock, directly facing the sea. It was hard to believe how green the place was. A magnificent spectacle no doubt, seen from the roadstead, splendid from a distance... On the spot, though, there was nothing to admire but the same overworked carcasses as in Fort-Gono, everlastingly sweating and pustulating. In a lucid moment I dismissed the blacks of my little caravan. They'd crossed a long stretch of jungle and feared for their lives going back, so they said. In leaving me, they wept in advance at the thought of the journey, but I didn't have the strength to feel sorry for them. I had suffered and sweated too much. And I was still at it.

By day and by night, to the best of my recollection, a lot of jabberers – they were decidedly in plentiful supply – crowded round my bed, which had been set up for that very purpose in the presbytery, since entertainment was rare in San Tapeta. The priest filled me with tisanes, a long gilded crucifix dangled over his belly, and when he came near me a loud clinking of coins rose from the depths of his soutane. Conversation with those people was out of the question. It exhausted me completely just to mumble a word or two.

I really thought it was all up with me, and I tried to take a last look at what could be seen of the world through the priest's window. I doubt if I could describe those gardens today without gross and outlandish mistakes. The sun was there, I can vouch for that, always the same, as if somebody had opened a big furnace in your face, and then behind it there was more sun and insane trees, whole avenues of them, those lettuces as big as oaks and those African dandelions, three or four of which would add up to a perfectly good chestnut tree in France. Throw in a toad or two, as hefty as spaniels, waddling furtively from one flowerbed to the next.

People, countries and objects all end up as smells. I kept my eyes closed because I really couldn't open them any more. Then from night to night the sharp smell of Africa was blunted. It became harder for me to recapture that heavy mixture of decaying soil, human crotches and ground saffron.

Time, patches of the past, then more time, and then at a certain moment I felt a series of jolts and twists, and then the jolting became more regular, a swaying, a rocking...

I was still lying down, that was sure, but whatever I was lying on was moving. I let myself go, I vomited, then I woke up again and fell asleep again. I was on the sea. I felt so faint that I barely had the strength to catch the new smell of ropes and tar. It was cool in the heaving niche where I was lying directly under a wide-open porthole. They'd left me alone. Evidently my journey was continuing... But what journey? I heard steps on the deck, a wooden deck right over my nose, and voices, and the waves lashing and melting against the ship's side.

Life seldom comes back to your deathbed, wherever you may be, except in the form of a low-down trick. The one those people in San Tapeta had played on me filled the bill. Taking advantage of my befuddled state, they'd sold me to the captain of a galley. A fine galley, to be sure, high of hull, well-fitted with oars, crowned with beautiful purple sails, gilt figurehead, superbly upholstered officers' quarters and on the prow a magnificent cod-liver-oil painting of the *Infanta Combitta** dressed for polo. The Infanta, I was told later on, was the ship's sponsor, offering it the protection of her name, her tits and her royal dignity. It was flattering.

After all, I reflected when I realized what had happened, in San Tapeta I was as sick as a dog, the whole world was spinning, and I'd certainly have died in that presbytery where the natives had left me... Return to Fort-Gono? Those accounts would certainly have got me fifteen years... Here at least I was moving, and that was ground for hope... Come to think of it, the captain of the *Infanta Combitta* had taken a big chance in buying me, even dirt cheap, from that priest before weighing anchor. It was a risky investment, for that captain could have lost all his money... He was counting on the brisk sea air to revive me. He deserved a reward and obviously he was winning his bet, for I was already recovering. I could see he was as pleased as Punch. I still raved quite a lot, but with a certain logic... After I opened my eyes, he often came to see me in my cubbyhole. He was always wearing his plumed hat. That's how I saw him.

It amused him to see me try to raise myself on my pallet in spite of my fever. "All right, shitarse!" he'd say. "You'll soon be able to row with the rest of them!" A kindly thought. He roared with laughter, giving me little strokes of his whip, but in a friendly kind of way, on the back of my neck, not on my rear end. He wanted me to laugh too, to share his pleasure at the business acumen he'd shown in acquiring me.

The food on board struck me as quite acceptable. My speech was still muddled. Soon, as the captain had foreseen, I recovered enough strength to join the boys at the oars. But where there were ten oarsmen, I saw a hundred: multiple vision.

The crossing wasn't strenuous, because most of the time we were under sail. Our conditions between decks were no more nauseating than those of the usual third-class passengers on a Sunday excursion train, and not nearly as perilous as what I'd endured on the *Admiral Bragueton* coming out. There was always plenty of breeze on this voyage from the east to the west of the Atlantic. The temperature dropped. Nobody complained about that between decks. The only trouble was that the trip seemed to be taking a long time. For my part, I had seen enough seascapes and jungle vistas to last me an eternity.

I'd have liked to ask the captain a few questions about the aim and purpose of this trip, but once I was definitely on the mend, he lost interest in me. Anyway, I was still drivelling too much for conversation. From then on I saw him only from a distance, like a real boss.

I started looking for Robinson among the galley slaves, and several times in the silence of the night I called him in a loud voice. There was no answer except for a few insults and threats from the other galley slaves.

Still, the more I thought about the details and circumstances of my adventure, the more likely it seemed to me that the same thing must have happened to him in San Tapeta. Except that Robinson must be rowing on some other galley. Those jungle Negros, I thought, must all have a hand in the racket. Why shouldn't they take their turn? They've got to live, haven't they? So naturally they sell the things and people they can't eat right away. The natives' relative kindness to me could be attributed to the most sordid of motives.

For weeks and weeks the *Infanta Combitta* sailed over the rolling Atlantic from fit of fever to fit of seasickness, and then one evening all was calm around us. My delirium was gone. We were bobbing at anchor. Waking next day, we realized on opening the portholes that we had reached our destination. And what a sight it was!

* * *

Talk of surprises! What we suddenly discovered through the fog was so amazing that at first we refused to believe it, but then, when we were face to face with it, galley slaves or not, we couldn't help laughing, seeing it right there in front of us...

Just imagine, that city was standing absolutely erect. New York was a standing city. Of course we'd seen cities, fine ones too, and magnificent seaports. But in our part of the world cities lie along the coast or on rivers, they recline on the landscape, awaiting the traveller, while this American city had nothing languid about her, she stood there as stiff as a board, not seductive at all, terrifyingly stiff.

We laughed like fools. You can't help laughing at a city built straight up and down like that. But we could only laugh from the neck up, because of the cold blowing in from the sea through a grey and pink mist, a brisk sharp wind that attacked our trousers and the chinks in that wall, I mean the city streets, which engulfed the wind-borne clouds. Our galley spun its narrow wake just outside the docks, at the end of the shit-coloured bay, asplash with schools of rowboats and avid, tooting tugs.

When you're down at heel, it's never much fun landing anywhere, but for a galley slave it's a lot worse, especially in America, because those people don't like the galley slaves that come over from Europe at all. "They're anarchists!" That's what they say. The only people they really welcome are tourists, who bring them dough, because all the currencies of Europe are relatives of the dollar.

I might have tried what others had succeeded in doing, swimming across the harbour and once on land start shouting: "Long live dollar!

Long live dollar!" It's a gimmick. A lot of people have landed that way and made a fortune. It's not certain, but so they say. Even worse things happen in dreams. I had a different plan in my head, along with my fever.

On board the galley I'd become an expert at counting fleas (not just catching them but adding and subtracting them, in short, compiling statistics), a subtle skill, which looks like nothing at all, but still it's a technique and I thought I'd make use of it. You can say what you like about the Americans, but when it comes to techniques, they're connoisseurs. They'd be crazy about my way of counting fleas, I was sure of that in advance. I was convinced that I couldn't fail.

I was about to offer them my services when suddenly our galley was ordered to its quarantine station, a sheltered cove nearby, within hailing distance of a small village at the end of a quiet bay, two miles east of New York.

There we remained under observation for weeks and weeks, long enough to acquire a daily routine. Every evening after supper, for instance, our water squad would go ashore and make its way to the village. To attain my ends I'd have to go along.

My shipmates knew what I had in mind, but the adventure didn't tempt them. "He's mad but harmless," they said. The food wasn't bad on board the *Infanta Combitta*, they got clubbed now and then, but not too badly, and all in all it was bearable. An average sort of job. And it had one sublime advantage: you couldn't be fired from a galley, and the King had even promised them a small pension at the age of sixty-two. That prospect made them happy, it gave them something to dream about, and another thing: they played at voting on Sundays, it gave them a feeling of freedom.

We were kept in quarantine for weeks, the men bellowed between decks, they fought and buggered one another by turns. But their main reason for not wanting to escape with me was that they were absolutely down on this America that I was so smitten with. We all have our bugbears, and theirs was America. They even tried to sour me on it. I told them I knew people there, my little Lola among others, who must have been loaded by then, and Robinson no doubt, who had surely carved himself a niche in the business world, but they clung to their aversion for the United States, their disgust, their hatred: "You'll always have a screw loose," they said. One day I made as if to join their expedition to the village water tap, and then I told them I wasn't going back to the galley. Goodbye!

They were a good bunch all in all, hard workers. They told me again that they didn't approve one bit of what I was doing, but they wished me good luck and plenty of fun all the same, in their own way. "Go!" they said. "Go right ahead! But we're warning you: you haven't got the right ideas for a beggar! It's your fever that scrambles your brains! You'll come back from that America of yours in worse condition than we are! Your fancy ideas will be the end of you! You want to learn things? You know too much already for the likes of you!"

I tried to tell them I had friends who were expecting me. I spluttered and stammered.

"Friends?" they said. "Your friends couldn't care less! Your friends forgot you long ago!…"

"But I want to see Americans," I insisted. "And besides, they've got women like nowhere else in the world!…"

"Come on back with us, you fool!" they said. "Believe us, it's not worth it. You'll make yourself sicker than you are! We'll tell you what Americans are like! They're either millionaires or skunks! There's nothing in between! The shape you're in you certainly won't be seeing any millionaires! But don't worry, you'll get your fill of skunks, you can be sure of that! And it won't be long, oh no!"

That's the way they spoke to me. A bunch of jerks, cocksuckers, subhumans, they made me sick! "Beat it, the whole lot of you!" I told them. "You're green with envy, that's all! We'll see if the Americans skin me alive! But one thing is sure, you've all got ladyfingers between your legs, and limp ones at that!"

I told them off, and after that I felt fine!

Night was coming on, and the galley was blowing the whistle for them. They all started rowing in cadence, all but one, me. I waited till I couldn't hear them any more, then I counted up to a hundred and ran to the village as fast as I could. That village was a pretty little place, well-lit, wooden houses just waiting to be used, lined up to the right and left of a chapel, all perfectly silent. Unfortunately I was shivering with malaria and fear. Here and there I came across a sailor from the garrison – those people seemed to be taking it pretty easy – and even a few children and then a young girl with delightful muscles. That was America! I had arrived. It's a pleasure to see that sort of thing after so many parched adventures. It's as life-giving as fruit. I'd stumbled on the one useless village in the whole country. A small garrison of sailors and their families kept its installations in readiness for the conceivable day when a raging plague, imported by a boat like ours, would threaten the metropolis.

Those installations would be used for killing off as many foreigners as possible, so as to keep the city population from catching anything. They even had a cemetery ready, with flowers all over. They were waiting. For sixty years they'd been waiting. Waiting was all they did.

Finding an empty shack, I slipped in and fell asleep instantly. In the morning the streets were full of sailors in short trousers, sturdy, well-built fellows, wielding brooms and sloshing water around my refuge and on all the streets and squares of that theoretical village. I tried to look unconcerned, but I was so hungry that in spite of my fears I headed for a place where there was a smell of cooking.

That's where I was spotted and cornered between two squads of sailors, determined to identify me. Their first idea was to chuck me in the water. Taken straight to the Head Quarantine Officer, I was in a bad way. Though constant adversity had led me to develop a certain crust, I still felt too steeped in fever to risk any of my brilliant improvisations. My mind was wandering, and my heart wasn't in it.

The best policy was to lose consciousness. Which I did. In the office where I later came to, some ladies in light-coloured dresses had replaced the men around me. They put me through a vague and benevolent interrogation, which would have been plenty for me. But benevolence never lasts in this world, and the next day the men started talking prison to me again. I took the opportunity to bring up fleas, just in passing, so to speak... How I could catch them... and count them... my speciality... as well as classify these parasites and compile flawless statistics. I saw that my approach interested my guards, I had captured their attention. They were listening. But as for believing me, that was a different kettle of fish.

Finally, the commanding officer of the station turned up. He was called the "Surgeon General", which would be a good name for a fish. He spoke roughly, but with more authority than the others. "What's this you're telling us, boy?" he said. "You say you can count fleas? Really now!..." He thought that would shut me up, but not at all. One-two-three I reeled off the little spiel I had prepared. "I believe in the enumeration of fleas! It's a civilizing factor, because enumeration is the basis of the most invaluable statistical data!... A progressive country must know the number of its fleas, broken down according to sex, age group, year and season..."

"Come, come, young man! Enough of your hogwash!" the Surgeon General broke in. "You're not the first! Other young scamps from Europe have been here before you, telling us the same kind of fairy tales, but in the end they turned out to be anarchists like the rest of them, only worse... They didn't even believe in anarchy any more! Enough of your boasting!... Tomorrow we'll try you out on the immigrants over there on Ellis Island, in the shower room! Major Mischief, my assistant, will tell me if you've been lying. For two months now Major Mischief has been clamouring for an expert flea counter. We'll assign you to him for a try! Dismissed! And if you've lied to us, we'll chuck you in the drink! Dismissed! And watch your step!"

I withdrew from the presence of that American authority as I had withdrawn from so many authorities, by presenting first my pecker and then, by a deft about-face, my rear end, accompanying the whole with a military salute.

This statistics racket, it seemed to me, was as good a way as any other of getting me to New York. The very next day, Mischief, the major in question, told me in a few words what my work would be. He was a fat, jaundiced-looking man, as short-sighted as it's possible to be, with enormous smoked glasses. He must have recognized me the way wild animals recognize their victims, by the general outline, because with those glasses he was wearing he couldn't possibly have distinguished any features.

On the job we got along fine. I even think that by the end of my stay Mischief had taken quite a liking to me. In the first place, not seeing a person is an excellent reason for taking a liking to him, and besides he was delighted at my brilliant flea-catching technique. Nobody else in the whole station could hold a candle to me when it came to catching and boxing the most restive, keratosed and impatient of fleas. I was able to classify them by sex before they had even been removed from the immigrant. I don't mind telling you, my work was amazing... In the end Mischief trusted my skill implicitly.

By late afternoon the nails of my thumb and forefinger were bruised from crushing fleas, but my day's work wasn't over, I still had to line up

the columns of my daily statistical table: so and so many Polish...
Yugoslavian... Spanish fleas... Crimean crabs... Peruvian chiggers...
every furtive, biting thing that travels on human derelicts ended
under my fingernails. As you see, my work was both monumental
and meticulous. Our calculations were completed in New York in a
special office equipped with electrical flea-counting machines. Every
day the little quarantine tug crossed the whole harbour, carrying our
figures to be processed or checked.

Days and days passed, my health picked up, but, as my fever and
delirium abated in those comfortable surroundings, my craving for
adventure and daring exploits revived and became imperious. At
thirty-seven degrees everything is boring.

Yet I could have stayed there, with not a thing to worry about, well-
fed at the station mess. Best of all, it seems worth adding, Major
Mischief's daughter, a stunning young lady of fifteen, used to turn
up in extremely short skirts after five o'clock and play tennis directly
under the window of our office. I've seldom seen finer legs, still
slightly on the mannish side perhaps, yet on their way to becoming
more delicate, a splendid specimen of burgeoning flesh. A challenge
to happiness, a promise to make a man shout for joy. Some of the
young ensigns of the detachment followed her everywhere.

Those young scamps had no need to justify themselves by doing
useful work like me! I didn't miss the slightest detail of their
caperings around my little idol. Just watching them, I found myself
blanching several times a day. After a while, I began to think that
maybe at night I could pass for a sailor myself. I was still fondling
that hope when, one Saturday in the twenty-third week of my stay,
the situation ripened. The man in charge of shuttling the statistics
back and forth, an Armenian, was suddenly promoted to the post
of executive flea-counter in Alaska, where he'd be dealing with the
prospectors' dogs.

A fine promotion if ever there was one, and true enough, the man
was delighted. The Alaskan dog teams are invaluable. Since they are
always needed, they are well cared for. Whereas nobody gives a damn
about immigrants, of whom there are always too many.

That left no one to take our figures to New York, and in a twinkling
I was assigned to the task. Before I shoved off, Mischief, my boss,
shook hands with me and urged me to be good and behave myself

in town. That was the last bit of advice that estimable man ever gave me, and just as he had never seen me up to that time, he never saw me again. As soon as we went ashore, the rain came down in buckets, penetrated my thin jacket and soaked the statistics, which gradually melted away in my hand. Nevertheless, I made a big wad with some of them and let it stick out of my pocket to make me look more or less like a businessman when I hit town. Thereupon, trembling with fear and emotion, I hurried off in quest of new adventures.

Raising my eyes to the ramparts, I felt a kind of reverse vertigo, because there were really too many windows and so much alike whichever way you looked that it turned my stomach.

Flimsily clad, chilled to the bone, I made for the darkest crevice I could find in that giant façade, hoping that the people would hardly notice me in their midst. My embarrassment was quite superfluous. I had nothing to fear. In the street I had chosen, really the narrowest of all, no wider than a good-sized brook in our part of the world and extraordinarily dirty, damp and dark at the bottom, there were so many other people, big and little, thin and fat, that they carried me along with them like a shadow. They were going to town like me, on their way to work no doubt. Poor people like everywhere else.

* * *

As if I knew where I was going, I put on an air of choosing and changed my direction, taking a different street on my right, one that was better lit. "Broadway" it was called. I read the name on a sign. High up, far above the uppermost stories, there was still a bit of daylight, with seagulls and patches of sky. We moved in the lower light, a sick sort of jungle light, so grey that the street seemed to be full of grimy cotton waste.

That street was like a dismal gash, endless, with us at the bottom of it, filling it from side to side, advancing from sorrow to sorrow, towards an end that is never in sight, the end of all the streets in the world.

There were no cars, only people and more people.

This was the priceless district, I was told later, the gold district: Manhattan. You can enter it only on foot, like a church. It's the banking heart and centre of the present-day world. Yet some of those people spit on the pavement as they pass. You've got to have your nerve with you.

It's a district filled with gold, a miracle, and through the doors you can actually hear the miracle, the sound of dollars being crumpled, for the dollar is always too light, a genuine Holy Ghost, more precious than blood.

I found time to go and see them, I even went in and spoke to the employees who guard the cash. They're sad and underpaid.

When the faithful enter their bank, don't go thinking they can help themselves as they please. Far from it. In speaking to Dollar, they mumble words through a little grill; that's their confessional. Not much sound, dim light, a tiny wicket between high arches, that's all. They don't swallow the Host, they put it on their hearts. I couldn't stay there long admiring them. I had to follow the crowd in the street, between those walls of smooth shadow.

Suddenly our street widened, like a crevasse opening out into a bright clearing. Up ahead of us we saw a great pool of sea-green light, wedged between hordes of monstrous buildings. And in the middle of the clearing stood a rather countrified-looking house, surrounded by woebegone lawns.

I asked several people in the crowd what this edifice was, but most of them pretended not to hear me. They couldn't spare the time. But one young fellow right next to me was kind enough to tell me it was City Hall, adding that it was an ancient monument dating back to colonial times, ever so historical… so they'd left it there… The fringes of this oasis formed a kind of park with benches, where you could sit comfortably enough and look at the building. When I got there, there was hardly anything else to see.

I waited more than an hour in the same place, and then towards noon, from the half-light, from the shuffling, discontinuous, dismal crowd, there erupted a sudden avalanche of absolutely and undeniably beautiful women.

What a discovery! What an America! What ecstasy! I thought of Lola! Her promises had not deceived me! It was true!

I had come to the heart of my pilgrimage. And if my appetite hadn't kept calling itself to my attention, that would have struck me as one of those moments of supernatural aesthetic revelation. If I'd been a little more comfortable and confident, the incessant beauties I was discovering might have ravished me from my base human condition. In short, all I needed was a sandwich to make me believe in miracles. But how I needed that sandwich!

And yet, what supple grace! What incredible delicacy of form and feature! What inspired harmonies! What perilous nuances! Triumphant where the danger is greatest! Every conceivable promise of face and figure fulfilled! Those blondes! Those brunettes! Those Titian redheads! And more and more kept coming! Maybe, I thought, this is Greece starting all over again. Looks like I got here just in time!

What made those apparitions all the more divine in my eyes was that they seemed totally unaware of my existence as I sat on a bench close by, slap-happy, drooling with erotico-mystical admiration and quinine, but also, I have to admit, with hunger. If it were possible for a man to jump out of his skin, I'd have done it then, once and for all. There was nothing to hold me back.

Those unlikely midinettes could have wafted me away, elevated me; a gesture, a word would have sufficed, and in that moment I'd have been transported, all of me, into the world of dreams. But I suppose they had other fish to fry.

I sat there for an hour, two hours, in that state of stupefaction. I had nothing more in the world to hope for.

You know about innards? The trick they play on tramps in the country? They stuff an old wallet with putrid chicken innards. Well, take it from me, a man is just like that, except that he's fatter and hungrier and can move around, and inside there's a dream.

I had to look at the practical side of things and not dip into my small supply of money right away. I didn't have much. I was even afraid to count it. I couldn't have anyway, because I was seeing double. I could only feel those thin, bashful banknotes through the material of my pocket, side by side with my phoney statistics.

Men were passing, too, mostly young ones with faces that seemed to be made of pink wood, with a dry, monotonous expression, and jowls so wide and coarse they were hard to get used to... Well, maybe that was the kind of jowls their womenfolk wanted. The sexes seemed to stay on different sides of the street. The women looked only at the shop windows, their whole attention was taken by the handbags, scarves and little silk bits and bobs, displayed very little at a time, but with precision and authority. You didn't see many old people in that crowd. Not many couples either. Nobody seemed to find it strange that I should sit on that bench for hours all by myself, watching the people pass. But all at once the policeman standing like an inkwell in the middle of the street seemed to suspect me of sinister intentions. I could tell.

Wherever you may be, the moment you draw the attention of the authorities, the best thing you can do is disappear in a hurry. Don't try to explain. Sink into the earth! I said to myself.

It so happened that just to one side of my bench there was a big hole in the pavement, something like the Métro at home. That hole seemed propitious, so vast, with a stairway all of pink marble inside it. I'd seen quite a few people from the street disappear into it and come out again. It was in that underground vault that they answered the call of nature. I caught on right away. The hall where the business was done was likewise of marble. A kind of swimming pool, but drained of all its water, a fetid swimming pool, filled only with filtered, moribund light, which fell on the forms of unbuttoned men surrounded by their smells, red in the face from the effect of expelling their stinking faeces with barbarous noises in front of everybody.

Men among men, all free and easy, they laughed and joked and cheered one another on, it made me think of a football game. The first thing you did when you got there was to take off your jacket, as if in preparation for strenuous exercise. This was a rite, and shirtsleeves were the uniform.

In that state of undress, belching and worse, gesticulating like lunatics, they settled down in the faecal grotto. The new arrivals were assailed with a thousand revolting jokes while descending the stairs from the street, but they all seemed delighted.

The morose aloofness of the men on the street above was equalled only by the air of intimate liberation and rejoicing that came over them at the prospect of emptying their bowels in tumultuous company.

The splotched and spotted doors to the cabins hung loose, wrenched from their hinges. Some customers went from one cell to another for a little chat, those waiting for an empty seat smoked heavy cigars and slapped the backs of the obstinately toiling occupants, who sat there straining with their heads between their hands. Some groaned like wounded men or women in labour. The constipated were threatened with ingenious tortures.

When a gush of water announced a vacancy, the clamour around the free compartment redoubled, and as often as not a coin would be tossed for its possession. No sooner read, newspapers, though as thick as pillows, were dismembered by the horde of rectal toilers. The smoke made it hard to distinguish faces, and the smells deterred me from going too close.

To a foreigner the contrast was disconcerting. Such free-and-easy intimacy, such extraordinary intestinal familiarity, and up on the street such perfect restraint. It left me stunned.

I returned to the light of day by the same stairway and went back to the same bench to rest. Sudden outburst of digestive vulgarity. Discovery of a joyous shitting communism. I ignored both these disconcerting aspects of the same adventure. I hadn't the strength for analysis or synthesis. My pressing desire was to sleep. O rare, delicious frenzy!

So I joined the line of pedestrians entering one of the neighbouring streets. We progressed by fits and starts because of the shop windows, which fragmented the crowd. At one point, the door of a hotel created a great eddy. People poured out onto the pavement through a big revolving door. I was caught up and poured the other way, into the big lobby inside.

Instant amazement... You had to divine, to imagine the majesty of the edifice, the generous proportions, because the lights were so veiled that it took you some time to know what you were looking at.

Lots of young women in the half-light, plunged in deep armchairs as in jewel cases. Around them attentive men, moving silently, with timid curiosity, to and fro, just offshore from the row of crossed legs and magnificent silk-encased thighs. Those miraculous beings seemed to be waiting for grave and costly events. Obviously they weren't giving me a thought. So, ever so furtively, I in my turn passed that long and palpable temptation.

Since at least a hundred of those divine leg owners were sitting in a single row of chairs, I reached the reception desk in so dreamy a condition, having absorbed a ration of beauty so much too strong for my constitution that I was reeling.

At the desk, a pomaded clerk violently offered me a room. I asked for the smallest in the hotel. I can't have had more than fifty dollars at the time. Also, I was pretty well out of ideas and self-assurance.

I hoped the room the clerk was giving me was really the smallest, because his hotel, the Laugh Calvin,* was advertised as the most luxurious and sumptuously furnished on the whole North American continent!

Over my head, what an infinity of furnished rooms! And all around me, in those chairs, what inducements to multiple rape! What abysses! What perils! Is the poor man's aesthetic torment to have no end? Is it to be even more long-lasting than his hunger? But there was no time to succumb; before I knew it, the clerk had thrust a heavy key into my hand. I was afraid to move.

A sharp youngster, dressed like a very junior brigadier general, stepped, imperious and commanding, out of the gloom. The smooth reception clerk rang his metallic bell three times, and the little boy started whistling. That was my send-off. Time to go. And away we went.

As black and resolute as a subway train, we raced down a corridor. The youngster in the lead. A twist, a turn, another. We didn't dawdle. We veered a bit to the left. Here we go. The lift. Stitch in my side. Is this it? No. Another corridor. Even darker. Ebony panelling, it looks like, all along the walls. No time to examine it. The kid's whistling. He's carrying my frail valise. I don't dare ask him questions. My job was to keep walking, that was clear to me. In the darkness here and there, as we passed, a red-and-green light flashed a command. Long lines of gold marked the doors. We had passed the 1800s long ago and then the 3000s, and still we were on our way, drawn by our invincible destiny. As though driven by instinct, the little bellboy in his braid and stripes pursued the nameless in the darkness. Nothing in this cavern seemed to take him unawares. His whistling modulated plaintively when we passed a black man and a black chambermaid. And that was all.

Struggling to walk faster in those corridors, I lost what little self-assurance I had left when I escaped from quarantine. I was falling apart, just as I had seen my shack fall apart in the African wind and the floods of warm water. Here I was attacked by a torrent of unfamiliar sensations. There's a moment between two brands of humanity when you find yourself thrashing around in a vacuum.

Suddenly, without warning, the youngster turned round. We had arrived. I bumped into a chair, it was my room, a big box with ebony walls. The only light was a faint ring surrounding the bashful greenish lamp on the table. The manager of the Laugh Calvin Hotel begged the visitor to look upon him as a friend and assured him that he, the manager, would make a special point of keeping him, the visitor, cheerful throughout his stay in New York. Reading this notice, which was displayed where no one could possibly miss it, added if possible to my depression.

Once I was left alone, it deepened. All America had followed me to my room, and was asking me enormous questions, reviving awful forebodings.

Reclining anxiously on the bed, I tried to adjust to the darkness of my cubbyhole. At regular intervals the walls on the window side trembled. An elevated-railway train was passing. It bounded between two streets like a cannonball filled with quivering flesh, jolting from section to section of this mercurial city. You could see it far away, its carcass trembling as it passed over a torrent of steel girders, which went on echoing from rampart to rampart long after the train had roared by at seventy miles an hour. Dinner time passed as I lay thus prostrate, and bedtime as well.

What had horrified me most of all was that furious elevated railway. On the other side of the court, which was more like a well shaft, the wall began to light up, first one, then two rooms, then dozens. I could see what was going on in some of them. Couples going to bed. These Americans seemed as worn out as our own people after their vertical hours. The women had very full, very pale thighs, at least the ones I was able to get a good look at. Before going to bed, most of the men shaved without taking the cigars out of their mouths.

In bed they first took off their glasses, then put their false teeth in a glass of water, which they left in evidence. Same as in the street, the sexes didn't seem to talk to each other. They impressed me as fat, docile animals, used to being bored. In all, I only saw two couples engaging, with the light on, in the kind of thing I'd expected, and not at all violently. The other women ate chocolates in bed, while waiting for their husbands to finish shaving. And then they all put their lights out.

There's something sad about people going to bed. You can see they don't give a damn whether they're getting what they want out of life or not, you can see they don't even try to understand what we're here for. They just don't care. Americans or not, they sleep no matter what, they're bloated molluscs, no sensibility, no trouble with their conscience.

I'd seen too many puzzling things to be easy in my mind. I knew too much and not enough. I'd better go out, I said to myself, I'd better go out again. Maybe I'll meet Robinson. Naturally that was an idiotic idea, but I dreamt it up as an excuse for going out again, because no matter how much I tossed and turned on my narrow bed, I couldn't snatch the tiniest scrap of sleep. Even masturbation, at times like that, provides neither comfort nor entertainment. Then you're really in despair.

The worst part is wondering how you'll find the strength tomorrow to go on doing what you did today and have been doing for much too long, where you'll find the strength for all that stupid running around, those projects that come to nothing, those attempts to escape from crushing necessity, which always founder and serve only to convince you one more time that destiny is implacable, that every night will find you down and out, crushed by the dread of more and more sordid and insecure tomorrows.

And maybe it's treacherous old age coming on, threatening the worst. Not much music left inside us for life to dance to. Our youth has gone to the ends of the earth to die in the silence of the truth. And where, I ask you, can a man escape to, when he hasn't enough madness left inside him? The truth is an endless death agony. The truth is death. You have to choose: death or lies. I've never been able to kill myself.

I'd better go out into the street, a partial suicide. Everyone has his little knacks, his ways of getting sleep and food. I'd need to sleep if I wanted to recover the strength I'd need to go to work next day. Get back the zip it would take to find a job in the morning, and in the meantime force my way into the unknown realm of sleep. Don't go thinking it's easy to fall asleep when you've started doubting everything, mostly because of the awful fears people have given you.

I dressed and somehow found my way to the lift, but feeling kind of foggy. I still had to cross the lobby, to pass more rows of ravishing enigmas with legs so tempting, faces so delicate and severe. Goddesses, in short, hustling goddesses. We might have tried to make an arrangement. But I was afraid of being arrested. Complications. Nearly all a poor bastard's desires are punishable by jail. So there I was on the street again. It wasn't the same crowd as before. This one billowed over the pavements and showed a little more life, as if it had landed in a country less arid, the land of entertainment, of night life.

The people surged in the direction of lights suspended far off in the darkness, writhing multicoloured snakes. They flowed in from all the neighbouring streets. A crowd like that, I said to myself, adds up to a lot of dollars in handkerchiefs alone or silk stockings! Or just in cigarettes for that matter! And to think that you can go out among all that money, and nobody'll give you a single penny, not even to go and eat with! It's heartbreaking to think how people shut themselves off from one another, like houses.

I too dragged myself toward the lights, a cinema, and then another right next to it, and another, all along the street. We lost big chunks of crowd to each of them. I picked a cinema with posters of women in slips, and what legs! Boyohboy! Heavy! Ample! Shapely! And pretty faces on top, as though drawn for the contrast, no need of retouching, not a blemish, not a flaw, perfect I tell you, delicate but firm and neat. Life can engender no greater peril than these incautious beauties, these indiscreet variations on perfect divine harmony.

It was warm and cosy in the movie house. An enormous organ, as mellow as in a cathedral, a heated cathedral I mean, organ pipes like thighs. They don't waste a moment. Before you know it, you're bathing in an all-forgiving warmth. Just let yourself go and you'll begin to think the world has been converted to loving kindness. I almost was myself.

Dreams rise in the darkness and catch fire from the mirage of moving light. What happens on the screen isn't quite real; it leaves open a vague cloudy space for the poor, for dreams and the dead. Hurry hurry, cram yourself full of dreams to carry you through the life that's waiting for you outside, when you leave here, to help you last a few days more in that nightmare of things and people. Among the dreams, choose the ones most likely to warm your soul. I have to confess that I picked the sexy ones. No point in being proud; when it comes to miracles, take the ones that will stay with you. A blonde with unforgettable tits and shoulders saw fit to break the silence of the screen with a song about her loneliness. I'd have been glad to cry about it with her.

There's nothing like it! What a lift it gives you! After that, I knew I'd have courage enough in my guts to last me at least two days. I didn't even wait for the lights to go on. Once I'd absorbed a small dose of that admirable ecstasy, I knew I'd sleep, my mind was made up.

When I got back to the Laugh Calvin, the night clerk, despite my greeting, neglected to say good evening the way they do at home. But his contempt didn't mean a thing to me any more. An intense inner life suffices to itself, it can melt an icepack that has been building up for twenty years. That's a fact.

In my room I'd barely closed my eyes when the blonde from the movie house came along and sang her whole song of sorrow just for me. I helped her put me to sleep, so to speak, and succeeded pretty well... I wasn't entirely alone... It's not possible to sleep alone...

* * *

To eat cheaply in America, you can buy yourself a hot roll with a sausage in it: it's handy, they sell them on street corners in the poor neighbourhoods, and they're not at all expensive. I didn't mind eating in poor neighbourhoods, but never meeting those splendid creatures designed for the rich – that bothered me. Under those conditions it wasn't worth eating.

True, at the Laugh Calvin, on those thick carpets, I could pretend to be looking for somebody among the too pretty women in the lobby. After a while I was able to face that sultry atmosphere without quailing. Thinking about it, I had to admit that the boys on the *Infanta Combitta* had been right: experience was teaching me that I didn't have sensible tastes for a poor slob. My shipmates on the galley had been right in giving me hell. Anyway, my morale was still low. More and more I dosed myself on movies, in this street or that street, but all they gave me was enough energy for a little stroll or two. No more. The loneliness in Africa had been pretty rough, but my isolation in this American anthill was even more crushing.

I'd always worried about being practically empty, about having no serious reason for living. And now, confronted with the facts, I was sure of my individual nullity. In that environment, too different from the one where my petty habits were at home, I seem to have disintegrated, I felt very close to nonexistence. I discovered that with no one to speak to me of familiar things, there was nothing to stop me from sinking into irresistible boredom – a terrifying, sickly-sweet torpor. Nauseating.

On the point of dropping my last dollar in this adventure, I was still bored. So profoundly that I even refused to envisage the most urgent steps I should have been taking. We are so trivial by nature that only amusements can stop us from dying for real. I clung to the movies with desperate fervour.

Leaving the delirious gloom of my hotel, I attempted a few excursions in the main streets round about, an insipid carnival of dizzy buildings. My weariness increased at the sight of those endless house fronts, that turgid monotony of pavements, of windows upon windows, of business and more business, that chancre of the world, bursting with pustulant advertisements. False promises. Drivelling lies.

Along the river I explored other streets, more and more of them. Here the dimensions were more normal; for instance, from the pavement where I was standing I might have smashed every window in the house across the street.

Those neighbourhoods were full of the smell of constant frying, the shops dispensed with pavement displays for fear of theft. Everything reminded me of the streets around my hospital in Villejuif, even the children with their crooked swollen knees all along the pavements, and the barrel organs. I'd have been glad to stay there with them, but poor people wouldn't have fed me any more than the rich; besides, I'd have had to look at them all, and their too much misery frightened me. So I finally went back to Richtown. "You no-good!" I said to myself. "Really, you have no virtue!" A man should be resigned to knowing himself a little better each day if he hasn't got the guts to put an end to his snivelling once and for all.

A tram was running beside the Hudson, heading for the midtown section, an ancient vehicle, trembling in every wheel and all its terrified carcass. It took a solid hour to get there. The passengers submitted without impatience to a complicated ritual: you paid by tossing coins into a kind of coffee mill stationed at the entrance. The conductor, dressed like ours, in the uniform of a Balkan prisoner of war, watched them doing it.

At last we arrived. Returning exhausted from those populist excursions, I once again passed that inexhaustible double row of beauties in my Tantalean lobby. Again and again I passed, pensive and prodded by desire.

My poverty was such that I didn't dare rummage through my pockets to make sure. If only, I thought, Lola hasn't picked this particular moment to leave town... But will she want to see me in the first place? Should I touch her for fifty or for a hundred dollars as a starter?... I hesitated. I felt that I wouldn't have the nerve till I'd eaten and slept properly for once. And then, if this first touch was successful, I'd go looking for Robinson right away – that is, as soon as I got my strength back. Robinson was nothing like me. He was determined! Courageous! Oh yes! I could bet he knew all about America by now, all the ins and outs! Maybe he knew some way of acquiring the certainty, the peace of mind in which I was so sadly lacking...

If, as I supposed, he too had come on a galley and trodden these shores before me, he'd be well launched on his American career by now! These jumpy lunatics wouldn't faze him! I myself, come to think of it, might have looked for a job in one of those offices, whose dazzling signs I saw outside... But at the thought of having to enter that sort of building I crumpled with fear. My hotel – that gigantic, loathsomely animated tomb – was enough for me.

Maybe those vast accretions of matter, those commercial honey-combs, those endless figments of brick and steel didn't affect the habitués the way they did me. To them perhaps that suspended deluge meant security, while to me it was simply an abominable system of constraints, of corridors, locks and wickets, a vast, inexpiable architectural crime.

Philosophizing is simply one way of being afraid, a cowardly pretence that doesn't get you anywhere.

I went out and watched my last three dollars wriggling in the palm of my hand under the electric signs on Times Square, that amazing intersection where the crowds engaged in picking their film showing are bathed in floods of advertising. In search of a cheap restaurant, I went into one of those rationalized public refectories, where the service is reduced to a minimum and the alimentary rite is cut down to the exact measure of nature's requirements.

They hand you a tray at the entrance, and you take your place in a line. You wait. The girls around me, delightful candidates for dinner, didn't say a word to me... It must feel really funny, I thought, to be able to go right up to one of those young ladies with the tidy, prettily shaped noses, and say: "Miss, I'm rich, very rich... just tell me what it might please you to accept..."

Everything that was so complicated a moment before would suddenly become so simple, so divinely simple... Everything would be changed, the forbiddingly hostile world would turn into a playful, docile, velvety ball, rolling at your feet. Then and there, perhaps, you'd throw off the tiresome habit of dreaming about successful people and enormous fortunes, because then you'd be able to put your hands on all that. The life of people without resources is nothing but one long rebuff and one long frenzy of desire, and a man can truly know, truly deliver himself only from what he possesses. As for me, I'd picked up and dropped so many dreams, my mind was cracked and fissured, full of draughts and disgustingly out of order.

In the meantime I was afraid to attempt even the most inoffensive conversation with these young things in the restaurant. I went ahead with my tray in well-behaved silence. When it came my turn to pass the earthenware hollows filled with sausages and beans, I took what was given me. That restaurant was so clean and well lit that, skimming its mosaic floor, I felt like a fly on milk.

Waitresses dressed like nurses stood behind the noodles, rice and stewed fruit. Each had her speciality. I took what the most attractive ones were dishing out. To my regret, they didn't smile at the customers at all. As soon as you were served, you had to leave your place in line and find yourself a table. You balance your tray and take little mincing steps as if it were an operating room. It was a change from the Laugh Calvin and my gold-bordered ebony cubbyhole.

But if they showered the customers with so much light, if they lifted us for a moment from the habitual darkness of our condition, there was method in their madness. The owner was up to something. I had my suspicions. After days of darkness it feels very strange to be suddenly bathed in torrents of light. It made me a little giddier than usual. Which wasn't difficult, I admit.

I couldn't manage to hide my feet under the immaculate little enamel-topped table I had landed at; they stuck out in all directions. I'd have liked my feet to be somewhere else, because we were being watched through the window by the line of people we had just left in the street. They were waiting for us to finish eating so they could come and take our tables. Actually that was the reason, to keep up their appetite, why we were so well lit and displayed so prominently; we were living advertisements, so to speak. The strawberries on my cake shimmered and sparkled so brightly that I couldn't bring myself to eat them.

You can't get away from American business enterprise.

171

Yet despite the dazzling glare and my cramped posture I perceived the comings and goings in my immediate vicinity of a very nice waitress and decided not to miss a single one of her delightful movements.

When my turn came to have her clear my table, I took careful note of the unusual shape of her eyes, the outer ends of which tilted upwards more sharply than is common among French women. The eyelids also inclined slightly towards the eyebrows on the temple side. A sign of cruelty, but just enough, the kind of cruelty you can kiss, an insidious tartness like the Rhine wines one can't help liking.

When she came close to me, I made little gestures of complicity, as if I knew her. She looked me over as if I'd been an animal, without indulgence but with a certain curiosity. "This," I said to myself, "is the first American woman who has been forced to look at me."

Once I'd finished my luminous cake, there was no help for it, I had to give up my place to someone else. Reeling slightly, instead of taking the obvious way to the exit, I braced myself and circled round the man at the cash desk who was waiting for all of us and our money. Sticking out like a sore thumb in the bright, disciplined light, I headed for the blonde.

The twenty-five waitresses at their posts behind the simmering dishes all signalled to me in unison that I was mistaken, headed the wrong way. In the plate-glass window I saw a great stir among the people waiting, and the people behind me, who were supposed to start eating, hesitated to sit down. I had broken the preordained order of things. All the people around me cried out in consternation: "It must be a foreigner!"

But I had my idea for what it was worth, I wasn't going to lose the beauty who had waited on me. The sweet thing had asked for it, she had looked at me. I was sick of being alone. I was sick of dreams. I wanted sympathy! Human contact!

"Miss," I said, "you hardly know me. But I already love you. Shall we get married?..." That's how I addressed her, most respectfully.

Her answer never reached me, for a giant guard, he too dressed all in white, stepped up at that exact moment and simply shoved me out into the night, without insults or brutality, like a dog that has misbehaved.

The whole thing went off like clockwork, there was nothing I could say.

I went back to the Laugh Calvin.

In my room the same thunders were still shattering their echoes, first the roar of the "El", which seemed to hurl itself at us from far away, smashing the city every time it passed by carrying away the aqueducts; and, in between, incoherent, mechanical sounds from far below, coming up from the street, plus the soft murmur of the eddying crowd, hesitant, monotonous, always starting up again, then hesitating again and starting up again. The great stewpot of people in a city.

From up high where I was, you could shout anything you liked at them. I tried. They made me sick, the whole lot of them. I hadn't the nerve to tell them so in the daytime, to their face, but up there it was safe. "Help! Help!" I shouted, just to see if it would have any effect on them. None at all. Those people were pushing life and night and day in front of them. Life hides everything from people. Their own noise prevents them from hearing anything else. They couldn't care less. The bigger and taller the city, the less they care. Take it from me. I've tried. It's a waste of time.

* * *

I have to admit it was only for need of money, but how very pressing, how imperious a need, that I started looking for Lola! If it hadn't been for that pitiful need, man would I have let that little bitch of a girlfriend grow old and die without ever setting eyes on her again! All in all – and when I thought about it I had no doubt whatsoever – her behaviour to me had been most crummily ruthless.

When, grown older, we look back on the selfishness of the people who've been mixed up with our lives, we see it undeniably for what it was, as hard as steel or platinum and a lot more durable than time itself.

As long as we're young, we manage to find excuses for the stoniest indifference, the most blatant caddishness, we put them down to emotional eccentricity or some sort of romantic inexperience. But later on, when life shows us how much cunning, cruelty and malice are required just to keep the body at thirty-seven degrees, we catch on, we know the score, we begin to understand how much swinishness it takes to make up a past. Just take a close look at yourself and the degree of rottenness you've come to. There's no mystery about it, no more room for fairy tales; if you've lived this long, it's because you've squashed any poetry you had in you. Life is keeping body and soul together.

I finally, with a good deal of trouble, found my little bitch on the twenty-third floor of a building on 77th Street. It's incredible how revolting people seem when you're about to ask them a favour. Her place was posh, pretty much what I'd imagined.

Having steeped myself in large doses of cinema, I was mentally in pretty good shape, almost out of the depression that had weighed on me ever since I landed in New York, so our first contact wasn't as unpleasant as I'd expected. Lola didn't even seem terribly surprised at seeing me; it was only when she recognized me that she seemed rather put out.

By way of preamble, I tried to strike up an inoffensive sort of conversation, drawing on our common past. I kept it as discreet as possible and mentioned the war just in passing, without any particular emphasis. There I was putting my foot in it. She didn't want to hear about the war, not one word. It aged her, and she didn't like that. She lost no time in getting back at me: age, she said, had so wrinkled, bloated and caricatured me that she wouldn't have known me in the street. In short, we exchanged compliments. If the little tart thought she could get me down with such foolishness! I didn't even deign to react to her sleazy impertinence.

Her furnishings didn't bowl me over with their elegance, but the place was cheerful enough, or at least I thought so after the Laugh Calvin.

There always seems to be a certain magic about getting rich quickly. Since the rise of Musyne and Madame Herote, I knew that a poor woman's arse is her gold mine. Those sudden female metamorphoses fascinated me, and I'd have given Lola's concierge my last dollar to make her talk.

But there was no concierge in the house. There were no concierges in the whole city. A city without concierges has no history, no savour, it's as insipid as a soup without pepper and salt, nondescript slop. O luscious scrapings! O garbage! O muck oozing from bedrooms, kitchens and attics, cascading down to the concierge's den, the centre of life – what luscious, tasty hellfire! Some of our concierges are victims of their profession, laconic, throat-clearing, delectable, struck dumb with amazement, martyrs, stupefied and consumed by the truth.

174

To counter the abomination of being poor, why deny it, we are in duty bound to try everything, to get drunk on anything we can, cheap wine, masturbation, movies. No sense in being difficult, "particular" as they say in America. Year in year out, we may as well admit, our concierges in France provide anyone who knows how to take it and coddle it close to his heart with a gratis supply of all-purpose hatred, enough to blow up the world. In New York, they're cruelly lacking in this vital spice, so sordid and irrefutably alive, without which the spirit is stifled, condemned to vague slanders and pallid bumbled calumnies. Without a concierge you get nothing that stings, wounds, lacerates, torments, obsesses and adds without fail to the world's stock of hatred, illumining it with thousands of undeniable details.

What made this lack all the more deplorable was that Lola, surprised in her native environment, inspired me with a new sort of disgust. I longed to pour out my revulsion at the vulgarity of her success, at her trivial, loathsome pride, but how could I? In that same moment, by the workings of an instant contagion, the memory of Musyne became equally hostile and repugnant to me. An intense hatred for those two women arose in me, it's still with me, it has become part and parcel of my being. I'd have needed a whole panoply of evidence to rid myself on time and for good of all present and future indulgence for Lola. We can't live our lives over again.

Courage doesn't consist in forgiveness, we always forgive too much! And it does no good, that's a known fact. Why was "the housemaid" put in the last row, after all other human beings? Not for nothing, we can be sure of that. One night while they're asleep, all happy people, believe me, ought to be put to sleep for real, that'll be the end of them and their happiness once and for all. The next day they'll all be forgotten, and we'll be free to be as unhappy as we please, along with the housemaid. But what's all this I'm telling you? Lola was pacing the floor without many clothes on, and in spite of everything her body still struck me as very desirable. Where there's a luxurious body there's always a possibility of rape, of a direct, violent breaking and entering into the heart of wealth and luxury, with no fear of having to return the loot.

Maybe she was just waiting for me to make a move, and then she'd have shown me the door. Anyway, I was careful, mostly because I was so abominably hungry. Eat first! Besides, she was going on and on about

175

the vulgar trivia of her daily life. The world would certainly have to be shut down for at least two or three generations if there were no more lies to tell. People would have practically nothing to say to one another. She finally got around to asking me what I thought of her America. I owned that I'd become so weakened, so terror-stricken, that almost everyone and almost everything frightened me, and that her country as such terrified me more than all the direct, occult and unforeseeable menaces I found in it, chiefly because of the enormous indifference towards me, which to my way of thinking was its very essence.

I had my living to make, I told her, so I'd soon have to cure myself of my excessive sensibility. In that respect, I admitted, I was very backward, and I assured her that I'd be exceedingly grateful if she could recommend me to some possible employer among her acquaintances... But please, as soon as possible... I'd be quite satisfied with a modest salary... And considerably more of this insipid hogwash... She took my modest but nevertheless indiscreet suggestion pretty badly. Her replies were discouraging from the start. She couldn't think of anyone at all who might give me a job or help me. Naturally that drove us back to talking about life in general and hers in particular.

We were still sizing each other up morally and physically when the bell rang. And then, with practically no pause or interval, four women swept into the room, painted, corpulent, middle-aged, muscular, bejewelled and very free and easy. Lola introduced us very summarily, she was visibly embarrassed and tried to drag them away somewhere, but, thwarting all her efforts, they competed for my attention, telling me everything they knew about Europe. Europe was an old-fashioned garden, full of old-fashioned, randy, grasping lunatics. They knew all there was to know about the Chabanais and the Invalides.*

Personally, I hadn't been to either of those places, the first being too expensive, the second too out of the way. In replying, I was overcome by a blast of automatic patriotism that made me even sillier than usual on such occasions. I told them their city gave me the creeps. A failed carnival, a nauseating flop, though the people in charge were knocking themselves out to put it over...

While perorating thus artificially and conventionally, I couldn't help realizing that there were other reasons than malaria for my physical prostration and moral depression. There was also the change in habits; once again I was having to get used to new faces in new surroundings and to learn new ways of talking and lying. Laziness is almost as compelling as life. The new farce you're having to play crushes you with its banality, and all in all it takes more cowardice than courage to start all over again. That's what exile, a foreign country is, that inexorable perception of existence as it really is, during those long lucid hours, exceptional in the flux of human time, when the ways of the old country abandon you, but the new ways haven't sufficiently stupefied you as yet.

At such moments everything adds to your loathsome distress, forcing you in your weakened state to see things, people, and the future as they are – that is, as skeletons, as nothings, which you will nevertheless have to love, cherish and defend as if they existed.

A different country, different people carrying on rather strangely, the loss of a few little vanities, of a certain pride that has lost its justification, the lie it's based on, its familiar echo – no more is needed, your head swims, doubt takes hold of you, the infinite opens up just for you, a ridiculously small infinite, and you fall into it...

Travel is the search for this nothing, this bit of intoxication for numbskulls...

Lola's four visitors had a good laugh listening to my wild confessions, my little Jean-Jacques act. They called me all sorts of names that I hardly understood because of their American mispronunciation and unctuous, indecent way of speaking. Pathetic cats.

When the black servant came in with tea, we all fell silent.

One of the visitors must have had more discernment than the others, for she announced in a loud voice that I was shaking with fever and must be frightfully thirsty. In spite of my shakes, I loved the food that was served. Those sandwiches, I can say without exaggeration, saved my life.

The conversation turned to the relative merits of the Paris brothels, but I didn't bother to join in. The ladies dabbled in various complicated drinks and then, flushed, warmed and communicative, started talking about "marriages". Busy as I was with the food, I couldn't help realizing in one corner of my mind that these were marriages of a very special kind, matings, I was pretty sure, between youths, and that the ladies collected a commission on them.

Lola saw that this talk caught my attention and aroused my curiosity. She gave me a pretty mean look. She had stopped drinking. The

American men Lola knew weren't like me, they never showed curiosity. Under her watchful eye I controlled myself with some difficulty. I'd have liked to ask those ladies a hundred questions.

Finally the guests left us, moving heavily, enlivened by drink, sexually stimulated. Bouncing and wriggling, they held forth with a curiously elegant and cynical eroticism. I sensed an Elizabethan something deep down, and I'd have liked to feel its undoubtedly choice and concentrated vibrations at the end of my organ. But much to my regret and increased sadness, I got no more than a presentiment of that biological communion, that vital message so essential for a traveller. Incurable melancholy.

As soon as they had left, Lola made no secret of her exasperation. That intermezzo had really annoyed her. I didn't say a word.

"Those hags!" she cried a few minutes later.

"How did you get to know them?" I asked her.

"I've always known them…"

No inclination to tell me more at the moment.

Judging by their rather arrogant manner towards her, I had the impression that in a certain society these women must have enjoyed greater prestige than Lola – a considerable authority, in fact. I never found out any more about it.

Lola said something about going downtown, but told me I could stay and wait for her and have some more to eat if I was still hungry. Seeing that I'd left the Laugh Calvin without paying my bill and had no intention of going back – with good reason – I was delighted with her suggestion – a few more moments of warmth before going out and facing the street, and – oh my aching back! – what a street!…

As soon as I was alone, I made for the hallway leading to the place the Negro servant had emerged from. We met halfway to the pantry, and I shook hands with him. He trusted me right off and led me to the kitchen – a fine, well-arranged place, much more logical and attractive than the living room.

Right away he started spitting on the beautiful tile floor as only black men know how to spit, abundantly and consummately. As a matter of politeness, I too spat as best I could. That did it, he took me into his confidence. Lola, he informed me, had a yacht on the river, two cars in the garage, a cellar stocked with liquor from all over the world. The Paris department stores sent her their catalogues. That was the story.

And he proceeded to repeat the same meagre information over and over again. I stopped listening.

I dozed beside him, and the past came back to me, the days when Lola had left me in wartime Paris. The chase that sly, glib, lying minx had led me, Musyne, the Argentines, their ships full of meat. Topo, the bedraggled cohorts on the Place Clichy, Robinson, the waves, the sea, poverty, Lola's gleaming white kitchen, her Negro servant. And me sitting there as if I were somebody else. Everything would go on. The war had burnt some and warmed others, same as fire tortures you or comforts you, depending on whether you're in it or in front of it. You've got to work the angles, that's all.

It was true what she'd said about my having changed, I couldn't deny it. Life twists you and squashes your face. It had squashed her face too, but less so. It's no joke being poor. Poverty is a giant, it uses your face like a mop to clear away the world's garbage. There's plenty left.

Still, it seemed to me that I'd noticed something new in Lola, moments of depression, of melancholy, gaps in her optimistic stupidity, the moments when a person has to stop and gather the strength to carry his life, his years, a little further, because they've become too heavy for the vitality he has left, his lousy little bit of poetry.

Suddenly the Negro began to jiggle and hop. Something had come over him. I was his new friend, and he was determined to stuff me full of cakes and load me with cigars. Finally, with infinite precautions, he removed a round, leaden object from a drawer.

"The bomb!" he cried furiously. I retreated. "*Libertà! Libertà!*" he shouted exultantly.

He put it back where it belonged and spat again, superbly. What emotion! What jubilation! His laughter, that gut sensation, infected me. Why not? A little thing like that, I said to myself, doesn't mean a thing. When Lola finally got back from her errands, she found us in the living room, plunged in smoke and laughter. She pretended not to notice.

The Negro quickly made himself scarce. She took me to her room. I found her sad, pale and trembling. Where could she have been? It was getting late. The time of day when Americans are at a loss because the pulse of life around them has gone into slow motion. Every second car is back in the garage. It's the time for half-confidences. But to benefit by it you've got to hurry. To put me in the mood she questioned me, but the tone she took when asking certain questions about the life I'd been leading in Europe stuck in my craw.

She made it quite clear that she thought me capable of every kind of beastliness. That hypothesis didn't make me angry, it only embarrassed me. She had a good idea that I'd come to ask her for money, and that in itself created a natural animosity between us. Such feelings verge on murder. We stuck to commonplaces, and I did my level best to avoid an out-and-out quarrel. She asked among other things about my sexual escapades, wanting to know if, somewhere in the course of my bummings-around, I hadn't abandoned a child she could adopt. A bug that had got into her. She was obsessed with the idea of adopting a child. She thought rather naively that a tramp like me must have sired clandestine families all over the world. She was rich, she confided, and not having a child to devote herself to was more than she could bear. She had read every available book on childcare, especially the ones that go into a lyrical swoon about motherhood, those books that cure you, if you really assimilate them, of all desire to copulate for ever and ever. Every virtue has its contemptible literature.

Since she wanted to sacrifice herself exclusively for a "little creature", I was out of luck. All I had to offer her was a big creature and one who struck her as too disgusting for words. Poverty doesn't draw unless it's properly presented, swathed in imagination. Our conversation languished. "Look, Ferdinand," she finally suggested, "we've had enough talk. I'm going to take you across town to see my little protégé. I enjoy looking after him, but his mother drives me crazy..." It was a strange time to be visiting. In the car on the way, we talked about her calamitous Negro.

"Did he show you his bombs?" she asked. I owned that he had put me through that ordeal.

"He's a maniac, Ferdinand, but not dangerous. He fills his bombs with my old bills... Years ago in Chicago he had his day... He belonged to a dangerous secret society for black emancipation... Horrible people, to judge by what he's told me... The police broke up the gang, but he still has a weakness for bombs... He never puts explosives in them... The spirit of the thing is enough for him... He's really an artist... He'll be a revolutionary as long as he lives. But I keep him, he's an excellent servant. And all things considered, he's probably more honest than the ones who aren't revolutionaries..."

And she came back to her adoption mania.

"It's really too bad you haven't a little girl somewhere. A dreamy nature like yours is no good at all for a man, but it would be fine for a woman…"

The rain poured down, closing the night around our car as it glided over the long band of smooth concrete. Everything was hostile and cold to me, even her hand, which I was holding tight in mine all the same. Everything came between us. We pulled up in front of a house that looked very different from the one we had just left. In an apartment on the second floor a little boy of about ten was waiting for us with his mother. The furniture had pretensions to Louis XV, and the cooking smells of a recent meal were still in the air. The child jumped up on Lola's lap and kissed her affectionately. The mother also seemed very fond of Lola. While Lola was talking to the child, I managed to take the mother into the next room.

When we came back, the boy was performing for Lola's benefit a dance step he had just learnt at the Conservatory. "He'll need a few more private lessons," Lola observed, "then I may introduce him to my friend Vera at the Globe Theatre. I wouldn't be surprised if the child had quite a future ahead of him." After these kind, encouraging words the mother thanked her tearfully and profusely. At the same time she accepted a small wad of green dollars, which she tucked away in her bosom like a love letter.

"I'd be rather pleased with that little boy," said Lola, once we were outside, "but I have to put up with the mother at the same time, and I don't care for mothers who are too sharp for their own good… Besides, the kid is too depraved… That's not the sort of attachment I want… What I long for is a purely maternal feeling… Do you understand me, Ferdinand?" When it comes to making a living, I can put up with anything, it's not a matter of intelligence, I just know I have to adapt.

She couldn't stop talking about her desire for purity. A few streets further on she asked me where I was planning to sleep that night and took a few more steps beside me. I said that if I didn't get hold of a few dollars I wouldn't be sleeping anywhere.

"All right," she said. "Come home with me. I'll give you a little change, then you can go where you please."

She was determined to put me out into the night as soon as possible. The usual thing. Always getting shoved out into the night like this,

I said to myself, I'm bound to end up somewhere. That's some consolation. "Chin up, Ferdinand," I kept saying to myself, to keep up my courage. "What with being chucked out of everywhere, you're sure to find whatever it is that scares all those bastards so. It must be at the end of the night, and that's why they're so dead set against going to the end of the night!"

After that it was very cold between us in her car. The streets we passed threatened us with all the armoured silence of their infinitely towering stone, with a kind of suspended deluge. A city lurking in ambush, an unpredictable monster, viscous with asphalt and rain. At last we slowed down. Lola went in ahead of me.

"Come up," she said. "Follow me!"

Her living room again. I wondered how much she'd part with to get this business over with and be rid of me. She took some banknotes out of a small handbag she had left on the table. I heard an enormous rustling of crumpled bills. Great moments! In the whole city there was no other sound. But I was so embarrassed that I asked her – I don't know why and it was most out of place – for news of her mother whom I had forgotten.

"My mother is ill," she said, turning around and looking me full in the face.

"Where is she now?"

"In Chicago."

"What's wrong with her?"

"Cancer of the liver... I've put her in the hands of the finest specialists in town... They're costing me a fortune, but they'll save her. They promised."

More and more details of her mother's condition in Chicago poured out of her. Her feeling for her mother made for familiarity, and in spite of herself she appealed to me for comfort. I had her where I wanted her.

"And you, Ferdinand, you believe they'll cure her, don't you?"

"No," I said briskly and firmly. "Cancer of the liver is absolutely incurable."

At that she went deathly pale. The bitch, that was the first time I'd ever seen anything disconcert her.

"But Ferdinand, the specialists assured me she'd recover! They guaranteed it... They gave it to me in writing!... They're great doctors, Ferdinand..."

"For cash, Lola, there will always be great doctors, luckily... I'd do the same for you myself if I were in their place... And so would you, Lola..."

Suddenly what I was saying struck her as so incontrovertible, so obvious that she couldn't even put up a fight.

For once, maybe for the first time in her life, she lost her nerve.

"But Ferdinand, don't you realize how terribly you're hurting me?... I love my mother, didn't you know that I love her?..."

Glad to hear it! Good grief! Who the hell cares whether she loves her mother or not!

Lola was sobbing in her emptiness.

"Ferdinand, you're a worthless monster!" she shouted in a rage. "You're wicked! Wicked!... Saying awful things like that is just your cowardly way of avenging yourself for the rotten situation you're in... And I just know you're doing my mother a lot of harm by talking that way!..."

In her despair I sniffed vestiges of the Coué method.*

Her fury didn't frighten me as much as that of the officers on the *Admiral Bragueton*, who'd wanted to annihilate me to give the bored ladies a kick.

I watched Lola closely as she was calling me every name in the book, and it gave me a certain feeling of pride to observe that by contrast the more she insulted me the more my indifference, no, my joy, increased. We're nice people deep down.

"Now," I figured, "she'll have to give me at least twenty dollars to get rid of me... Maybe even more..."

I took the offensive: "Lola, lend me the money you promised or I'll sleep here, and you'll hear me repeat all I know about cancer, its complications, its hereditary character, because you know, Lola, cancer is hereditary, and don't forget it!"

As I developed and refined on the details of her mother's case, I saw Lola blanch, weaken, crumple before my eyes. "Oh, the bitch!" I said to myself. "Keep a good hold on her! For once you've got the good end!... Don't let her off the line! You won't find such a good one in a hurry!..."

She was beside herself. "Here!" she screamed. "Take it! Take your hundred dollars and get out and never come back, hear, never!... Out! Out! Out! You beast!..."

"Won't you kiss me all the same, Lola? Come on!... We're still friends, aren't we?" I suggested, to see how far I could go in disgusting her. At that point she took a revolver out of a drawer, and she wasn't joking. The stairs were good enough for me, I didn't even ring for the lift.

That good solid fight restored my taste for work and picked up my morale. The next day I took the train to Detroit, where, I'd been assured, it was easy to get hired and there were lots of little jobs that were well paid and didn't take too much out of you.

* * *

The passers-by spoke to me the way the sergeant had spoken to me in the forest. "You can't go wrong," they said. "Just follow your nose."

And true enough I saw some big squat buildings all of glass, enormous dollhouses, inside which you could see men moving, but hardly moving, as if they were struggling against something impossible. Was that Ford's? And then all around me and above me as far as the sky, the heavy, composite, muffled roar of torrents of machines, hard, wheels obstinately turning, grinding, groaning, always on the point of breaking down but never breaking down.

"So this is the place..." I said to myself. "It's not very promising..." Actually, it was worse than everywhere else. I went closer, up to a door where it was written on a slate that men were wanted.

I wasn't the only one waiting. One of the men cooling their heels told me he had been there, on the same spot, for two days. The poor sucker had come all the way from Yugoslavia for this job. Another deadbeat spoke to me; he said he'd decided to work just for the fun of it – a nut, a phoney.

Hardly anybody in that crowd spoke English. They eyed each other distrustfully like animals who had often been beaten. They gave off a smell of urinous crotches, like in the hospital. When they spoke to you, you kept away from their mouths, because in there poor people smell of death.

Rain was falling on our little crowd. The files of men stood compressed under the eaves. People looking for work are very compressible. What he liked at Ford's, an old Russian in a confiding frame of mind told me, was that they didn't care who or what they hired. "But watch your step," he added for my instruction, "don't get uppity, because if you get uppity they'll throw you out in two seconds and in two seconds you'll be replaced by one of those mechanical machines that he always keeps on hand, and it's no soap if you try to get back!" That Russian spoke good Parisian, because he'd been a taxi driver for years, but then he'd been fired because of some cocaine business in Bezons, and in the end he'd staked his cab in a game of *zanzi* with a fare and lost it.

It was true what he told me, that they took on anybody at all at Ford's. He hadn't lied. I had my suspicions, though, because down-and-outers like that tend to be off their rockers. There's a degree of destitution when the mind doesn't always stay with the body. It's too uncomfortable. What's talking to you is practically a disembodied soul. And a soul isn't responsible for what it says.

Naturally they stripped us stark naked for a starter. The examination was given in a kind of laboratory. We filed slowly past. "You're in terrible shape," said the medical assistant the moment he laid eyes on me, "but it doesn't matter."

And me with my worry about being turned down because of my African fevers in case they chanced to palpate my liver! Not at all, they seemed delighted at the cripples and weaklings in our batch.

"For the kind of work you'll be doing here," the doctor assured me, "your health is of no importance!"

"Glad to hear it," I said. "But you know, Doctor, I'm an educated man, I even studied medicine at one time..."

At that he gave me a dirty look; I saw that I'd put my foot in it again, to my detriment.

"Your studies won't do you a bit of good around here, son! You're not here to think, you're here to make the movements you're told to. We don't need imaginative types in our factory. What we need is chimpanzees... Let me give you a piece of advice. Never mention your intelligence again! We'll think for you, my boy! A word to the wise."

Lucky for me that he warned me. It was just as well that I should know the manners and customs of the house. I'd already made enough stupid blunders to last me at least ten years. From then on I was determined to pass for a quiet little drudge. When we had our clothes back on, we were sent off in slow-moving files, hesitant groups, in the direction where the stupendous roar of machinery came from. Everything trembled in the enormous building, and we ourselves, from our ears to the soles of our feet, were gathered into this trembling, which came from the windows, the floor, and all the clanking metal, tremors that shook the whole building from top to bottom. We ourselves became machines, our flesh trembled in the furious din, it gripped us around our heads and in our bowels and rose up to the eyes in quick continuous jolts. The further we went, the more of our companions we lost. In leaving them we gave them bright little smiles, as if all this were just lovely. It was no longer possible to speak to them or hear them. Each time three or four of them stopped at a machine.

Still, you resist; it's hard to despise your own substance, you'd like to stop all this, give yourself time to think about it and listen without difficulty to your heartbeat, but it's too late for that. This thing can never stop. This enormous steel box is on a collision course; we, inside it, are whirling madly with the machines and the earth. All together. Along with the thousands of little wheels and the hammers that never strike at the same time, that make noises which shatter one another, some so violent that they release a kind of silence around them, which makes you feel a little better.

The slow-moving little car full of hardware has trouble passing between the machine tools. Gangway! The workers jump aside to let the hysterical thing through. And the clanking fool goes on between the belts and flywheels, bringing the men their ration of servitude.

It's sickening to watch the workers bent over their machines, intent on giving them all possible pleasure, calibrating bolts and more bolts, instead of putting an end once for all to this stench of oil, this vapour that burns your throat and attacks your eardrums from inside. It's not shame that makes them bow their heads. You give in to noise as you give in to war. At the machines you let yourself go with the two-three ideas that are wobbling about at the top of your head. And that's the end. From then on everything you look at, everything you touch, is hard. And everything you still manage to remember more or less becomes as rigid as iron and loses its savour in your thoughts.

All of a sudden you've become disgustingly old.

All outside life must be done away with, made into steel, into something useful. We didn't love it enough the way it was, that's why. So it has to be made into an object, into something solid. The regulations say so.

I tried to shout something into the foreman's ear; he grunted like a pig in answer and made motions to show me, very patiently, the simple operation I was to perform for ever and ever. My minutes, my hours, like those of the others, all my time, would go into passing linchpins to the blind man next to me, who had been calibrating these same linchpins for years. I did the work very badly from the start. Nobody reprimanded me, but after three days of that first job, I was transferred, already a failure, to pushing the little trolley full of washers that went jolting along from machine to machine. At one machine I left three, at another a dozen, at still another only five. Nobody spoke to me. Existence was reduced to a kind of hesitation between stupor and frenzy. Nothing mattered but the ear-splitting continuity of the machines that commanded all men.

At six o'clock, when everything stops, you carry the noise away in your head. I had enough noise to last me all night, not to mention the smell of oil, as if I'd been given a new nose and a new brain for all time.

By dint of renunciation I became, little by little, a different man... a new Ferdinand. It took several weeks. But then the desire to see people came back to me. Naturally not the factory hands – they were mere echoes and smells of machines like myself, lumps of flesh convulsed with vibrations. I wanted to touch a real body, a pink body made of soft, quiet life.

I didn't know a soul in that city, least of all any women. Finally, after a good deal of trouble, I obtained the vague address of a "house", a clandestine brothel, at the north end of town. On several evenings in a row, after work, I strolled around the neighbourhood on reconnaissance. The street was like any other, though maybe a little cleaner than the one where I lived.

I located the house in question: it had a garden around it. To get in, you had to move quickly so the cop on duty nearby wouldn't notice. That was the first place in America where I was received without brutality, amiably in fact, for my five dollars. And what beautiful young women, well rounded, bursting with health and graceful strength, almost as beautiful, come to think of it, as the ones at the Laugh Calvin.

And these, at least, you could come right out and touch. I couldn't help myself. I got to be a regular customer. It used up all my pay. When night came, I needed the erotic promiscuity of those splendid, welcoming creatures to restore my soul. The movies were no longer enough, that mild antidote was powerless to fight the physical horror of the factory. To survive, I needed lecherous tonics, drastic elixirs. In that house I didn't have to pay much, they gave me friendly terms, because I brought the girls a few little refinements from France. Except on Saturday nights: then there was no time for refinements, business boomed, and I had to make way for baseball teams on a spree, magnificently vigorous young bruisers, to whom happiness came as easily as breath.

While the baseball teams were at it, I, likewise in high spirits, would sit alone in the kitchen, writing my short stories. I'm sure those athletes' enthusiasm for the ladies of the establishment didn't measure up to my own slightly impotent fervour. Confident in their own strength, those baseball players were blasé about physical perfection. Beauty is like drink or comfort: once you get used to it, you stop paying attention.

They visited the brothel mostly to make whoopee. Often they'd end up having terrible fights. The police would burst in and take them all away in little trucks.

Towards Molly, one of the lovely girls there, I soon developed an uncommon feeling of trust, which in frightened people takes the place of love. I remember her kindness as if it were yesterday, and her long, blond, magnificently strong, lithe legs, noble legs. Say what you like, the mark of true aristocracy in humankind is the legs.

We became intimate in body and mind, and took walks around town for a few hours every week. She was comfortably off, since she took in about a hundred dollars a day in the whorehouse, while I made barely ten at Ford's. The lovemaking she did for a living didn't tire her in the least. Americans do it like birds.

In the evening, when I'd finished pushing my little delivery wagon around, I'd meet her after dinner and force myself to put on a cheerful face. You've got to be cheerful with women, in the beginning at least. A vague desire came over me to suggest things we could do, but I hadn't the strength. She understood the industrial blues, she was used to factory workers.

One evening, just like that, apropos of nothing, she presented me with fifty dollars. First I looked at her. I didn't dare. I thought about my mother and what she'd have said. And then it came to me that my mother, poor thing, had never given me that much. To please Molly, I went right out with her dollars and bought a lovely tan "four-piece" suit, which was what they were wearing that spring. They had never seen me arrive at the whorehouse looking so natty. The madam played her big phonograph just to teach me how to dance.

Later Molly and I went to the movies to break in my new suit. She asked me on the way if I was jealous, because the suit made me look sad and not want to go back to the factory. A new suit always throws you off. She gave my suit passionate little kisses when nobody was looking. I tried to think of something else.

What a woman my Molly was! What generosity! What a body! What fullness of youth! A feast of desires! And then I was worried again. Was this pimping?... Those were my thoughts.

To make matters worse, Molly pleaded: "Don't go back to Ford's! Get yourself a little job in an office... as a translator, for instance... That's the thing for you... You like books..."

Her advice was kindly given, she wanted me to be happy. For the first time somebody was taking an interest in me, looking at me from the inside so to speak, taking my egoism into account, putting herself in my place, not just judging me from her point of view like everyone else.

If only I had met Molly sooner, when it was still possible to choose one road rather than another! Before that bitch Musyne and that little turd Lola crimped my enthusiasm! But it was too late to start being young again. I didn't believe in it any more! We grow old so quickly and, what's more, irremediably. You can tell by the way you start loving your misery in spite of yourself. Nature is stronger than we are, no two ways about it. She tries us in one particular mould, and we're never able to throw it off. I had started out as the restless type. Little by little, without realizing it, you begin to take your role and fate seriously, and before you know it, it's too late to change. You're a hundred per cent restless, and it's set that way for good.

Very lovingly Molly tried to keep me with her, to dissuade me... "Life can be just as pleasant here as in Europe, Ferdinand! We won't be unhappy together." And in a sense she was right. "We'll invest our savings... We'll buy a little business... We'll be like other people..." She said that to quiet my scruples. Plans for the future. I agreed with her. I was even rather ashamed of all the trouble she was taking to hold me. I was very fond of her, but I was even fonder of my vice, my mania for running away from everywhere in search of God knows what – driven, I suppose, by stupid pride, by a sense of some sort of superiority.

I was afraid of hurting her. She understood and anticipated my concern. She was so nice that I finally told her about the mania that drove me to clear out of wherever I happened to be. She listened to me for days and days while I held forth, laying myself disgustingly bare, fighting with fantasies and points of pride, and she never lost patience, far from it. She only tried to help me get over my foolish and futile anxiety. She didn't quite get the point of my ravings, but she always took my part against my phantoms or with them, whichever I preferred. She was so gentle and persuasive that I grew accustomed to her kindness and took it almost personally. But I felt that I was beginning to cheat on my so-called destiny, my *raison d'être* as I called it, and stopped telling her everything that passed through my mind. I crawled back into myself all alone, just delighted to observe that I was even more miserable than before, because I had brought a new kind of distress and something that resembled true feeling into my solitude.

All that is commonplace. But Molly was gifted with angelic patience and had an unshakable belief in "vocations". For instance, her younger sister at the University of Arizona had been smitten with a craze for photographing birds in their nests and wild animals in their dens. So to enable her to study that astonishing speciality, Molly regularly sent this photographer sister of hers fifty dollars a month.

A really unbounded heart, containing something sublime, convertible into cash and not phoney like mine and so many others. Molly would have liked nothing better than to take a financial interest in my dotty career. Though at times I struck her as pretty well off the beam, she thought my convictions real and not to be discouraged. She offered me an allowance and only asked me to draw up a little budget. I couldn't make up my mind to accept. A last vestige of delicacy prevented me from banking any further, from speculating on her really too noble and kindly nature. And that's how I deliberately got myself in bad with Providence.

I was so ashamed of myself that I even made a feeble attempt to go back to Ford's. Nothing came of my heroic little gesture. I got as far as the factory gate, but at that liminal point I froze. The thought of all those machines whirring as they lay in wait for me demolished my feeble work impulse once and for all.

I stationed myself outside the glass front of the main power plant, that multiform giant which roars as it pumps something or other God knows where and brings it back again through a thousand gleaming pipes as intricate and menacing as lianas. One morning, as I stood there in drooling contemplation, my Russian taxi driver came by. "Hey, you old rascal," he says to me. "You've been fired!... It's been three weeks since you showed up... They've already put a machine in your place... I warned you..."

"At least," I said to myself, "that finishes it... No need to come back..." And I beat it back to town. On the way home I dropped in at the Consulate to ask if by any chance they'd had news of a Frenchman by the name of Robinson.

"Oh yes!" said the consuls. "Yes indeed! He's been in here to see us twice, with false papers what's more... Actually he's wanted by the police! Do you know him?..." I let it go at that.

After that I expected to meet Robinson any minute. I felt it in my bones. Molly was as kind and affectionate as ever. Once she felt sure I was planning to go away for good, she was even nicer than before. There was no point in being nice to me. Often on Molly's free afternoons we took trips to the outskirts.

Bare little hills, clumps of birches around tiny little lakes, people here and there reading dingy magazines under a sky heavy with leaden clouds. Molly and I avoided elaborate confessions. She knew the score. She was too sincere to say much about her grief. She knew what went on inside, in her heart, and that was enough for her. We kissed. But I didn't kiss her properly as I should have, on my knees if the truth be known. I was always partly thinking about something else at the same time, about not wasting time and tenderness, as if I wanted to keep them for something magnificent, something sublime, for later, but not for Molly and not for this particular kiss. As if life would carry away everything I longed to know about it, about life in the thick of the night, and hide it from me, while I was expending my passion in kissing Molly, and then I wouldn't have enough left, I'd have lost everything for want of strength, and life – Life, the true mistress of all real men – would have tricked me as it tricks everyone else.

We went back to the crowds, and then I'd leave her outside her house, because the customers would keep her busy all night until early morning. While she was taking care of them, I can't deny I was sad, and my sadness spoke to me so plainly of her that I felt she was with me even more than when she really was. I went to the movies to kill time. After the show, I'd board a tram going this way or that way and tour around in the night. After two o'clock flocks of timid passengers would get on, a type you seldom see before or after that hour, always pale and sleepy, in docile groups, bound for the suburbs.

With them you could go a long way. Much farther than the factories, to vague housing developments, little streets of shapeless bungalows. On pavements sticky with the small rain of dawn the daylight glistened blue. My tram companions vanished along with their shadows. They closed their eyes on the day. It was hard to make those spectres talk. Too tired. They didn't complain, not at all: they were the men who cleaned stores and more stores during the night, and all the offices in the city, after closing time. They didn't seem as anxious as us day people. Maybe because they'd sunk to the very bottom of things.

One of those nights when I'd taken still another tram and we'd got to the last stop and everybody was quietly getting off, I thought I heard someone calling me by name: "Ferdinand! Hey, Ferdinand!" Naturally it sounded outrageous in that dim light, I didn't like it. Above the rooftops the sky was coming back in cold little patches, cut out by the eaves. Sure enough, someone was calling me. I turned around and instantly recognized Léon. He came over to me, speaking in a whisper, and we filled each other in.

He'd been cleaning an office like the rest of them. That was as much of a gimmick as he'd managed to find. He walked heavily, with a certain true majesty, as if he had been doing dangerous and in a way sacred things in the city. Actually I'd noticed that all those night cleaners had that look. In fatigue and solitude men emanate the divine. His eyes were also full of it when, in the bluish half-light where we were standing, he opened them wider than eyes usually open. He too had cleaned endless rows of toilets and made whole mountains of silent offices sparkle.

"Ferdinand," he said. "I recognized you right away! By the way you got into the tram… By the sad look on your face when you saw there were no women on board. Am I right? Isn't that your style?" He was right, it was my style. Unquestionably, my soul was as obscene as an open fly. So his observation was apt and nothing to be surprised at. What I hadn't expected was that he too was a failure in America. That came as a surprise.

I told him about the galley at San Tapeta. But he didn't know what I was talking about. "You're delirious!" he said simply. He'd come over on a freighter. He'd have tried for a job at Ford's, but his papers were just too phoney, he wouldn't have dared show them. "They're barely good enough to keep in my pocket," he said. For cleaning offices they didn't much care who you were. They didn't pay much either, but they looked the other way... This work was a kind of Foreign Legion of the night.

"What about you?" he asked me then. "What are you doing? You still cracked? Still chasing rainbows? Still got the travel bug?"

"I want to go back to France," I said. "I've seen enough, you're right..."

"Best thing you can do," he said. "For us the jig is up... We've aged without noticing it, I know... I'd like to go home too, but there's still this trouble with my papers... I'll wait a while and try and get hold of some good ones... I can't complain about the work I'm doing... There's worse. But I'm not learning English... Some of the guys have been at it for thirty years and all they've learnt is 'exit', because it's written on the doors they polish, and 'lavatory'. You get the drift?"

I got the drift. If Molly should ever fail me, I'd have to go into night work myself.

No reason why that should ever stop.

The fact is that when you're at war you say peace will be better, you bite into that hope as if it were a chocolate bar, but it's only shit after all. You don't dare say so at first for fear of making people mad. You try to be nice. When you're good and sick of wallowing in muck you speak up. Then everybody thinks you were raised in a barn. And there you have it.

I met Robinson two or three times after that. He wasn't looking at all well. A French deserter, who made bootleg liquor for the gangsters of Detroit, let him occupy a corner of his shop. The business tempted Robinson. "I'd make a little rotgut for those bastards to pour down their throats," he confided, "but you know, I've lost my nerve... The first going-over a cop gave me, I know I'd fold up... I've been through too much... Besides, I'm sleepy all the time... Not to mention the dust in those offices, my lungs are full of it... See what I mean?... It wears you down..."

We arranged to meet another night. I went back to Molly and told her the whole story. She tried not to show how bad I was making her feel, but it wasn't hard to see she was miserable. I kissed her more often now, but her unhappiness was deep, more real than in other people, because most of us tend to talk as if things were worse than they are. American women are different. We're afraid to understand, to admit it. It's rather humiliating, but this is real unhappiness, not pride, not jealousy, there are no scenes, it's genuine heartbreak. We may as well admit that we haven't got it in us and that when it comes to the pleasure of being really unhappy we're bone-dry. We're ashamed of not being richer in heart and everything else, and also of having judged humanity worse than it really is.

Now and then Molly would let go and say something mildly reproachful, but it was always said gently and kindly.

"You're sweet, Ferdinand," she'd say. "I know you try hard not to be as beastly as other people, but sometimes I wonder if you really know what you want... Think it over! You'll have to find a way of earning your living when you get back there, Ferdinand... You won't be able to roam around all night dreaming the way you do here... the way you enjoy so much... while I'm working... Have you thought of that, Ferdinand?"

In a way she was dead right, but I couldn't help being the way I was. I was afraid of hurting her. She was so easy to hurt.

"Believe me, Molly, I love you, I always will... as best I can... in my own way."

My own way didn't amount to much. And yet Molly had a perfect body, she was very tempting. But I had that lousy weakness for phantoms. Maybe I wasn't entirely to blame. Life forces you to spend too much of your time with phantoms.

"You're very affectionate, Ferdinand," she reassured me. "Don't worry about me... You've got this sickness... always wanting to know more and more... That's all... Anyway, you have to live your own life... Out there, all alone... You'll go farther travelling alone... Will you be leaving soon?"

"Yes, I'll finish medical school in France, and then I'll come back," I had the gall to assure her.

"No, Ferdinand, you won't be back... And I won't be here either..."
She was nobody's fool.

It came time for me to go. One evening shortly before she'd have to start working, we went to the station. I'd said goodbye to Robinson during the day. He wasn't happy either to see me go. I was always leaving people. On the station platform, while we were waiting for the train, some men passed, they pretended not to know her, but they exchanged whispers.

"You're already far away, Ferdinand. You're doing exactly what you want, aren't you? That's the main thing... It's the only thing that counts..."

The train pulled in. I wasn't so sure of my plans once I saw the engine. I kissed Molly with all the spirit I had left... I was sad for once, really sad, for everybody, for myself, for her, for everybody.

Maybe that's what we look for all our lives, the worst possible grief, to make us truly ourselves before we die.

Years have passed since I left her, years and more years... I wrote many times to Detroit and all the other addresses I remembered where I thought she might be known. I never received an answer.

The house is closed now. That's all I've been able to find out. Good, admirable Molly, if ever she reads these lines in some place I never heard of, I want her to know that my feelings for her haven't changed, that I still love her and always will in my own way, that she can come here any time she pleases and share my bread and furtive destiny. If she's no longer beautiful, hell, that's all right too! We'll manage! I've kept so much of her beauty in me, so living and so warm, that I've plenty for both of us, to last at least twenty years, the rest of our lives.

To leave her I certainly had to be mad, and in a cold, disgusting way. Still, I've kept my soul in one place up to now, and if death were to come and take me tomorrow, I'm sure I wouldn't be quite as cold, as ugly, as heavy as other men, and it's thanks to the kindness and the dream that Molly gave me during my few months in America.

* * *

Getting back from the Other World isn't the half of it! You pick up the sticky, precarious thread of your days just as you left it dangling. It's waiting for you.

For weeks and months I hung around the Place Clichy, where I'd started from, and environs, the Batignolles for instance, doing odd jobs. Ghastly! Under the rain, or in the heat of the cars when June came, that burns your throat and nose, almost like at Ford's. For fun I'd watch them pass, people and more people, on their way to the theatre or the Bois in the evening.

Always more or less alone in my free time, I'd mull over books and newspapers and all the things I'd seen. I resumed my studies, all the while working for a living, and finally managed to pass my examinations. Science, take it from me, is closely guarded, the Faculty of Medicine is a well-locked cupboard. Plenty of jars and very little jam. But after braving five or six years of academic tribulations I got my degree, a very high-sounding piece of paper. Then I put up my shingle in the suburbs, my sort of place, at La Garenne-Rancy,* right after the Porte Brancion* on your way out of Paris.

I had no great opinion of myself and no ambition, all I wanted was a chance to breathe and to eat a little better. I put my nameplate over the door and waited.

The neighbourhood people came and eyed my nameplate suspiciously. They even went to the police station to ask if I was a real doctor. Yes, they were told. He's filed his diploma, he's a doctor all right. The news spread all over Rancy that a real doctor had set up shop in addition to all the others. "He'll never make a living!" my concierge predicted. "There are too many doctors around here already!" She was perfectly right.

In the suburbs it's mostly by tram that life turns up in the morning. Starting at dawn, whole strings of them would come clanking down the Boulevard Minotaure, carrying loads of dazed citizens to work.

The young ones actually seemed happy about it. They'd cheer the traffic on and cling to the running boards, laughing for all they were worth, the darlings! It's hard to believe. But when you've known the telephone booth of the corner café for twenty years, so filthy you always mistake it for the crapper, you lose all desire to joke about serious things and about Rancy in particular. Then you realize where they've put you. These houses are your prison, pissy within, flat façades, their heart belongs to the landlord. You never see him. He wouldn't dare show his face. The bastard sends his agent. Yet the neighbourhood people say he's affable enough when you meet him. It doesn't cost him a thing.

The sky in Rancy is the same as in Detroit, a smoky soup that bathes the plain all the way to Levallois. Cast-off buildings bogged down in black muck. From a distance the chimneys, big ones and little ones, look like the fat stakes that rise out of the muck by the seaside. And inside it's us.

You need the courage of a crab at Rancy, especially when you're not as young as you used to be and you know you'll never get away. There at the end of the tram line a grimy bridge spans the Seine, that enormous sewer which displays everything that's in it. Along the banks, on Sunday and at night, men climb up on the piles of garbage to take a leak. Flowing water makes men meditative. They urinate with a sense of eternity like sailors. Women never meditate. Seine or no Seine. In the morning the tram carries away its crowds to get themselves compressed in the Métro. Seeing them all fleeing in that direction you'd think there must have been some catastrophe at Argenteuil, that the town was on fire. Every day in the grey of dawn it comes over them, whole clusters cling to the doors and handrails. One enormous rout! Yet all they're going to Paris for is a boss, the man who saves you from starvation. The cowards, they're scared to death of losing him, though he makes them sweat for their pittance. For ten years you stink of it, for twenty years and more. It's no bargain.

Plenty of bitching in the tram, just to get into practice. The women gripe even worse than the kids. If they caught somebody without a ticket, they'd stop the whole line. It's true that some of those women are already drunk, especially the ones headed for the market at Saint-Ouen, the semi-bourgeoises. "How much are the carrots?" they ask long before they get there, to show they've got money to spend.

Compressed like garbage in this tin box, they cross Rancy, stinking good and proper especially in the summer. Passing the fortifications,* they threaten one another, they let out one last shout, and then they scatter, the Métro swallows them up, limp suits, discouraged dresses, silk stockings, sour stomachs, dirty feet, dirty socks. Hard-wearing collars as stiff as boundary posts, pending abortions, war heroes, all scramble down the coal-tar and carbolic-acid stairs into the black pit, holding their return ticket which all by itself costs as much as two breakfast rolls.

The nagging dread of being fired without ceremony, something (accompanied by a tight-lipped reference) that can happen to a tardy worker any time the boss decides to cut down on expenses. Never-dormant recollections of the "slump", of the last time they were unemployed, of all the newspapers they had to buy for the classifieds, five sous a piece... the queuing at employment offices... Such memories can strangle a man, however well protected he may seem in his "all-weather" coat.

The city does a good job of hiding its crowds of dirty feet in those long electric sewers. They won't rise to the surface again until Sunday. You'd better stay indoors when they emerge. Just one Sunday watching their attempts to amuse themselves will permanently spoil your taste for pleasure. Around the Métro entrance, near the bastions, you catch the endemic, stagnant smell of long-drawn-out wars, of spoilt, half-burnt villages, aborted revolutions and bankrupt businesses. For years the ragpickers of the "Fortified Zone"* have been burning the same damp little piles of rubbish in ditches sheltered from the wind. Half-arsed barbarians, undone by red wine and fatigue. They take their ruined lungs to the local dispensary instead of pushing the trams off the embankment and emptying their bladders in the tollhouse.* No blood left in their veins. When the next war comes, they'll get rich again selling rat skins, cocaine and corrugated-iron masks.

For my practice I had found a small apartment at the edge of the "Zone", from which I had a good view of the embankment and the workman who's always standing up top, looking at nothing, with his arm in a big white bandage, the victim of a work accident, who doesn't know what to do or what to think and hasn't enough money to buy himself a drink and fill his mind.

Molly had been right, I was beginning to understand her. Study changes a man, puts pride into him. You need it to get to the bottom of life. Without it you just skim the surface. You think you're in the know, but trifles throw you off. You dream too much. You content yourself with words instead of going deeper. That's not what you wanted. Intentions, appearances, no more. A man of character can't content himself with that. Medicine, even if I wasn't very gifted, had brought me a good deal closer to people, to animals, everything. Now all I had to do was plunge straight into the heart of things. Death is chasing you, you've got to hurry, and while you're looking you've got to eat, and keep away from wars. That's a lot of things to do. It's no picnic.

In the meantime I wasn't getting many patients. It takes time to get started, people said to comfort me. At the moment the patient was mostly me.

Nothing, it seemed to me, can be gloomier than La Garenne-Rancy when you've got no patients. No doubt about it. You shouldn't think in a place like that, and I'd come, from the other end of the earth what's more, precisely to think at my ease! Wasn't I in luck. Stuck-up simpleton! Black and heavy it came over me... No joke, and it stayed with me. There's no tyrant like a brain.

Below me lived Bézin, the little junk dealer. Whenever I stopped outside his door he said to me: "You got to choose, Doctor! Play the races or drink, it's one or the other!... You can't have everything!... I prefer my aperitif! I don't care for gambling..."

His favourite aperitif was gentian-cassis. Not a bad-natured man ordinarily, but unpleasant after a few drinks... When he went to the Flea Market to stock up, he'd stay away for three days, his "expedition" he called it. They'd bring him back. And then he'd prophesy:

"I can see what the future will be like... An endless sex orgy... With movies in between... You can see how it is already..."

On those occasions he could see even further: "I also see that people will stop drinking... I'll be the last drinker in the future... I've got to hurry... I know my weakness..."

Everybody coughed in my street. It keeps you busy. To see the sun you have to climb up to Sacré-Cœur at least, because of the smoke.

From up there you get a beautiful view; then you realize that way down at the bottom of the plain it's us and the houses we live in. But if you try to pick out any particular place, everything you see is so ugly, so uniformly ugly, that you can't find it.

Still further down it's always the Seine, winding from bridge to bridge like an elongated blob of phlegm.

When you live in Rancy you don't even realize how sad you've become. You simply stop feeling like doing anything much. What with scrimping and going without this and that, you stop wanting anything.

For months I borrowed money right and left. The people were so poor and so suspicious in my neighbourhood that they couldn't make up their minds to send for me before dark, though I was the cheapest doctor imaginable. I spent nights and nights crossing little moonless courtyards in quest of ten or fifteen francs.

In the morning there was such a beating of carpets the whole street sounded like one big drum.

One morning I met Bébert on the pavement; his aunt, the concierge, was out shopping, and he was holding down the lodge for her. He was raising a cloud from the pavement with a broom.

Anybody who didn't raise dust at seven o'clock in the morning in those parts would get himself known all up and down the street as an out-and-out pig. Carpet-beating was a sign of cleanliness, good housekeeping. Nothing more was needed. Your breath could stink all it liked, no matter. Bébert swallowed all the dust he raised in addition to what was sent down from the upper floors. Still, a few spots of sunlight reached the street, but like inside a church: pale, muffled, mystic.

Bébert had seen me coming, I was the neighbourhood doctor who lived near the bus stop. Bébert had the greenish look of an apple that would never get ripe. He was scratching himself, and watching him made me want to scratch too. The fact is I had fleas myself, I'd caught them from patients during the night. They like to jump up on your overcoat, because it's the warmest and dampest place available. You learn that in medical school.

Bébert abandoned his carpet to come and say good morning. From every window they watched us talking.

If you've got to love something, you'll be taking less of a chance with children than with grown-ups, you'll at least have the excuse of hoping they won't turn out as crummy as the rest of us. How are you to know?

I've never been able to forget the infinite little smile of pure affection that danced across his livid face. Enough gaiety to fill the universe.

Few people past twenty preserve any of that affection, the affection of animals. The world isn't what we expected! That's it! So our looks change! They change plenty! We made a mistake! And turned into a thorough stinker in next to no time! Past twenty it shows in our face! A mistake! Our face is just a mistake.

"Hey, Doctor!" Bébert sings out. "Is it true that they picked up a guy on the Place des Fêtes last night? Throat cut open with a razor? You were on duty, weren't you? Is it true?"

"No, Bébert. I wasn't on duty, it wasn't me, it was Dr Frolichon*..."

"That's too bad, cos my aunt said she wished you'd have been on duty and you'd have told her all about it..."

"Maybe next time, Bébert."

"Do they often kill people round here?" Bébert asked.

I passed through the dust, but just then the municipal street-sweeper whished past and, whirling up from the gutters, a howling typhoon filled the whole street with new clouds, more dense and stinging than the others. We couldn't see each other any more. Bébert jumped up and down, sneezing and shouting for joy. His haggard face, his greasy hair, his emaciated monkey legs, the whole of him danced convulsively at the end of his broom.

Bébert's aunt came home from shopping; she had already downed a glass or two. I have to add that she sniffed ether now and then, a habit contracted when she was working for a doctor and having such trouble with her wisdom teeth. The only teeth she had left were two in front, but she never failed to brush them. "When you've worked for a doctor like I have, you don't forget your hygiene." She gave medical consultations in the neighbourhood, and as far away as Bezons.

I'd have been interested to know if Bébert's aunt ever thought of anything. No, she thought of nothing. She talked a lot without ever thinking. When we were alone with no one listening, she'd touch me for a free consultation. It was flattering in a way.

"Bébert, Doctor, I have to tell you because you're a doctor, he's a little pig!... He 'touches' himself! I noticed it two months ago, and I wonder who could have taught him such a filthy habit... I've always brought him up right!... I tell him to stop... but he keeps right on..."

I gave her the classic advice: "Tell him he'll go crazy."

Bébert, who'd been listening, wasn't pleased.

"I don't touch myself, it's not true. It's the Gagat* kid who suggested..."

"See?" said the aunt. "I suspected as much. The Gagats, you know, the people on the fifth floor... They're all perverts. It seems the grandfather runs after female lion tamers... Really, I ask you, lion tamers... Look, Doctor, while you're here, couldn't you prescribe a syrup to make him stop touching himself?..."

I followed her to her lodge to write out an anti-vice-syrup prescription for Bébert. I was too easy with everybody, I knew that. Nobody paid me. I treated them all free of charge, mostly out of curiosity. That's a mistake. People avenge themselves for the favours done them. Bébert's aunt took advantage of my lofty disinterestedness. In fact she imposed on me outrageously. I let things ride. I let them lie to me. I gave them what they wanted. My patients had me in their clutches. Every day they snivelled more, they had me at their mercy. And while they were at it they showed me all the ugliness they kept hidden behind the doors of their souls and exhibited to no one but me. The fee for witnessing such horrors can never be high enough. They slither through your fingers like slimy snakes.

I'll tell you the whole story some day if I live long enough.

"Listen, you scum! Let me do you favours for a few years more. Don't kill me yet. Looking so servile and defenceless; I'll tell the whole story. You'll fade away like the oozing caterpillars in Africa that came into my shack to shit... I'll make you into subtler cowards and skunks than you are, and maybe it'll kill you in the end."

"Is it sweet?" Bébert asked about the medicine.

"Don't make it sweet whatever you do," said the aunt. "For that little creep... He doesn't deserve to have it sweet, he steals enough sugar from me already! He has every vice, he'll stop at nothing. He'll end up murdering his mother!"

"I haven't got a mother," said Bébert peremptorily. He had his wits about him.

"Damn you!" cried the aunt. "None of your back talk, or I'll give you the cat-o'-nine-tails!" Then and there she takes it down off the hook, but he'd already beat it out into the street. "Cocksucker!" he shouted back at her from the corridor. The aunt went red in the face and came back to me. Silence. We changed the subject.

"Maybe, Doctor, you ought to go and see the lady on the mezzanine at 4 Rue des Mineures... Her husband used to be a notary's clerk... She's heard about you... I told her what a wonderful doctor you are, so nice to the patients."

I know she's lying. Her favourite doctor is Frolichon. She always recommends him when she can and runs me down at every opportunity. As far as she's concerned, my humanitarianism has earned me an animal hatred. Because, don't forget, she's an animal. Except that this Frolichon she admires makes her pay cash, so she consults me on the run. If she recommends me, this must be a strictly non-paying patient, or there's something very shady somewhere. As I'm leaving, I remember Bébert.

"You ought to take him out," I said. "The child doesn't get out enough..."

"Where do you want us to go? I can't go very far on account of my lodge..."

"Take him to the park at least on Sundays..."

"But there are even more people and more dust in the park than here... It's so crowded."

There's some sense in what she says. I try to think of another place to suggest.

Diffidently I propose the cemetery.

The cemetery of La Garenne-Rancy is the only open space of any size in the neighbourhood with a few trees in it.

"Say, that's true, I hadn't thought of that. Maybe we'll go!"

Bébert had just come in.

"How about it, Bébert? Would you like to go for a walk in the cemetery? I have to ask him, Doctor, because I don't mind telling you, he's as stubborn as a mule about taking a walk!..."

Actually, Bébert has no opinion. But the idea appeals to his aunt, and that's enough. She has a weakness for cemeteries, like all Parisians. It looks as if she were about to start thinking. She examines the pros and cons. The fortifications are too low class... The park is definitely too dusty... While the cemetery, sure enough, isn't bad... The people who go there on Sunday are mostly respectable folk who know how to behave... And another thing that makes it really convenient is that on the way back you can shop on the Boulevard de la Liberté, where some of the shops keep open on Sunday.

And she concluded: "Bébert, take the doctor to see Madame Henrouille on the Rue des Mineures... You know where Madame Henrouille lives, don't you, Bébert?"

Bébert knew where everything was, if only it gave him a chance to roam around.

* * *

Between the Rue Ventru and the Place Lénine it's all apartment houses. The contractors have taken over practically all the fields that were left around there, at Les Garennes, as the area was called. There was just a tiny bit of country at the end, a few empty lots after the last gas lamp.

Wedged in between apartment buildings, a few private houses are still holding out, four rooms with a big coal stove in the downstairs hallway; true, for reasons of thrift, the stove is seldom lit. The dampness makes it smoke. These remaining private houses belong to people who have retired on small incomes. The moment you go in, the smoke makes you cough. The people who've stayed in the neighbourhood haven't got big incomes, especially these Henrouilles I was being sent to. They had a little something though.

In addition to the smoke, as you stepped in, the Henrouilles' house smelt of the toilet and stew. They'd just finished paying for the place, it represented the savings of at least fifty years. The first time you saw them, you noticed something was wrong and wondered what it was. Well, the unnatural side of the Henrouilles was that for fifty years they had never spent one sou without regretting it. They'd put their flesh and spirit into that house of theirs, like a snail. But the snail doesn't know what it's doing.

The Henrouilles had spent a lifetime acquiring a house, and once it was theirs they couldn't get over it. Like people who've just been dug out of an earthquake, they were flabbergasted. Folks who've just been let out of a dungeon must get a funny look on their faces.

The Henrouilles had thought about buying a house even before they were married. First separately, then together. For half a century they had refused to think about anything else, and when life had forced them to think about something else, the war for instance and especially their son, it made them very unhappy.

When as newly-weds they had moved into their house, each with the savings of ten years, it wasn't quite finished and it was still in the middle of the fields. To reach it in winter, they had to put on sabots; they'd leave them at the grocery store on the corner of the Rue de la Révolte in the morning when they set out for work in Paris, three kilometres distant, by horse car, two sous a ticket.

You need a sturdy constitution to get through a whole lifetime on such a schedule. There was a picture of them over the bed on the upper floor, taken on their wedding day. Their bedroom furniture had all been paid for, ages ago in fact. All the receipted bills that had accumulated in the last ten, twenty, forty years, lie pinned together in the top bureau drawer, and the account book, fully up to date, is downstairs in the dining room where they never eat. Henrouille will show you all that if you ask him. On Saturdays he balances the accounts in the dining room. They've always eaten in the kitchen.

I learnt these things little by little from them and other people and some from Bébert's aunt. When I knew them a little better, they themselves told me about the terror that had haunted them all their lives, the fear that their only son, who was in business, might find himself in difficulties. For thirty years that ugly thought had more or less kept them awake nearly every night. The boy had set himself up in the feather business! The ups and downs of feathers in the last thirty years are almost unimaginable! Perhaps there's no worse, no more unstable business in all the world than feathers.

Some businesses are so shaky that no one would think of borrowing money to put them back on their feet, but there are others where the question of a loan keeps coming up almost constantly. When it occurred to them, even now that the house was paid for, that their son might approach them for a loan, the Henrouilles stood up from their chairs, looked at each other, and went red in the face. What would they do if that happened? They would refuse.

Their minds had been made up from the first to turn down all requests for a loan... Because of their principles and so as to have a nest egg waiting for him, a legacy, a house, an inheritance. That was their way of thinking. There was no nonsense about their son, but in business it's so easy to go wrong...

When they asked me for my opinion, it was the same as theirs.

My own mother was in business; her business had never brought us anything but misery, a little bread and a lot of trouble. So naturally I was down on business. I had no difficulty in understanding the perils facing the boy, the risk involved in a loan he might be forced to envisage if hard-pressed. I needed no explanations. For fifty years old man Henrouille had been a petty clerk in a notary's office on the Boulevard Sébastopol. He knew how fortunes can go to rack and ruin, and told me some hair-raising stories about it. Beginning with his own father, whose bankruptcy had prevented Henrouille from studying to be a teacher on leaving school and obliged him to go right into clerking. You remember things like that.

Well, now that their house was bought and paid for and they didn't owe a single sou, they had nothing to worry about on the security side. They were both sixty-five.

Just then Henrouille became aware of a strange ailment, or rather, he'd felt it for a long time but hadn't thought about it because there was still the house to be paid for. Once that was all settled and signed, he began to dwell on his strange trouble – dizzy spells and a whistling as of steam in both ears.

About that time he began buying the newspaper, because then they could afford it. And in the paper he saw an advertisement describing exactly what he felt in his ears. He bought the medicine it recommended, but it didn't do his ailment a bit of good; on the contrary, the whistling seemed to get worse. Maybe just from thinking about it. They finally decided on a visit to the dispensary. "It's high blood pressure," the doctor told them.

Those words came as a shock. But his new obsession came at just the right time. He had worried about the house and his son's bills for so many years that they had left a kind of hole in the tissue of fears that had gripped him body and soul for forty years and raised him to the same pitch of anguished trepidation every time a bill came due. Now that the doctor had spoken of blood pressure, he listened to the pressure beating against his ears from deep inside. He'd get up out of bed to feel his pulse and stand motionless beside his bed, feeling a faint quaver run through his body at every heartbeat. All this, he said to himself, was his death. He had always been afraid of life, and now he attached his fear to something different, to death, to his blood pressure, just as for forty years he had attached it to the peril of not being able to finish paying for the house.

He had always been just as unhappy, but now he quickly had to find a good new reason for being unhappy. That's not as easy as it sounds. Just saying "I'm unhappy" won't do. You've got to prove it, to make absolutely sure. That's all he wanted: to be able to state a good substantial motive for his fear. According to the doctor, his blood pressure was twenty-two. Twenty-two is something. The doctor had taught him to find the way to his own death.

Their son in the feather business hardly ever came to see them. Once or twice around New Year's, no more. There wasn't much point in his coming any more! His father and mother had nothing left to lend. So he hardly ever turned up.

It took me longer to get to know Madame Henrouille; she had no fears, not even the fear of her own death, which she couldn't conceive of. She only complained of old age, but without really thinking about it, just to be like other people, and about the high cost of living. Their life's labour was behind them. The house was paid for. To speed up the final payments she'd even taken to sewing buttons on waistcoats for one of the department stores. "The amount of buttons you've got to sew on for five francs, you wouldn't believe it!" she'd say. And delivering her work on the bus, she rode second class and things were always happening. One afternoon a woman had bumped into her. Madame Henrouille had given her a piece of her mind. The woman was a foreigner, the first and only foreigner Madame Henrouille had ever spoken to.

The walls of the house had kept good and dry in the old days when there was still air circulating around them, but now that there were tall apartment buildings next door, everything oozed and trickled with humidity – even the curtains had a musty smell.

Once the house was really theirs, Madame Henrouille had been all smiles for a whole month, as blissful as a nun after communion. In fact she was the one who had suggested: "Look, Jules, suppose we buy a newspaper every day, now we can afford it!..." Just like that. She had thought of her husband, she had looked at him. But then she looked round her and after a while she thought of his mother, her mother-in-law Henrouille. At that the daughter-in-law went suddenly serious again, the way she had been before they finished paying for the house. That thought brought them back to square one, it meant they would have to go on saving for the old woman, her husband's mother, whom the two of them never mentioned to each other or to anyone outside.

She lived at the far end of the garden with an accumulation of old brooms, old chicken crates, and the shadows of buildings. Her home was a low shed, from which she seldom emerged. Just getting meals in to her was a long complicated business. She wouldn't admit anyone to her lair, not even her son. She was afraid of being murdered, so she said.

When the daughter-in-law thought of embarking on a new course of savings, she first said a few words to her husband to sound him out: why, for instance, wouldn't they send the old woman to St Vincent's Convent, where the Sisters took care of feeble-minded old women like her? The son said neither yes nor no. He was busy with something else at the moment, those sounds in his ears that never stopped. What with thinking about that abominable whistling and listening to it, he'd convinced himself that it would prevent him from sleeping. And true enough, instead of falling asleep, he'd listen to his whistling, drummings and hummings – a new torture that kept him busy day and night. He had all those noises inside him.

Little by little, though, his anxiety wore itself out, and there wasn't enough left to keep him busy all by itself. So then he and his wife started going back to the market at Saint-Ouen. Everyone said it was the cheapest for miles around. They'd leave home in the morning, and it took them all day, because of all the figures they added up and the discussions they'd have about the prices of things and the money they might have saved by buying one thing rather than another... Back home at about eleven that night, they'd be seized again by the fear of being murdered. That fear hit them regularly, especially the wife. He was more concerned with the sounds in his ears, he'd cling to them desperately at that hour when the street was perfectly still. "I'll never be able to sleep!" he'd repeat to himself out loud to increase his terror. "You can't imagine!"

But she never tried to understand what he meant, or to imagine why this buzzing in his ears should trouble him so. "You hear me when I speak, don't you?" she'd ask him.

"Yes," he'd say.

"Well, then you're all right!... And it would make more sense to start thinking about your mother, who's been costing us a fortune what with prices going up ever day... And the stink in that shack of hers!..."

The cleaning woman came in for three hours a week to do the washing, she was the only visitor they had had for years. She also helped Madame Henrouille to make her bed. Every time they had turned the mattress in the last ten years, Madame Henrouille, wanting it to be repeated all over the neighbourhood, had told the cleaning woman in the loudest voice she could manage: "We never keep money in the house!" Just as a precaution, to discourage thieves and prospective murderers.

Before going up to their room together, they would close all the doors and windows with great care, each checking up on the other. Then they'd go out in the garden to make sure the mother-in-law's lamp was still burning. A sign she was still alive. She consumed quantities of oil. She never put her lamp out. She, too, was afraid of murderers and afraid of her son and daughter-in-law. In all the twenty years she'd been living there she had never opened her windows summer or winter and never let her lamp go out.

Her son kept his mother's money, a small pension. He took care of it. They left her meals outside the door. They kept her money. It worked fine that way. But she complained about the arrangement, and that wasn't all; she complained about everything. She'd shout through the door at anybody who approached her shack. The daughter-in-law would try to pacify her: "It's not our fault if you're getting old. All old people get the same pains…"

"Old my arse! You slattern! You scum! It's you that's killing me with your filthy lies!"

She denied her age ferociously. And through her door she battled irreconcilably against the evils of the whole world. She rejected the fatalities and compromises of the life outside as a base imposture. She refused all contact with such things, she wouldn't hear of them. "It's all a pack of lies!" she'd scream. "You made it up!"

She defended herself bitterly against everything that happened outside her hovel and rejected all temptation to compromise or be reconciled. She was sure that if she opened the door hostile forces would burst in, grab her, and finish her off once and for all.

"They're sly nowadays!" she would scream. "They have eyes all around their heads and mouths all the way down to their arseholes and then some, all to tell lies with… It's them all over…"

She had the gift of the gab, she had picked it up as a girl, peddling bric-a-brac at the Temple Market with her mother… She harked back to the days when the common people hadn't yet learnt to listen to themselves growing old.

"If you won't give me my money I'm going out to work!" she'd shout at her daughter-in-law. "Hear, you slut? I'm going out to work, I want to work!"

"But grandmother, you're not strong enough!"

"Oh! I'm not strong enough! Try and get in here and you'll see if I'm not strong enough!"

So one more time they left her barricaded in her shack. But they were dead set on my seeing the old woman; that's what I'd come for. It took some doing before she let us in. To tell the truth, I couldn't quite see what they wanted of me. It was the concierge, Bébert's aunt, who had told them what a nice doctor I was, so kind and considerate… They asked me if I couldn't give her some medicine to keep her quiet… But what they (especially the daughter-in-law) wanted even more was for me to get the old woman committed once and for all. After we'd knocked for a good half-hour, she suddenly flung the door open, and there she was in front of me with her watery, red-rimmed eyes… But there was a look in those eyes that danced merrily over her grey, shrunken cheeks; it caught your attention and made you forget the rest;

it gave you a feeling in spite of yourself of lightness and pleasure, a feeling of youth that you tried instinctively to hold on to.

That bright look lit up everything in the darkness around her with a youthful joy, a frail but pure delight that we no longer have at our command. Her voice, which cracked when she screamed, gave her words a cheery ring when she consented to talk like other people, it made her phrases and sentences hop, skip and jump as brightly as you please, the way people were able to do with their voices and the things around them in the days when not being able to sing or tell a story properly was looked upon as stupid, shameful and sick.

Age had covered her, like a sturdy old tree, with smiling branches.

Grandma Henrouille was merry; discontented and filthy, but merry. The destitution in which she had lived for more than twenty years had not marked her soul. Her dread, on the contrary, was the outside world, as though cold, horror and death could come to her only from that direction and not from within. She evidently feared nothing from within, she seemed absolutely sure of her mind, as of something undeniable, acknowledged and certified, once and for all.

And to think that I had been chasing mine halfway around the world!

They called the old woman "mad" – that's easy to say. She hadn't set foot outside her den more than three times in the last twelve years, and that's all there was to it! She may have had her reasons... She was afraid of losing something... She wasn't going to tell them to people like us, people who were no longer inspired by life.

Her daughter-in-law brought up her commitment project again. "What do you say, Doctor? Don't you think she's mad?... We can't get her to go out any more!... It would do her good to get out now and then!... Oh yes, grandmother, it would do you good!... Don't say it wouldn't... It would do you good!... I assure you." The old woman shook her head. She shut herself in, stubborn and savage, when that kind of pressure was put on her...

"She won't let us take care of her... She'd rather relieve herself in the corners... It's cold in her shack, and there's no fire... We really can't let her go on like this... Don't you agree, Doctor, that we can't?..."

I pretended not to understand. Henrouille had stayed home beside the stove; he preferred not to know exactly what his wife and mother and I were cooking up...

The old woman flew off the handle again.

"Give me back everything that's mine and I'll go away!... I have money to live on!... And that's the last you'll ever hear of me!..."

"Money to live on! But grandmother! You can't expect to live on your three thousand a year!... The cost of living has gone up since the last time you went out!... You tell her, Doctor, wouldn't it be better for her to go and live with the Sisters like we told her?... The Sisters are good and kind..."

But the thought of the Sisters gave her the creeps.

"The Sisters!... The Sisters!..." she rebelled. "I've never stayed with any Sisters!... Why not send me to live with the priest while you're at it!... If I haven't got enough money, as you say, I'll go to work!..."

"Work, grandmother? Where? Oh, Doctor, would you listen to her! Work at her age! She'll soon be eighty! It's madness, Doctor. Who'd want her? Why, you're insane, grandmother!..."

"Insane! Nobody! Nowhere!... Aren't you somewhere?... You lump of shit, you!..."

"Listen to her, Doctor! She's raving and insulting me! How can you expect us to keep her here?"

The old woman turned to confront me, the new peril.

"How does he know if I'm crazy or not? Is he inside my head? Is he inside yours? He'd have to be to know!... Beat it, both of you!... Get out of my home!... The way you keep at me you're meaner than six months of winter!... Go and examine my son instead of standing there jabbering in the henbane! He needs a doctor a sight more than I do! Not a tooth left in his head, and they were perfect when I was taking care of him! Go on, beat it, get out, the both of you!" And she slammed the door in our faces.

From behind her lamp she watched us retreating across the yard. When we'd reached the other side, when we were far enough away, she started sniggering again. She'd given a good account of herself.

When we got back from that disagreeable incursion, Henrouille was still standing by the stove, with his back to us. His wife went on pestering me with questions, all aimed in the same direction... She had a dark, sly little face. Her elbows hugged her body when she spoke. She never gestured. She was determined that this medical consultation shouldn't be wasted, she wanted it to serve some purpose... The cost of living was going up all the time... Her mother-in-law's pension wasn't enough any more... They were getting old themselves after all... They couldn't go on for ever living in fear that the old woman would die without proper care... that she'd set the house on fire... in her fleas and filth... instead of going to a perfectly good institution, where she'd be taken care of...

Since I put on an air of agreeing with them, they were both as affable as could be... they promised to sing my praises in the neighbourhood... if only I'd help them... take pity on them... rid them of the old woman... who was miserable herself, living in the conditions she brought on herself with her obstinacy...

"We could even rent her little house," suggested the husband, who had suddenly woken up... He'd made a faux pas, saying that in front of me. His wife stepped on his foot under the table. He didn't understand why.

While they were wrangling, I thought about the thousand francs I could pocket just by making out a certificate of commitment. They seemed to want it badly... Bébert's aunt had probably told them all about me and assured them that I was the most down-at-heel doctor in all Rancy... and would do anything they asked... They'd never have expected Frolichon to do a thing like that! He was virtuous!

I was deep in these reflections when the old woman burst into the room where we were plotting. She must have suspected something. What a spectacle! She had bunched her ragged skirts over her belly, and there she was, all tucked up, screaming at us and at me in particular. She'd come in from the far end of the garden for that express purpose.

"Blackguard!" she yelled at me point-blank. "You can go home! Didn't I tell you to beat it! You won't gain anything by hanging around!... I'm not going to the nuthouse!... Nor to the Sisters either!... Do your damnedest, lie your head off!... You won't get me, you bought and paid-for pimp!... They'll go before I do, the thieves, robbing an old woman!... And you, too, you rotter, you'll end up in jail, I'm telling you, and it won't be long!"

I was certainly out of luck. For once I'd had a chance of making a thousand francs at one stroke! I took to my heels.

When I was out in the street, she leant over the little peristyle to shout after me in the darkness. "Scoundrel!... Scoundrel!" she shrieked. And the echo came back. The rain was coming down. I ran from lamp-post to lamp-post as far as the urinal on the Place des Fêtes. The first available shelter.

* * *

In that public convenience, at hip height, I found Bébert. He too had gone there for shelter. He had seen me running out of the Henrouille house. "So that's where you've been," he said. "Now you'll have to go up and see the people on the fifth floor of our house – it's for their daughter..." The girl he was referring to, I knew her well... wide hips, beautiful thighs, long and silky... There was something tender yet wilful about her, and in her movements the precise grace that you often find in women who are sexually fit. She had consulted me several times about her pains in the abdomen. At twenty-five, after her third abortion, she was having complications. Her family called it anaemia.

You should have seen her, so solidly built and with a taste for coitus unusual in females. Discreet in her ways, modest in dress and speech. Not the least bit hysterical. But well-endowed, well-fed, well-balanced, a champion in her line. An athlete of pleasure. No harm in that. She only went with married men. And only with connoisseurs, men capable of recognizing and appreciating nature's triumphs, who won't settle for some vicious little slut. No, her soft skin, her sweet smile, her way of walking, and the nobly mobile fulness of her hips earned her the heartfelt, well-merited enthusiasm of certain office managers who knew their stuff.

Unfortunately these office managers couldn't divorce their wives on her account. On the contrary, she helped them to stay happily married. So every time she found herself three months gone, it never failed, she went to the midwife. When you're a hot number and you haven't got a sucker handy, life is no bed of roses.

Her mother opened the door by a crack, as cautiously as if she'd been expecting a murderer. She spoke in whispers, but they were so loud, so intense, she might just as well have been cursing.

"Oh, Doctor, what have I done to deserve such a daughter! Oh, Doctor, you won't breathe a word to anyone in the neighbourhood, will you?... I trust you!" She went on and on, airing her fears and spluttering about what the neighbours might think. She was having an attack of knuckleheaded anxiety. Those attacks last a long time.

She gave me time to get used to the dim light in the hallway, the smell of leeks in the soup, the wallpaper with its idiotic leaves and flowers, and her strangled voice. Finally, amid bumblings and exclamations, we reached her daughter's bedside. She lay prostrate, her mind wandering. I'd have like to examine her, but she was losing so much blood, there was such a gooey mess I couldn't see anything in her vagina. Blood clots. A glug-glug between her legs like in the decapitated colonel's neck in the war. All I could do was put back the big wad of cotton and pull up the blanket.

The mother was looking at nothing and listening to nothing but herself. "It'll kill me, Doctor! I'll die of shame!" I made no attempt to dissuade her. I didn't know what to do. We could see the father pacing back and forth in the little dining room next door. Apparently he hadn't finished composing his attitude for the occasion. Maybe he was waiting for things to come to a head before selecting a posture. He was in a kind of limbo. People live from one play to the next. In between, before the curtain goes up, they don't quite know what the plot will be or what part will be right for them, they stand there at a loss, waiting to see what will happen, their instincts folded up like an umbrella, squirming, incoherent, reduced to themselves – that is, to nothing. Cows without a train.

But the mother had the leading part as intermediary between her daughter and me. The stage could cave in, she didn't give a damn, she was happy and convinced of her goodness and beauty.

I couldn't count on anyone but myself to break this sickening spell.

I risked suggesting that the girl should be sent straight to the hospital for an emergency operation.

A big mistake! I'd given her the cue for her finest speech, the one she'd been waiting for.

"Oh God, the disgrace! The hospital! Oh, Doctor! The disgrace of it! All we needed! The last straw!"

There was nothing I could say. I sat down and listened to the mother thrashing about more tumultuously than ever, entangled in her tragic absurdities. Too much humiliation, too much misery culminate in total inertia. The world is too much for you to bear. You give up. While she invoked and provoked Heaven and Hell, thundering disaster, I looked down in defeat and, looking, saw a small puddle of blood forming under the girl's bed, from which a thin trickle oozed slowly along the wall towards the door. A drop fell regularly from the bed springs. Drip drip. The towels between her legs were soaked red. I managed to ask, very timidly, whether the whole placenta had been ejected. The girl's hands, pale and bluish at the tips, hung down on either side of the bed. It was the mother again who answered my question with a flood of disgusting jeremiads. I should have reacted, but I hadn't the strength.

I myself had been so obsessed by my bad luck for so long, I was sleeping so badly that I was just drifting, I didn't care whether one thing happened rather than another. My only thought was that if I had to listen to this screeching mother I was better off sitting than standing. It doesn't take much to please you once you're thoroughly resigned. And anyway, where would I have found the fortitude to interrupt this wild woman who "didn't know how she was going to save the family's honour". What a part! And how she ranted! After every abortion, I knew from experience, she let loose in the same way, trying, it goes without saying, to outdo herself each time! How long it went on she alone could decide! Today she seemed determined to increase the effect.

She, it occurred to me, must have been beautiful herself, as luscious as you please in her day; but more voluble, I'm pretty sure, more wasteful of energy, more demonstrative than her daughter, whose concentrated intimacy had been one of nature's truly admirable achievements. Those things haven't been studied as closely as they deserve. The mother sensed her daughter's animal superiority and instinctively condemned it out of hand, the unforgettable depth of her fucking, her way of coming like a continent.

In any case she was delighted with the theatrical aspect of the disaster. Her mournful tremolos monopolized the attention of our little group, as thanks to her we floundered in chorus. And there was no hope of getting her out of there. I ought to have tried, though. To do something... It was my duty, as they say. But I was too comfortable sitting and too uncomfortable standing.

Their place was a bit more cheerful than the Henrouilles', just as ugly but more comfortable. Cosy. Not sinister like the Henrouilles'. Just plain ugly.

Dazed with fatigue, I glanced around the room. Little things without value that had always been in the family, especially the mantelpiece cover with its little pink velvet bells that you can't buy any more, and the porcelain Neapolitan figurine, and the sewing table with the bevelled mirror, a present no doubt from an aunt in the provinces who had had two of them. I said nothing to the mother about the puddle of blood I saw forming under the bed or the drops that kept falling regularly, she'd have screeched even louder and wouldn't have listened to me any more. She was never going to stop complaining and venting her indignation. She was dedicated.

Just as well to keep still and look out of the window as the grey velvet of evening took hold of the avenue, house by house, first the smallest, then the others; in the end the big ones are taken, too, and the people moving about in between, more and more faint, vague and blurred, hesitating as they pass from pavement to pavement before vanishing into the darkness.

Further away, far beyond the fortifications, strings and rows of lights scattered through the night like tacks to hang forgetfulness over the city, and other little lights, red and green, boats and more boats, a whole flotilla come from all directions, tremulously waiting for the great gates of night to open behind the Tower.*

If that mother had taken a moment to breathe, or better still, if there had been a long moment of silence, I might have dropped everything and tried to forget that it was necessary to live. But she kept at me.

"Couldn't I give her an enema, Doctor? What do you think?" I didn't say yes or no, but once again, since she gave me a chance to speak, I advised immediate removal to the hospital. The only response was more yelping – sharper, more resolute, more strident than ever. There was nothing to be done.

I made slowly and quietly for the door.

The shadows now lay between us and the bed.

I could scarcely see the girl's hands resting on the sheet, because the two pallors were so much alike.

I went back and felt her pulse, which was weaker, more furtive than before. Her breath came in gasps. I could still hear her blood dripping on the floor like a watch ticking more and more slowly, more and more faintly. I couldn't do a thing. The mother went ahead of me to the door.

"Especially, Doctor," she said in a paroxysm of terror, "promise you won't say a word to anyone!" She implored me. "Give me your word!"

I promised anything she wanted. I held out my hand. She gave me twenty francs. She closed the door behind me, little by little.

Downstairs Bébert's aunt was waiting for me with her most solemn expression. "Is it bad?" she enquired. I realized that she'd been waiting for half an hour to collect her usual commission of two francs. To make sure I wouldn't get away. "And how about the Henrouilles? Everything all right?" she asked. She was hoping to collect a cut for them too. "They didn't pay me," I replied. Which was true. Her prepared smile turned to a pout. She didn't believe me.

"It's really too bad, Doctor, if you can't get people to pay you! How can you expect people to respect you?... Nowadays people pay right away or not at all!" That too was true. I beat it. I had put my beans on to cook before leaving. Now was the time, at nightfall, to go and buy my milk. During the day people smiled to see me with my bottle. Naturally. No maid.

Winter dragged on, stretching out over months and months. We were always deep in rain and mist; they were at the bottom of everything.

There were plenty of patients, but not many who were willing and able to pay. Medicine is a thankless profession. When you get paid by the rich, you feel like a flunkey; by the poor, like a thief. How can you take a fee from people who can't afford to eat or go to the movies? Especially when they're at their last gasp. It's not easy. You let it ride. You get soft-hearted. And your ship goes down.

When the quarterly rent came due in January, I first sold my sideboard; I told the neighbourhood people I needed the space, because I was planning to give physical-culture classes in my dining room. I wonder if anyone believed me. In February, to pay my taxes, I sold my bicycle and the phonograph Molly had given me as a going-away present. It played 'No More Worries'. The tune is still running through my head. It's all I've got left. As for the records, Bézin had them in his shop for a long time, and then in the end he sold them.

To make myself sound even richer, I told people I was going to buy a car as soon as the warm weather set in and in preparation I wanted to take in a little cash. I suppose I just didn't have the gall to practise medicine seriously. When I was being escorted to the door after giving the family plenty of advice and handing them my prescription, I'd start talking about everything under the sun just to postpone the moment of payment a little longer. I was no good at playing the prostitute. Most of my patients were so wretchedly poor and foul-smelling, so disagreeable too, that I always wondered where they would ever find the twenty francs owing to me and whether they mightn't murder me to get them back. And yet I needed those twenty francs badly. Shameful! I still blush to think of it.

"Fees!…" as my colleagues persisted in saying. It didn't stick in their craw. As if the word made it perfectly natural and there were no need to explain… "Shameful!" I couldn't help thinking, you can't get around it. Everything can be explained, I know that. But that doesn't change the fact that the man who takes a hundred sous from the poor and the wicked will be a louse to his dying day. Ever since then, in fact, I've been sure of being as slimy a customer as anyone else. It's not that I've committed orgies and follies with their hundred sous and their ten francs. Certainly not! The landlord took most of it, but that's no excuse either. I wish it were, but it isn't. The landlord is shittier than shit, but that's another story.

What with eating my heart out and walking in the icy showers of the season, I was beginning to look tubercular myself. Naturally. That's what happens when you have to forgo practically every pleasure. Now and then I'd buy a few eggs, but my diet consisted mainly of beans and lentils. They take a long time to cook, I'd spend hours in the kitchen watching them boil after my visiting hours, and since I lived on the second floor I had a fine view of the back court. Back courts are the dungeons of row houses. I had plenty of time to look at my court, and especially to hear it.

That's where the shouts and yells of the twenty houses round about crash and rebound, even the cries of the concierges' little birds, rotting away as they pipe for the spring they will never see in their cages beside the privies, which are all clustered together out at the dark end with their ill-fitting, banging doors. A hundred male and female drunks inhabit those bricks and feed the echoes with their boasting quarrels and muddled, eruptive oaths, especially after lunch on a Saturday. That's the intense moment in family life. Shouts of defiance as the drink pours down. Papa is brandishing a chair, a sight worth seeing, like an axe, and Mama a log like a sabre! Heaven help the weak! It's the kid who suffers. Anyone unable to defend himself or fight back – children, dogs and cats – is flattened against the wall. After the third glass of wine, the black kind, the worst, it's the dog's turn, Papa stamps on his paw. That'll teach him to be hungry at the same time as people. It's good for a laugh when he crawls under the bed, whimpering for all he's worth. That's the signal. Nothing arouses a drunken woman so much as an animal in pain, and bulls aren't always handy. The argument starts up again, vindictive, compulsive, delirious, the wife takes the lead, hurling shrill calls to battle at the male. Then comes the mêlée, the smash-up.

The uproar descends on the court, the echo swirls through the half-darkness. The children yap with horror. They've found out what Mama and Papa have in them! Their yells draw down parental thunders.

I spent whole days waiting for what sometimes happens after these family scenes to happen.

It happened on the third floor, across from my window, in the house on the other side.

I couldn't see a thing, but I heard it clearly.

There's an end to everything. It's not always death, it's often something else and possibly worse, especially when there are children.

That's where those tenants lived, at the level where the shadow begins to pale. If the father and mother were alone on the days when this kind of thing happened, they'd first have a long argument and then there'd be a long silence. The situation was building up. They had a bone to pick with the little girl. They called her. She knew. She started whimpering right away. She knew what she was in for. To judge by her voice, she must have been about ten. It took me quite a few times before I understood what the two of them did to her.

First they tied her up; it took a long time, like getting ready for an operation. That gave them a kick. "You little skunk!" cried the father. "The filthy slut!" went the mother. "We'll teach you!" they'd shout together, and bawl her out for all sorts of things that they probably made up. I think they tied her to the bedposts. Meanwhile the child was squeaking like a mouse in a trap. "That won't help you, you little scum. You've got it coming! Oh yes! You've got it coming!" Then came a volley of oaths, you'd have thought she was cursing at a horse. All steamed up. "Stop talking, Mama," said the little girl gently. "Stop talking, Mama! Hit me, but stop talking!" They gave her a terrible thrashing. I listened to the end to make sure I wasn't mistaken, that this was really happening. I couldn't have eaten my beans with that going on. I couldn't close the window either. I was no good for anything. I was helpless. I just stayed there listening, same as everywhere and always. Still, I believed I gained strength listening to such things, the strength to go further, a strange sort of strength, next time I'd be able to go down even deeper and lower, and listen to other plaints that I hadn't heard before or had had difficulty in understanding, because beyond the plaints we hear, there always seem to be others that we haven't yet heard or understood.

When they had beaten her so much she couldn't howl any more, a little sob continued to come out every time she breathed.

And then I heard the man saying:

"All right, old girl! Step lively! In there!" As happy as a lark.

He said that to the mother, and then the door into the next room would slam behind them. Once she said to him, I heard her: "Oh, Julien, I love you so much, I could eat your shit, even if you made turds this big..."

That was their way of making love, their concierge told me, they'd do it in the kitchen, leaning against the sink. They couldn't do it any other way.

I learnt those things about them little by little in the street. When I met them, the three of them together, there was nothing to attract attention. They'd be out for a walk like a normal family. And now and then I'd see the father outside his shop on the corner of the Boulevard Poincaré, where they sold "shoes for sensitive feet". He was the head salesman.

Most of the time our court had only unrelieved horrors to offer. Especially in the summer, it thundered with threats and echoes and blows, with falling objects and people, and unintelligible insults. The sun never reached the bottom. The walls seemed to be painted with dense blue shadows, especially in the corners. The concierges had their own little privies, clustered like so many beehives. At night when they went out to pee they'd bump into the garbage cans, which would boom like thunder.

Washing, strung from window to window, would be trying to dry.

After dinner, when there were no brutalities under way, what you heard was mostly arguments about the races. But those sporting polemics also ended badly as often as not, with assorted swats and wallops, and behind one of the windows, for one reason or another, someone was always knocked cold in the end.

In the summer everything smelt strong. There was no air left in the court, only smells. The prevailing smell by far is cauliflower. A cauliflower can beat ten toilets, even if they're overflowing. It's a known fact. The ones on the second floor were always overflowing. Madame Cézanne, the concierge at No. 8, would come up with her rattan unplugger. I'd watch her working away, and in the end we got to talking. "If I were you," she advised me, "I'd take care of the pregnant women on the quiet... Some of the women in this neighbourhood really live it up... You'd hardly believe it!... They'd like nothing better than to use your services!... Take it from me! It's better than treating cheap clerks for varicose veins... Besides, they pay cash."

Madame Cézanne had an enormous aristocratic contempt, I don't know where she got it, for anybody who worked...

"The tenants here are never satisfied, you'd think they were in jail, they've got to make trouble for everybody!... One day their toilets are plugged up... Another day they have a gas leak... Or their letters are being opened!... Always making nuisances of themselves... Pests! The other day one of them spat in his rent envelope... Did you ever hear the like?"

Sometimes she'd have to give up trying to unplug a toilet, it was too hard. "I don't know what they put in there, but at least they shouldn't let it dry!... I know them... They always send for me too late... If you ask me, they do it on purpose!... In the place where I used to work, it was so hard they had to melt the pipe!... I can't imagine what those people eat... It's double strength!..."

* * *

You'd have a hard time talking me out of the idea that Robinson wasn't mostly to blame for my trouble starting up again. At first I didn't pay much attention to my spells. I somehow kept dragging myself from one patient to the next, but I'd become even uneasier than before, more and more so, like in New York, and I was beginning to sleep even worse than usual.

In short, meeting Robinson again had given me a shock, and I seemed to be falling sick again.

With the misery painted all over his face, I felt he was bringing back a bad dream that I'd been unable to get rid of all those years. It was driving me nuts.

All of a sudden he turned up. I'd never see the last of him. He must have been looking for me in the neighbourhood, I certainly wasn't looking for him... He was bound to come back again and make me think about his rotten life. Actually everything conspired to make me think of his repulsive substance. Even those people I saw out the window, who didn't look like anything much, just walking in the street, chewing the fat in doorways, rubbing shoulders, made me think of him. I knew what they were after and what they were hiding behind their innocent look. To kill and get killed, that's what they wanted, not all at once of course, but little by little like Robinson, with all the old sorrows they could summon up, all the new miseries and still nameless hatreds, except when they do it with out-and-out war, and then it's quicker.

I didn't even dare go out, for fear of meeting him.

My patients would have to send for me two or three times in a row before I'd make up my mind to visit them. Usually they had called in someone else by the time I got there. My head was a shambles like life itself. I was called to 12 Rue Saint-Vincent, third floor, where I'd been only once before. Actually, they came to get me in a car. I recognized the old man right away, he wiped his feet elaborately on my doormat. A furtive type, grey and stooped, his grandson was sick and he wanted me to hurry.

I remembered his daughter too, another strapping wench, a little faded, but strong and silent, she always came home to her parents for her abortions. They never scolded her, but all the same they wished she'd finally get married, all the more so since she already had a little boy of two staying with the grandparents.

For no reason at all this child was always getting sick, and when he was sick, the grandfather, the grandmother and the mother wept together. What made them weep all the more was that he had no legitimate father. It's at times like this that families are most afflicted by irregular situations. The grandparents were convinced, without quite admitting it to themselves, that illegitimate children are more delicate and prone to illness than others.

The father – at any rate the putative father – had cleared out for good. They had talked marriage to him so much that he couldn't take it any more. He'd beat it so fast that if he was still running he must have been far away by then. Nobody could understand why he had run out on her like that, least of all the girl herself, because he had really enjoyed fucking her.

Now that the fickle lover had gone, all three of them contemplated the child and blubbered. She had given herself to that man "body and soul", as they say. In her opinion that explained everything, it was bound to happen. The baby had come out of her body and left her thighs all wrinkled. The mind is satisfied with phrases, but not the body, the body is more fastidious, it wants muscles. A body always tells the truth, that's why it's usually depressing and disgusting to look at. It's true that I've rarely known a single childbirth to demolish so much youth. All that mother had left, in a manner of speaking, was feelings and a soul. No one wanted her any more.

Before that clandestine birth, the family had lived in the Filles-du-Calvaire quarter; they had lived there for years. If they exiled themselves to Rancy, it wasn't for the pleasure of it, it was to hide, to get themselves forgotten, to disappear.

As soon as it became impossible to conceal the pregnancy from the neighbours, they decided to leave their Paris neighbourhood to avoid all comments. A removal for honour's sake.

In Rancy they didn't need the respect of their neighbours. In the first place no one knew them in Rancy, and in the second place the municipal government was known all over France for its abominable politics; not to mince words, they were anarchists, thugs. In that kind of community public opinion is of no account.

The family had punished themselves voluntarily, cutting themselves off from all their old relations and old friends. Their tragedy was complete. Nothing more to lose, so they said. Declassed. When you're determined to lose your name, you go among the common people.

They found no fault with anyone. They merely tried to discover by feeble little acts of rebellion what Destiny could have had in mind the day it had played them such a dirty trick.

Living in Rancy gave the daughter only one consolation, but that was a big one. Now she could talk freely to all and sundry about "her new responsibilities". In deserting her, her lover had awakened a passion for heroism and singularity that had lain dormant in her nature. As soon as she felt sure that she would never for the rest of her days lead the same sort of life as most women of her class and background, and that she would always be in a position to invoke the tragedy of a life ruined by her very first love, she adjusted with alacrity to the great disaster that had befallen her and, all things considered, the ravages of fate became tragically welcome. She glorified in her unmarried-mother role.

In the dining room, as her father and I went in, the economy lighting stopped at half-tints and faces appeared only as pale spots, blobs of flesh mumbling words that hung suspended in a penumbra heavy with the smell of old pepper that all heirloom furniture exudes.

The child, lying swaddled on his back in the middle of the table, let me palpate him. To begin with, I pressed the wall of his abdomen, ever so carefully and slowly, from the navel to the testicles, and then still very gravely I auscultated him.

His heartbeat was like a kitten's, sharp and nervous. Then the child had enough of my exploring fingers and began to yell as children can do incredibly at that age. That was too much. Since Robinson's return I'd been feeling very funny in body and mind, and the little innocent's screams made an abominable impression on me. What screams! Heavens above, what screams! I was at the end of my rope.

Another idea must have helped to provoke my idiotic behaviour. In my exasperation, I couldn't stop myself from blurting out all the rancour and disgust I had been holding in for too long.

"Hey," I said to that little bellower, "don't be in such a hurry, you little fool, you'll have plenty of time for bellowing! Never fear, you little idiot, there'll be time to spare. Save your strength. There'll be enough misery to melt your eyes and your head and everything else if you don't watch out!"

The grandmother gave a start:

"What are you saying, Doctor?"

"There will be plenty!" I repeated simply.

"What?" she asked in horror. "Plenty of what?"

"You have to understand!" I said. "You have to understand. You're always having things explained to you! That's the whole trouble! Try to understand! Make an effort!"

"What will be left?... What's he saying?" they all three asked one another. The daughter "with the responsibilities" made a strange face and started emitting prodigiously long screams. Here was a marvellous occasion for a fit, and she wasn't going to miss it. She meant business. She kicked! She choked! She squinted horribly! I'd done it all right! You should have seen her! "Mama, he's mad!" She bellowed so hard she almost choked. "The doctor's gone mad! Mama, take my baby away from him!" She was saving her child.

I shall never know why, she began in her agitation to take on a Basque accent. "He's saying such awful things! *Mameng!*... He's insane!..."

They snatched the baby out of my hands as if they were rescuing him from the flames. The grandfather, who had been so deferential only a short while ago, unhooked an enormous mahogany thermometer from the wall, it was as big as a club... And he pursued me at a distance to the door, which he slammed violently behind me with a big kick.

Naturally they took advantage of the incident not to pay for my call...

When I found myself back on the street, I wasn't exactly pleased with what had happened. Not so much because of my reputation, which couldn't have been worse in the neighbourhood than people had already made it with no help from me, as because of Robinson, from whom I had hoped to deliver myself with my outburst of frankness, to find the strength never to see him again by deliberately creating a scandal, by stirring up this hideous scene with myself.

Here's what I figured: by my little experiment I'd see how much of a stink it's possible to kick up at one throw! The trouble with scenes and tantrums is that you're never finished, you never know how far you'll be forced to go in your frankness... What people are still hiding from you... And what they'll show you some day... if you live long enough... if you go far enough into the heart of their cock-and-bull stories... The whole business would have to be started all over again.

I too, just then, was in a hurry to hide. I started for home by way of the Impasse Gibet, then I took the Rue Valentines. It was quite a distance. Time to change my mind. I headed for the lights. On the Place Transitoire I met Péridon the lamp-lighter. We exchanged a few innocent remarks. "On your way to the movies, Doctor?" he asked me. That gave me the idea. A good one, I thought.

The bus gets you there quicker than the Métro. After that shameful incident I'd have been glad to leave Rancy for good if I'd been able to.

When you stay too long in the same place, things and people go to pot on you, they rot and start stinking for your special benefit.

* * *

In spite of everything it was just as well that I went back to Rancy next day, because of Bébert, who fell sick just then. My colleague Frolichon had just gone off on his vacation. Bébert's aunt hesitated, then she asked me to take care of her nephew after all, probably because I charged less than any other doctor she knew.

It was after Easter. The weather was looking up. The first south winds were passing over Rancy, the ones that blew all the soot from the factories down on our window panes.

Bébert was sick for weeks and weeks. I went to see him twice a day. The neighbourhood people would wait for me outside the lodge, pretending to be just passing by, and on the doorsteps of their houses. It gave them something to do. People would come a long way to find out if he was better or worse. The sunshine has too many things to pass through; it never gives the street anything better than an autumn light full of regrets and clouds.

People gave me lots of advice in connection with Bébert. The fact is, the whole neighbourhood took an interest in his case. Some thought well, others poorly, of my intelligence. When I went into the lodge, a critical, rather hostile and most of all crushingly stupid silence set in. The lodge was always full of the aunt's cronies, it smelt strongly of petticoats and rabbit piss. Each had her own favourite doctor, who was cleverer and more learned than any other. I presented only one advantage, but one that's hard to forgive, I charged hardly anything. A gratis doctor is bad for the reputation of a patient and his family, however poor they may be.

Bébert wasn't delirious yet, he had just lost all desire to move. He was losing weight by the day. A bit of yellow, flabby flesh still clung to his bones and quivered from top to bottom every time his heart beat. He'd got so thin in over a month of illness that his heart seemed to be all over his body. He'd look at me with a lucid smile when I came to see him. Sweetly he ran a temperature of thirty-nine, then of forty, and there he lay with a pensive look on his face for days and weeks.

After a while Bébert's aunt had shut up and stopped bothering us. She had said everything she knew. That took the wind out of her sails, so she'd go and blubber in one corner of her lodge after another. Grief had come to her when she ran out of words, and she didn't seem to know what to do with it. She'd try to wipe it off with her handkerchief, but it came back in her throat all mixed with tears, and she'd start all over again. She'd get it all over her and manage to be a little dirtier than usual. That would upset her and she'd cry out: "Oh dear! Oh dear!" That was all. She had cried so much she was exhausted, her arms would fall to her sides, and she'd stand there in front of me, absolutely bewildered.

But then after all she'd go back into her grief and give herself a jolt and start sobbing again. These comings and goings in her misery went on for weeks. I couldn't dispel the feeling that this illness would end badly. It was a kind of malignant typhoid that baffled all my efforts: baths, serum, dry diet, vaccines... Nothing helped. I did everything I could think of... all in vain. Bébert was going, being carried away irresistibly, smiling all the while. He was high up, balanced on top of his fever, and I was down below making a fool of myself. Naturally a lot of people were advising the aunt, pressing her to dismiss me in no uncertain terms and call in another, more imposing and more experienced doctor in a hurry.

The incident of the girl "with the responsibilities" had gone the rounds and been liberally commented on. The whole neighbourhood was gargling with it.

But since the other doctors, once informed of the nature of Bébert's illness, showed no eagerness to take the case, I was kept on in the end. As long as Bébert had fallen to my lot, my colleagues figured, I might as well see him through.

All I could do was go to the bistro now and then and phone various doctors in the Paris hospitals, with whom I was more or less acquainted, and ask those sage, widely respected luminaries what they would do if faced with a case of typhoid like the one that was driving me mad. They all gave me excellent, ineffectual advice, but all the same it pleased me to hear them making an effort free of charge for the benefit of the unknown child I had taken under my wing. After a while you start taking pleasure in the merest trifles, the small consolations life deigns to give us.

While I was busying myself with such subtleties, Bébert's aunt was collapsing on every chair and staircase in the house; she'd emerge from her daze only to eat. But she never missed a meal. Her neighbours wouldn't have let her forget. They watched over her. They stuffed her between sobs. "It'll keep your strength up!" they declared. She even began to put on weight.

Speaking of Brussels sprouts, the smell rose to orgiastic heights at the peak of Bébert's illness. It was the season. Everyone was making her presents of Brussels sprouts, ready-cooked and steaming hot. "It's true," she was glad to admit, "they give me strength!... And besides, they make me urinate!"

227

Before bedtime, because of the doorbell, so as to sleep lightly and hear the very first ring, she'd fill herself full of coffee. That way the tenants wouldn't wake Bébert by ringing two or three times. Passing by the house in the evening, I'd go in to see if maybe it was all over. She'd speculate out loud: "Don't you think it may have been the rum and camomile tea he drank at the fruit store the day of the bicycle race that made him sick?" That idea had been plaguing her from the start. The stupid fool.

"Camomile!" Bébert murmured faintly, an echo submerged in his fever. Why try to tell her different? I'd go through the two or three professional motions she expected of me, and then I'd go and face the night, not at all pleased with myself, because, like my mother, I could never feel entirely innocent of any horrible thing that happened.

About the seventeenth day I decided that it might not be a bad idea to drop in at the Joseph Bioduret Institute* and ask them what they thought about a typhoid case of this kind. Maybe they'd give me a bit of advice or recommend some vaccine. That way, if Bébert were to die, I'd have done everything possible, tried everything, however out of the way, and then perhaps I wouldn't feel eternally guilty. At about eleven o'clock one morning I arrived at the Institute near La Villette at the other end of Paris. First they sent me wandering through laboratories and more laboratories, looking for a man of science. There wasn't a soul in those laboratories at that hour, neither laymen nor men of science, only various objects in wild disorder, the gutted bodies of small animals, cigarette butts, chipped gas jets, cases and jars with mice suffocating inside them, retorts, bladders, broken stools, books, dust and more cigarette butts, which, mingled with the effluvia of the urinals, made up the prevailing smell. Since I was early, I thought, while I was at it, I'd go and visit the tomb of that great scientist, Joseph Bioduret, which was right there in the basement of the Institute, in with the gold and marble. A bourgeois-Byzantine fantasy in the best of taste. The collection was taken on your way out of the crypt, and the guard was grumbling because someone had slipped him a Belgian coin. In the last half-century the shining example of this Bioduret had led any number of young people to choose the scientific career. And the scientific career had produced as many failures as the Conservatory. After a certain number of years of failure, scientists turn out to be pretty much alike. In the mass graves of the great debacle a Doctor of

Medicine is as good as a "Prix de Rome". The only difference is that they don't take the bus at exactly the same time of day. That's all.

I had to wait quite a long while in the garden of the Institute, a combination of prison yard and city square, with flowers carefully lined up along malignantly decorated walls.

At last some underlings began to turn up. Several, dragging their feet listlessly, were carrying provisions from the nearby market in large shopping bags. Then, in small, unshaven, whispering groups, the men of science came sauntering through the gate, more slowly and diffidently than their humble assistants, and dispersed down different corridors, scraping the paint off the walls as they passed. Grey-haired, umbrella-carrying schoolboys, stupefied by the pedantic routine and intensely revolting experiments, riveted by starvation wages for their whole adult lives to these little microbe kitchens, there to spend interminable days warming up mixtures of vegetable scrapings, asphyxiated guinea pigs and other nondescript rubbish.

They themselves, when all's said and done, were nothing but monstrous old rodents in overcoats. Glory, in our time, smiles only on the rich, men of science or not. All those plebeians of research had to keep them going was their fear of losing their niches in this heated, illustrious and compartmented rubbish bin. What meant most to them was the title of official scientist, thanks to which the pharmacists of the city still trusted them more or less to analyse, for the most niggardly pay incidentally, their customers' urine and sputum. The slimy wages of science.

Arriving in his compartment, the methodical researcher would spend a few moments gazing ritually at the bilious, decaying viscera of last week's rabbit, which was on classic and permanent display in one corner of the room, a putrid font. When the smell became really intolerable, another rabbit would be sacrificed, but not before, because of the fanatic thrift of Professor Jaunisset,* who was then Secretary General of the Institute.

Thanks to this thrift, some of the rotting animals gave rise to unbelievable by-products and derivatives. It's all a matter of habit. Some of the more practised laboratory technicians had become so accustomed to the smell of putrefaction that they would have had no objection to cooking in an operational coffin. These modest auxiliaries of exalted scientific research sometimes outdid the thrift of Professor

229

Jaunisset himself, taking advantage of the Bunsen burners to cook themselves countless ragouts and other still riskier concoctions.

After absently examining the viscera of the ritual guinea pig and rabbit, the men of science slowly proceeded to the second act of their scientific daily life, the smoking of cigarettes. Thus they strove to neutralize the ambient stench and their boredom with tobacco smoke, and managed, from butt to butt, to get through the day. At five o'clock they put the various putrefactions back in the ramshackle incubator cabinet to keep them warm. Octave, the technician, hid the string beans he had cooked behind a newspaper to get them safely past the concierge. Subterfuges. Taking them home to Gargan all ready for supper. The man of science, his master, was still writing a little something, diffidently, doubtingly, in one corner of his laboratory book, with a view to a forthcoming and utterly pointless paper that he would feel obliged to present before long to some infinitely impartial and disinterested academy, and that would serve to justify his presence at the Institute and the meagre advantages it conferred.

A true man of science takes at least twenty years on an average to make the great discovery – that is, to convince himself that one man's lunacy is not necessarily another man's delight, and that all of us here below are bored with the bees in our neighbours' bonnets.

The coldest, most rational scientific madness is also the most intolerable. But when a man has acquired a certain ability to subsist, even rather scantily, in a certain niche with the help of a few grimaces, he must either keep at it or resign himself to dying the death of a guinea pig. Habits are acquired more quickly than courage, especially the habit of filling one's stomach.

I ransacked the Institute for Parapine, I'd come all the way from Rancy to see him, so naturally I kept on looking. It was no small order. I made several false starts, hesitating a long while before choosing among so many corridors and doors.

Parapine was an old bachelor, he never ate lunch and I doubt if he ate dinner more than two or three times a week, but then enormously, with the frenzy of the Russian student, all of whose outlandish ways he had retained.

Parapine was an undisputed eminence in his special field. He knew all there was to know about typhoid in animals as well as human beings. His reputation went back twenty years to the day when certain

German authors claimed to have isolated the Eberthella bacteria in the vaginal excreta of an eighteen-month-old girl, so creating an enormous stir in the Halls of Truth. Only too delighted to take up the challenge in the name of the National Institute, Parapine had outdone those Teutonic braggarts by breeding the same microbes, now in its pure form, in the sperm of a seventy-two-year-old invalid. Instantly famous, he managed to hold the limelight for the rest of his life by publishing a few unreadable columns in various medical journals. This he had done without difficulty ever since his day of audacity and good fortune.

The serious scientific public trusted him implicitly and consequently had no need to read him.

If those people were to start getting critical, no further progress would be possible. They would spend a whole year over every page.

When I came to the door of his cell, Serge Parapine was spitting steady streams into all four corners of his laboratory, with a grimace of such disgust that it made you wonder. Parapine shaved now and then, but he always had enough hair on his cheeks to make him look like an escaped convict. He was always shivering or at least he seemed to be, though he never removed his overcoat, which presented a large assortment of spots and still more of dandruff that he would scatter far and wide with little flicks of his fingernails, at the same time bringing his always oscillating forelock back into position over his red-and-green nose.

In the course of my laboratory work in medical school, Parapine had given me some instruction in the use of the microscope and had shown me unquestionable kindness on several occasions. I hoped he had not forgotten me completely since those remote days and that he might consent to give me valuable advice in connection with Bébert, with whose case I was really obsessed.

Undoubtedly, I was much more interested in preventing Bébert from dying than if he had been an adult. You never mind very much when an adult passes on. If nothing else, you say to yourself, it's one less stinker on earth, but with a child you can never be so sure. There's always the future.

Once acquainted with my difficulties, Parapine asked nothing better than to help me and to orient my perilous therapy, but unfortunately, in twenty years, he had learnt so many, so diverse, and so often contradictory things about typhoid that by that time he was just about

231

unable to formulate any clear and definite opinion concerning that most commonplace ailment and its treatment.

"First of all, my dear colleague," he said. "Do you believe in serums? Huh? Give me your honest opinion... And vaccines?... What do you really think?... Some of the best minds today have no use for vaccines at all... That of course is a bold way of thinking... Yes, indeed... but even so... in the last analysis... Don't you think there's a certain truth in that sort of negativism?... What do you think?"

The sentences issued from his mouth in terrifying bursts, amid avalanches of tremendous Rs.

While he was struggling like a lion against other enraged and desperate hypotheses, Jaunisset, the illustrious Secretary General of the Institute, who was still alive at the time, passed our windows frowning superciliously.

At the sight of him, Parapine turned if possible paler than ever and abruptly changed the subject in his haste to show me all the disgust aroused in him by the mere daily sight of this Jaunisset, who was glorified by just about everyone else. In half a second he disposed of Jaunisset as a crook and maniac of the first water, accusing him of enough monstrous, unprecedented and secret crimes to fill a penal colony for a century.

I was powerless to stop Parapine from giving me hundreds of hate-ridden pointers about the clownish trade of medical research, which he was obliged to practise if he wanted to eat. This hatred of his was more precise, more scientific you might say, than the hatreds emanating from other men occupying similar positions in offices or shops.

He spoke in a very loud voice, and I was amazed at his outspokenness. His technician was listening to us. He too had finished his bit of cookery and was still moving about, for form's sake, between incubator and test tubes, but he had grown so accustomed to listening to Parapine pouring out his more or less daily maledictions that he had come to regard these tirades, however extravagant, as absolutely academic and meaningless. Certain little private experiments that this technician pursued with great seriousness in one of the laboratory's incubators struck him, on the other hand, as prodigiously and deliciously instructive compared to Parapine's outpourings. Parapine's rages in no way tempered his enthusiasm. Before leaving, he tenderly, scrupulously shut the door of the incubator on his private microbes, as if it were a tabernacle.

"Did you notice that technician of mine, my dear colleague?" said Parapine as soon as he had gone. "Did you notice that old fool? He's been cleaning up my rubbish for almost thirty years, and all he ever hears people talk about is science, but that most abundantly and sincerely... Well, far from being disgusted, he, unlike everyone else in the whole place, has come to believe in it! After handling my cultures for years, he thinks they're marvellous! He dotes on them... The most meaningless of my buffooneries enchants him! Isn't it the same with all religions? Hasn't the priest stopped believing in God years ago, while his sacristan goes on believing... Heart and soul! It's sickening!... That old fool carries absurdity to the point of aping the dress and goatee of the illustrious Joseph Bioduret! Did you notice?... Between you and me, the great Bioduret wasn't so very different from my technician except for his worldwide reputation and the intensity of his manias... That giant of experimental science with his mania for rinsing his bottles with care and observing the hatching-out of moths in incredible detail has always struck me as monstrously vulgar... Take away his prodigious pettiness, his housekeeping and, I ask you, what's left to admire about the great Bioduret? All right, I'll tell you: the hateful look of a malignant, cantankerous concierge. That's all. In his twenty years of membership in the Academy he had ample time to exhibit his vile, contemptible character... nearly everyone hated him, he quarrelled... and what quarrels!... with just about everyone in sight. The man was an ingenious megalomaniac... Nothing more."

Parapine was slowly getting ready to leave. I helped him put a scarf around his neck and a sort of mantilla over his eternal dandruff. Then he remembered that I'd come to see him about something precise and urgent. "My word!" he said. "Here I've been boring you with my own little problems and forgetting your patient! Forgive me, colleague, and let's get back to our subject! But after all, what can I tell you that you don't already know? Among so many shaky theories and questionable experiments, reason, in the last analysis, forbids us to choose! Just do your best, colleague! Since you have to do something, do your best! Personally, I must tell you in confidence that typhoidal infections have come to disgust me beyond all measure! Beyond all imagination! When I came to typhoid as a young man, there were only a few of us prospecting the field, we were able to help one another... to advance one another's reputations... While now, what can I say? They pour

233

in from Lapland, my friend! From Peru! More and more every day! Specialists are turning up from all over the world! In Japan they roll off the assembly line! In less than a few years I've seen the world become a hotbed of universal and preposterous publications on this same hackneyed subject. To maintain and more or less defend my position I've resigned myself to writing and rewriting my same little article from congress to congress, from journal to journal, throwing in a few subtle, innocuous and quite tangential modifications towards the end of each season... Believe me, colleague, typhoid in our time is as botched and bungled as the mandolin or banjo. It's maddening! Everyone wants to play some little tune in his own way. I may as well admit it, I haven't the strength to drive myself any more; what I'm looking for, to see me through to the end of my days, is some quiet little backwater of research that will bring me neither enemies nor disciples, but only the mediocre celebrity without jealousy which I sorely need and with which I shall gladly content myself. Among other absurdities, I have considered studying the comparative influence of central heating on haemorrhoids in northern and southern countries. What do you think of it? The role of hygiene? Of diet? That kind of thing is fashionable nowadays. Such a study, properly handled and ingeniously dragged out, is sure to be favourably received by the Academy, since the majority of its members are old men to whom these problems of heating and haemorrhoids can hardly be indifferent. Look what they've done for cancer, which concerns them so closely!... Don't you think the Academy might vote me one of its hygiene awards? Why not? Ten thousand francs? Not bad... Enough for a trip to Venice... Yes, my young friend, I was in Venice once as a young man... Oh yes! You can starve there just as well as anywhere else... But you breathe a sumptuous aroma of death that's not easy to forget..."

By then we were out on the street, but had to hurry back for his galoshes, which he'd forgotten. That delayed us. Then we rushed through the streets, but he didn't tell me where we were going.

Making our way down the long Rue de Vaugirard strewn with vegetables and other encumbrances, we approached a square surrounded by chestnut trees and policemen, and we slipped into the back room of a small café, where Parapine sat down at a curtained window.

"Too late!" he moaned. "They've gone!"

"Who?"

"The little girls from the Lycée... Some of them are charming... I know their legs by heart. I ask for nothing more at the end of my day... Let's get out of here! I'll see them another day..."

And we left each other as good friends.

* * *

I'd have been glad if I'd never have had to go back to Rancy. Since the morning when I'd left it, I had almost forgotten my daily cares; they were so deeply encrusted in Rancy that they didn't follow me. Perhaps they'd have died of neglect like Bébert if I hadn't gone back. They were suburban cares. Even so, on the Rue Bonaparte, reflection came back to me, the gloomy kind, though it's a street that would normally be pleasing to a passer-by. Few streets are so smiling and so gracious. But on approaching the Seine, I began to worry. I strolled aimlessly about. I couldn't make up my mind to cross the river. Everybody can't be Caesar! Across the bridge, on the opposite bank, my troubles would begin. I reserved the right to wait on the Left Bank until nightfall. At least, I said to myself, I'd be saving a few hours of sunlight.

The water lapped against the bank where the fishermen were, and I sat down to watch them. I really was in no hurry at all, no more than they were. I'd pretty well come to the point – the age, you might say – when a man knows what he's losing with every hour that passes. But he hasn't yet built up the wisdom to pull up sharp on the road of time, and anyway, even if you did stop you wouldn't know what to do without the frenzy for going forward that has possessed you and won your admiration ever since you were young. Even now you're not as pleased with your youth as you used to be, but you don't yet dare admit in public that youth may be nothing more than a hurry to grow old.

In the whole of your absurd past you discover so much that's absurd, so much deceit and credulity, that it might be a good idea to stop being young this minute, to wait for youth to break away from you and pass you by, to watch it going away, receding in the distance, to see all its vanity, run your hand through the empty space it has left behind, take a last look at it, and then start moving, make sure your youth has really gone, and then calmly, all by yourself, cross to the other side of time to see what people and things really look like.

The fishermen on the bank weren't catching anything. They didn't even seem to care very much whether they caught any fish or not. The fish must have known them. They were all just pretending. A fine last glow of sunshine maintained a little warmth around us and sent reflections sprinkled with blue and gold leaping over the water. A cool wind came over to us through the big trees on the far side, a smiling wind blowing through thousands of leaves in gentle gusts. A nice place to be. For two whole hours we stayed there, catching nothing, doing nothing. Then the Seine darkened and the corner of the bridge turned red with the sunset. The people on the bank above had forgotten us as we sat there between the embankment and the water.

The night came out from under the arches and climbed along the chateau,* taking the façade and, one by one, the sunset-flaming windows.

Again there was nothing I could do but go away.

The booksellers on the bank were shutting up their boxes. "Are you coming?" a woman shouted over the parapet to her fisherman husband beside me, who was putting away his tackle, camp chair and worms. He grumbled and the other fishermen grumbled after him, and up we went, all of us grumbling, to the river bank. I spoke to his wife, just to be saying something pleasant before night took everything away. Then and there she wanted to sell me a book. She had forgotten, so she said, to put it away in her box. "I'll let you have it at half-price, for next to nothing…" A little old Montaigne, absolutely authentic, for one franc. For that little money I was glad to give her pleasure. I took her Montaigne.

Under the bridge the water looked dark and heavy. I had lost all desire to go anywhere. On the boulevards I drank a *café crème* and opened the book she had sold me. I just chanced to open it at a letter Montaigne once wrote to his wife after a son of theirs had died. That passage caught my interest at once, probably because it made me think of Bébert. Roughly, this is what Montaigne says to his wife: "Ah, my dear wife, don't eat your heart out! Cheer up!… Everything will turn out all right!… It always does… And by the way, rummaging through some old papers belonging to a friend of mine, I've just found a letter that Plutarch wrote to his wife under circumstances very similar to ours… That letter, dear wife, struck me as so apt, so much to the point, that I'm sending it on to you!… A splendid letter! Well, I won't keep you waiting any longer, just let me know if it doesn't do a good job of healing your sorrow!... Dear wife! I'm sending you Plutarch's fine letter! It's really something! I'm sure you'll like it!... Pay close attention, dear wife! Read it carefully! Show it to your friends! And read it over! Now my mind is at rest... I'm sure it will set you up!... Your devoted husband, Michel." Now that, I said to myself, is a good job. How happy his wife must have been to have a husband like her Michel, who never let anything get him down. Well, it's their business. Maybe we go wrong when we try to judge other people's hearts. Maybe they felt real grief? Period grief?

But as far as Bébert was concerned, my day hadn't been so good. I had no luck with Bébert, dead or alive. It seemed to me that there was nothing for him on earth, not even in Montaigne. Maybe, come to think of it, it's the same for everybody, nothingness. No getting around it, I'd left Rancy that morning, and now I had to go back, empty-handed. I had absolutely nothing to offer him, or his aunt either.

A short stroll around the Place Blanche before going back.

I see people all up and down the Rue Lepic, even more than usual. So I go up too, to see what's going on. The crowd was outside a butcher shop. You had to squeeze into the circle to see what was going on. It was a pig, an enormous pig. He was groaning in the middle of the circle, like a man who's being pestered, but louder. The people were tormenting him, they never stopped. They'd twist his ears just to hear him squeal. He'd tug at his rope and try to escape and squirm and wriggle his feet in the air. Other people would poke him and prod him, and he'd bellow even louder with the pain. Everybody was laughing more and more.

The pig couldn't manage to hide in the little straw he had, it would fly away when he grunted and puffed into it. He couldn't escape from those people, and he knew it. He kept urinating the whole time, but that didn't help him either. Any more than his grunting and bellowing. No hope. Everybody was laughing. The butcher back in his shop was exchanging signs and jokes with his customers and gesticulating with a big knife.

He was happy too. He had bought the pig and tied it up as an advertisement. He couldn't have had a better time at his daughter's wedding.

More people kept arriving outside the shop to watch the pig crumpling in big pink folds after every attempt to escape. But that wasn't enough yet. They put a vicious little dog on the pig's back and incited it to jump and snap at the fat bulging flesh. They were having such a wonderful time that they blocked off the street completely. The police had to come and disperse the crowd.

When you get to the top of the Caulaincourt Bridge* at about that hour, you see the first lights of Rancy beyond the great lake of night that covers the cemetery. To get there you have to go all the way around. It's a long way. You need so much time and so many steps to get around the cemetery to the fortifications, you get the feeling you're going round the night itself.

When you get to the Porte and the toll station, you pass the stinking old office where the little green official is rotting away. The dogs of the Zone are at their barking posts. In spite of everything you see some flowers in the light of a gas lamp, they belong to the flower woman who is always there, waiting for the dead who pass from day to day, from hour to hour. The cemetery, another cemetery next to it, and then the Boulevard de la Révolte with all its street lamps, heading straight into the night. You just turn left and follow it. That was my street. There was really no fear of meeting anyone. Even so, I'd have liked to be somewhere else and far away. I'd also have liked to be wearing slippers so no one would hear me going in. Yet I was in no way to blame if Bébert wasn't getting better. I had done all I could. I had nothing to reproach myself with. It wasn't my fault if such cases are hopeless. I passed his door – without being noticed, I thought. Upstairs I didn't open the blinds, I looked through the slits to see if there were still people talking outside Bébert's. Some visitors were still coming out of the house, but they didn't look the same as yesterday's visitors. A neighbourhood cleaning woman I knew was crying as she left. "It looks bad." I said to myself. "He's certainly no better... Maybe he's dead? If one of them is in tears already!..." The day was over.

I racked my brains: was I really not at all to blame? It was cold and still in my place. Like a little night just for me, in a corner of the big one.

Now and then the sound of steps rose up to me and the echo came in louder and louder, droning, then dying away... Silence. I looked out again to see if anything was happening across the way. Nothing was happening except inside me, still asking myself the same questions.

I was so tired from walking and finding nothing that I finally fell asleep in my coffin, my private night.

* * *

Why kid ourselves, people have nothing to say to one another, they all talk about their own troubles and nothing else. Each man for himself, the earth for us all. They try to unload their unhappiness on someone else when making love, they do their damnedest, but it doesn't work, they keep it all, and then they start all over again, trying to find a place for it. "You're pretty, Mademoiselle," they say. And life takes hold of them again until the next time, and then they try the same little gimmick. "You're very pretty, Mademoiselle!..."

And in between they boast that they've succeeded in getting rid of their unhappiness, but everyone knows it's not true and they've simply kept it all to themselves. Since at that little game you get uglier and more repulsive as you grow older, you can't hope to hide your unhappiness, your bankruptcy, any longer. In the end your features are marked with that hideous grimace that takes twenty, thirty years or more to climb from your belly to your face. That's all a man is good for, that and no more, a grimace that he takes a whole lifetime to compose. The grimace a man would need to express his true soul without losing any of it is so heavy and complicated that he doesn't always succeed in completing it.

Just then I was busy improving my soul with bills I couldn't pay, insignificant as they were, my impossible rent, my overcoat that was much too light for the season and the grocer who laughed up his sleeve every time he saw me counting my pennies, hesitating to buy a piece of Brie and blushing when the price of grapes started going up. And then my patients, who were never satisfied. Bébert's death hadn't done me any good in the neighbourhood. His aunt didn't hold it against me, though. No, I can't say she behaved badly under the circumstances. It was more from the Henrouilles in their private house that trouble and worry suddenly began raining down on me.

One day Grandma Henrouille walked out of her shack without so much as a by-your-leave, ignoring her son and daughter-in-law, and decided entirely on her own to come and see me. She had a head on her shoulders. After that she came many times and asked me if I really thought she was insane. Questioning me like that gave the old woman something to do. She'd wait in my so-called waiting room. Three chairs and a little three-legged table.

When I got back that evening, I found her in the waiting room, comforting Bébert's aunt by telling her all about the relatives she herself had lost along the way before arriving at her age, nieces by the dozen, an uncle here and there, a father way back in the middle of the last century, any number of aunts and her daughters, who had passed on here and there, she couldn't quite remember where or how. Her own daughters had become so vague in her mind that she had to imagine them more or less, but still with deep sorrow when she spoke of them to someone else. By that time her own children were even less than memories. Around her aged loins she gathered a whole nation of humble ancient deaths, shades long silent, imperceptible sorrows, which, when I arrived, she was trying with considerable difficulty to rouse to a little life for the consolation of Bébert's aunt.

And then Robinson dropped in to see me. Introductions all around. Friends.

In fact it was then, as I later recollected, that Robinson got into the habit of meeting Grandma Henrouille in my waiting room. They'd sit and talk. Bébert was to be buried the next day. "Are you coming?" the aunt asked everyone she met. "I'd appreciate it if you came…"

"Of course I'll come," said the old woman. "It's nice to have people around one at such times." There was no keeping her in her hovel. She'd turned into a gadabout.

"Oh, I'm so glad you're coming!" the aunt thanked her. "And you, Monsieur, will you come too?" she asked Robinson.

"Oh, I'm afraid of funerals, Madame, you mustn't take it amiss," he said to get out of it.

And then each of them talked a lot, all about his own affairs, almost violently, even Grandma Henrouille joined in. They all talked much too loudly, like in a nuthouse.

So I went in and took the old woman to my consulting room next door.

I didn't have much to say to her. But she had questions for me. I promised not to go through with the commitment proceedings. We went back to the waiting room and sat down with Robinson and the aunt. We all talked for a good hour about the sad case of Bébert. Everyone in the neighbourhood agreed that I had knocked myself out trying to save him, that you can't fight fate, and that all in all, to everybody's surprise, I had behaved pretty well. When Grandma Henrouille heard the child's age,

240

seven, she seemed to feel better, that relieved her in a way. The death of so young a child was just an accident in her opinion, not the same as a normal death, which might have given her food for thought.

Robinson started again telling us about the acids that burned his stomach and lungs, suffocated him, and made him spit black phlegm. But Grandma Henrouille didn't spit anything at all, and she didn't work with acids, so what Robinson had to say on the subject was of no interest to her. She had only come to size me up. She looked at me out of the corner of her lively bluish eyes as I spoke, and none of the latent tension between us escaped Robinson. It was dark in my waiting room, the big building on the other side of the street was paling before giving in to the night. After that there were only our voices between us, and all that voices seem on the point of saying but never say.

Once alone with Robinson, I tried to make it plain that I had no desire whatever to see him any more, but that didn't stop him from coming back towards the end of the month, and almost every evening after that. It's true that his lungs were in bad shape.

"Monsieur Robinson has been asking for you again..." said my concierge, who liked him. "He doesn't seem to be getting better, does he?..." she added. "He was coughing again when he came..." She knew it annoyed me to hear her talk about him.

It's true that he coughed. "It's hopeless," he himself said. "I'll never get over it..."

"Wait till summer! A little patience! You'll see... It'll just stop..."

You know, the kind of thing you say in such cases. I couldn't cure him as long as he was working with acids... But I tried to cheer him up all the same.

"It'll just stop?" he'd say. "You give me a pain!... Do you think it's funny breathing like I do?... I'd like to see you with a thing like this in your chest... This kind of thing in the chest gets a man down... Take it from me..."

"You're depressed, you're having a bad time, but when you feel better... Even a little better, you'll see..."

"A little better? I'll feel a little better when I'm eight feet under! I should have got killed in the war, then I'd feel really better! For you there was some sense in coming back! You can't complain!"

People cling to their rotten memories, to all their misfortunes, and you can't pry them loose. These things keep them busy. They avenge themselves for the injustice of the present by smearing the future inside them with shit. They're cowards deep down, and just. That's their nature.

I stopped answering him. That made him angry.

"You see? You think the same as I do!"

To get him to leave me in peace, I made him up some cough syrup. It seems his neighbours complained that he coughed all the time and it kept them awake. While I was filling the bottle, he went on wondering out loud where he could have caught this stubborn cough. He also wanted me to give him injections of gold salts.

"If the injections killed me, I wouldn't mind, you know!"

Naturally I wouldn't have anything to do with this heroic therapy. Mostly I wanted him to go away.

Just seeing him hanging around, I'd lost all my pleasure in life. It was already hard enough for me to keep from drifting with the current of my own failure, from giving in to my impulse to close up shop once and for all. Twenty times a day I'd say to myself: "What for?" So listening to his lamentations in addition was really too much.

"You have no spirit, Robinson!" I finally told him… "You ought to get married, maybe that would give you some zest for life…" If he'd got himself a wife, it would have taken him off my hands. The suggestion made him angry, and he left me. He didn't care for my advice, especially that kind. On the marriage issue he didn't even answer me. And I must admit, that was a pretty silly piece of advice.

One Sunday when I wasn't on duty we went out together. We settled on the terrace of a café at the corner of the Boulevard Magnanime and ordered a small cassis and a *diabolo*.* We didn't talk much, we didn't have much to say to each other. What good are words anyway when you know the score? You'll only come to blows. There aren't many buses on Sunday. Sitting on the terrace, it's almost a pleasure to see the boulevard so neat and clean, all rested like the people. The phonograph was playing in the café behind us.

"Hear that?" says Robinson. "His phonograph is playing American tunes. I recognize them. It's the ones they played at Molly's place in Detroit…"

In the two years he'd spent there he hadn't gone very far into American life. Still, he'd been touched in a way by their brand of music, where they too try to get away from the weight of routine and the crushing misery of having to do the same thing every day. While it's playing, they can shuffle about for a while with a life that has no meaning. Bears on both sides of the ocean.

He was thinking so hard about all that that he had hardly touched his cassis. A little dust was rising on all sides. Some children with big bellies and smudged faces were wandering around under the plane trees; they too were attracted by the phonograph records. Nobody can really resist music. You don't know what to do with your heart, you're glad to give it away. At the bottom of all music you have to hear the tune without notes, made just for us, the tune of death.

A few shops still have the obstinacy to open on Sunday: the slipper woman comes out of her shop and parades her pounds of varicose veins from display to display, stopping to chat here and there.

At the news-stand the morning papers hang yellow and limp, an enormous artichoke of news going bad. A dog takes a quick piss on them, the news woman is dozing.

An empty bus is heading back to its depot in a hurry. Thoughts have their Sundays too, come to think of it. We're even more dazed than usual. Here we sit, empty, bewildered, contented. We have nothing to talk about, because nothing happens to us any more, we're too poor, maybe life is sick of us. Why not?

"Can't you think of something I could do to get out of this job that's killing me?"

He had surfaced from his reflections.

"I want to get out of that racket, see? I'm sick of working like a dog... I want to roam around too... Wouldn't you know somebody who needs a chauffeur by any chance?... You know so many people."

Sunday ideas, gentleman's ideas had come over him. I was afraid to argue, to insinuate that no one would entrust his motor car to a man with the mug of an impoverished murderer, that with or without a uniform he would always look too peculiar.

"You're not very encouraging, are you?" he said. "So you think I'll never get out of the ditch?... You think there's not even any point in my trying?... In America you said I was too slow... In Africa I couldn't stand the heat... Here I'm not intelligent enough... But that's all a lot of hooey, you can't tell me different! If only I had plenty of money!... Everybody would think I was adorable... here... there... and everywhere... Even in America... Ain't it the truth? What about

243

you?… All we need is to own an apartment house with half a dozen tenants paying good stiff rents…"

"You've got something there," I said.

He had come to that major conclusion all by himself, and he couldn't get over it. Then he gave me a funny look, as if he had suddenly discovered something all too nauseating about me.

"Come to think of it," he said, "you've got the good end. You sell your hokum to sick people, and you haven't a thing to worry about… Nobody riding you… You come and go when you like, you're free… You're nice enough on the surface but what a bastard underneath!…"

"You're being unfair, Robinson!"

"All right, then find me something!"

He was determined to pass on his acid job to someone else…

We started off through the little side streets. In the late afternoon you'd think Rancy was a village. The big house door is ajar. The yard is empty, and so is the dog's kennel. One afternoon like this, years ago, the peasants left their homes, driven away by the city creeping out from Paris. There are only one or two taverns left from those days, unsaleable, crumbling away, overgrown by limp wisteria vines, hanging down over walls reddened with posters. The grating hung between two gargoyles has rusted till it can't rust any more. All this past – nobody touches it any more. It's dying without any help from anyone. The present tenants are much too tired when they come home at night to do anything about the outside of their house. They just pile up, family by family, in what's left of the common rooms and drink. The ceiling is marked with rings of smoke left by the wobbly hanging lamps of those days. The whole neighbourhood is shaken uncomplaining by the continuous rumble of the new factory. Moss-covered tiles crash down on high, humpbacked cobblestones, the kind you'll find today only in Versailles and in venerable prisons.

Robinson accompanied me to the little town park hemmed in by warehouses, where all the strays in the neighbourhood come and misbehave on the mangy lawn, on the senile boule ground, around the incomplete Venus, and on the sand pile for playing and peeing.

The conversation started up again, about this and that. "My trouble is that drink doesn't agree with me." A bee in his bonnet. "When I drink, I get cramps, it's unbearable. Worse!" And by throwing up several times he demonstrated that even our little cassis that afternoon hadn't agreed with him… "See what I mean?"

He left me outside his door. "The Palace of Draughts," he said and vanished. I thought I wouldn't be seeing him for a while.

That night it looked as if my business might be picking up.

I got two urgent calls from the same house, the one over the police station. On Sunday evening everybody lets go, their sighs, their feelings, their impatience. Human dignity goes on a holiday spree. After a whole day of alcoholic freedom the slaves are stirring, there's no holding them, they sniff, they snort, they clank their chains.

In the house over the police station two tragedies were in progress at once. On the second floor a man was dying of cancer, on the fourth there had been a miscarriage that was more than the midwife could handle. That worthy matron was giving everybody absurd advice, all the while washing out napkins and more napkins. Between two douches she'd slip away to give the cancer patient downstairs an injection, at ten francs an ampoule, of camphorated oil if you please. A good day for her.

Every family in the house had spent the day in dressing gowns and shirtsleeves, lending a helping hand, well reinforced by highly seasoned food. Every stairway and corridor smelt of garlic and other more mysterious odours. The dogs were having a fine time, running up as far as the sixth floor. The concierge was determined to keep abreast of events. You couldn't move without running into her. She only drank white wine, because red wine gives you discharges.

The elephantine midwife in her smock was directing both tragedies, on the first floor and on the third, bounding, sweating, delighted, vindictive. My arrival infuriated her. She had been holding her audience since morning, she was the star.

I tried my best to spare her feelings, to make myself as inconspicuous as possible, to approve of everything (when in reality everything she had done was preposterous), but my being there and every word I said went against her grain. It was to be expected. A supervised midwife is as friendly as a hangnail. You can't think of any place to put her where she'll do as little harm as possible. From the kitchen the family overflowed through the apartment and out onto the staircase, where they mingled with the relatives of other tenants. And what multitudes of relatives! Fat ones and thin ones gathered in somnolent clusters

245

under the hanging lamps. It was getting late, and more were arriving from the provinces, where people go to bed earlier than in Paris. They were fed up. Everything I said to the relatives of those tragedies, upstairs and down, was taken amiss.

The death agony on the first floor didn't last long. Which had its pros and cons. Just as his last gasp was coming up, Dr Omanon, his regular doctor, drops in to see if his patient is dead, and starts bawling me out or pretty near for being there at the bedside. I explained to Omanon that I was on municipal Sunday duty, so my presence was perfectly natural. Whereupon, with dignity, I climbed up to the third floor.

Upstairs the woman's arse was still bleeding. It wouldn't have surprised me if she too had taken it into her head to die without bothering to wait. A minute to give her an injection, and down again to Omanon's patient. It was definitely all over. Omanon had just left. But the bastard had pocketed my twenty francs. Another dud. After that I was determined to stick to my post beside the miscarriage. So I ran upstairs as fast as I could.

Her vulva was still bleeding, and I explained a few things to the family. Naturally the midwife disagreed. It almost looked as if she was being paid for contradicting me. But there I was, I had to do something, who cared if she was happy or not? So let's not fool around! This case was worth at least a hundred francs to me if I handled it right and stuck to my guns! A man of science keeps his temper, damn it! It's hard work standing up to the remarks and questions steeped in white wine that hurtle implacably through the air over your innocent head – it's no joke. Belching and sighing, the family impart their opinions. The midwife is waiting for me to make a fool of myself, clear out, and leave her the hundred francs. But the midwife has another thing coming! What about my rent? Who's going to pay it? This labour had been twiddling its thumbs since this morning, I won't deny it. She's bleeding, I won't deny that either, but it's not coming out, I've got to hold my ground!

Now that the cancer patient has died downstairs, his deathbed audience has crept up here. As long as you're losing a night's sleep, as long as you're making the sacrifice, you may as well take in all the entertainment the neighbourhood has to offer. The downstairs family comes up to see if maybe this tragedy is going to end as badly as theirs. Two deaths in the same building, on the same night, would be a sensation to last them a lifetime! Nothing less! Everybody's dogs can be heard tinkling their bells as they scamper up and down the stairs. They come in too. More people from far away pour in, whispering. Some teenage girls have suddenly discovered the "facts of life", as their mothers call it and now, in the face of tragedy, they're putting on a tenderly knowing air. The female consoling instinct. A cousin has been watching them since morning. He's fascinated, he hasn't stirred from their side. They come as a revelation in his fatigue. Everyone's clothes are askew. The cousin will marry one of them, he wishes he could see their legs while he's about it, to make it easier to choose.

The fetus refuses to come out, the passage must be dry, it won't slip through, nothing but blood. This would have been her sixth child. Where's the husband? I ask for him.

The husband had to be found if I was going to send his wife to the hospital. A relative had suggested the hospital. She had a family at home and wanted to get to bed on account of the children. But when the word hospital was brought up, they couldn't come to an agreement. Some were in favour, others were dead set against, because of what people would say. They wouldn't even hear of it. Some very hard words were exchanged between relatives, words that would never be forgotten and would go down in the family. The midwife despised everybody. What preoccupied me was finding the husband, I wanted to consult him, so we could make up our minds one way or the other. He finally emerges from one of the groups, even more undecided than everyone else. But the decision was up to the husband. Hospital? No hospital? What does he think? He doesn't know. He wants to look. So he looks. I show him his wife's hole, the blood clots, the glug-glug, his whole wife seeping away. She's groaning like a big dog that's been run over by a car. He doesn't know what he wants. Somebody gives him a glass of white wine to pick him up. He sits down.

He still can't make up his mind. He's a man who works hard all day. Everyone knows him in the market and especially at the freight station, where he totes sacks, and no small loads, big heavy things, been toting them for the last fifteen years. He's famous. His trousers are vast and shapeless, likewise his jacket. They don't fall off, but he doesn't seem to be very much attached to his trousers and jacket. He only seems attached to the earth and standing upright on it, with his two feet spread wide as if the earth would start quaking under him any minute. His name is Pierre.

We're all waiting. "Well, Pierre," they all ask him. "What do you think?" Pierre scratches himself and goes and sits down right next to his wife's face, as if he had trouble recognizing this woman who was always bringing so much pain into the world, and then he sheds a kind of tear and stands up. We all fire the same question. I make out a certificate of admission for the hospital. "Try and think, Pierre!" everyone pleads. He tries but makes a sign meaning it won't come. He gets up and staggers out to the kitchen, taking his glass with him. Why wait any longer? That husband's indecision, everybody realized, was likely to go on all night. We might as well be going.

For me it was a hundred francs lost, that's all! But one way or another I'd have had trouble with the midwife… that was sure. On the other hand, I wasn't going to risk any surgical manipulations in front of all those people and in my state of fatigue! "Too bad!" I said to myself. "No use hanging around! Maybe next time… May as well resign myself! Let Nature take her course, the bitch!"

I'd hardly reached the stairs when they all called me back and he came running after me. "Hey, Doctor!" he yelled. "Don't go!"

"What do you want me to do?" I asked him.

"Wait, I'll go with you, Doctor!… Please, Doctor!…"

"All right," I said, and let him go down with me. I was in the lead, so I stopped at the first floor to say goodbye to the dead cancer patient's family. The husband went into the room with me, and we came right out again. In the street he fell into step with me. There was a nip in the air. We came across a puppy who was practising how to answer the other dogs of the Zone with long howls. He was very persistent and very plaintive. He had already mastered the art. He'd soon be a real dog.

"Hey, that's Egg Yolk," says the husband, delighted at recognizing him and at changing the subject… "The daughters of the laundryman on the Rue des Gonesses brought him up on a baby's bottle, Egg Yolk… Do you know the laundryman's daughters?"

"Yes," I said.

As we were walking he told me about ways they had of feeding puppies on milk without its costing too much. But behind those words he was looking all the while for an idea in connection with his wife.

A bar was open near the Porte.

"Coming in, Doctor? I'll buy you a drink…"

I wasn't going to hurt his feelings. "All right!" I said. "Two coffees." I took the opportunity to talk about his wife. My talking about her turned him dead serious, but I still couldn't get him to make up his mind. There was a big bouquet on the bar counter. For the owner Martrodin's birthday. "A present from the children!" he himself told us. So we had a vermouth with him and drank his health. The Law on Drunkenness and a framed school diploma were hanging on the wall. When he saw that, the husband absolutely insisted on the owner reciting the Subprefectures of the Loir-et-Cher Department, because he had learnt them in school and still knew them. Then he claimed it wasn't the owner's name on the diploma but somebody else's; that made the owner sore, so the husband came back and sat with me. He was in the throes of doubt again, so tormented that he didn't even see me leave…

I never saw that husband again. Never. I was badly disappointed by the events of that Sunday and tired besides.

I had hardly gone a hundred metres in the street when I saw Robinson coming my way, loaded down with all kinds of boards, big ones and little ones. I recognized him in spite of the darkness. He was embarrassed at seeing me and tried to get away, but I stopped him.

"Why aren't you in bed?" I asked him.

"Not so loud!…" he said. "I've come from the building site!…"

"And what are you doing with all that wood? Building what?… A coffin?… You stole it, I bet?…"

"No. A rabbit hutch…"

"You raising rabbits now?"

"No, it's for the Henrouilles…"

"The Henrouilles? They've got rabbits?"

"Yes, three. They're going to keep them in the little yard, you know, where the old woman lives…"

"You're building them a rabbit hutch at this time of night? Funny time to…"

"It was his wife's idea…"

"Some idea!… What's she going to do with rabbits? Sell them? Make top hats?"

"You'll have to ask her when you see her. As long as she comes across with the hundred francs, I…"

This business with the rabbit hutch struck me as very odd, at that time of night. I kept at him.

He changed the subject.

"But what were you doing at their house?" I asked. "You didn't know the Henrouilles."

"The old lady took me to see them... that day I met her in your office... The old woman is a big talker once she gets started... You can't imagine... No getting away from her... So now I'm sort of pals with her and with them too... Some people like me, you know!..."

"You never said a word about all that... But since you see them, maybe you know if they're managing to get the old woman committed..."

"No, not from what they tell me..."

He wasn't enjoying this conversation at all, I could feel that, he didn't know how to get rid of me. But the more slippery he got the more I wanted to know...

"Life is hard, you've got to admit it... the things a man has to do..." he said vaguely. But I brought him back to the subject. I was determined to make him come clean...

"They say the Henrouilles have more money than meets the eye... What do you think, now that you've been seeing them?"

"Yes, maybe they have, but one thing is sure, they want to get rid of the old woman!"

Robinson had never been much good at deception.

"It's because of the cost of living, you know, that keeps going up, that's why they want to get rid of her. They told me one time that you refused to certify her... Is that true?"

Then quickly, without insisting on an answer, he asked me which way I was going.

"Been visiting a patient?"

I told him something about my adventures with the husband I had just lost by the wayside. That gave him a good laugh, but it also made him cough.

His cough doubled him up so bad I could hardly see him though he was right next to me. All I could vaguely make out was his hands, folded in front of his mouth like a big livid flower, trembling in the night. He couldn't stop. "It's the draughts!" he finally said when the cough had spent itself and we'd come to the door of his house.

"One thing my pad is full of is draughts! And fleas! Have you got fleas in your place too?…"

I had. "Naturally," I told him. "I bring them home from my patients."

"Sick people smell of piss, don't they?" he said.

"Yes, and sweat…"

"All the same," he said slowly after thinking it over. "I'd have liked to be a hospital orderly."

"Why?"

"I'll tell you… because people with nothing wrong with them, you can't get around it, are frightening… Especially since the war… I know what they're thinking… They don't always know it themselves… but I know what they're thinking… As long as they're up, they think about killing you… but when they're sick, no two ways, they're not as frightening… You've got to be prepared for anything, I tell you, as long as they're up. Don't you see it that way?"

"Yes!" I had to say.

"Is that why you decided to become a doctor?" he asked.

Thinking it over, I realized that maybe Robinson was right. But then he had another of his coughing fits.

"Your feet are wet," I said. "You'll come down with pleurisy wandering around like this at night… Go home," I advised him. "Go to bed…"

His nerves were on edge from all that coughing.

"I wouldn't be surprised if Grandma Henrouille came down with the flu!" he said, laughing and coughing into my ear.

"What makes you say that?"

"You'll see!…" he said.

"What have they dreamt up now?"

"That's all I can tell you… You'll see…"

"Come on, Robinson, you stinker, tell me. You know I never spill the beans…"

Suddenly he wanted to make a clean breast of it, maybe in part to convince me that he wasn't as resigned and lily-livered as he looked.

"Go on!" I prodded him in a whisper. "You know I never talk…"

That was all the encouragement he needed.

"That's a fact," he admitted. "You know how to keep your mouth shut." And right away he starts to come seriously clean. You wanted it, here it is…

There wasn't a soul around us at that time of night on the Boulevard Coutumance.

"Do you remember," he starts up, "the story about those carrot pedlars?"

Offhand I didn't remember any story about carrot pedlars.

"Come off it," he insists. "You know... You told me the story yourself!..."

"That's right!..." All at once it came back to me. "The brakeman on the Rue des Brumaires?... The one who got his balls blown off while stealing rabbits?"

"Yes, that's it, from the grocer on the Quai d'Argenteuil..."

"Yes!..." I say. "I remember now. So what?" I still didn't see the connection between that ancient incident and Grandma Henrouille.

He came out with it soon enough.

"Don't you see?"

"No," I said... but soon I was afraid to see.

"You're being awfully slow!..."

"It's just that it looks like a nasty business for you to be getting into..." I couldn't help commenting. "You can't be going to murder Grandma Henrouille just to please the daughter-in-law?"

"Of course not. I'm just building the rabbit hutch they asked for... The fireworks are up to them... They'll do the rest... if they want to..."

"How much have they given you for all this?"

"A hundred francs for the wood and two hundred and fifty for my work and a thousand more for the idea... And, you understand... this is only a beginning... a story like that... if properly told... is as good as a pension!... Well, son... now do you see?..."

I saw very well, and I wasn't surprised. It only made me sad, a little sadder than before. Anything you can say to dissuade people in a case like that is bound to be feeble. Has life been kind to them? So why would they take pity on anybody? What for? What are other people to them? Has anybody ever been known to go down to hell to take someone else's place? No. They send other people down, that's all.

The vocation for murder that had suddenly come over Robinson struck me in a way as an improvement over what I'd observed up until then in others, always half-hateful, half-benevolent, always boring with their vagueness, their indirection. I had definitely learnt a thing or two by following Robinson in the night.

But there was a danger: the law. "The law is dangerous," I told him. "If you're caught, you with the state of your health, you'll be sunk... You'll never leave prison alive... It'll kill you!..."

"That's just too bad," he said. "I'm fed up with honest work... I'm getting old... still waiting my turn to have some fun, and when it comes... if it does, with plenty of patience... I'll have been dead and buried long ago... Honest work is for suckers... You know that as well as I do..."

"Maybe... but crime, you know, everybody'd go in for it if there weren't risks... And the police are rough... There's the pros and cons..." We examined the situation.

"I won't say different, but doing my kind of work, in my condition, coughing, not sleeping, doing jobs that no horse would touch... Nothing worse can happen to me now... That's how I feel about it... Nothing..."

I didn't dare tell him that all in all he was right, because he'd have held it up to me later on if his new racket misfired.

To cheer me up he listed a few good reasons why I shouldn't worry about the old woman, first of all because any way you looked at it she hadn't long to live, she was already too old as it was. He would just be arranging for her departure.

All the same it was a very nasty business. The whole thing had been worked out between him and the couple. Seeing as the old woman had taken to leaving her shack, they'd send her to feed the rabbits one evening... The fireworks would be carefully placed... They'd go off full in her face the moment she touched the door... Exactly what happened at the grocer's... The neighbourhood people already thought she was mad, the accident wouldn't come as a surprise to anybody... They'd say they had warned her never to go near the rabbits... And she had disobeyed them... At her age there was certainly no chance of her surviving an explosion like the one they were fixing for her... right square in the puss.

No two ways, that was some story I had told Robinson.

* * *

And the music came back with the carnival, the music you've heard as far back as you remember, ever since you were little, that's always playing somewhere, in some corner of the city, in little country towns, wherever poor people go and sit at the end of the week to figure out what's become of them. "Paradise!" they call it. And music is played for them, sometimes here, sometimes there, from season to season, it tinkles and grinds out the tunes that rich people danced to the year before. It's the mechanical music that floats down from the wooden horses, from the cars that aren't cars any more, from the railways that aren't at all scenic, from the platform under the wrestler who hasn't any muscles and doesn't come from Marseille, from the beardless lady, the magician who's a butter-fingered jerk, the organ that's not made of gold, the shooting gallery with the empty eggs. It's the carnival made to delude the weekend crowd.

We go in and drink the beer with no head on it! But under the cardboard trees the stink of the waiter's breath is real. And the change he gives you has several peculiar coins in it, so peculiar that you go on examining them for weeks and weeks and finally, with considerable difficulty, palm them off on some beggar. What do you expect at a carnival? Gotta have what fun you can between hunger and jail, and take things as they come. No sense complaining, we're sitting down, aren't we? Which ain't to be sneezed at. I saw the same old Gallery of the Nations, the one Lola caught sight of years and years ago on that avenue in the park of Saint-Cloud. You always see things again at carnivals, they revive the joys of past carnivals. Over the years the crowds must have come back time and again to stroll on the main avenue of the park of Saint-Cloud… taking it easy. The war had been over long ago. And say, I wonder if that shooting gallery still belonged to the same owner? Had he come back alive from the war? I take an interest in everything. Those are the same targets, but in addition, they're shooting at airplanes now. Novelty. Progress. Fashion. The wedding was still there, the soldiers too, and the town hall with its flag. Everything. Plus a few more things to shoot at than before.

But the people were getting a lot more fun out of the dodgem cars, a recent invention, because of the collisions you kept having and the terrible shaking they gave your head and innards. More howling lunatics kept pouring in for the pleasure of smashing ferociously into one another and getting scattered in all directions and fracturing their spleens at the bottom of their tubs. Nothing would make them stop. They never begged for mercy, it looked as if they'd never been so happy. Some were delirious. They had to be dragged away from their smash-ups. If they'd been offered death as an extra attraction for their franc, they'd have gone right in. At about four o'clock the town band was supposed to play in the middle of the carnival ground. It took some doing to collect the musicians, because of the neighbourhood bars, all of which wanted a turn at them. A last one was always missing. The rest waited. Some went looking for him. While waiting for them to come back, the others would be stricken with thirst and two more would disappear. They had to start all over again.

Incrusted with dust, the gingerbread pigs turned into relics and gave the prize-winners a devastating thirst.

Family groups are waiting for the fireworks before going home to bed. Waiting is part of the carnival too. Thousands of empty bottles jiggle and clink in the shadow under the tables. Restless feet consent or say no. The tunes are so familiar you hardly hear the music or the wheezing motor-driven cylinders behind the booths, which put life into things it costs two francs to see. When you're tipsy with fatigue your heart pounds in your temples. Bim! Bim! It beats against the velvet around your head and inside your ears. One of these days you'll burst. So be it! One of these days, when the movement inside catches up with the movement outside, when your thoughts scatter far and wide and rise up at last to play with the stars.

A lot of crying went on all over the carnival, children getting accidentally squeezed between chairs and others being taught to resist their longings, to forgo the enormous little pleasure of another ride on the merry-go-round. For character-building the carnival hasn't its equal. It's never too soon to start. The little darlings don't know yet that everything costs money. They think it's pure generosity that makes the grown-ups behind the brightly lit counters incite the public to treat themselves to the marvels which they have amassed and which they guard with their raucous smiles. Children don't know the law. Their parents slap them to teach them the law and protect them from pleasure.

There's never a real carnival except for the shopkeepers, and then it's deep down and secret. The shopkeeper rejoices at night when all the unsuspecting yokels, the public, the profit fodder, have gone home, when silence returns to the avenue and the last dog has squirted his last drop of urine at the Japanese billiard table. That's when the accounts are totted up, when the shopkeepers register their receipts and take stock of their powers and their victims.

On the last Sunday evening of the carnival, Martrodin's barmaid cut her hand pretty badly slicing sausage.

Late that night, the things around us suddenly became quite distinct, as if they were sick of wobbling from one side of fate to the other and had all come out of the shadow at once and started talking to me. But you'd better not trust things and people at such times. You think objects are going to talk but they don't say a thing, and often enough the night swallows them up before you can understand what they were trying to tell you. Anyway that's been my experience.

Be that as it may, I ran into Robinson that same night at Martrodin's café just as I was getting ready to dress the barmaid's wound. I remember the circumstances exactly. There were some Arab customers nearby, a whole raft of them were dozing on the benches. They didn't seem interested in anything that was going on around them. Speaking to Robinson, I was careful not to bring up our conversation of the other night, when I'd caught him carrying boards. I had trouble sewing up the barmaid's cut, because I couldn't see very well at the back of the bar. I had to pay close attention, and that kept me from talking. As soon as I'd finished, Robinson drew me into a corner and informed me without my asking that everything was all set for his scheme, it would be coming off soon. His telling me that didn't suit me at all, I could have easily done without it.

"Soon? What?"

"You know as well as I do…"

"What? The same old business?…"

"Guess how much they're giving me?"

I had no desire to guess.

"Ten thousand!… Just to hold my tongue…"

"That's a lot of money!"

"It'll save my life, that's all," he said. "Those are the ten thousand francs I've needed all along!… The first ten thousand!… See?… I've never really had a trade, but now with ten thousand francs!…"

He must have started blackmailing them already…

He listed his projects, all the things he'd be able to do with ten thousand francs... leaning against the wall, in the shadow. He gave me time to think about them. A new world. Ten thousand francs!

Yes, but thinking it over, I wondered if I wasn't running some risk myself, if I wasn't slipping into some sort of complicity by not trying to talk him out of his scheme. Actually I should have reported him. Not that I gave a damn about morality, any more than anyone else. What business was it of mine? But all the nasty stories, all the complications the law stirs up when a crime has been committed, just to entertain the taxpayer, the prurient bastard!... When that happens, it's hard to clear yourself... I'd seen it happen. Trouble for trouble, I preferred the quiet kind that's not splashed all over the newspapers.

To make a long story short, I was fascinated and horrified at the same time. I'd gone this far, and once again I hadn't the courage to get really to the bottom of things. Now that the time had come to open my eyes in the darkness, I almost preferred to keep them shut. But Robinson seemed to want me to open them, to know all about it.

To change the subject a bit, as we roamed around the room, I started talking about women. He didn't think much of women.

"You know," he said, "I can get along fine without women, their big arses, their fat thighs, their rosebud lips, their bellies that always have something growing in them – if it's not a brat it's a disease... Their smiles won't pay your rent for you! Take me in my pad: if I had a woman, it wouldn't do me a bit of good to show the landlord her arse on the fifteenth of the month, he wouldn't reduce the rent!..."

Robinson had a thing about independence. He said so himself. But Martrodin was getting sick of our private conversation, our little plots in the corner.

"Robinson, dammit, the glasses!" he sings out. "Do you expect me to wash them for you?"

Robinson starts up.

"You see," he informs me. "I'm filling in here!"

It was carnival time all right. Martrodin was having a hard time counting up the take, it was getting on his nerves. The Arabs left except for the two who were still dozing by the door.

"What are they waiting for?"

"The barmaid!" says Martrodin.

"How's business?" I asked, just to say something.

"Pretty good... But it's not easy! See, Doctor, I bought this place for sixty thousand before the crash. I'd need to get at least two hundred out of it... See what I mean?... It's true, the place is full, but it's mostly Arabs... And those people don't drink... They haven't caught the habit yet... Poles is what I need. Take it from me, Doctor, the Poles are drinkers... In the Ardennes, where I was before, I had Poles, they worked in the enamelling ovens, get the idea? Those ovens really heated them up!... That's what we need here!... Thirst!... On Saturdays they spent everything they had!... Christ! That was something! Their whole pay! Bing!... These greasers here aren't interested in drinking, they're more interested in buggering each other... It seems drinking's prohibited by their religion and buggery isn't..."

Martrodin had it in for the Arabs. "A bunch of perverts! It seems they even do it to my barmaid!... They're fanatics! Crazy way to behave! Doctor, I ask you..."

With his stubby fingers Martrodin squeezed the little serous pouches he had under his eyes. "How are your kidneys doing?" I asked him when I saw him doing that. I was treating him for his kidneys. "I hope you've cut out the salt at least."

"There's still some albumin, Doctor. I had the pharmacist analyse it only the other day... Oh, I don't care if I conk out, from albumin or something else, what bugs me is working the way I do... for practically nothing!..."

The barmaid had finished washing her dishes, but her bandage had got so greasy I had to change it. She held out a five-franc note. I didn't want to accept her five francs, but she insisted. Her name was Séverine.

"Why, Séverine," I observed, "you've had your hair cut."

"Had to!" she says. "It's the style! And besides, with the cooking in this place, long hair picks up all the smells..."

"Your arse smells a damn sight worse!" Martrodin breaks in. Our chatter was interfering with his accounts. "And it doesn't keep your customers away..."

"Yes, but it's not the same thing," says Séverine, who was good and mad. "Every part has its own smell... And look here, boss, you want me to tell you what you smell like... Not just one part, all over?"

Séverine was really worked up. Martrodin didn't want to hear the rest. He just grumbled and went back to his wretched accounts.

Séverine's feet were so swollen from the day's work that she couldn't manage to get out of her felt slippers and into her shoes. She prepared to leave in her slippers.

"I'll sleep all right with them on!" she finally said aloud.

"Go put the light out in the back!" Martrodin ordered her. "Anybody could guess that you don't pay the electricity bills!"

"I'll sleep all right!" Séverine repeated with a sigh, as she was getting up.

Martrodin was still at his accounts. To reckon better he'd taken off his apron, then his vest. He was sweating blood. From the invisible depths of the bar we could hear a clatter of saucers, that was Robinson and the other dishwasher at work. Martrodin was tracing his big childish numbers with a blue pencil squeezed between his thick murderer's fingers. In front of us the barmaid was dozing, sprawled all over her chair. Now and then she'd regain a spark of consciousness in her sleep.

"Oh, my feet! Oh, my feet!" she'd say and fall back into her doze.

But then Martrodin woke her with a yell.

"Hey, Séverine! Get your greasers out of here! I'm sick of them!... Clear out, the whole lot of you, Christ almighty! It's time."

The Arabs didn't seem to be in any hurry at all in spite of the hour. Séverine finally woke up. "It's true, I gotta go!" she finally agreed. "Thanks, boss!" She took both greasers along with her. They had joined forces to pay her.

"I'll do them both tonight," she told me as she was leaving. "Cos next Sunday I won't be able to on account of I'm going to Achères to see my kid. Cos next Saturday is visiting day."

The Arabs got up and followed her. They didn't seem the least bit insolent. Still, Séverine looked at them kind of dubiously, because she was so tired. "I don't agree with the boss," she says. "I like greasers better! Arabs aren't brutal like Poles, but they're perverts... Boy, are they perverts... Well, let 'em do what they please, I don't think that'll keep me from sleeping! All right, boys!" she called them. "Let's go!"

Off they go, all three, she a step or two ahead of them. We saw them cross the square, littered with the wreckage of the carnival, the last gas lamp at the end whitened their group for an instant, and then the night took them in. We heard their voices for a while and then nothing at all. There was nothing left.

I left the bistro without talking to Robinson again. Martrodin bade me a polite goodnight. A policeman was pacing the boulevard. In passing each other we stirred up the silence. Here and there the sound startled a shopkeeper bogged down in his aggressive figuring, like a dog gnawing a bone. A family on a bender filled the whole street, yelling on the corner of the Place Jean-Jaurès. They weren't getting ahead at all, they stood at the end of an alley, hesitating to go in, like a fishing fleet in a gale. The father went stumbling from one side of the street to the other and couldn't seem to stop pissing.

The night had come home.

* * *

I remember another night about that time because of what happened. First, shortly after dinner time, I heard a terrible sound of garbage cans being moved. People often made a racket with the garbage cans in my stairway. Then a woman moaning, sighing. I opened my door a crack, but I didn't move.

If I came out after an accident without being called, they'd probably think of me as a helpful neighbour, and my medical assistance wouldn't have to be paid for. If they wanted me, they'd just have to send for me officially, and then it would cost them twenty francs. Poor people persecute altruism implacably, meticulously, and the kindest impulses are punished without mercy. So I waited for someone to ring my bell, but no one came. For reasons of economy no doubt.

I had almost stopped waiting when a little girl appeared at my door, trying to read the names on the bells. As it turned out, she was looking for me. Madame Henrouille had sent her.

"Who's sick?" I asked.

"A gentleman. He's hurt himself…"

"A gentleman?" I thought of Henrouille himself.

"The husband?… Monsieur Henrouille?"

"No… A friend, but he's in their house…"

"Somebody you know?"

No, she'd never seen this friend.

It was cold out, the child ran, I walked fast.

"How did it happen?"

260

"I don't know."

We skirted a small park, the remains of an old forest, where at night the long, slow winter mists would catch between the trees. One little street after another. We soon came to the house. The child didn't say goodbye to me, she was afraid to go nearer. Madame Henrouille, the daughter-in-law, was standing on the front steps under the awning, waiting for me. Her oil lamp was flickering in the wind.

"This way, Doctor! This way!" she called out.

"Has your husband hurt himself?" I asked her.

"Go right in!" she said rather brusquely, without even giving me time to think. I ran smack into the old woman, who began to yap and light into me while I was still in the hallway. A broadside.

"Oh, the monsters! The bandits! Doctor! They tried to kill me!"

So they'd come a cropper.

"Kill you?" I said with an air of surprise. "Why would they want to do that?"

"Because I was taking too long to die! Use your brains, damn it! Naturally I don't want to die!"

"Mother! Mother!" the daughter-in-law broke in. "You've taken leave of your wits! How can you say such awful things to the doctor!..."

"Awful things, is it? Well, you slut, you've got a bloody nerve! Taken leave of my wits, have I? I've got wits enough to see the whole lot of you hanged! Believe you me!"

"But who's hurt? Where is he?"

"You'll see who!" the old woman puts in. "The murderer! He's upstairs on their bed! A fine mess he's made of your bed, you hussy! Got his no-good blood all over your mattress! His blood, not mine! What filthy rotten blood that must be! You won't wash that out in a hurry! Take it from me, that murderer's blood will stink for a long time to come! Some people go to the theatre for excitement! Not us, we've got a theatre right here! It's upstairs, Doctor! Real theatre, no make-believe. Don't miss it! Hurry hurry! Maybe the dirty dog will be dead before you get there! And then you won't see a thing!"

The daughter-in-law tried to hush her up, for fear she'd be heard on the street. In spite of the situation, the daughter-in-law didn't seem terribly upset, only put out that their scheme had misfired, but her opinions were unchanged. In fact she was dead sure she'd been right.

"Oh Doctor, listen to her! Isn't it shameful! When I've always tried so hard to make her life pleasant! You know that!… Didn't I keep urging her to go and stay with the Sisters…"

Hearing about the Sisters again was too much for the old woman.

"To Paradise! Yes, you slut, that's where you all wanted to send me! Oh, you bandits! That devil upstairs! That's why you and your husband brought him here! To kill me, that's right, not to send me to any Sisters! He botched it, the man's all thumbs if you ask me! Go on, Doctor, go and see what that bastard upstairs has done to himself, oh yes, him and nobody else!… I hope he croaks! Go on, Doctor! Go see him before it's too late!…"

If the daughter-in-law didn't seem dejected, the old woman was even less so. The plot had almost wiped her out, but she wasn't as indignant as she put on. It was all an act. Actually that bungled murder had revived her, raised her up from the creeping tomb she'd been shut up in all those years at the back of the mouldering garden. Late in life an indestructible vitality had come back and was running through her veins. She was indecently relishing not only her victory but also the prospect of having something to torment her mean-hearted daughter-in-law with for the rest of her life. She had her where she wanted her now. She was bent on my knowing every detail of the miscarried plot and how it had all happened.

"And do you know where I met that murderer?" she went on in the same exalted register, especially for my benefit. "In your waiting room… That's right, Doctor, and I didn't trust him!… I didn't trust him this far!… Do you know what he first suggested to me? He wanted to bump you off, you bitch! That's right, you slut! And cheap too! I assure you! He has the same propositions for everybody! It's common knowledge!… So you see, you hussy, I know how he makes his living! I know all about him! His name is Robinson!… Deny it if you dare! Tell me that's not his name! As soon as I saw him whispering in corners with you two, I had my suspicions… And a good thing too!… If I hadn't been suspicious, where'd I be now?"

Over and over again the old woman told me how it had all happened. The rabbit had moved while he was fastening the fireworks to the door of the hutch. Meanwhile she had been watching him from her shack, she'd had a "ringside seat", as she put it. The contraption was loaded with buckshot… it had gone off in his face while he was connecting it up, right in his eyes. "A man's not easy in his mind when he's plotting murder," she concluded. "What would you expect?"

Anyway, for butter-fingered incompetence, it took the cake.

"That's what they've done to men lately!" the old woman went on. "That's right! Matter of habit! They have to kill to eat! They're not satisfied any more to steal their daily bread... Or kill their grandmothers!... Nobody's ever seen anything like it... Never!... It's the end of the world! Wickedness is all they're good for! And you now! Up to your necks in it!... And him gone blind! You'll have him on your hands for the rest of your days!... What do you think of that?... Him and his slimy tricks!..."

The daughter-in-law didn't say a word, but she must have worked out her plan. She was a really concentrated villain. While we were busy with our reflections, the old woman went looking through the rooms for her son.

"And you know, Doctor, I have a son! Where's he got to? What's he up to now?"

She staggered down the corridor, shaken by non-stop laughter.

Old people don't usually laugh so hard, except in the nuthouse. When you hear a thing like that, you wonder what the world's coming to. She was bent on finding her son. He'd escaped into the street. "All right, let him hide! He can live for ever for all I care! Now he'll have to live with that scum upstairs, serves him right, live with the two of them, including our friend who'll never see again! And support him! Hee hee! Square in the face! I saw it! I saw it from start to finish! Boom boom! I saw it all right! And it wasn't a rabbit, I assure you! Damn it all, Doctor, where's my son? Haven't you seen him? There's another dirty dog, always been even deeper than her, but now finally the viciousness of his crummy character has come out, oh yes, it's come out all right! It takes a long time for a low character like his to come out! But when it does, it's rotten to the core! You can't deny it, Doctor! Something worth seeing!" She was having a fine time. She wanted to impress me with her superiority to the situation and to confound us all, to humiliate us, so to speak.

She had hit on a good role and was working it for all it was worth. An emotional binge. Which is always a pleasure. There's no limit to our happiness as long as we're capable of playing a part. She was sick of old folks' jeremiads, the only part she'd been given in the last twenty years. She'd never let go of this new, virulent, unhoped-for role that had come her way. Old age means not having a passionate role to play any more, seeing your theatre fold up on you, so there's nothing but death to look forward to. All of a sudden the old woman's zest had come back to her with her new and ardent role: the avenger. She didn't want to die any more, not in the least. She radiated the desire to live, the affirmation of life. In melodrama she had found new fires, real fire.

She was warming herself, she had no desire to leave the new fire, to leave us. For a long while she had almost ceased to believe there was any fire. She hadn't known what to do to stop herself from dying at the back of her dim-witted garden. And then suddenly this tempest of hard, hot reality had hit her.

"My death!" Grandma Henrouille was shrieking now. "That's something I want to see! Do you hear! I've still got my two eyes! I want to get a good look at it!"

She never wanted to die, never. That was definite. She had stopped believing in her death.

* * *

Everybody knows that such situations are hard to manage and that managing them is always very expensive. In the first place we didn't even know where to put Robinson. In the hospital? Obviously that would make for loose tongues, all sorts of gossip... Send him back to his pad? Unthinkable, with his face in that condition. Like it or not, the Henrouilles had to keep him.

He lay in bed upstairs, in a pitiful state. He was terrified of being thrown out and prosecuted. Not hard to see why. It was one of those things that you really can't tell anyone about. We kept the blinds in his room carefully drawn, but people, the neighbours, started passing through that street more often than usual, just to look up at the shutters and ask for news of the injured man. We gave them news all right, we told them fairy tales. But how were we to stop them from smelling a rat? From gossiping? Besides, they embroidered on what we told them. How could we stop them from speculating? Luckily nobody had gone to the law. That was something. As far as his face was concerned, I was doing all right. The wound was very jagged and a lot of dirt had got into it, but no infection had set in. As for his eyes, I foresaw scars in the corneas, through which light would pass with difficulty, if at all.

We'd manage to patch up some sort of eyesight if there was anything left to patch. For the moment we'd concentrate on what was most urgent, above all we'd have to prevent the old woman from getting us all into trouble with her horrible yapping in front of the neighbours. True, most of them thought she was mad, but that doesn't always account for everything.

If the police really started prying, God knows where it would lead us. Preventing the old woman from making a spectacle of herself in her little yard had become a ticklish business. We all took turns trying to calm her down. It was no good if she thought we were browbeating her, but gentleness didn't always work very well either. In a frenzy of vindictiveness, she was blackmailing us, neither more nor less.

I went to see Robinson at least twice a day. He groaned under his bandages as soon as he heard me climbing the stairs. He was really in pain, but not as much as he wanted me to think. He'd have cause, I foresaw, for much worse distress when he realized exactly what had happened to his eyes... I was evasive about the future. He complained of stinging in his eyelids. He thought that was what prevented him from seeing anything.

The Henrouilles were taking good care of him, in accordance with my instructions. No trouble on that score.

Nobody mentioned the plot any more. We didn't speak of the future either. As I was leaving them in the evening, we all took turns looking at one another, so intensely I always had a feeling that we were about to do away with one another once and for all. When I thought it over, that culmination struck me as logical and expedient. I could scarcely imagine the nights in that house. But there they would be in the morning, and together we'd face the world together just where we left it together the night before. Madame Henrouille would help me renew the dressing with permanganate, and we'd open the blinds a bit as a test. The result was always the same. Robinson didn't even notice that we had just opened the blinds...

So the earth makes its way through the vastly menacing, silent night.

Every morning the son would welcome me with a little peasant phrase: "Well, well, Doctor... Looks like another late frost!" he would observe, glancing up at the sky from under the little peristyle. As if the weather mattered. His wife would go out and try again to parley with her mother-in-law, but only succeed in redoubling her fury.

While we kept Robinson's eyes bandaged, he told me about his beginnings in life. When he was eleven, his parents had apprenticed him to a high-class shoemaker. One day he delivered a pair of shoes to a lady customer, and she invited him to share a pleasure which up until then he had known only in his imagination. He was so horrified by what he had done that he never went back to his boss. In those days fucking a customer was still an unforgivable crime. The lady's chemise, especially, all of chiffon, had had a phenomenal effect on him. Thirty years later he remembered that chemise in every detail. The lady swishing through her apartment full of cushions and fringed portières, her pink and perfumed flesh, had given young Robinson food for interminable and despairing comparisons to last him the rest of his life.

Yet a good many things had happened since. He'd seen continents and been through whole wars, but he'd never recovered from that revelation. It gave him pleasure to think about it, to tell me about the brief moment of youth he had enjoyed with the lady customer. "Having my eyes closed like this makes me think," he observed. "It's like a parade... Like having a movie show in my bean..." I didn't dare tell him that he'd have time to get awfully sick of his little movie show. Since all thought leads to death, a day would come when he'd see nothing else in his movie show.

Not far from the Henrouilles' house there was a little factory with a big engine in it. It shook their house from morning to night. And there were other factories a little further away that thumped and pounded the whole time, even at night. "We'll be gone when the roof caves in," Henrouille would joke, but he was kind of worried all the same. "It'll happen sooner or later!" It was true that bits of plaster were falling from the ceiling. An architect tried to reassure them, but whenever you stopped in that house to listen to what was going on, you felt as if you were on a ship, sailing from one fear to another. Passengers, shut up between decks, making plans even sadder than life, economizing and dreading the darkness as well as the light.

Henrouille would go up to the bedroom after lunch to read a while to Robinson, as I'd asked him to. The days passed. He treated Henrouille, too, to the story about that marvellous lady customer he had laid in the days of his apprenticeship. After a while the story became a kind of collective joke for everyone in the house. That's what happens to our secrets when we spread them abroad. There's nothing terrible inside us or on earth or possibly in heaven itself except what hasn't been said yet. We won't be easy in our minds until everything has been said once and for all, then we'll fall silent and we'll no longer be afraid of keeping still. That will be the day.

In the weeks while his eyelids were suppurating, I was able to entertain him with fairy tales about his eyes and the future. Sometimes I'd pretend the window was closed when it was wide open and sometimes that it was very dark outside.

But one day when my back was turned he went to the window himself to see what was what, and before I could stop him he had slipped the bandage off his eyes. He hesitated for quite a while. He touched the window frame first on the right, then on the left. He couldn't believe it, but in the end he had to. There was no getting around it.

"Bardamu!" he shouted. "Bardamu! It's open! The window's open, I tell you!" – I didn't know what to say. I stood there like an idiot. He was holding both arms out of the window, in the fresh air. Naturally he couldn't see a thing, but he felt the air. He stretched his arms out in his darkness as far as he could, as if he were trying to touch the end of it. He didn't want to believe it. His own private darkness. I pushed him back into his bed and said things to comfort him, but he didn't believe me any more. He was crying. He too had come to the end. There was nothing more we could say to him. A time comes when you're all alone, when you've come to the end of everything that can happen to you. It's the end of the world. Even grief, your own grief, doesn't answer you any more, and you have to retrace your steps, to go back among people, it makes no difference who. You're not choosy at times like that, because even to weep you have to go back where everything starts all over, back among people.

"What will you do with him when he's better?" I asked the daughter-in-law at lunch after this scene. They had asked me to stay and eat with them in the kitchen. Neither of them had any serious idea of how to get out of the mess they were in. The cost of buying him a pension terrified them, especially her, because she knew more about the price of arrangements for invalids. She had even gone to the Public Welfare and taken steps. Steps they avoided mentioning to me.

One evening after my second visit Robinson did everything he could think of to keep me with him, he wanted me to stay a bit later than usual. He went on rehashing all the memories he could muster about the things we had done and the places we had been together, even things we had never tried to remember before. He remembered things we had never had time to bring up. In his seclusion the world we had explored seemed to pour back on him with all the moans, the kindnesses, the old clothes, the friends we had left behind us; in his eyeless head he had opened a shop full of outworn emotions.

"I'll kill myself!" he announced when his misery seemed too great to bear. And yet he managed to bear his misery a little longer, like a weight that was much too heavy and infinitely useless, misery on a road where he met no one to whom he could speak of it, it was just too big and complicated. He couldn't have explained this misery of his, it exceeded his education.

He was a natural-born coward, I knew it, and so did he; he kept hoping we'd save him from the truth, but on the other hand I was beginning to wonder if there was anywhere such a thing as a real coward... It looks like any man has things he is willing to die for, quickly and gladly. Except that a chance to die pleasantly, the chance he's looking for, doesn't always materialize. So he goes off somewhere to die as best he can... He sticks around on earth and everybody takes him for a jerk and a coward, but the truth is that he simply lacks conviction. He only seems to be a coward.

Robinson was not prepared to die under the conditions offered. Under different conditions he might have been delighted.

All in all, death is something like marriage.

This particular death didn't appeal to him, that was the long and the short of it.

Then he'd have to resign himself and accept his helplessness and distress. But for the moment he was frantically busy splotching his soul with misery and distress. Later he'd put order into his misery and then a real new life would begin. He'd have to.

"You may not believe me," he said to me that evening after dinner, piecing bits of memories together. "I've never had much of a gift for languages, but do you know, towards the end in Detroit I managed to carry on a bit of a conversation in English... I've forgotten it now, all except one little phrase... Two words... They've been coming back to me ever since this thing happened to my eyes… 'Gentlemen first!' That's just about all I can say in English now, I don't know why… of course, it's an easy thing to remember… 'Gentlemen first!'" To take his mind off his troubles, we tried talking English together. We kept repeating "Gentlemen first!" over and over again like idiots apropos of everything and nothing. A private joke. In the end we even taught it to Henrouille, who'd come up for a while to keep tabs on us.

While stirring up memories, we started wondering what might be left of all that… of all the things we'd known together… We wondered what could have become of Molly, our sweet Molly… As for Lola, I'd just as soon have forgotten her, but come to think of it I'd have welcomed news of them all, even little Musyne while I was at it… who was probably living in Paris, nearby. Practically next door, in fact… Still, I'd have had to bestir myself to find out about her… There were so many people whose names, mannerisms and addresses I had lost, whose friendliness and even their smiles, after so many years and years of trouble and worrying about the next meal, must have turned into pathetic grimaces, like old cheeses… Even memories have their youth… When you let them grow old, they turn into revolting phantoms dripping with selfishness, vanity and lies… They rot like apples… So we talked about our youth, mulling it over. We didn't trust it… Which reminded me, I hadn't been to see my mother in a long time… And those visits had never done my nervous system any good… When it came to sadness, my mother was worse than me… Still in her little shop, she seemed after all those years and years to make a point of piling up disappointments around her… When I went to see her, she'd say: "You know, Aunt Hortense died two months ago in Coutances… Maybe you should have gone… And Clémentin, you remember Clémentin?… The floor polisher who played with you when you were little… Well, they picked him up the day before yesterday on the Rue d'Aboukir… He hadn't eaten in three days…"

Robinson's childhood had been so dismal he didn't know what to say when he thought of it. Except for the episode with the lady customer, he couldn't find anything, even in the far recesses, that didn't make him sick with despair; it was like a house full of repugnant, foul-smelling objects: brooms, slop jars, housewives and smacks in the face… Monsieur Henrouille had nothing to say of his own youth including his military service, except that he'd had his picture taken with a pompon, and that picture was still hanging over the wardrobe.

When he'd gone back down, Robinson told me how worried he was that he'd never get the promised ten thousand francs now... "Don't count on them!" was my advice. I thought it best to prepare him for that new disappointment.

Some bits of shot left over from the explosion kept surfacing at the edges of his wound. I removed them in several instalments, a few each day. The pain was bad when I probed just above the conjunctiva.

We had taken every possible precaution, but the neighbourhood people gossiped right and left all the same. Luckily Robinson suspected nothing, it would have made him a lot sicker than he was. No doubt about it, there was suspicion all around us. Moving about the house in her slippers, Madam Henrouille was quieter and quieter. You weren't expecting her and then she'd be right on top of you.

What with the reefs all around us, the least doubt could wreck us all. Then the whole ship would crack, split, crash, come apart at the seams, and wash up on the shore. Robinson, the grandmother, the fireworks, the rabbit, his eyes, the unlikely son, the murdering daughter-in-law – we'd all end up with our garbage and our rotten secrets in the office of some furious examining magistrate. I wasn't very pleased with myself. Not that I'd done anything positively criminal. I hadn't. But I felt guilty all the same. I was especially guilty of wishing deep down that this whole business would go on. In fact I couldn't see any objection to all of us together drifting deeper and deeper into the night.

To tell the truth, there was no need of wishing, things were moving all by themselves, and moving fast!

* * *

The rich don't have to kill to eat. They "employ" people, as they call it. The rich don't do evil themselves. They pay. People do all they can to please them, and everybody's happy. They have beautiful women, the poor have ugly ones. Clothing aside, they're the product of centuries. Easy to look at, well fed, well washed. After all these years, life can boast no greater accomplishment.

It's no use trying, we slide, we skid, we fall back into the alcohol that preserves the living and the dead, we get nowhere. It's been proved. After all these centuries of watching our domestic animals coming into the world, labouring and dying before our eyes without anything more unusual ever happening to them either than taking up the same insipid fiasco where so many other animals had left off, we should have caught on. Endless waves of useless beings keep rising from deep down in the ages to die in front of our noses, and yet here we stay, hoping for something... We're not even capable of thinking death through.

The women of the rich, well fed, well lied to, well rested, tend to be good-looking. That's a fact. And maybe, after all, it's enough. How do I know? Maybe that's a reason for living.

"Don't you think the women in America were prettier than the ones here?" – Robinson had been asking me things like that ever since he'd started chewing on his travels. He was getting curious, he even started talking about women.

I wasn't going to see him quite so often now, because about that time I was put in charge of a small neighbourhood dispensary for tuberculosis. I may as well call a spade a spade: it brought in eight hundred francs a month. My patients were mostly people from the zone, that village of sorts, which never succeeds in picking itself entirely out of the mud and rubbish, bordered by paths where precocious snot-nosed little girls play hookey under the fences to garner a franc, a handful of French fries and a dose of gonorrhoea from some sex fiend. A setting for avant-garde films where the trees are poisoned with laundry and lettuces drip with urine on Saturday night. In those few months of specialized practice I performed no miracles. Miracles were sorely needed. But my patients weren't at all eager for me to perform miracles, they were banking on their tuberculosis to move them from the state of absolute misery in which they'd been mouldering ever since they could remember to the state of relative misery conferred by microscopic government pensions. Their more or less positive sputum had been getting them periodically rejected for military service ever since the war. They got thinner and thinner, thanks to fever maintained by eating little, vomiting a lot, drinking enormous quantities of wine and working in spite of it all, one day out of three, to tell the truth.

The hope of a pension possessed them body and soul. One day a pension would come to them like grace if only they had the strength to wait a little while before snuffing out completely. You can't know what it is to come back and wait for something if you haven't seen all the coming back and waiting poor people expecting a pension can do.

While the rain came down outside, they'd spend whole afternoons and evenings hoping in the corridor and doorway of my run-down dispensary, stirring up their hopes of percentages, their longing for definitely positive sputum, genuine hundred-per-cent tubercular sputum. Their hope of getting cured came far behind their hope for a pension... Of course they also thought about getting cured, but very little, they were much too dazzled by their dreams of an income, however infinitesimal. This ultimate, uncompromising desire left room only for negligible wishes, and even their death became by comparison a side issue, a sporting risk. Death after all is only a matter of a few hours, a few minutes, but a pension is like poverty, it lasts a whole lifetime. Rich people are drunk in a different way, they can't understand this frenzy about security. Being rich is another kind of drunkenness, the forgetful kind. That, in fact, is the whole point of getting rich: to forget.

Little by little I'd broken my bad habit of promising my patients good health. The prospect of getting well didn't thrill them. Good health can't be anything but second best. Getting well means you can work. Isn't that lovely? While a government pension, however negligible, is purely and simply divine.

When you have no money to offer the poor, you'd better keep your trap shut. If you talk to them about anything but money, you'll almost always be deceiving them, lying. It's easy to amuse the rich, all you need, for instance, is mirrors for them to see themselves in, because in the whole world there's nothing better to look at than the rich. To keep the rich cheerful all you've got to do is move them up a notch in the Legion of Honour every ten years, like a sagging tit, that'll keep them busy for another ten years. And that's the truth. My patients were poor and selfish; they were materialists, shrunk to the measure of their sordid hope that positive sputum streaked with blood would get them a pension. Nothing else meant a thing to them. Not even the seasons meant a thing. They were aware of the seasons only insofar as the seasons affected their cough and the state of their health; in the winter, for instance, you're a good deal more likely to catch cold than in the summer, but on the other hand you're more likely to spit blood in the springtime, and during the summer heat it's not difficult to lose as much as five pounds a week... Sometimes I heard them talking among themselves when they were waiting for their turn, and they thought I wasn't there... They told endless horror stories about me and lies that would make you blow your imagination out. Running me down like that probably picked them up, gave them some sort of mysterious courage that they needed to be more and more ruthless, hard and vicious, to stick it out, to last. Having someone they could slander, despise and threaten seems to have made them feel better. And yet I did all I could to please them, I went to bat for them, I tried to help them, I gave them plenty of iodine to make them spit up their filthy bacilli, but I never succeeded in neutralizing their cussedness...

When I questioned them, they stood there in front of me, smiling like servants, but they didn't like me, mostly because I was helping them, but also because I wasn't rich, and having me for a doctor meant they were being treated free of charge, which is never flattering for a sick person, even if he is hoping for a pension. No slander would have been too great for them to spread behind my back. Most of the doctors in the neighbourhood had cars, I didn't, and to their way of thinking my walking was a kind of infirmity. If anyone gave them the slightest encouragement, something my colleagues were always glad to do, they'd avenge themselves, or so it seemed, for all my kindness, for my devotion and readiness to help. Which is perfectly normal. Nevertheless the time passed.

One evening when my waiting room was almost empty, a priest came in to see me. I didn't know that priest, I almost showed him the door. I didn't like priests, I had my reasons, especially since the time they'd shanghaied me at San Tapeta. But hard as I tried to place this one, searching my mind for something definite to reproach him with, the fact is that I'd never seen him before. Still, he must, like me, have gone about quite a lot in Rancy by night, he lived nearby. Maybe he avoided me on his rounds. I thought it over. Maybe somebody had told him I didn't like priests. You could see that by the weaselling way he started his spiel. One thing is sure – we had never jostled each other around the same sickbeds. He had been officiating, he told me, at a church nearby for the last twenty years. Plenty of parishioners, but not many who paid. A kind of beggar, come to think of it. We had that much in common. The soutane he was wearing struck me as a most uncomfortable sort of drapery for plodding through the muck of the Zone. I said as much. I went so far as to stress the extravagant discomfort of such a garment.

"You get used to it!" he said.

The impertinence of my remark didn't put him off, he became more affable than ever. Obviously he had something to ask of me. His voice seldom rose above a certain confidential monotone which, or so at least I imagined, came from his calling. While he was cautiously preambling, I tried to form a picture of all he did each day to earn his calories, all his grimaces and promises, pretty much like my own... And then, to amuse myself, I imagined him all naked at his altar... It's a good habit to get into: when somebody comes to see you, quick, reduce him to nakedness, and you'll see through him in a flash, regardless of who it is, you will instantly discern the underlying reality, namely, an enormous, hungry maggot. It's good sleight-of-the-imagination. His lousy prestige vanishes, evaporates. Once you've got him naked, you'll be dealing with nothing more than a bragging, pretentious beggar, talking drivel of one kind or another. It's a test that nothing can withstand. In a moment you'll know where you're at. There won't be anything left but ideas, and there's nothing frightening about ideas. With ideas nothing is lost, everything can be straightened out. Whereas it's sometimes hard to stand up to the prestige of a man with his clothes on. Nasty smells and mysteries cling to his clothes.

This Abbé had very bad teeth, decayed, discoloured, ringed with greenish tartar – in short, a fine case of alveolar pyorrhoea. I was going to talk to him about his pyorrhoea, but he was too busy telling me things. The things he was telling me kept squirting against the stumps of his teeth under the impulse of a tongue, no movement of which escaped me. In a number of spots the edges of his tongue were bruised and bleeding.

This kind of meticulous observation was a habit, you might say a hobby, of mine. When you stop to examine the way in which words are formed and uttered, our sentences are hard put to survive the disaster of their slobbery origins. The mechanical effort of conversation is nastier and more complicated than defecation. That corolla of bloated flesh, the mouth, which screws itself up to whistle, which sucks in breath, contorts itself, discharges all manner of viscous sounds across a fetid barrier of decaying teeth – how revolting! Yet that is what we are adjured to sublimate into an ideal. It's not easy.

Since we are nothing but packages of tepid, half-rotted viscera, we shall always have trouble with sentiment. Being in love is nothing, it's sticking together that's difficult. Faeces on the other hand make no attempt to endure or to grow. On this score we are far more unfortunate than shit: our frenzy to persist in our present state – that's the unconscionable torture.

Unquestionably we worship nothing more divine than our smell. All our misery comes from wanting at all costs to go on being Tom, Dick or Harry, year in year out. This body of ours, this disguise put on by common jumping molecules, is in constant revolt against the abominable farce of having to endure. Our molecules, the dears, want to get lost in the universe as fast as they can! It makes them miserable to be nothing but "us", the jerks of infinity. We'd burst if we had the courage, day after day we come very close to it. The atomic torture we love so is locked up inside us with our pride.

Since I was silent, stunned by the thought of these biological ignominies, the Abbé, thinking he had me in his pocket, assumed a benevolent, almost familiar manner. With infinite precautions he broached the subject of my medical reputation in the neighbourhood. My reputation, he gave me to understand, might have been better if I had taken a very different course at the start, during the first few months of my practice in Rancy.

"Don't forget, my dear doctor, that the sick are basically conservative... As you must doubtless know, they live in fear that heaven and earth will fail them..."

In other words, I should have made my peace with the Church from the start. That was his eminently practical as well as spiritual conclusion. Not a bad idea. I was careful not to interrupt him, but waited patiently for him to come to the point of his visit.

The weather couldn't have been gloomier or more confidential. It was so vile, so coldly and emphatically vile, it gave you the feeling that if you went out you'd never see the rest of the world again, that the world would have melted away in disgust.

My nurse had finally brought her case histories up to date, every last one. She had no excuse whatever for staying there listening to us. So she left us, but miffed, slamming the door behind her, and plunged into a furious downpour.

* * *

In the course of our conversation this priest told me his name: Abbé Protiste he called himself. Between exercises in evasiveness, he informed me that he and Madame Henrouille had for some time been taking steps with a view to getting the old woman and Robinson, the two of them together, into an inexpensive religious institution. They were still at it.

Looking closely at this Abbé Protiste, I might have taken him for a salesman in a department store, maybe even a section manager – wet, greenish and many times dried. There was something really plebeian in the humility of his insinuations. In his breath too. When it comes to breath, I never go wrong. There was a man who ate too fast and drank white wine.

Madame Henrouille, he told me as a starter, had called on him at the presbytery soon after the incident so see if he could help them out of the mess they had got themselves into. In telling me that, he seemed to be looking for excuses, explanations, as if he were ashamed of his part in the affair. There was really no need of putting on airs on my account. I knew the lie of the land. He was simply joining us in the night, that's all. That was his lookout. Little by little, what with the money involved, this priest had developed an extraordinary crust. That too was his lookout! Since my dispensary was steeped in silence and night had settled on the Zone, he lowered his voice to a whisper, wanting to confide in me alone. But whisper or not, everything he said struck me as monstrous and intolerable, probably because of the quiet all around me, which seemed to be full of echoes. Or were they only in my head? "Hush!" I kept wanting to say in the intervals between his words. I was so frightened my lips trembled a little, and at the end of his sentences I made myself stop thinking.

Now that he had joined us in our terror, the priest didn't quite know how to go about following the four of us in the darkness. A small group. He wanted to know how many of us were already mixed up in the affair. And where we were headed. So that he too, hand in hand with his new friends, might direct his steps towards the goal we would have to reach all together or not at all. We were all in the same boat now. The priest would have to learn to walk in the dark like the rest of us. He was still unsteady on his pins. He asked me what he should do to keep from falling. He didn't have to come if he was afraid! We'd get to the end together, and then we'd know what we'd been looking for in our adventure. That's what life is, a bit of light that ends in darkness.

But on the other hand, maybe we'd never know, maybe we wouldn't find anything. That's death.

The essential for the moment was to grope our way carefully. At the point we had got to we couldn't go back. We had no choice. Their lousy justice with its laws was everywhere, at the bend of every corridor. Madame Henrouille was holding the old woman's hand, her son and I were holding theirs and Robinson's as well. We were all in it together. I explained all that to the priest without delay. And he understood.

Like it or not, I told the Abbé, in our present situation it wouldn't do us a bit of good to be noticed and exposed by the passers-by, I made that very clear. If we met anybody, we should pretend to be just taking a walk. Those were the instructions. Act natural. So now the Abbé knew the ins and outs, he understood. He gave me an ardent handshake. Naturally he too was scared to death. A beginner. He hesitated, he floundered like an innocent. At that point there was neither road nor light, and in their place only words of caution, which we passed back and forth but didn't greatly believe in ourselves. The words people say to reassure each other at times like that fall on empty air. The echo sends back nothing, you've walked out on society. Fear says neither yes nor no. Fear swallows up everything we say, everything we think.

Nor does it help at times like that to stare wide-eyed into the darkness. It's horror wasted, that's all. The night has taken everything, even the light of our eyes. It has drained us. Even so, we have to join hands or we'll fall. Day people can't understand us. Between them and us stands our fear, which will weigh on us until this thing ends one way or another and we can get back together, in death or life, with the other bastards of this world.

For the moment the Abbé had only to help us and find things out in a hurry, that was his job. Actually that's what he had come for, to knock himself out finding a home as quickly as possible, first for Grandma Henrouille and then for Robinson, with the nuns in the provinces. He thought such an arrangement possible, and so did I. Except we'd have to wait months for a vacancy, and we were sick of waiting. We were fed up.

The daughter-in-law was quite right, the sooner the better. They should beat it and good riddance! So Protiste came up with another scheme which, I agreed on the spot, seemed most ingenious. Best of all, it would mean a commission for both of us, the priest and me. The arrangement was to go into effect almost immediately, and I'd have my own little part to play. It consisted in persuading Robinson to go south, to give him a bit of friendly but firm advice.

Not knowing either the bottom or the underside of Protiste's scheme, I ought perhaps to have expressed certain reservations, tried to protect my friend a little... Because the scheme Abbé Protiste put forward was indeed pretty wild. But we were all so harried by circumstances that our chief concern was haste. I promised everything they asked, to help and to keep my mouth shut. Ticklish situations of this kind seemed to be nothing new to this Protiste, and something told me that he would make things a lot easier for me.

But where were we to begin? We'd have to arrange for Robinson to leave quietly for the south. How would Robinson feel about the south? Not to mention leaving with the old woman, whom he had come very close to murdering... I'd insist... That's all!... He'd simply have to, for all sorts of reasons, not all of them very good, but sound, yes, sound...

The job that had been found for Robinson and the old woman in the south was certainly weird. In Toulouse. A beautiful city, Toulouse! We'd be seeing Toulouse! We'd go visit them down there! I promised I'd go to Toulouse as soon as they were settled in their lodgings and their work and all.

Then, thinking it over, it bothered me a little that Robinson should be leaving so soon, but at the same time I was glad, mostly because for once I was making a bit of real profit on the deal. A thousand francs they were giving me. It was all settled. All I had to do was work up Robinson's enthusiasm for the south, convince him that there was no better climate for damaged eyes, that he'd be blissfully well off down there, and that all things considered he was pretty damn lucky to get off so easily. That ought to do it.

After five minutes of rumination along these lines, I myself was steeped in conviction and prepared for a decisive confrontation. Strike while the iron is hot, that's my opinion. After all, he'd be no worse off down there than here. Protiste's idea, when I thought it over, seemed perfectly reasonable. You've got to admit it, those priests know how to bury the worst scandals.

All things considered, the deal being offered Robinson and the old woman wasn't so bad. If I wasn't mistaken, it was some sort of mummy show. The mummies were in the cellar of some church, and tourists could visit them for a fee. A fine business, Protiste assured me. I almost believed him, and that made me a little jealous. It's not every day that you can get the dead to work for you.

I locked up the dispensary and started resolutely through the sludge with the priest, heading for the Henrouilles. This was really something new. A thousand francs' worth of hope! I had changed my mind about the priest. When we got to the house, we found the Henrouilles, man and wife, with Robinson in his room on the second floor. But what a state Robinson was in!

"So there you are!" he screeches frantically as soon as he hears my steps on the stairs. "There's something going on! I can feel it!... Tell me the truth!" he gasps.

He starts snivelling before I can say a word. The Henrouilles are making signs while he appeals to me for help: "A pretty mess!" I say to myself. "They're in too much of a hurry!... Always have been!... They've broken it to him cold! Without preparation! Without waiting for me!..."

Luckily I was able to retell the whole story, so to speak, in different words. Robinson was more than willing to see the same facts in a different light. All right by him. The priest in the hallway didn't dare come into the room. He was reeling with fright.

"Come in!" the daughter-in-law finally called out. "Come right in! You're very welcome, Monsieur l'Abbé! You've caught a poor, stricken family, that's all!... The doctor and the priest!... Always together in life's most painful moments! Isn't that right?"

She was making phrases. Her new-found hope of extricating herself from the shit and the darkness was making the old bag lyrical in her repulsive way.

The bewildered priest lost all control and started sputtering with excitement at some distance from the sickbed. His excitement communicated itself to Robinson, who resumed his raving: "They're lying! They're all lying to me!" he yelled.

Talk! Talk! And about what? Appearances! Emotional outpourings. Always the same. Still, it sparked me up, revived my nerve. I drew the daughter-in-law into a corner and put it to her plainly, because I saw that the only person capable of getting them out of this mess was yours truly. "A down payment!" I said to her. "And I want it now!" When there's no trust, as the saying goes, there's no reason to use kid gloves. She got the drift and deposited a thousand-franc note right in the middle of my palm. And then another to be on the safe side. I had thrown my weight. So while I was at it, I set to work, bringing Robinson around. He'd just have to go south, and that was that.

It's easy to speak of betrayal. But to betray somebody you need an opportunity, and once you have it you've got to take it. It's like opening a window in jail. Everybody would like to, but you don't often get the chance.

* * *

Once Robinson had left Rancy, I thought things would pick up, for instance that I'd have a few more patients than usual, but nothing of the kind. In the first place, there was a slump in those parts, a wave of unemployment, which is the worst thing that can happen. And then, in spite of the winter, the weather turned dry and mild, when what the medical profession needs is damp cold. No epidemics either – in short a bad season, a flop.

I even saw some of my colleagues making their rounds on foot, which goes to show, smiling as if it amused them to walk, but actually very much put out, their only purpose being to save money by giving their cars a rest. All I had to wear outside was a raincoat. Was that what gave me my obstinate cold? Or could it have been the habit I'd got into of eating much too little? How do I know? Or had my fevers come back? Be that as it may, there was a cold snap just before spring, and after that I never stopped coughing, I was really sick. A disaster. One morning I simply couldn't get up. Bébert's aunt was just passing the house. I got someone to call her. She came up. I sent her to collect a small bill that was still owing to me in the neighbourhood. The last and only. I collected half, and it did me for ten days, in bed.

Flat on your back for ten days you have time to think. As soon as I felt better, I'd get out of Rancy, that's what I decided. I hadn't paid my rent for six months... So goodbye my four sticks of furniture! I'd slip quietly away, naturally without a word to anyone, and I'd never be seen again in La Garenne-Rancy. I'd leave without trace or address. When the hyenas of poverty are on your trail, why argue? If you're smart, you'll shut up and clear out.

With my MD, it was true, I could practise anywhere... But anywhere else it would be neither better nor worse... Yes, a little better at first, because it takes a while for people to find out about you, to get into the swing, and pick up the knack of doing you harm. While they're still looking for your most vulnerable spot, you have a little peace, but once they've found your funny bone it's the same all over. All things considered, the best time is the few weeks while you're still unknown in a new place. After that, the crumminess starts all over. It's their nature. The main thing is not to wait till they've spotted your weaknesses. Squash a bedbug before it can slip into its crack. Am I right?

As for sick people, patients, I had no illusions... In another neighbourhood they'd be no less grasping or jug-headed or weak-kneed than the ones here. The same wine, the same movies, the same sports talk, the same enthusiastic submission to the natural needs of the gullet and the arse would produce the same crude, filthy horde, staggering from lie to lie, bragging, scheming, vicious, brutal between two fits of panic.

But just as a sick man changes sides in bed and in life, so we too are entitled to move from side to side, it's the only thing we can do, the only defence that's ever been found against Fate. No good hoping to drop off your misery somewhere on the way. Misery is like some horrible woman you've married. Maybe it's better to end up loving her a little than to knock yourself out beating her all your life. Since obviously you won't be able to bump her off.

Anyway, I slipped away from my mezzanine pad in Rancy very quietly. At my concierge's they were all sitting around the table over wine and chestnuts when I passed the lodge for the last time. They didn't see a thing. She was scratching herself, and he, bent over the stove, befuddled by the heat, was so far gone in drink that he couldn't keep his eyes open.

As far as those people were concerned, I was slipping into the unknown, a kind of endless tunnel. It feels good to have three less people knowing you – that is, spying on you and doing you dirt – three people without the faintest idea what's become of you. It's great. Three, because I'm counting their daughter, their little girl Thérèse, who scratched her fleas and bedbug bites so hard that she was all broken out and festering with boils. It's true that you got so badly bitten at my concierge's that going into their lodge was like crawling into a scrubbing brush.

Falling on the people who passed in the street, the long, naked, whistling finger of gas in the entrance turned them instantly into ghosts, gaunt or stout, framed in the black doorway. The same passers-by would then go and find themselves a bit of colour here and there, in the light of windows or street lamps, and finally lose themselves, as black and shapeless as myself, in the night.

I was no longer under any obligation to recognize these passers-by. Still, I'd have liked to stop them for just one second in their aimless roaming, just long enough to tell them once and for all that I was clearing out, getting lost far far away, so far that I didn't give a shit for any of them and they had no way of hurting me now, it was no use trying...

When I got to the Boulevard de la Liberté, the vegetable wagons were bumping along the road to Paris. I went the same way. I was almost out of Rancy. It was kind of chilly, so to warm myself I made for Bébert's aunt's lodge, which was a little out of my way. Her lamp was a spot in the darkness at the end of the corridor. "I really have to say goodbye to his aunt," I said to myself. "Then it'll really be over."

She was sitting as usual in her chair, among the smells of her lodge. A small stove warmed the room, and there was her old face that always seemed about to burst into tears now that Bébert was gone. On the wall, over her sewing box, hung a big school photo of Bébert in his school smock, with his beret and his cross. It was an enlargement, she'd paid for it with coffee coupons. I woke her.

She started up. "Good morning, Doctor." I still remember her exact words. "You look sick!" she said first thing. "Sit down... I'm not very well myself..."

"I was taking a little walk," I said, feeling silly to be turning up like that.

"It's late for a little walk, especially since you're headed for Place Clichy... There's a cold wind on the avenue at this time of night!"

She stood up and, stumbling this way and that, started making us a hot grog, at the same time talking about everything under the sun, but mostly the Henrouilles and Bébert.

There was nothing I could do to make her stop talking about Bébert, though it made her miserable and was bad for her and she knew it. I listened without interrupting, I was in a torpor. She wanted to remind me of all Bébert's endearing qualities, she set them out in a kind of display, taking a great deal of trouble because she was determined not to forget a single one of Bébert's qualities. She kept starting over, and when she had them all in order and had told me everything that could possibly be told about bottle-feeding him as a baby, she'd remember some little quality that would have to be lined up beside the others. She'd start once again from the beginning, and even so she'd forget something, and when that happened she had no recourse but to burst into tears of frustration. She was so tired her mind wandered. She sobbed herself to sleep. She hadn't strength enough to retrieve her little memories of little Bébert, whom she had loved so dearly, from the darkness for very long. Nothingness was always close to her now and to some extent upon her. A bit of grog and fatigue and there it was, she fell asleep and snored like a distant airplane being carried away by the clouds. She had no one left on earth.

While she sat crumpled among the smells, I thought I'd go away and probably never see Bébert's aunt again. After all, Bébert had slipped away, quietly and for good, and his old aunt would be following him before long. Her heart was sick and very old. It pumped blood into her arteries as best it could, but then the blood had a hard time climbing back into the veins. She'd be going to the big cemetery nearby, where the crowds of dead are waiting. That's where she took Bébert to play before his illness. And then it would really be over. They'd come and repaint her lodge, and then it would seem as if we had all retrieved ourselves like Japanese billiard balls on the brink of the hole, shilly-shallying before they end it all.

Billiard balls also start out with vigour and brio, but they never get anywhere in the end. Neither do we, and the whole earth is good for nothing else than to help us all get together. Bébert's aunt no longer had far to go; there was practically no vigour left in her. We can't get together while we're alive. There are too many colours to distract us and too many people moving around us. We can only get together in silence, when it's too late, like the dead. I knew all that, but it didn't help. I too had to move and go somewhere else... I couldn't stay there with her.

My diploma in my pocket made a big bulge, much bigger than my money and my papers. Outside the police station the patrolman was on duty, waiting to be relieved at midnight. He kept spitting. We bade each other good evening.

After the on-and-off light over the gas pump on the corner of the boulevard came the toll station with its clerks, verdant in their glass cage. The trams had stopped running. This was a good time to drop in on the toll clerks and talk about life, which is getting harder and harder, more and more expensive. There were two of them, a young one and an old one, both with dandruff, bent over enormous ledgers. Through their window you could see the fortifications, enormous shadowy piers jutting far out into the night as they waited for ships from so far away, ships so noble that you'll never see such boats. That's for sure. But we can hope for them.

I chatted for quite a while with those clerks, we even drank a bit of coffee that was warming on the cast-iron stove. They asked me as a joke if I was going on holiday, at night like that with my little bundle. "That's right," I said. No use talking to those clerks about anything too peculiar. They couldn't have helped me to understand. Still, I was miffed at their little joke and felt the need of saying something striking, of impressing them sort of, so I started talking off the cuff, about the campaign of 1816,* the one that had brought the Cossacks to the exact spot where we were then, to the Barrier, on the heels of the great Napoleon.

All this, of course, as nonchalantly as you please. Having convinced those lugs of my superior culture and sprightly erudition, I felt reassured and started down the avenue to the Place Clichy.

You've doubtless noticed the two prostitutes waiting at the corner of the Rue des Dames. They fill in the few weary hours separating deep night and early dawn. Thanks to them, life perseveres through the darkness. With their handbags chock-full of prescriptions, all-purpose handkerchiefs and photos of children in the country, they are the connecting link. Be careful when approaching them in the darkness, for those women are so specialized – barely alive enough to respond to the two or three sentences which sum up everything one can do with them – that they barely exist. They are insect ghosts in buttoned boots.

Don't speak to them, don't go too near them. They're dangerous. I had plenty of room. I started running between the car tracks. The avenue is long.

At the end of it you'll see the statue of Marshal Moncey. He has been defending the Place Clichy since 1816 against memories and oblivion, against everything and nothing, with a wreath of not very expensive beads. I came running down the deserted avenue and got there 112 years too late. No more Russians, no more battles, no more Cossacks, no more soldiers, nothing except a ledge of the pedestal that you could sit down on, just under the wreath. And the little brazier with three shivering derelicts around it, squinting into the acrid smoke. Not a very good place to be.

A few cars now and then raced desperately for the exits.

In times of crisis you remember the Grands Boulevards as a place that's not as cold as other places. What with my fever, it cost me an effort of the will to make my brain function. Under the influence of Bébert's aunt's grog, I descended the slope in flight from the wind, which isn't quite so cold when it comes at you from behind. Near the Saint-Georges Métro station an old woman in a little round hat was wailing about her granddaughter in the hospital, stricken with meningitis, so she said. With that as an excuse, she was taking up a collection. With me she was out of luck.

All I could give her was words. I told her about little Bébert and also about a little girl I'd taken care of in Paris, who had died of meningitis while I was in medical school. It had taken her three weeks to die, and her mother in the bed next to hers was so unhappy she couldn't sleep, so she masturbated the whole three weeks, and even when it was all over there was no way of stopping her.

Which goes to show that we can't do without our pleasures for so much as a second, and that it's very hard to be really unhappy. Life is like that.

The grieving old woman and I parted outside the Galeries. She was on her way to Les Halles to unload carrots. She'd been plodding the vegetable trail, and so had I, the same.

But I was drawn to the Tarapout.* It's plunked down on the boulevard like a big luminous cake. And people come to it from all directions, in a frantic hurry, like grubs. They emerge from the night with wide-open eyes, all ready to stock up on images. The ecstasy that never ends. It's the same people as in the Métro. But here outside the Tarapout they're happy, same as in New York they scratch their bellies at the box office, secrete a little change, and rush, happy and resolute, into the glaring apertures. There was so much light on the people, on their movements, globes and garlands of light, that it practically undressed them. You couldn't have talked about anything personal in that lobby, it was the exact opposite of night.

Rather dazed myself, I went to a café nearby. At the table next to mine, when I looked up, who should I see but Parapine, my one-time professor, having a beer, with his dandruff and all. We get together. There have been big changes in his life. It takes him ten minutes to tell me about them. No laughing matter. Professor Jaunisset had been so mean to him, had so persecuted him that he, Parapine, had been obliged to leave, to resign, and give up his laboratory. And then the mothers of the little girls at the Lycée had waylaid him at the gates of the Institute and beaten him up. Scandal. Investigation. Trouble.

At the last moment, thanks to an ambiguous advertisement in a medical journal, he had managed in the nick of time to secure another paltry means of support. Nothing much, of course, but down his alley and not demanding. The job was based on an ingenious application of Professor Baryton's recent theories concerning the role of the cinema in the education of cretin children. A significant step forward in the exploration of the unconscious. The latest thing. The talk of the town.

Parapine took his special patients to the Tarapout, because it was so modern. He picked them up at Baryton's rest home in the suburbs, and after the show took them back again – dazed, glutted with visions, safe, happy, sound and wonderfully modernized. That was all he had to do. Once they were seated in front of the screen they needed no supervision. A perfect audience. Everybody was happy. The same film ten times in a row would have delighted them. They were without memory. Continuous surprise – what a joy! Their families were delighted. So was Parapine. So was I. We chortled with well-being and drank beer after beer to celebrate the material reinstatement of Parapine in the modern world. We'd stay there, we decided, until two in the morning, until after the last show at the Tarapout, then we'd pick them up and hurry them back to Dr Baryton's establishment at Vigny-sur-Seine by cab. A good deal.

Delighted to see each other, we started talking just for the pleasure of exchanging fantasies, first about our travels and then about Napoleon, who cropped up in connection with Moncey on the Place Clichy.

Everything becomes a pleasure when two people want nothing more than to get on together, because then you finally feel free. You forget your life – that is, you forget all about money matters.

One thing leading to another, we even thought up some funny things to say about Napoleon. Parapine knew the history of Napoleon well. It had fascinated him in secondary school back in Poland, he told me. Parapine had been properly educated, not like me.

So Parapine told me that during the retreat from Russia Napoleon's generals had a hell of a time stopping him from going to Warsaw to get himself sucked off just once more by the Polonaise of his heart. That was Napoleon all over, even in the midst of the worst reverses and calamities. Absolutely irresponsible. Think of his Josephine! He was her eagle, but it made no difference! Ants in his pants, come hell and high water. If you've got a taste for wine and women, nothing can stop you. And we all have it, that's the sad part. That's all we think about! In the cradle, at the café, on the throne, in the toilet. Everywhere! Everywhere! Our peckers! Napoleon or not! Cuckold or not! Pleasure first! To hell, says the Great Defeated One, with those four hundred thousand fanatics, emberezina'd* to the gills... as long as old 'Poleon gets one last squirt! What a swine! Never mind! Life is like that! That's how everything ends. In absurdity. Long before the audience, the tyrant is bored with the play he's acting. When he's good and sick of secreting delirium for the benefit of the public, he goes and gets laid. When that happens, he's washed up! Destiny drops him in two seconds flat! His fans have no objection to his massacring them with might and main! None whatever! That's nothing! They forgive him a hundred per cent! What they won't forgive is when he starts boring them all of a sudden. Good work is tolerated only when hammed up. Epidemics stop only when the microbes get disgusted with their toxins. Robespierre was guillotined because he kept saying the same thing, and what did for Napoleon was over two years of Legion-of-Honour inflation. That lunatic's headache was having to supply half of sedentary Europe with a longing for adventure. An impossible job. It killed him.

Whereas the cinema, that new little factotum of our dreams, can be bought, hired for an hour or two like a prostitute.

Nowadays people are so bored that artists have been posted everywhere as a precaution. People are bored even in the houses where artists have been installed, with their overflow of emotion, their sincerities tumbling from floor to floor till the doors rattle. Each one of them is out to throb more outrageously and passionately, to abandon himself more intensely than his neighbour. Nowadays they decorate the public loos and slaughterhouses and pawnshops, and all that to entertain you, to cheer you up, to distract you from your fate.

Just plain living, what a drag! Life is a classroom, and boredom is the monitor, always keeping an eye on you, you have to look busy at all costs, busy with something fascinating, otherwise he comes and corrodes your brain. A day that's nothing more than a lapse of twenty-four hours is intolerable. Like it or not, a day should be one long almost unbearable pleasure, one long coitus.

Disgusting thoughts of this kind come to you when you're crazed by necessity, when a desire for a thousand other things and places is squeezed into each one of your seconds.

Robinson, too, in his way, was harried by the infinite before his accident, but now he was through, or so I thought.

Seeing as we were quietly settled at the café, I talked, I told Parapine everything that had happened since our last meeting. He understood things, even my kind, and I confessed to him that I had broken my medical career by leaving Rancy in such a cavalier fashion. That was the only way to put it. It was no joke. Under the circumstances I couldn't dream of going back to Rancy. Parapine agreed.

While we were talking thus pleasantly, confessing as it were, the Tarapout had an intermission, and all in a heap the movie-house musicians came over to the bistro. So we all had a drink together. Parapine was well known to the musicians.

In the course of the conversation, it came out that a pasha was needed for the stage show. A silent part. The guy who'd played it before had left without notice. Yet it was a good part, and well paid. Not at all strenuous. And in addition, let's not forget, charmingly surrounded by a sumptuous flock of English dancing girls, thousands of precise and agile muscles. Just my line and just what I needed.

I smirked and smiled and waited for the manager to make me an offer. In other words, I applied for the job. Since it was late and they hadn't time to go looking for another actor at the Porte Saint-Martin,* the manager was delighted to have me right on the spot. It saved him shoe leather. Me too. He barely looked at me. In fact he took me there and then. And put me to work. It might have bothered them if I'd limped, but even there I'm not so sure…

Penetrating the lovely warm padded basement of the Tarapout, I found a veritable hive of perfumed dressing rooms, where the English girls, while waiting for their number, passed the time romping suggestively and swearing. Overjoyed to have reconnected with my bread and butter, I hastened to make friends with my easy-going young colleagues. They welcomed me charmingly. Angels. Discreet angels. Besides, it's pleasant to be neither confessed nor despised. That's England for you.

The Tarapout was raking it in. Even backstage all was luxury, well-being, legs, lights, soaps and sandwiches. I believe the sketch we appeared in was set in Turkestan. It was a pretext for choreographic high jinks, musical contortions and violent drumming.

My part was slight but essential. Puffed up with gold and silver, I had some difficulty at first in finding a place to stand in among so many unstable lamps and doodads, but I got used to it, and thus displayed to my best advantage, I had nothing to do but daydream under the opalescent spotlights.

For a good fifteen minutes twenty cockney bayadères knocked themselves out with song and bacchanalian dance, supposedly to convince me of the reality of their charms. I'd have been satisfied with less. It seemed to me that going through that routine five times a day was a lot to expect of a poor girl. Those girls never weakened, they waggled their bottoms implacably, with the slightly boring energy typical of their race, the unflagging persistence of an ocean liner, ploughing its way through endless seas…

* * *

Why struggle, waiting is good enough, since everything is bound to end up in the street. Basically, only the street counts. Why deny it? It's waiting for us. One of these days we'll have to make up our minds and go down into the street, not one or two or three of us, but all. We stand on the brink, we simper and fuss, but never mind, the time will come.

Interiors are no good. As soon as a door closes on a man, he begins to smell and everything he has on him smells too. Body and soul, he deteriorates. He rots. It serves us right if people stink. We should have looked after them. We should have taken them out, evicted them, exposed them to the air. All things that stink are indoors, they preen themselves, but they stink all the same.

Speaking of families, I know a pharmacist on the Avenue de Saint-Ouen who had a marvellous sign in his window, a lovely advertisement: One bottle (price three francs) will purge the whole family! Isn't that great! They all belch! They shit together, as a family. They hate one another's guts, the essence of home life, but no one complains because after all it's cheaper than living in a hotel.

Which brings us to hotels. A hotel is more unsettled, less pretentious than an apartment, you don't feel so guilty. The human race is never free from worry, and since the last judgement will take place in the street, it's obvious that in a hotel you won't have so far to go. Let the trumpeting angels come, we hotel dwellers will be the first to get there.

In a hotel you try not to attract too much notice. It doesn't do a bit of good. As soon as you shout too loud or too often, they put their finger on you. Pretty soon, the way sound carries from room to room, you'll almost be afraid to piss in the washbasin. So naturally you improve your manners, the way officers do in the navy. Heaven and earth can start quaking from one minute to the next, we'll be prepared, it won't faze us, for already, just colliding in the hotel corridors, we beg and obtain pardon ten times a day.

I'd advise you to familiarize yourself with the toilet smell of everyone on your floor: it comes in handy. It's hard to harbour illusions at a rooms-by-the-month hotel. The guests don't cut much of a figure. They journey discreetly through life from day to day, the hotel is a ship that's rotting and full of holes, and they know it.

The one I moved to was patronized mostly by students from the provinces. As soon as you set foot on the stairs, it smelt of breakfast and old cigarette butts. At night you could recognize the place from a distance, because of the flame of grey light over the door and the gap-toothed gilt letters hanging from the balcony like an enormous dental plate. A monstrous lodging machine, distempered by sordid goings-on.

We'd pay one another visits from room to room. After years of crummy undertakings in the world of practical affairs, of so-called adventures, I was back again with students.

Their desires were still the same, intense and putrid, neither more nor less insipid than in the old days when I'd left them. The people had changed, but the ideas were the same. They still went at more or less regular hours to the other end of the neighbourhood to nibble bits of medicine, odds and ends of chemistry, a pill or two of law and heaps of zoology. The war, in passing over their age group, hadn't changed a thing, and if out of sympathy you took an interest in their dreams, they led you straight to their fortieth birthday. These young men gave themselves twenty years, 240 months of dogged thrift, in which to achieve happiness.

Their notions of happiness and success were conventional images, but carefully drawn. They saw themselves at the last square, surrounded by a small but incomparably precious family. Yet they would seldom have looked at this family. What for? One thing a family isn't meant for is to be looked at. And a father's distinction and happiness consist in kissing his family – his poetry – without ever looking at it.

By way of novelty, they'd have motored to Nice with their dowered bride and possibly have adopted the use of cheques for making payments. As for the shameful reaches of the soul, they would no doubt have taken their wife to a whorehouse one evening. No more. The rest of their world would be shut up in their daily papers and guarded by the police.

Staying at that flea-bitten hotel made my friends a trifle shameful and irritable for the moment. The young bourgeois student feels that he's being punished, and since it's taken for granted that he can't start saving yet, he drowns his sorrow in Bohemia and more Bohemia, in coffee-house despair.

At the beginning of each month we went through a short but acute fit of eroticism, the whole hotel shook with it. We washed our feet. An erotic expedition was arranged. Money orders arrived from the provinces, and that is what made up our minds. I might have obtained just as good coituses from my English chorus girls at the Tarapout, and free of charge at that, but thinking it over, I rejected the easy way because of the complications and the rotten jealous little pimps who were always hanging around backstage, waiting for the girls.

Since we read several pornographic magazines at our hotel, we knew the ropes and addresses needed for getting fucked in Paris! You have to admit that addresses are fun. You let yourself be tempted... even I, who had known the Passage des Bérésinas and travelled and experienced no end of complications in the pornographic line, never seem to have exhausted the hope of intimate revelations. Where the arse is concerned, there's always a residue of curiosity. You say to yourself that the arse has nothing more to tell you, that you haven't one more minute to waste on it, and then you start again just to make absolutely sure that the subject is exhausted, you learn something new about it after all, and that suffices to launch you on a wave of optimism.

You pull yourself together, you think more clearly than before, you start hoping again even if you'd given up hope altogether, and inevitably you revert once more to the arse, the same old story. Indeed, there are always, at all ages, discoveries to be made in the vagina. So one afternoon three of us from the hotel set out in search of an inexpensive piece. It was quick work, thanks to the connections of Pomone,* who operated an agency in the Batignolles quarter for every kind of erotic arrangement or combination that anyone could desire. His books were full of offers at all prices. This providential man officiated without ostentation of any kind at the back of a court; his exiguous premises were so poorly lit that you needed as much tactile sense and gift of dead reckoning to find your way as in an unfamiliar urinal. Your nerves would be unsettled by the layers of curtain you had to part before reaching the procurer, who was always to be found seated in an artificial confessional twilight.

Because of that dim light, to tell the truth, I never really managed to get a good look at Pomone, and though we had long conversations and even worked together for a time, though he made me all sorts of propositions and confided any number of sensitive secrets, I should be quite incapable of recognizing him today if I met him in hell.

I remember only that the furtive enthusiasts in the sitting room, waiting their turn for an interview, always behaved correctly, never any familiarity between them, in fact they were as reserved as if they'd been waiting for some eccentric dentist who disliked noise and didn't care much for light either.

I made the acquaintance of Pomone through a medical student. The student cultivated him as a means of making a bit of extra money out of his cock, because, you see, the lucky bastard was gifted with a monumental penis. He and his amazing equipment would be hired to bring animation into little intimate gatherings in the suburbs. The ladies made a great fuss over him, especially those who wouldn't have believed that anyone could have "such a big one". Overwhelmed young girls would dream and rave. In the police records our student figured under the alarming pseudonym of Balthazar!*

The waiting customers seldom strike up a conversation. Suffering exhibits itself; pleasure and the needs of the flesh hang their heads in shame.

Say what you please, it's a sin to be a lecher and poor. When Pomone heard about my situation and my medical past, nothing could stop him from telling me about his suffering. A vice was wearing him out. It consisted in "touching" himself continuously under his desk, while conversing with his customers, hunters afflicted with an itching perineum. "It's my work, you see! How do you expect me to control myself... with all the horrors they tell me, the swine!..." In short, his customers tempted him to vice, like those obese butchers who can't help gorging themselves on meat. In addition, I believe his bowels were constantly inflamed as a result of a malignant fever originating in his lungs. And the fact is that he was carried off by tuberculosis a few years later. He was also exhausted in a different sense by the chatter of his pretentious lady customers, always cheating, always making up ridiculous stories about nothing or about their sexual apparatus, the like of which, to hear them talk, you wouldn't find if you ransacked all four corners of the earth.

What the men wanted most and what had to be found for them was mostly consenting and admiring partners for their erotic whims. Incredible the quantities of love those men had to share, as much as Madame Herote's customers. A single morning's mail would bring the Pomone Agency enough unsatisfied love to extinguish all the wars in the world for ever. But these deluges of sentiment never went beyond the arse. The more's the pity.

His desk disappeared beneath that disgusting mass of passionate banalities. In my desire to know more, I decided to help him for a while in classifying that vast epistolary ragout. Just as with neckties or diseases, he explained, you grouped them according to types, the lunatics on one side, the masochists and sadists on another, the flagellants over here, the ones looking for a "governess" on a different page, and so on. It's not long before your amusement becomes a chore. We've been expelled from Paradise all right! No doubt about that! Pomone was of the same opinion with his moist hands and his everlasting vice, which gave him pleasure and remorse at the same time. After a few months I knew enough about his business and himself. My visits became less frequent.

At the Tarapout they continued to regard me as quite acceptable, a quiet, punctual extra, but after a few weeks of calm, my customary ill luck sought me out from an unusual quarter, and I was obliged to abandon my work as an extra and resume my miserable journey.

Seen in perspective, those days at the Tarapout were only a sort of forbidden and insidious port of call. Admittedly, I was always well dressed during those four months, once as a prince, twice as a centurion, one day as an aviator, and well and regularly paid. At the Tarapout I ate enough to last me for years. I led the life of a coupon clipper without the coupons. Treachery! Disaster! One night, I don't know why, they changed our number. The scene of the new sketch was the London Embankment. My misgivings were immediate, our little English girls were expected to sing, off key and ostensibly on the banks of the Thames at night, while I played the part of a policeman. A totally silent role, walking up and down in front of the parapet. Suddenly, when I'd stopped thinking about it, their singing grew louder than life itself and steered fate in the direction of calamity. While they were singing, I couldn't think of anything but all the poor world's misery and my own, those tarts with their singing made my heart burn like tuna fish. I thought I'd digested it, forgotten the worst! But this was the worst of all, a song that couldn't make it... And as they sang, they wiggle-waggled, to try and bring it off. A fine mess, all of a sudden we were knee-deep in misery... No mistake! Mooning about in the fog! Their lament was dripping with misery, it made me grow older from minute to minute. Panic oozed from the very stage set. And nothing could stop them. They didn't seem to understand all the harm their song was doing us all... They laughed and flung out their legs in perfect time, while lamenting their whole life... When it comes to you from so far, with such sureness of aim, you can't mistake it and you can't resist.

Misery was everywhere, in spite of the luxurious hall; it was on us, on the set, it overflowed, it drenched the whole earth. Those girls were real artists... Abject misery poured out of them, and they made no attempt to stop it or even understand it. Only their eyes were sad.

The eyes aren't enough. They sang the calamity of existence, and they didn't understand. They mistook it for love, nothing but love, the poor little things had never been taught anything else. Supposedly, they were singing about some little setback in love! That's what they thought! When you're young and you don't know, you mistake everything for love trouble...

Where I go... where I look...
It's only for you... ou...
Only for you... ou...

That's what they sang.

It's a mania with the young to put all humanity into one arse, just one, the dream of dreams, mad love. Maybe later they would find out where all that ended, when their rosiness had fled, when the no-nonsense misery of their lousy country had engulfed them, all sixteen of them, with their hefty mares' thighs and their bobbing tits... The truth is that misery already had the darlings by the neck, by the waist, they couldn't escape. By the belly, by the breath, by every cord of their thin, off-key voices.

Misery was inside them. No costume, no spangles, no lights, no smile could fool her, delude her about her own, Misery finds her own wherever they may hide; it just amuses her to let them sing silly songs of hope while waiting their turn... Those things awaken Misery, caress and arouse her...

That's what our unhappiness, our terrible unhappiness comes to, an amusement.

So to hell with people who sing love songs! Love itself is misery and nothing else, misery lying out of our mouths, the bitch, and nothing else. She's everywhere, don't wake her, not even in pretence. She never pretends. And yet those English girls went through their routine three times a day, with their backdrop and accordion tunes. It was bound to end badly.

I didn't interfere, but don't worry, I saw the catastrophe coming.

First one of the girls fell sick. Death to cuties who stir up calamity! Let 'em croak, we'll all be better off! And while we're at it, don't hang around street corners near accordion players, as often as not that's where you'll catch it, where the truth will strike. A Polish girl was hired to take the place of the sick one in their act. The Polish chick coughed too, when she wasn't doing anything else. She was tall and pale, powerfully built. We made friends right away. In two hours I knew all about her soul – as far as her body was concerned, I had to wait a while. This girl's mania was mutilating her nervous system with impossible crushes. Naturally, what with her own unhappiness, she slid into the English girls' lousy song like a knife into butter. Their song began very nicely, like all popular songs it didn't seem to mean a thing, and then your heart began to droop, it made you so sad that listening to it you lost all desire to live, because it's true that everything, youth and all that, comes to nothing, and then you started harking to the words, even after the song was over and the tune had gone home to sleep in its own bed, its honest-to-goodness bed, the tomb where everything ends. Two choruses, and you felt a kind of longing for the sweet land of death, the land of everlasting tenderness and immediate foggy forgetfulness. As a matter of fact their voices were foggy too.

All of us in chorus repeated their plaint, reproachful of everybody who was still around, still dragging their living carcasses from place to place, waiting along the river banks, on all the river banks of the world, for life to finish passing, and in the meantime doing one thing and another, selling things to other ghosts, oranges and racing tips and counterfeit coins, policemen, sex fiends, sorrows, telling each other things in this patient fog that will never end...

Tania was the name of my new pal from Poland. Her life at the moment, I gathered, was one compact frenzy, because of a little forty-year-old bank clerk, whom she had known since Berlin. She wanted to go back to Berlin and love him in spite of everything and at all costs. She'd have done anything to get back to him.

She pursued theatrical agents, those promisers of engagements, to the ends of their pissy stairways. While waiting for answers that never came, those rotters pinched her buttocks. But she was so totally enthralled by her faraway love that she hardly noticed their manipulations. This state of affairs hadn't prevailed for a week when disaster struck. For months she had been loading destiny with temptations, like a cannon.

Flu carried off her marvellous lover. The news came to us one Saturday afternoon. Dishevelled and haggard, she dragged me to the Gare du Nord. That in itself was nothing unusual, but in her frenzy she clamoured at the ticket window, insisting that she had to be in Berlin in time for the funeral. It took two stationmasters to dissuade her, to get her to understand that it was much too late.

In the state she was in, I couldn't think of leaving her. She was intent on her tragedy, and still more intent on exhibiting it to me in full flood. What an opportunity! Love thwarted by poverty and distance is like a sailor's love: no two ways, it's irrefutable and sure-fire. In the first place, when you're unable to meet too often, you can't fight, which is that much gained. Since life consists of madness spiked with lies, the farther you are from each other the more lies you can put into it and the happier you'll be. That's only natural and normal. Truth is inedible.

Nowadays, for instance, it's easy to talk about Jesus Christ. Did Jesus Christ go to the toilet in front of everybody? It seems to me his racket wouldn't have lasted very long if he'd taken a shit in public. Very little presence, that's the whole trick, especially in love.

Once Tania had been thoroughly assured that there was no possible train to Berlin, we made up for it in telegrams. At the Bourse* post office, we composed an extremely long one, because we didn't know whom to address it to. We didn't know anybody in Berlin except the dead man. From that moment on, there was nothing we could do but exchange words about the dead man's death. Words helped us to walk around the Bourse two or three times. Then we had to do something to soothe Tania's sorrow, so we strolled slowly up towards Montmartre, garbling words of grief.

On the Rue Lepic you start meeting people on their way to the top of the city in search of merriment. They're in a hurry. When they get to Sacré-Cœur, they look down at the night, a big dense hollow with houses piled at the bottom.

On the little square we went into the café that looked the least expensive. By way of consolation and gratitude Tania let me kiss her wherever I pleased. She also liked to drink. Tipsy merrymakers were already asleep on the benches around us. The clock at the top of the little church started striking the hours and more hours, and on and on. We had reached the end of the world, that was becoming obvious. We couldn't go any farther, because farther on there were only dead people.

The dead began on the Place du Tertre, two steps away. From where we were it was easy to see them. They were passing over the Galeries Dufayel,* to the east of us.

Even so, you've got to know how to find them – namely, from inside with your eyes almost closed, because the electric signs with their great copses of light make it very hard to see the dead, even through the clouds. I realized at once that these dead had Bébert with them. Bébert and I even gave each other the high sign, and then not far from him I saw the pale girl from Rancy, she had finally finished aborting, this time her guts had been taken out of her, and we too signalled to each other.

There were old patients of mine here and there, male and female, that I'd long stopped thinking about, and still others, the black man in a white cloud, all alone, the one they had given one lash too many down there in Topo, and old man Grappa, the lieutenant of the virgin forest! I'd thought of them all from time to time, of the lieutenant, the tortured black, and also of my Spaniard, the priest, he had come down from heaven that night with the dead to say prayers, and his golden crucifix was getting in his way, making it hard for him to fly from sky to sky. It got tangled up in the clouds, the dirtiest and yellowest of them, and as time went on I recognized more dead people, more and more... So many you can't help feeling ashamed of not having had time to look at them while they were living here beside you, all those years...

There's never enough time, it's true, not even for thinking of yourself.

Well, anyway, all those sons of bitches had turned into angels without my noticing! Whole clouds full of angels, including some very far-out and disreputable ones, all over the place. Roaming around, high over the city! I looked for Molly among them, a golden opportunity, my sweet, my only friend, but she hadn't come with them... She'd always been so nice that she probably had a little heaven all to herself, right next to God... I was glad not to find her with all those thugs, oh yes, the ghosts assembled over the city that night were really just the dregs of the dead, just scoundrels, scum and riff-raff. Especially from the cemetery nearby they came, more and more of them, though it's not a big cemetery, not at all high-class. There were even Communards, all drenched with blood, with their mouths wide open as if they wanted to yell some more and couldn't... The Communards were waiting with the others, waiting for La Pérouse, La Pérouse of the Islands, who was in command of the whole rally that night... La Pérouse* was taking a hell of a long time to get ready, because of his wooden leg, which he'd put on backwards... he'd always had trouble with that wooden leg, and besides he couldn't find his big spyglass.

He refused to come out of the clouds without his spyglass round his neck, crazy idea, the famous spyglass of his adventures, a laugh, it made you see people and things far away, farther and farther away through the small end, and naturally becoming more and more desirable because and in spite of your getting closer to them. Some Cossacks, who were tucked away not far from the Moulin,* couldn't manage to get clear of their graves. They were trying so hard it was terrifying, but they had tried many times before... They kept toppling back into their graves, they'd been drunk since 1820.

Nevertheless, a shower made them shoot up, and there they were over the city, refreshed. Then they scattered far and wide and painted the night with their turbulence, from cloud to cloud... The Opéra in particular seemed to attract them, with its enormous brazier of electric signs in the middle. Spurting from it, the ghosts bounded to the other end of the sky, so numerous and so active they made your head spin. Ready at last, La Pérouse wanted them to hoist him up at the last stroke of four. They held him in place and strapped him to the saddle. Finally astride and settled, he went right on waving his arms and gesticulating. The clock striking four almost made La Pérouse lose his balance as he was buttoning his coat. But then he led the mad rush across the sky. A hideous rout. Twisting and turning, the phantoms pour from all directions, the ghosts of a thousand heroic battles... They pursue, they challenge, they charge one another, centuries against centuries. For a long while, the north is cluttered with their abominable mêlée. The bluish horizon detaches itself, at last the day rises through the big rent they've made in the night while escaping.

After that it becomes very hard to find them. You have to get outside of time.

If you do manage to find them, it will be over towards England, but on that side the fog is always so dense, so compact that it's like sails rising one after another from the earth to the highest heaven and for all time. With practice and close attention you can find them even so, but never for very long, because of the wind that keeps blowing rain squalls and mists from the open sea.

The tall woman who is there, guarding the island, is the last of all. Her head is even higher than the uppermost mists. By now she is the only halfway-living thing on the island. Her red hair, high over everything else, still puts a little gold into the clouds: that's all there is left of the sun.

They say she's trying to make herself a cup of tea.

She may as well try, because she'll be there for all eternity. She'll never bring her tea to a boil, because of the fog, which has become too dense and penetrating. For a teapot she uses the hull of a ship, the most beautiful, the largest of ships, the last she could find in Southampton, and she heats up her tea in it, waves and waves of it... She stirs... She stirs it about with an enormous oar... That keeps her busy.

Serious for all time, bent over her tea, she doesn't look at anything else.

The whole dance has passed over her, but she hasn't even moved, she's used to having these ghosts from the continent losing themselves over there... That's the end of it.

With her fingers she stirs, that's good enough for her, the coals under the ashes between two dead forests.

She tries to revive the fire, it's all hers now, but her tea will never boil again.

There's no life left for the flames.

No more life in the world for anyone, only a wee bit for her and everything is almost over...

* * *

Tania woke me up in the room where we had finally gone to bed. It was ten in the morning. To get rid of her I told her I wasn't feeling very well and wanted to stay in bed awhile.

Life was starting up again. She pretended to believe me. So, soon as she'd gone, I went out myself. There really was something I wanted to do. The saraband of the night before had left me with a strong taste of remorse. The memory of Robinson came back to plague me. It was true that I'd abandoned the man to his fate and, worse, to the mercies of Abbé Protiste. No need to say more. True, I'd heard that everything was just fine down there in Toulouse and that Grandma Henrouille was being good and kind to him now. In certain situations, however, you only hear what you want to hear and what seems most convenient... Come right down to it, those vague rumours didn't prove a thing.

Anxious and curious, I headed for Rancy in quest of news, something definite, the real thing. To get there I had to take the Rue des Batignolles, where Pomone lived. It was on my way. As I approached his house, I was surprised to see Pomone in person on the corner, apparently shadowing a little man at some distance. Since Pomone never went out, I figured something big must be going on. I recognized the character he was following, a client, in his correspondence he referred to himself as "the Cid". But we had been tipped off that "the Cid"* worked in the post office.

For years he'd been pestering Pomone to find him a well-bred girlfriend: that was his dream. But the young ladies that were introduced to him were never well bred enough to suit him. They committed gaffes, so he claimed. On close consideration, there are two main classes of girlfriend, the "broad-minded" ones and the ones who've had "a good Catholic upbringing". Two equally crummy ways of feeling superior, two ways of titillating anxious, frustrated men, the "shrinking violet" type and the "girl about town".

This search had gone on month after month and engulfed all "the Cid's" savings. His transactions with Pomone had brought him to the end of his resources and the end of his hopes. Later on I heard that "the Cid" had committed suicide in a vacant lot that same afternoon. Actually, I knew something cockeyed was afoot the moment I saw Pomone leave his house. So I followed them quite a way through that neighbourhood, which loses its shops as it goes along, and even its colours one after another, till there's nothing left but ramshackle bistros as you approach the toll gate. When you're not in a hurry, it's easy to get lost in those streets, befogged by the sadness and utter indifference of the place. So great is your ennui that if you had a little money you'd jump into a cab and escape. The people you pass are burdened with a fate so heavy that you feel embarrassed on their account. It's practically certain that behind their curtained windows some of those small pensioners have left their gas on. Nothing you can do about it. "Christ!" you say. Which isn't much.

There's not even a bench to sit down on. Everywhere you look it's brown and green. When it rains, it rains from all directions, from the front and sides, and the street is as slippery as the back of a big fish with a parting of rain in the middle. You can't even speak of disorder in that neighbourhood, it's more like an almost well-kept prison, a prison that has no need of doors.

Roaming around like that, I finally lost Pomone and his suicide, right after the Rue des Vinaigriers. That put me so near La Garenne-Rancy I couldn't resist the temptation to cast a glance across the fortifications.

From a distance, La Garenne-Rancy doesn't look bad, you can't deny it, because of the trees in the big cemetery. You could swear you were in the Bois de Boulogne.

When you really want information about someone, you have to go to the people who know. After all, I said to myself, what have I got to lose by paying the Henrouilles a little visit? They must know what's going on in Toulouse. So then I made a mistake. You can never be careful enough. Before you know it, you're deep in the noisome regions of the night. It doesn't take long for disaster to strike. The merest trifle can bring it on, and besides, in the first place, there are certain people you shouldn't dream of going back to see. Especially those people! Once it's done, you're sunk.

Roaming at random, I was finally drawn by habit to the vicinity of the Henrouilles' house. Still in the same place, I couldn't get over it. Suddenly the rain was coming down. There was no one in the street but me. I didn't dare go any closer. I was about to turn back when the door of the house opened just enough for the daughter-in-law to motion me to come in. That woman saw everything. She'd seen me on the opposite pavement, looking fuddled. I had lost all desire to go closer, but she insisted. She even called me by my name.

"Doctor!... Oh, hurry!"

That's how she called me, not a moment's hesitation... I was afraid of attracting attention, so I hurried up her front steps. Again I saw the little corridor with the stove in it, the whole layout. I have to admit, it gave me the same old uneasy feeling. Then she started telling me that her husband had been very sick for two months and was getting steadily worse.

Naturally I had my suspicions.

"What about Robinson?" I hastened to ask her.

At first she eluded my question. Then finally she decided to answer. "They're both fine... Their business in Toulouse is doing well," she finally said, but talking very fast. That was all, then she shifted back to her sick husband. She wanted me to see him that minute, there was no time to lose... seeing that I was so devoted... that I knew her husband well... blah blah blah... that he had confidence in no one but me...

that he'd refused to see any other doctor... that they didn't have my address... Bullshit, in short.

I had good reason to suspect that there was more to her husband's illness than met the eye. I knew the lady well and the ways of the household. Nevertheless, my idiotic curiosity made me climb the stairs to the bedroom.

He was lying in the same bed where I'd treated Robinson after his accident some months before.

A room changes in a few months, even if you don't move anything. Old and run-down as things may be, they still find the strength, the Lord knows where, to get older. Everything had changed around us. Not that anything had moved, no, of course not, the things themselves had actually changed, in depth. Things are different when you go back to them, they seem to have more power to enter into us more sadly, more deeply, more gently than before, to merge with the death which is slowly, pleasantly, sneakily growing inside us, and which we train ourselves to resist a little less each day. From moment to moment, we see life languishing, shrivelling inside us, and with it the things and people who may have been commonplace or precious or imposing when we last left them. Fear of the end has marked all that with its wrinkles, while we were chasing around town in search of pleasure or bread.

Soon our past will be attended only by inoffensive, pathetic, disarmed things and people, mistakes with nothing to say for themselves.

The wife left me alone with her husband. He was in bad shape. Not much circulation left. The trouble was in his heart.

"I'm going to die," he simply kept repeating.

Cases like this were my special form of luck. I listened to his heartbeat just to be doing something, the few gestures people expect under those circumstances. His heart was racing, no doubt about it; shut up behind his ribs, it ran after life in fits and starts, but run or not, it would never catch up with life. His goose was cooked. Soon, the way it was stumbling, his heart would fall in the muck, all juicy and red, gushing like a crushed pomegranate. That's how his flabby old heart would look on the marble, cut open with a knife at the autopsy that would take place in a few days. All this would end in a lovely court-ordered autopsy. That's what I foresaw, considering that everyone in the neighbourhood would be relaying some highly seasoned rumours after his death, which would look very fishy after the other business.

The neighbours had it in for his wife with all the accumulated and still-undigested suspicions aroused by the previous affair. This would come up a little later. At the moment the husband didn't know how to live or die. He was already part way out of life, but he couldn't quite get rid of his lungs. He expelled air, and air came back. He'd have been glad to let himself die, but he had to live to the end. It was rough work, and it was driving him up the wall.

"I can't feel my feet any more..." he groaned. "I'm cold up to my knees..." He tried to touch his feet, but he couldn't.

He couldn't drink either. It was almost over. Handing him the tisane his wife had made him, I wondered what she could have put in it. That tisane didn't smell very good, but smell proves nothing. Valerian smells vile all by itself. And the way he was suffocating, it didn't make much difference whether the tisane was spiked or not. Still, he was going to a lot of trouble, working like mad with all the muscles he had left under his skin to keep suffering and breathing. He was struggling as much against life as against death. In a case like that the right thing would be to burst. When nature stops giving a damn, there wouldn't seem to be any limits. Behind the door his wife was listening to our consultation, but I knew his wife like a book. I tiptoed over and caught her. "Gotcha!" I said. She wasn't the least bit put out, she even whispered something in my ear.

"You should get him to remove his plate..." she murmured. "It must interfere with his breathing..." It was all right with me. Why indeed shouldn't he remove his plate?

"But you tell him!" I advised her. It was ticklish saying a thing like that to someone in his condition.

"No! No! It would be better coming from you!" she insisted. "Coming from me it would upset him to know I knew..."

"Really?" I asked in amazement. "Why?"

"He's been wearing it for thirty years and never said a word about it to me..."

"In that case," I suggested, "why not let him keep it? As long as he's used to breathing with it in..."

"Oh no, I'd never forgive myself!" she replied with a kind of quaver in her voice..

I went quietly back into the room. He heard me approaching. He was glad I'd come back. Between fits of suffocation he spoke to me. He made an effort to be friendly, asked how I was getting along, if I had built up a new clientele… "Oh, yes!" I said in reply to all his questions. It would have been much too long and complicated to go into detail. Not the right time. Hidden behind the door, his wife made signs at me, meaning I should ask him to remove his plate. I went close to his ear and whispered, advising him to remove it. Mistake! "I threw it down the toilet!…" he said, his eyes more frightened than ever. Vanity, that's what it was. After that he let out a long groan.

An artist makes do with what happens to be at hand. All his life Henrouille had taken aesthetic pains with his dental plate.

That was a good time for confessions. I'd have liked him to take advantage and give me his opinion about his mother and what had been done to her. But he couldn't. His mind was wandering. He began to drool copiously. The end. Impossible to get another sentence out of him. I wiped his lips and went back downstairs. His wife in the corridor wasn't at all pleased, she almost lit into me about the plate, as if it were my fault.

"It was gold, Doctor!… I know! I know how much he paid for it!… They don't make them like that any more!…" She went on and on! She made me so nervous I offered to go up and try again. But only if she went with me.

That time the husband hardly recognized us. Just a little. The groans weren't as loud when we were both with him; it was as if he wanted to hear everything his wife and I said to each other.

I didn't go to the funeral. The autopsy that I had kind of feared never came off. It was all done on the quiet. But after that the widow Henrouille and I were no longer on speaking terms because of the dental plate.

* * *

Young people are always in such a hurry to go and make love, in such a rush to grab hold of anything that's been advertised as a pleasure. When it comes to sensation they never think twice. It's a little like those travellers who go and eat anything that's given them at the station buffet while waiting for the whistle to blow. As long as you provide young people with the two or three phrases likely to steer a conversation in the direction of fucking, that's all they need, they'll be as happy as larks. Happiness comes easy to the young, why wouldn't it when they come as often as they please?

Youth is a glorious beach at the edge of the water, where women seem at last to be freely available, where they're so beautiful they don't need the falsehood of our dreams.

So naturally when winter comes it's hard for us to go home, to tell ourselves that it's all over, to admit it. We'd be glad to stay on, even in the cold of age, we go on hoping. That's not hard to understand. We're contemptible. No one's to blame. Pleasure and happiness come first. I think so too. When you start hiding from people, it's a sign that you're afraid to play with them. That in itself is a disease. We should try to find out why we refuse to get cured of loneliness. A character I met in the hospital during the war, a corporal, spoke to me about that kind of feeling. Too bad I never saw him again! "The earth is dead," he said to me. "We people are just worms on top of it, worms on its fat, revolting carcass, eating its entrails and all its poisons... Nothing can help us, we were born rotten... There you have it!"

True, they hauled this thinker off to the fortress one night, proof that he was still good enough to be shot. I even remember that it took two MPs to hold him, a tall one and a short one. At the court martial they said he was an anarchist.

Sometimes, when you think about it years later, you wish you could retrieve the words certain people said and the people themselves, so as to ask them what they were trying to tell you... But they're as gone as gone can be!... We weren't educated enough to understand them... We'd like to know if maybe they've changed their minds... But it's much too late... It's over and done!... Nobody knows anything about them any more. So we just have to go on alone in the night. We've lost our true companions, and we didn't even ask them the right question, the real one, when there was still time. When we were with them, we didn't know. Lost men. Anyway, we're always late. Vain regrets won't make the kettle boil.

Well, luckily at least Abbé Protiste came to see me one fine morning to split the commission we'd made on Grandma Henrouille's crypt. Actually I'd given up expecting that priest. He dropped like a gift from heaven... We each had fifteen hundred francs coming to us! At the same time he brought me good news of Robinson. It seems his eyes were a good deal better. The lids had even stopped suppurating. And they were all asking for me down there. True enough, I'd promised to go and see them. Even Protiste insisted.

From what he told me I also gathered that Robinson was going to be married soon to the daughter of the woman who sold candles in the church next to the burial vault, the one that had jurisdiction over Grandma Henrouille's mummies. The thing was as good as done.

Naturally all this started us talking about the death of Monsieur Henrouille, but we didn't go into it very deeply. More pleasantly, the conversation came back to Robinson's future, and then to the city of Toulouse, that I didn't know at all and that Grappa had talked about in the old days, and then to the weird business the two of them were engaged in down there, and finally to the young girl who was due to marry Robinson. In other words, we talked about everything under the sun, a little of this and a little of that... Fifteen hundred francs! That made me indulgent, and optimistic, so to speak. Everything he told me about Robinson's plans struck me as wise, sensible, judicious and well suited to the circumstances... Everything would be all right. So at least I thought. And then the priest and I started talking about age. We had both spent more than thirty years on inhospitable and little-regretted shores. There was no point in even turning around to look back on those shores. We hadn't lost much by growing older. "A man, after all, must be very degraded," I concluded, "to regret one year more than another!... You and I, Mr Priest, can grow old with gusto! And enthusiasm! Was yesterday such a bargain? Or last year?... What did you think of it?... Regret what?... I ask you!... Youth?... You and I never had any youth!...

"The poor, it's true, get younger inside as they go along, and towards the end, provided that on the way they've made some attempt to jettison all the lies and fear and contemptible eagerness to obey they were given at birth, they're less revolting than at the start. The rest of what exists on earth isn't for them! It doesn't concern them! Their job, their only job, is to get rid of their obedience, to vomit it up. If they manage that before kicking in, then they can boast that they haven't lived for nothing."

I was definitely in good form... Those fifteen hundred francs had sparked me off. I went on: "The only real youth, Mr Priest, is loving everyone without distinction, that alone is true, that alone is young and new. Well, Mr Priest, do you know many young people who are

307

like that?... I don't!... All I see is crusty old stupidities fermenting in more or less recent bodies, and the more these sordid absurdities ferment the more they stimulate the young and the more they boast how fantastically young they are! But it's not true, it's bullshit... They're young the way a boil is young, no more, because of the pus inside that hurts and makes them swell up."

My talking to him like that upset Protiste... Not wanting to irritate him any more, I changed the subject... For one thing, he'd been very kind to me, providentially so in fact... It's hard to stop yourself from going back to a subject that's as much on your mind as that was on mine. It scrambles your brains. To get free, you try to unload some part of it on everybody who comes to see you, and that exasperates them. Being alone is to train for death. "A man," I went on, "should die more abundantly than a dog and take a thousand minutes to do it. Each minute will be new all the same and laced with enough fear and trembling to make him forget all the pleasure he may have had in making love during the preceding thousand years... Happiness on earth would be to die with and while having pleasure... The rest is nothing at all, a fear that we don't dare avow, art."

Hearing me rave that way, Protiste thought I must have fallen sick again. Maybe he was right and maybe I was wrong about everything. In my isolation, searching for a way to punish man's universal egoism, it's true that I was jerking off my imagination, looking for punishment everywhere, even in death. You amuse yourself as best you can when you're short of money and don't often get a chance to go out, much less to emerge from yourself and fuck.

I admit it wasn't exactly sensible to needle Protiste with philosophical ideas contrary to his religious convictions. But the fact is his whole person exuded a nasty little smell of superiority that must have got on quite a few people's nerves. As he saw it, all we humans on earth were in a kind of waiting-for-eternity room, each with a number. His number, I don't have to tell you, was first-class, good for Paradise. He didn't give a shit about anything else.

Such convictions are unbearable. On the other hand, when he offered that same afternoon to advance me the price of the trip to Toulouse, I stopped needling and contradicting him. My dread of having to face Tania and her ghost again at the Tarapout made me accept his invitation without a word of argument. A week or two of the easy life, if nothing else, that's what I said to myself. When it comes to tempting you, the Devil has millions of tricks! We'll never know them all. If we lived long enough, we wouldn't know where to go to start a new happiness. We'd have strewn aborted happinesses all over, the whole earth would stink of them, unbreathably. The ones in the museums, the real abortions, turn some people's stomachs, the mere sight of the things makes them want to vomit. And our loathsome attempts to be happy are miscarried enough to sicken you long before you die for real.

If we didn't forget them, we'd simply waste away. Not to mention the trouble we've taken to get where we are, to make our hopes, our degenerate joys, our passions and lies interesting... Want some? Help yourself. And what of our money? And our little affectations that go with it... And the things we get other people to swear to and that we ourselves swear to, things we thought no one had ever said or sworn to before, before they filled our minds and mouths, and perfumes and caresses and mimicries – in short, everything it takes to hide all that as much as possible, so we'll never have to speak of it again, for fear it will come back at us like vomit. Our trouble isn't lack of perseverance, it's that we're not on the right road that leads to an easy death.

Going to Toulouse was another piece of damn foolishness. Thinking it over, I suspected as much. So I had no excuse. But following Robinson in his adventures, I had developed a taste for shady undertakings. Already in New York when I couldn't sleep, I racked my brains wondering if it mightn't be possible to go further and still further with Robinson. You sink, at first you're afraid in the darkness, but all the same you want to understand, and after that you never leave the depths. But there's too much. You can't understand so many things at once. Life is too short. You don't want to be unjust to anyone. You have scruples, you hesitate to make snap judgements and, worst of all, you're afraid to die while you're hesitating, because then you'd have been on earth for nothing whatsoever. And that's the worst of all.

Hurry, hurry, don't be late for your death. Sickness, the poverty that disperses your hours and years, the insomnia that paints whole days and weeks grey, the cancer that may even now, meticulous and blood-spotted, be climbing up from your rectum.

You'll never have time, you tell yourself! Not to speak of war, which is also, what with the criminal boredom of men, ready to rise up from the cellar that poor people shut themselves up in. Do we kill enough poor people? Not sure... It's a moot point... Maybe all those who don't understand should have their throats cut... And perhaps other, new poor people should be born, and so forth and so on, until we get a crowd who understand the joke, the whole joke... Just as you mow a lawn until the grass is really right, really soft.

On leaving the train at Toulouse I was in doubt what to do. But a bottle of beer at the station buffet set me strolling through the streets. An unfamiliar city is a fine thing! That's the time and place when you can suppose that all the people you meet are nice. It's dream time. And because you're in a dream you can afford to waste a little time in the park. Still, after a certain age, unless you have gilt-edged reasons, people will think you've gone to the park to chase little girls like Parapine. So better not. You'll be safer in the pastry shop just before the park gate, the beautiful shop on the corner, as fancy as a brothel stage set, bevelled mirrors studded with little birds. Deep in thought, you catch yourself eating burnt almonds ad infinitum. A place for seraphim. The young ladies who work there babble furtively about their private affairs as follows:

"So I told him he could call for me on Sunday... My aunt heard him and made a terrible stick because of my father..."

"But hasn't your father remarried?" her friend breaks in.

"What has that got to do with it?... Even if he's remarried, he still has a right to know who his daughter's going out with..."

The other young lady in the shop was of the same opinion. The consequence was an impassioned controversy involving all three. Not wanting to disturb them, I sat quietly in my corner, stuffing myself uninterruptedly with tarts and cream puffs – which were excellent by the way – hoping that my discretion would help them solve their delicate problem of family priorities more quickly; but they made no progress. Nothing came of their discussion. Their speculative incompetence restricted them to an imprecise sort of hatred. Those shop girls were bursting with illogicality, vanity and ignorance. Drooling with rage, they whispered insults by the dozen.

I couldn't help it, I was fascinated by their nasty passion. I attacked the rum babas. I stopped counting the babas. So did they. I was hoping they'd come to some conclusion before I had to leave... But passion made them deaf and soon dumb in my presence.

Tense, their venom spent, they rested in the shelter of the pastry counter, each one invincible, shut up in her shell, pinched, ruminating plans for a still more embittered comeback. At the first opportunity, she would – promptly this time – spew out all the angry, cutting absurdities she happened to know about her little friend. And the occasion wouldn't be long in coming, she'd see to that... Scrapings of arguments aimed at nothing at all. In the end I sat down, the better for them to befuddle me with the unceasing sound of their words, intentions, thoughts, as on a shore where the ripples of unceasing passions never manage to get organized...

You listen, you wait, you hope, here, there, in the train, at the café, in the street, in drawing rooms, at the concierge's, you listen and wait for evil to get organized as in wartime, but there's only waste motion, nothing is ever done, either by those unfortunate young ladies or by anyone else. No one comes to help us. An enormous babble, grey and monotonous, spread over life like an enormously discouraging mirage. Two ladies came in, and the muddle-headed charm of the ineffectual conversation spread out between the counter girls and myself was broken. The girls gave the new arrivals their eager and undivided attention, anticipating their requests and their least desires. They chose here and there and nibbled at the tarts and petits fours. When it came time to pay, they gushed polite phrases, and each insisted on offering the others little pastries to nibble that very minute.

One declined most graciously, explaining at length and in confidence to the other ladies present, who took a keen interest, that her doctor had forbidden her all sweets, that her doctor was a genius, that he had done wonders in combating constipation in Toulouse and elsewhere, that he was well on his way to curing her of a retention of "number two", from which she had been suffering for more than ten years, thanks to a very special diet and a miraculous medicine known to him alone. The other ladies were not going to let themselves be outdone so easily in matters of constipation. Their own constipation defied comparison. They were up in arms. They demanded proofs. In response to their doubts, the lady observed simply that when moving her bowels she now broke wind, that it sounded like fireworks... that because of her new-style bowel movements, all well-moulded, solid and substantial, she was obliged to take extra precautions... Sometimes these marvellous new faeces of hers were so hard they gave her excruciating pain in the rectum... a tearing sensation!... So now she had to use Vaseline before moving her bowels. Irrefutable.

Thus convinced, the voluble ladies left the Petits Oiseaux pastry shop, accompanied to the threshold by the smiles of the entire staff.

The park across the way was a good place in which to rest, meditate briefly and put my thoughts in order before going to look for my friend Robinson.

In provincial parks the benches, offering a view of flower beds overstuffed with cannas and daisies, are almost always empty on weekday mornings. Near the rock garden, on strictly captive waters, a small tin boat, encircled by floating ashes, was moored to the shore by a mouldy rope. A sign announced that the skiff operated on Sunday and that a tour of the lake cost two francs.

How many years? Students? Phantoms?

In the corners of all parks there lie forgotten any number of little coffins garlanded with dreams, thickets charged with promises, handkerchiefs full of everything. All a big joke.

But that's enough daydreaming! Let's go looking for Robinson and his church of Sainte-Éponime, and that crypt where he and the old woman are taking care of mummies. That's what I'd come for, so I'd better get going.

I took a carriage, and we meandered this way and that at a leisurely sort of trot, through the dark sunken streets of the old town, where the light catches between the roofs. Over cobbles and bridges we drove with a great clatter of wheels, behind a horse that was all shoes. They haven't burnt any cities in the south for a long time. They've never been so old. Wars don't pass that way any more.

We pulled up in front of Sainte-Éponime on the stroke of noon. The crypt was a little farther on, under a calvary. It was pointed out to me, in the middle of a small, parched garden. You entered the crypt through a sort of barricaded hole. From a distance I saw the caretaker, a young girl, and asked for news of my friend Robinson. She was just closing the door. She answered with a friendly smile, and the news she gave me was good.

From where we were standing in that noonday light everything around us turned pink, and the worm-eaten stones of the church rose skywards, as though ready to melt into the air.

Robinson's little friend must have been about twenty, with firm, wiry legs, a small, perfectly charming bust, and surmounting it a delicate, precisely etched face. Just the eyes may have been a little too black and attentive for my taste. Not at all the dreamy type. It was she who wrote Robinson's letters, the ones I had received. She went ahead of me to the vault with her precise gait, her shapely feet and ankles. She had the build of a good lay, and must have spread her legs very nicely when circumstances demanded. Short, hard hands with a strong grip, the hands of an ambitious working girl. A brisk little movement to turn the key. Shimmering heat all around us. Once she had the door open, she decided, in spite of the lunch hour, to show me through the vault. I was beginning to feel a little more relaxed. Behind her lantern we descended into increasing coolness. It was very nice. I pretended to stumble between two steps as an excuse for grabbing her by the arm. That made us laugh, and when we reached the clay floor at the bottom I kissed her a little on the neck. She protested at first, but not very much.

After a brief moment of affection, I wriggled round her belly like a love worm. Lecherously we moistened and remoistened our lips for our soul conversation. With one hand I crept slowly up her tensed thighs, it's fun with the lantern on the floor, because at the same time you can watch the muscles rippling over her legs. It's a position I can recommend. Ah! Such moments are not to be missed! They put your eyes out of joint, but it's worth it. What gusto! What sudden good humour! The conversation resumed in a new tone of confidence and simplicity. Now we were friends. Arses first! We had just saved ten years.

"Do you often show people around?" I asked, puffing and putting my foot in it. But I quickly covered up: "Doesn't your mother sell candles at the church next door?... Father Protiste has told me about her."

"I only take Madame Henrouille's place during lunch hour," she answered. "In the afternoon I work for a dressmaker... On the Rue du Théâtre... Did you pass the theatre on your way here?"

Again she reassured me about Robinson. He was much better, in fact the specialist thought he'd soon see well enough to go out by himself. All that was most encouraging. As for Grandma Henrouille, she seemed delighted with the vault. She was doing good business and saving money. Only one difficulty: in the house where they were living, the bedbugs kept everybody awake, especially on stormy nights. So they burned sulphur. It seemed that Robinson often spoke of me, pleasantly what's more. One thing leading to another, we came around to the projected marriage, the circumstances and all.

I have to admit that with all that talk I still hadn't asked her name. Her name was Madelon.* She'd been born during the war. Their marriage plans, after all, suited me fine. Madelon was an easy name to remember. I figured she must know what she was doing in marrying Robinson... Even if he was getting better, he'd always be an invalid... And besides, she thought only his eyes were affected... But his nerves were shot, and so was his morale and everything else! I was almost going to tell her so, to warn her... I've never known how to steer conversations about marriage, or extricate myself from them.

To change the subject, I expressed a keen and sudden interest in the cellar and its occupants. People came a long way to see it, so as long as I was there why not take a look?

With her little lantern Madelon and I made the shadows of the corpses emerge from the wall one by one. They must have given the tourists food for thought! Those ancient stiffs were lined up against the wall as if a firing squad had worked them over... They weren't exactly skin and bone any more, or clothing either... Just a little of all that... In a very grimy state, and full of holes. Time had been gnawing at their skin for centuries and was still at it... Here and there it was still tearing away bits of their faces... enlarging all the holes and even finding long strips of epidermis that death had left clinging to their cartilage. Their bellies had emptied of everything, and now there were little cradles of shadow where their navels had been.

Madelon explained that to get into this condition the bodies had had to spend more than five hundred years in a quicklime cemetery. You wouldn't have taken them for corpses. Their corpse days were far behind them. By easy stages they had come closer and closer to dust.

In that cellar there were big ones and little ones, twenty-six in all, who asked for nothing better than to enter into eternity. They weren't being admitted yet. Two women with bonnets perched on top of their skeletons, a hunchback, a giant and even a complete baby, with a kind of bib, lace if you please, around his tiny dried-out neck, and some bits and pieces of swaddling clothes.

Grandma Henrouille was making a lot of money out of these scrapings of the centuries. To think that when I last saw her she herself had looked very much like these spooks… So then Madelon and I went slowly back, passing them by again. One by one their so-called heads stood silent in the harsh circle of lamplight. It's not exactly night they have in their eye sockets, it's almost a gaze, but gentler, like the gaze of those who know. More disturbing is their smell of dust, it catches in your nose.

Whenever a party of tourists showed up, Grandma Henrouille was on the spot. She made those stiffs work like circus performers. At the height of the summer season, they brought her in a hundred francs a day.

"Don't they look sad?" Madelon asked me. A ritual question.

Death didn't mean a thing to that cutie. She had been born during the war, when death came easy. But I knew well how people die. Something I had learnt. It's very painful. It's all right to tell the tourists that these dead are happy. They can't speak for themselves. Grandma Henrouille even clouted them on the belly when there was enough parchment left on it, and it went "boom boom". But even that's no proof of good cheer.

Finally Madelon and I got back to our own affairs. So it was true that Robinson was better. That was good enough for me. Our little friend seemed bent on this marriage! She must have been bored to death in Toulouse. You didn't often meet a man who had travelled as much as Robinson. What stories he had to tell! True ones and not so true. He'd already spoken to them at length of America and the tropics. Lovely.

I'd been in America and the tropics too. I knew stories about them too and offered to tell her some. Come to think of it, I had travelled with Robinson, and that's how we'd got to be friends. The lantern went out. We lit it ten times while arranging the past and the future. She wouldn't let me touch her breasts, said they were much too sensitive.

But seeing that Grandma Henrouille would be coming back from her lunch any minute, we had to climb back to the daylight over the steep, rickety staircase, which was as difficult to negotiate as a ladder. I made a note of those stairs.

* * *

315

Because of the treacherous narrow stairs Robinson didn't often go down to the mummy cellar. Most of the time he stood at the door, giving the tourists a bit of sales talk and getting used to taking in a few specks of light here and there.

Meanwhile in the depths, Grandma Henrouille managed very well. She knocked herself out with the mummies, enlivening the tourists' visit with a little speech about her parchment stiffs. "They're not at all repulsive, ladies and gentlemen, because, as you see, they were preserved in quicklime... for more than five centuries... Our collection is the only one of its kind in the whole world... The flesh is gone, of course... Only the skin is left, but it's tanned... They're naked, but not indecent... You will observe that a baby was buried at the same time as its mother... The baby is also extremely well preserved... And that tall man with the lace shirt that he still has on... He's got every one of his teeth... You will observe..." At the end of the tour she clouted them all on the chest – it sounded like a drum. "Observe, ladies and gentlemen, that this one has only one eye left... all dried out... and the tongue too... it's like leather!" She gave it a pull. "He's sticking his tongue out, but he's not nasty... You can give what you like as you leave, ladies and gentlemen, but the usual is two francs each and half-price for children... You can touch them before you go... convince yourself... but please, ladies and gentlemen, don't pull too hard... they're extremely fragile..."

Grandma Henrouille had wanted to raise the prices as soon as she got there, she applied to the diocese. But it wasn't so simple, because of the priest at Sainte-Éponime, who demanded a third of the take all for himself, and also because of Robinson, who kept griping, because in his opinion she wasn't giving him a big-enough rake-off.

"I've been had," he concluded. "Taken for a sucker... Again... I never have any luck!... The old bag's cellar, you know... it brings in a fortune!... Believe you me, she's raking it in."

"But you didn't put any money into the business!" I argued to calm him down and put some sense into him... "And you're well fed!... Well taken care of!..."

But Robinson was as stubborn as a mule, he felt persecuted, and that was that. He refused to understand, to resign himself.

"All in all," I said, "you've come out of a nasty business pretty well!... So don't complain! You'd have gone straight to Cayenne* if they'd nabbed you… Here nobody's bothering you!… And you've found little Madelon who's a sweet kid and willing to put up with you… despite the state of your health!… So what have you got to complain about?… Especially now that your eyes are getting better…"

"You seem to be saying I don't know what I'm complaining about," he said then. "But I feel I've got to complain… that's the way it is… it's all I've got left… that's right… It's the only thing they let me do… Nobody's forced to listen."

True enough, he did nothing but complain whenever we were alone. I had come to dread those confidential moments. I looked at him with his blinking eyes which still oozed a little in the sunlight, and I said to myself that all things considered Robinson was not endearing. There are animals like that, they can be innocent, unhappy, anything you please, you know it, and still you don't like them. There's something wrong with them.

"You could have died in jail…" I tried again, determined to make him think.

"I've been in jail… It's no worse than where I am now!… You're out of date…"

He hadn't told me he'd been in prison. That must have been before we met, before the war. He pressed his point and concluded: "Take it from me. There's only one kind of freedom, only one, to see properly and have your pockets full of cash. The rest is bullshit!…"

"So what, exactly, do you want?" I asked him. When he was challenged like that to make up his mind, to speak up, he deflated. And that's just when it might have been interesting…

During the day, while Madelon was working for the dressmaker and Grandma Henrouille was exhibiting her mummies, we went to a café under the trees. Robinson was crazy about that café under the trees, probably because of the noise the birds made up above us. Millions of them! Especially about five o'clock, when they came home to their nests, all keyed up by the summer. They swooped down on the square like a storm. There was a story about a barber who had his shop across from the park and had gone crazy just from hearing them cheep for years and years. It's true we couldn't hear each other talk. Robinson thought it was cheerful.

"If only she'd give me twenty centimes per visitor and be regular about it, I'd be satisfied!"

About every fifteen minutes he'd get back to his preoccupation. In between, the colours of times past seemed to come back to him, incidents too, stories, among others, about the Compagnie Pordurière in Africa, which both of us had known well after all, and some hairy tales that he'd never told me before. Maybe he hadn't dared. He was kind of reticent in a way, I'd even say secretive.

Speaking of the past, what I remembered best when I was in good spirits was Molly, like the echo of a clock striking in the distance. When something pleasant popped into my mind, I always thought of her.

After all, when our egoism lets us go for a while, when it comes time to throw it off, the only women whose memory you cherish in your hearts are the ones who really loved men a little, not just one man, even if it was you, but the whole lot.

When we left the café that evening, we hadn't done a thing, we could have been retired non-coms.

During the season, there was a steady flow of tourists. They hung around the crypt, and Grandma Henrouille always got them to laugh. Her jokes weren't exactly to the priest's taste, but, since he was collecting more than his share, he didn't say boo, and besides smutty jokes were over his head. Be that as it may, Grandma Henrouille was worth seeing and hearing in the midst of her corpses. She looked you straight in the eye, she wasn't in the least afraid of death; wrinkled and shrivelled as she was, you'd have thought she was one of them, coming along with her lantern to shoot the shit right in what passed for their faces.

When we got back to the house and gathered for dinner, we discussed the day's take, and Grandma Henrouille called me her "little old Dr Jackal" because of the dealings we'd had in Rancy. All in a bantering tone, of course. Madelon bustled about in the kitchen. That joint where we were staying got only the measliest light, it was an annex of the sacristy, very cramped, all cluttered with joists and struts and dusty crannies. "Yes," said the old woman, "it's practically always night in here, so to speak, but you can still find your bed, your pockets and your mouth. That's good enough for me!"

She hadn't grieved for long after her son's death. "He was always very delicate," she said to me one evening. "Look, I'm seventy-six and I've never complained!... He complained all the time, it was his way, exactly like your Robinson... just to give you an example. Take the stairs to the

318

crypt, for instance... They're tough, you'll agree... You've been down there... They knock me out, of course they do, but some days they're worth as much as two francs a step to me... I've figured it out... Well, for that price I'd climb up to heaven if anyone asked me to!"

Madelon put lots of spices in our food, and tomatoes as well. It was great. And we drank rosé. Even Robinson had taken to wine now that he was living in the south. He had already told me everything that had happened since his arrival in Toulouse, so I had stopped listening. To tell the truth, I was kind of disappointed in him, and disgusted. "You're a bourgeois!" I told him finally (at that time I could think of no worse insult). "All you ever think of is money... Once you recover your eyesight, you'll be the worst of the whole bunch!"

Hard words couldn't get him down. They seemed on the contrary to give him a lift. Besides, he knew it was true. The man's all set, I said to myself, no need to trouble my head about him... You can't get around it, a little woman like that, slightly on the violent, depraved side, will change a man beyond recognition... For a long time, I said to myself, I thought this Robinson was made for adventures, but cuckold or not, blind or not, he's only a cheap punk... Neither more nor less.

In addition, Grandma Henrouille had contaminated him with her mania for saving, and so had Madelon with her desire to be married. That settled it. He was washed up. Especially as he'd got to like the girl more and more. I knew something about that. I'd be lying if I said I wasn't a little jealous: it wouldn't be true. Madelon and I got together for short moments now and then, before dinner in her room. But those meetings were hard to arrange. We never spoke of them. We were as discreet as could be.

Don't go thinking on that account that she didn't love her Robinson. There's no connection. It was just that he was playing at being engaged, so naturally she played at being faithful. That's how it was between them. As long as they saw eye to eye, that was the main thing. As he told me, he wasn't going to touch her until they were married. It was his idea. So he'd have eternity, and I'd have the here and now. He was also planning, so he told me, to set himself up in a small restaurant with Madelon, and run out on Grandma Henrouille. He really meant business. "She's nice, the customers will like her," he foresaw in his more cheerful moments. "And say, you've tasted her cooking... When it comes to grub, she hasn't her equal!"

He even thought he could touch Grandma Henrouille for a bit of capital to start with. All right with me, but I suspected that he'd have a hard time persuading her. "You see everything through rose-coloured glasses," I said, just to calm him down and make him think a little. At that he began to cry and call me a heartless bastard. To tell the truth, you should never discourage anybody. I admitted that I was wrong, that my trouble was my black thoughts, and that all things considered, they were what had wrecked my life. Robinson's gimmick before the war had been copperplate engraving, but he wouldn't have anything more to do with it, not at any price. That was his business. "With my lungs I need fresh air, and anyway my eyes will never be the same." In a way he was right. What could I say? When we walked through busy streets together, people turned around to pity the blind man. People have plenty of pity in them for the infirm and the blind, they really have love in reserve. I'd often sensed that love they have in reserve. There's an enormous lot of it, and no one can say different. But it's a shame that people should go on being so crummy with so much love in reserve. It just doesn't come out, that's all. It's caught inside and there it stays, it doesn't do them a bit of good. They die of love – inside.

After dinner Madelon would devote herself to her "little Léon", as she called him. She read the newspaper out loud. He was wild about politics at the time, and the papers in the South pustulated with politics, of the juiciest kind.

Around us in the evening the house would sink into the dilapidation of the centuries. That's the time, after dinner, when the bedbugs come out for the corrida and also the time to test the corrosive formula which I hoped to sell to some pharmacist at a small profit later on. A modest racket. My invention amused Grandma Henrouille, and she helped me with my experiments. Together we went from nest to nest, from crack to cranny, and sprayed their swarms with my vitriol. They scurried and vanished in the light of the candle that Grandma Henrouille conscientiously held for me.

While at our work, we talked about Rancy. Just thinking about the place gave me the collywobbles, I'd have stayed in Toulouse for the rest of my life. What more did I want, after all, than my daily bread and some time to myself? Happiness in short. Still, I had to think about going back to work. Time was passing, and so were the Abbé Protiste's bonus and my savings.

Before leaving, I thought I'd teach Madelon a thing or two, and give her a bit of advice. Of course it's better to give money when you can afford it and you want to help. But you can also do good by warning a person, telling them exactly what's what and especially about the risks of fucking right and left. That's what I said to myself, because I was really worried about Madelon catching something. She was a smart little number, but no one could have been more ignorant about microbes. So I started explaining in great detail that she should take a close look before responding to advances. If it was red... if there was a drop at the end... In short, the classical and exceedingly useful things that everyone should know. After listening attentively and hearing me out, she protested for the sake of form. She even made something of a scene, assuring me... that she was a "respectable" girl... that I should be ashamed of myself... that I had a foul opinion of her... because she'd done it with me... that I despised her... that all men were beastly...

Anyway, the kind of thing they say in a case like that... I might have expected it... Window-dressing. What mattered to me was that she had listened carefully to my advice and grasped the essential. The rest didn't mean a thing. After hearing what I had to say, what really saddened her was that you could catch all those things I'd been telling her about just from affection and pleasure. Even if nature was to blame, she thought I was fully as disgusting as nature, and that offended her. I carried the matter no further, except for a few words about condoms, which are so convenient. After that we played psychologist and tried to analyse Robinson's character just a little. "He's not exactly jealous," she said to me. "But he has his difficult moments."

"That's neither here nor there!..." I said, and launched into a description of Robinson's character, as if I knew his character, but I noticed right away that I didn't know Robinson at all, except for a few obvious and glaring features. Nothing more.

It's amazing how hard it is to imagine what can make one person pleasing to another... You want to do someone a favour, to be helpful, and all you do is make a fool of yourself... It's pitiful, the moment you open your mouth... you flounder.

Nowadays it's not easy to be La Bruyère.* The whole unconscious skedaddles the moment you go near it.

* * *

Just as I was about to buy my ticket, they got me to stay, for another week, we agreed. The idea was to show me the country around Toulouse, the cool banks of the river I'd heard so much about, and especially they wanted me to see the beautiful vineyards on the outskirts, that everyone in town seemed to take pleasure and pride in, as if they were all part-owners. They wouldn't think of letting me leave like that, when I hadn't seen anything but Grandma Henrouille's corpses. It was unthinkable! Well anyway, soft soap...

I was paralysed by so much kindness. I didn't dare seem too eager to stay, because of my intimacy with Madelon, which was getting kind of dangerous. The old woman was beginning to suspect something between us. A strain in the air.

But the old woman wasn't coming with us on this excursion. In the first place she didn't want to close her crypt, not for a single day. So I agreed to stay on, and one Sunday morning we set out for the country. Robinson walked between us, we held him by the arms. At the station we took second-class tickets. Even so, the compartment smelt strongly of sausage, just the same as third class. We got off at a place called Saint-Jean. Madelon seemed familiar with the region, and right away she began meeting acquaintances from this village and that village. It looked like a fine day coming on. As we walked along, we had to tell Robinson everything we saw. "Here there's a garden... That's a bridge over there, and on top of it there's a man fishing... He's not catching anything... Watch out for the bicycle..." But the smell of fries gave him his direction all right. In fact it was he who dragged us to a bar where they served fries for fifty centimes a portion. I'd always known that Robinson was fond of fries. So am I. It's a Parisian taste. Madelon preferred vermouth, dry and straight.

Rivers aren't happy in the south. They seem to be sick, always drying up. Hills, sun, fishermen, fish, boats, ditches, wash troughs, vines, weeping willows – all want some, all clamour for water. Much too much water is demanded of them, so there isn't much left in the river bed. In places it looks more like a badly flooded road than a genuine river. Seeing as we'd come for pleasure, we had to hurry up and find some. When we'd finished our fries, we thought we'd take a little boat ride before lunch, that would be fun, me rowing of course, the two of them, Robinson and Madelon, facing me, hand in hand.

So off we go, merrily down the stream as they say, scraping the bottom here and there, she letting out squeals and he not quite easy in his mind either. Flies and more flies. Dragonflies everywhere, watching the river out of their big eyes and giving frightened little flicks of their tails. Amazing heat that makes the surface steam. We glide over the water from those long flat eddies back there to this tangle of dead branches... We hug the burning bank, looking for whiffs of shade that we grab as best we can under a few trees not too riddled with sunshine. Talking makes you even hotter, if that's possible. On the other hand, you're afraid to admit you're not comfortable.

Robinson, naturally enough, was the first to be fed up with navigation. I suggested landing near a restaurant. We weren't the only ones to have that little idea. Every fisherman on that reach of the river was already settled at the bistro before us, jealously nursing his aperitif, entrenched behind a siphon. Robinson didn't dare ask me if this café I had chosen was expensive, but I set his mind at rest by assuring him that the prices were posted and perfectly reasonable. It was true. He never let go of his Madelon's hand the whole while.

Now it can be told that we paid our bill at the restaurant as if we had eaten, but we had only tried to eat. The less said of the dishes they served us the better. They're still there.

After that, to spend the afternoon, it would have been too complicated to arrange a fishing party, and it would have made Robinson unhappy because he wouldn't even have seen his float. As for me, I was sick and tired of rowing, just from the morning's effort. That had been plenty. The training I'd had on the rivers of Africa was far behind me. I had aged in that as in everything else.

For a change of exercise, I suggested that a little walk along the bank would do us a lot of good, at least as far as the tall grass you could see up there less than a kilometre away, not far from that line of poplars.

So there we went, Robinson and I arm in arm, and Madelon a few steps ahead of us. It was easier that way through the grass. At a bend in the river we heard accordions. The sound came from a barge, a beautiful barge moored at that point in the river. The music attracted Robinson. Which was understandable in his situation, and besides he had always had a weakness for music. Glad to have found something that amused him, we parked right there on the grass, which wasn't as dusty as on the slanting bank nearby. We could see that it wasn't any ordinary barge. It was neat and well turned out, not meant for hauling anything, more of a houseboat than a barge, with flowers all over it and even a spanking little kennel for the dog. We described the houseboat to Robinson. He wanted to know all about it.

"I'd like to live on a clean little boat like that myself," he said then. "How about you?" he asked Madelon...

"I see what you mean," she replied. "But that's an expensive idea you've got, Léon! I'm sure it would cost you a lot more than an apartment house!"

We all started reckoning how much that kind of a houseboat might cost, and we couldn't get together... Each of us insisted on his own figure... Regardless of what we were counting, our class of people used to do it out loud... Meanwhile, the accordion music came over to us as caressingly as you please, we could even hear the words of a song they were singing... Finally we agreed that the houseboat, just as it was, must be worth at least a hundred thousand francs... A figure to set you dreaming...

Close your lovely eyes, for the hours are short...
In the wonderful land, the beautiful land of drea-eams...

That's what they were singing inside the boat, men's and women's voices mixed, a little out of tune, but very pleasant all the same because of the setting. It went with the heat and the country and the time of day and the river.

Robinson persisted in driving his estimates sky-high. The way we'd described the houseboat, he was sure it would cost a lot more... Because it had a big glass window to let in more light and brass fittings all over, luxury in short...

"Léon, you're knocking yourself out." Madelon tried to quiet him. "Why don't you stretch out on this nice thick grass and rest a while... A hundred thousand or five hundred thousand, who cares?... You haven't got it and neither have I... So really there's no sense in working yourself up..."

He lay down, but he kept working himself up about the price all the same, he wanted to know for sure, and he wanted to see this houseboat that cost so much...

"Has it got an engine?" he asked... We didn't know.

Just to please him, since he insisted, I took a look at the stern, to see if I'd spot the exhaust pipe of a small engine...

Close your lovely eyes, for life is a dream...
Love is a fan-ta-sy...
Close your lovely eyes!

The people in there went on singing. We were drooping with fatigue... They were putting us to sleep.

Suddenly a spaniel came bounding out of the kennel and stood on the gangplank barking in our direction. We woke with a start, and we gave the spaniel hell! He had frightened Robinson.

So then a character who seemed to be the owner came out on deck through the little cabin door. He said he wouldn't stand for anybody shouting at his dog, and we talked back! But when he noticed that Robinson was as good as blind, the man calmed down and felt foolish. He changed his mind about bawling us out and even let us call him a few names to get even. To make up for his rudeness, he invited us to come and have coffee on his boat, to celebrate, he added, his birthday. He wouldn't hear of our baking out there in the sun, and so forth and so on... And besides it was lucky we'd turned up, because they were thirteen at table... He was a young man, an eccentric. He liked boats, he explained... We could see that. But his wife was afraid of the sea, so they had moored their boat out here, on the beach, so to speak... We went aboard, and everybody seemed glad to have us... First of all his wife, a fine-looking woman, who played the accordion like an angel. Anyway, it was nice of them to have us over for coffee! We could have been almost anybody! It was trusting of them... We realized right off that it wouldn't do to shame our charming hosts... Especially in front of their guests... Robinson had his faults, but as a rule he had a certain fine feeling. Just by the sound of their voices he realized that we had to behave and abstain from bad language. True, we weren't very well dressed, but we were neat and clean. The owner of the houseboat, I looked him over, must have been about thirty, with artistic brown hair and a nice sailor-type suit, but custom-made. And his attractive wife had really "velvety" eyes.

They had just finished lunch. Plenty of leftovers. We didn't say no to a piece of cake, certainly not! Or a glass of port to go with it. I hadn't heard such high-class voices in a long time. High-class people have a certain way of talking that intimidates you and frightens me personally, especially their women. It's really just a lot of half-baked, pretentious phrases, but as highly polished as antique furniture. Meaningless as they are, their phrases are terrifying. When you try to answer, you're afraid of slipping up. And even when they take the tone of the gutter and amuse themselves singing the songs of the poor, they hang on to that high-class accent, which inspires suspicion and antipathy. That accent always has the kind of whiplash that's needed for talking to servants. It's sexy, but it makes you want to tumble their women, just to see their dignity, as they call it, melt away.

In a whisper I told Robinson about the furniture, all antiques. The place reminded me a little of my mother's shop, except naturally it was cleaner and more orderly. My mother's shop always smelt of old pepper.

The walls all around were hung with paintings by the owner. A painter, as his wife told me with lots of simper and gush. His wife loved her man all right. He was an artist, nice penis, nice hair, nice income, everything needed to make a woman happy; in addition, she had her accordion, her friends, her reveries on the meagre, swirling water, she was quite content never to go anywhere... Here they had all that plus all the sweet coolness in the world, enclosed between the half-curtains and the breath of the ventilator. And God-given security besides.

Seeing as we were there, we thought we might as well make ourselves at home. Iced drinks, then strawberries and cream, my favourite dessert. Wriggling and simpering, Madelon accepted a second helping. She too was improving her manners. The men were taken with Madelon, especially the rich father-in-law. He seemed delighted to have Madelon beside him and went to no end of trouble to make her happy. He ransacked the whole table for delicacies just for her, and she lit into them with such enthusiasm that the tip of her nose was soon covered with whipped cream. To judge by the conversation, the father-in-law was a widower. If so, he'd forgotten it. Soon, what with the liqueurs, Madelon was tipsy. The suit Robinson was wearing, and mine too, showed signs of fatigue, of seasons and more seasons, but maybe in that dim light no one would notice. Still, I felt rather humiliated among those people, so comfortable in all respects, as clean as Americans, so well-washed and well-groomed, fit for a fashion parade.

Once liquored up, Madelon didn't behave so well. Aiming her little profile at the pictures, she started talking rubbish. The hostess noticed and took to the accordion again to gloss it over. Everybody sang, the three of us joined in under our breaths, but listlessly and out of tune, the same song as we'd been listening to outside, and then another.

Robinson had managed to strike up a conversation with an elderly gentleman who seemed to know all there was to know about growing cocoa trees. A splendid subject. A get-together between colonials. To my amazement I heard Robinson saying: "When I was out in Africa – I was working for the Compagnie Pordurière in those days as their agronomist in chief – I used to mobilize a whole village to harvest the crop…" And more of the same. He couldn't see me, so he gave himself free rein… The sky was the limit… Phoney memories… He really gave the old gentleman an earful… A pack of lies… Anything he could think of to put himself in the class of the old gentleman, who was really an expert. It exasperated and dismayed me to hear Robinson, who had always been rather reserved in company, shooting his mouth off like that.

They'd given him a place of honour in the depths of a big scented sofa. In his right hand he held a glass of brandy, while his left hand, with sweeping gestures, evoked the majesty of the untamed forests and the fury of the equatorial tornado. He was launched, well launched… Alcide would have had a good laugh if he could have been there in the corner. Poor Alcide!

I can't deny it, we were very comfortable on their houseboat, especially as a light breeze had come up on the river and, framed in the windows, the fluted curtains began to flutter like merry and cool little flags.

More ices were served and then another round of champagne. It was the owner's birthday, he told us so a dozen times. For once he had decided to give everyone, even the wayfarer, pleasure. For once that was us. For an hour or two or possibly three, we would all be reconciled under his aegis, we'd all be pals, the known, the unknown, even strangers, even the three of us whom they had picked up on the river bank for want of anything better, so as not to be thirteen at table. I was going to start singing my little song of good cheer, but then I changed my mind, suddenly too proud, too conscious. At that point, to justify their invitation that lay heavy on my mind, I saw fit to reveal that in my person they were entertaining one of the most distinguished physicians of Greater Paris! They could hardly have suspected it from my dress! Or from the low estate of my companions for that matter! But the moment they knew who I was, they declared themselves delighted and flattered, and every one of them started telling me about his very special little ailments. I took the opportunity to make friends with a tycoon's daughter, a sturdy young cousin of the skipper's, who suffered from hives and developed heartburn on the slightest provocation.

When you're not used to the comfort and luxuries of the table, they go to your head in no time. Truth is always glad to leave you. With next to no encouragement it will set you free. And we manage very nicely without it. Amid this sudden plethora of comforts a fine megalomaniacal delirium finds no difficulty in overwhelming you. I started telling tall ones in my turn, intermittently discussing hives with the young cousin. You extricate yourself from your daily humiliations by trying, like Robinson, to put yourself on a level with the rich by means of lies, the currency of the poor. We're all ashamed of our ungainly flesh, our inadequate carcasses. I couldn't make up my mind to show them my truth; it was as unworthy of them as my rear end. I had to make a good impression at all costs.

I started answering their questions with fantasies, same as Robinson had done in his confab with the old gentleman. I, too, was invaded by pride!... My enormous clientele!... The dreadful overwork!... My friend Robinson... the agronomist who had offered me the hospitality of his chalet... on the outskirts of Toulouse...

And besides, when your table companion has eaten well and had plenty to drink, he's easily convinced. Luckily! Anything goes! Robinson had preceded me in the furtive delights of impromptu cock-and-bull; it cost me very little effort to follow in his footsteps.

Because of the smoked glasses he was wearing, the people couldn't see exactly what was wrong with Robinson's eyes. We generously attributed his misfortune to the war. From then on we were sitting pretty, raised first socially, then patriotically, to the level of the other guests, who had been rather taken aback at first by the whimsy of the painter husband, though to be sure his status as a fashionable artist obliged him now and then to do something weird and unexpected... The guests began to find all three of us ever so charming and inconceivably interesting.

Maybe Madelon didn't play her role of fiancée as modestly as she should have; she got everybody – including the women – so hot and bothered I was afraid the party would end in an orgy. It didn't. Gradually the sentences became undone, defeated by slobbering attempts to go beyond words. Nothing happened.

Tangled in phrases and cushions, fuddled by our collective effort to make one another happy, more deeply, more warmly happy by the spirit alone since our bodies were replete, we did everything possible to suffuse the present moment with all the pleasure in the world, with every marvel known to us in and outside of ourselves, so that our neighbour might at last get the full advantage of it and confess to us that this was the very miracle he was looking for, that this gift from us was just what had been lacking for so and so many years to his eternal happiness! That we at last had revealed to him the reason of his own being! And he was going to tell all and sundry that he had found the reason of his being! So we'd down another bumper together to celebrate our joy! May our joy endure for ever! And may this charm never be broken! May we, above all, never ever relapse into those abominable days when there were no miracles, the days before we met and miraculously found one another!... All of us together from this moment on! At last! And for ever!

The skipper couldn't restrain himself from breaking the charm.

He had this mania for talking about his painting, it was really too much on his mind, about his pictures, come what may and apropos of anything or nothing. Thanks to his obstinate idiocy, crushing banality returned, drunk as we were, to our midst. Defeated, I went over to the skipper and delivered myself of a few heartfelt and high-flown compliments, the sweet words in which artists delight. Just what he needed. My compliments hit him like an orgasm. He slumped down on one of the overblown sofas and fell asleep almost instantly, as sweetly as you please, palpably happy. The others meanwhile studied the contours of one another's faces with a leaden gaze of mutual fascination, torn between almost irresistible somnolence and the delights of heaven-sent digestion.

As for me, I suppressed my desire to doze, saving it up for the night. Only too often the day's lingering fears banish sleep, so when you're lucky enough to build up a small stock of beatitude, you have to be a born fool to squander it in futile preliminary catnaps. Keep it for the night, that's my motto! Always be thinking of the night. Besides, we'd been invited to dinner, so it was time to be working up a fresh appetite...

We took advantage of the prevailing stupor to slip away. The three of us managed a discreet exit, dodging the slumbering guests dispersed around the hostess's accordion. Softened by music, the hostess's eyes blinked in search of darkness. "See you later," she said as we passed. Her smile ended in a dream.

We didn't go very far, only to the place where I'd noticed a bend in the river, between two rows of tall, pointed poplars. From there you can see the whole valley, and in the distance a village in its hollow, huddled round a church tower planted like a nail in the reddening sky.

Madelon was anxious. "What time is there a train back?" she asked.

"Don't worry!" we assured her. "They'll take us by car... It's all arranged... The skipper said so... They've got one..."

That was enough for Madelon. She was dreamy with happiness. It had really been a splendid day.

"Léon," she asked him. "How do your eyes feel now?"

"Much better. I didn't want to tell you before because I wasn't sure, but I think, especially with the left eye, it's getting so I can count the bottles on the table... I drank quite a lot, did you notice? Good stuff too!..."

"The left is the heart side!" said Madelon joyfully. Naturally she was happy about his eyes being better.

"Come," she suggested, "you kiss me and I'll kiss you!" Their effusions were making me feel in the way. But it was hard for me to leave, because I didn't know where to go. I made as if to do my business behind a nearby tree and stayed there, waiting for their seizure to pass. They said things full of tenderness. I heard them. The dullest love dialogues are kind of amusing when you know the people. And I'd never heard them talk like that before.

"Do you really love me?" she asked.

"I love you as much as I love my eyes!" was his answer.

"Oh Léon, that's a beautiful thing to say!... But you haven't seen me yet, Léon... Maybe when you see me with your own eyes and not just through other people's, you won't love me so much... When that time comes, you'll see other women, and maybe you'll love them all... The way your friends do..."

That remark, made in an undertone, was a dig at me. I hadn't the slightest doubt... She thought I was far away and couldn't hear her...

So she let loose... She lost no time... Robinson started protesting. "Hey there!..." Slander, malicious gossip, he assured her...

"Me! Certainly not! Oh no, Madelon!" he defended himself. "That's not my way at all! What makes you think I'm like him?... When you've been so good to me!... I'm the faithful sort! I'm no skirt-chaser! When I give my word it's for always! You're beautiful, I know that already, but you'll be even more beautiful when I see you... There! Are you happy now? Not crying any more? What more can I tell you?"

"Oh Léon! You're so sweet!" she said, cuddling up to him. Then they were swearing to love each other for ever and ever and nothing could stop them, the heavens weren't big enough.

"I want you to always be happy with me..." he said very gently. "With nothing to do and everything you need all the same..."

"Oh, how good you are, my sweet Léon! You're even better than I thought... So tender! So faithful! So everything!..."

"It's because I adore you, my pussycat..."

And they worked each other up even further by necking. And then, as if to shut me out of their intense happiness, they gave me a kidney punch...

She started off: "Your friend the doctor! Isn't he a nice one!" And then she repeated, as if the thought of me stuck in her craw. "He's a nice one all right!... I wouldn't want to say anything against him, because he's a friend of yours... But I have a feeling that he's a brute with women... I don't like to say anything bad about him, because I think he's really fond of you... But, you know, he's not my type... I'll tell you something... You're sure it won't make you mad?" No, nothing would make Léon mad. "Well, I'd say the doctor is too hot on women... Kind of like a dog, see what I mean?... What do you think?... I get the feeling that he's ready to jump every last one of them! He does his nasty business, and then he makes himself scarce... Don't you think so? Don't you think he's like that?"

The bastard thought everything she wanted him to think, in fact he agreed that in addition to being right, everything she said was screamingly funny. So funny he could die laughing. He encouraged her to go on and almost split a gut.

"Yes, Madelon, what you say is perfectly true! Ferdinand isn't a bad sort, but delicacy isn't his strong point, I don't mind telling you, nor fidelity either!... Take my word for it!..."

"Has he had lots of mistresses? You must know, Léon."

The bitch. She was fishing for information.

"Plenty," he replied with assurance, "but you know... he's not hard to please!..."

Some conclusion had to be drawn from this exchange, and Madelon proceeded to draw one.

"Doctors are mostly all pigs, everybody knows that... But if you ask me, he's a champion!..."

"You've never said truer words," my good and faithful friend approved her. And he went on: "It's so bad, he's such a sex fiend, I've often thought he took drugs... And say, the man's equipment! If you could see it! Huge! Monstrous! It's not natural!..."

"Really?" said Madelon, perplexed, trying to remember my equipment. "You think he's got some disease?" She was worried, suddenly dismayed by those intimate revelations.

"I don't know about that," he was regretfully obliged to admit. "I can't tell for sure... But it wouldn't surprise me with the life he leads."

"Yes, you're right... he must take drugs... That must be why he's so strange sometimes..."

Madelon's little head was working hard, and she added: "We'd better be careful from now on..."

"What's the matter?" he asked. "You afraid of him? He isn't anything to you, I hope?... He hasn't ever made you any advances, has he?"

"No, of course not. I wouldn't have let him! But you never know what he might take into his head... Suppose he threw a fit, for instance... Those dope fiends have fits, you know!... But one thing is sure, I'd never go to him if I were sick!..."

"Neither would I, now you bring it up!" Robinson approved. After which there was more mushing and petting...

"Honey lamb!..." she cooed.

"Kitten!... Kitten!..." he replied. And silences in between, punctuated by barrages of kisses.

"See how many times you can tell me you love me while I kiss you as far as your shoulder..."

That little game began at the top of the neck.

"I'm as red as a beet!" she cried, panting... "I'm suffocating!... Air! Air!" But he didn't let her breathe. He started all over again. Sitting in the grass nearby, I tried to see what would happen. He took her nipples between his lips and toyed with them. Innocent pastimes. I was all red in the face myself for a variety of reasons and in addition amazed at my own indiscretion.

"We'll be very happy, won't we, Léon? Tell me you're sure we'll be happy."

Then came an intermission. And then endless plans for the future, enough plans to make a whole new world, but a world only for the two of them. I, most especially, wasn't in it at all. It looked as if they'd never finish getting rid of me, sweeping my nasty image out of their life.

"Have you been friends with Ferdinand a long time?"

The question was nagging at her...

"Oh yes, for years... in different places..." he answered. "First we just happened to meet, on our travels... He likes going to strange places... So do I in a way, and for a long time we travelled together... See?..." He reduced our life together to the flattest banality.

"Well," she said with crisp determination. "You're not going to be such good friends any more... From now on!... It's going to stop!... It is going to stop, isn't it, pussycat?... From now on I'll be your only companion... Understand?... How about it, sweetie?..."

"What's wrong? You jealous of him?" In spite of himself he was rather disconcerted, the dope.

"No, I'm not jealous of him, but you see, Léon, I love you too much, I want you all to myself... I don't want to share you with anybody... And he's not the kind of person you should associate with now that I love you, Léon... He's too immoral... Understand? Tell me you adore me, Léon! Tell me you understand!"

"I adore you..."

"That's good."

* * *

We got back to Toulouse that same night.

The accident happened two days later. It was time for me to be leaving after all, and I was just packing my suitcase before starting for the station when I heard someone shouting outside the house. I listened... They wanted me to come quick and hurry down to the crypt... I couldn't see the person who was shouting that way... But to judge by the tone of voice, it must have been terribly urgent... They wanted me to go there right away, apparently.

"Just a minute," I say. "Where's the fire?" I didn't feel like hurrying... It must have been about seven o'clock, just before dinner time. We were supposed to say goodbye at the station, we'd arranged it that way. That was convenient for everybody, because the old woman would be coming home a little later than usual. She was expecting a whole crowd of pilgrims at the crypt that evening.

"Come, quick, Doctor!" The voice in the street shouted again. "Madame Henrouille has had an accident!"

"OK! OK! OK!... I'll be right down!" I said. "I understand... I'm coming down!"

But in less than a moment I'd thought it over. "You go ahead," I said. "Tell them I'm coming right away... I'm hurrying... Soon as I put my trousers on..."

"But it's terribly urgent!" the voice cried... "She's unconscious, I tell you!... She seems to have broken a bone in her head!... She fell down the stairs!... Down to the bottom of her vault!"

"That'll do!" I said to myself when I heard that lovely story. No need to think any longer. I beat it straight to the station. I knew all I wanted to know.

I caught my train at seven fifteen, but only by a whisker.

We never did say goodbye.

*　*　*

The first thing Parapine said when he saw me was that I wasn't looking well.

"You must have worn yourself to a frazzle in Toulouse," he said, suspicious as usual.

It's true that I'd had a scare down there in Toulouse, but nothing to complain about, since I'd managed to keep clear of serious trouble, or so I thought, by slipping away at the critical moment.

I told Parapine the story in detail and aired my suspicions as well. He wasn't convinced that I'd been very bright, but we didn't have time to go into it very thoroughly, because by then the question of a job for me had become so urgent that I had to do something about it. There was no time to be lost in discussion... I had only a hundred and fifty

francs left to my name and no idea where to turn. The Tarapout?...
They weren't hiring any more... the Depression. Back to La Garenne-
Rancy? Try and retrieve my practice? I considered it for a while in
spite of everything, but only as a last resource and very reluctantly.
Nothing is quenched so easily as the sacred fire.

It was Parapine who finally came to the rescue. He found me a
small job at the institution where he himself had been working for
some months.

Their business was still pretty good. In addition to taking cretins
to the movies, Parapine was in charge of the sparks. Twice a week,
at scheduled hours, he unleashed magnetic storms over the heads of
the melancholies assembled for that purpose in a hermetically sealed
and pitch-black room. Mental gymnastics in sum, a brilliant idea
emanating from Dr Baryton, his boss. A skinflint, incidentally, this
colleague of ours. He took me on at a very low salary but with a
contract a mile long, full of clauses entirely to his advantage. In short,
a boss.

We were hardly paid at all at that rest home, but the food wasn't
at all bad and the lodging was excellent, with facilities for laying
the nurses, which was tolerated and tacitly permitted. Baryton, the
boss, had no objection whatever, in fact he had noticed that erotic
tolerance attached the staff to the house. A wise man looks the other
way.

And besides, in the first place, it was no time to ask questions
or make demands when he was offering me a nice little chunk of
wherewithal in the nick of time. Thinking it over, I couldn't quite see
why Parapine was suddenly taking such an active interest in me. His
attitude weighed on my mind. To give him credit for brotherly love...
would really be gilding his character... It had to be something more
complicated. But you never can tell...

We all ate lunch together, that was the custom, gathered around
Baryton, our boss, the esteemed alienist, with his pointed beard
and short beefy thighs, a nice man except for his thrift, but on that
point he could be utterly revolting, all he needed was a pretext or
opportunity.

He certainly gave us plenty of noodles and harsh Bordeaux.
Somebody had left him a whole vineyard, so he told us. Which was
our tough luck. A very inferior vintage, I assure you.

His asylum at Vigny-sur-Seine was always full. It was called a "Rest Home" in the prospectuses, because it was in the middle of a big garden, where the nuts went walking on nice days. They walked as if they had trouble keeping their heads balanced on their shoulders: they seemed in constant fear of stumbling and spilling the contents. All sorts of misshapen things, things they were dreadfully attached to, were bobbing and bumping about in there.

When the patients spoke of their mental treasures, it was always with anguished contortions or airs of protective condescension that made you think of powerful and ultra-meticulous executives. Not for an empire would those lunatics have gone outside their minds. A madman's thoughts are just the usual ideas of a human being, except that they're hermetically sealed inside his head. The world never gets into his head, and that's the way he wants it. A sealed head is like a lake without an outlet, standing, stagnant.

Baryton bought his noodles and vegetables wholesale in Paris. So naturally we weren't very popular with the shopkeepers of Vigny-sur-Seine. I'd go so far as to say that they detested us. Their animosity didn't spoil our appetites. At the beginning of my stay, Baryton, at the table, would distil philosophical conclusions from our disjointed remarks. But seeing that he had spent his life among lunatics and made his living by his association with them, sharing their meals, neutralizing their lunacies as best he could, nothing bored him so much as having to talk about their manias at table. "They have no place in the conversation of normal people!" he declared in peremptory self-defence. He himself observed that rule of mental hygiene strictly.

He was fond of conversation, and there was a kind of terror in the way he insisted on its being amusing, reassuring and above all thoroughly sane. He just didn't want to think about the loonies. His feeling towards them was one of instinctive antipathy, and with that he contented himself once and for all. On the other hand, he loved hearing us talk about our travels. We couldn't tell him enough. My arrival liberated Parapine from the need to talk. For him it was providential: now I could entertain the boss during meals. All my peregrinations were served up, related at length, doctored of course, made suitably literary, amusing. Baryton made an enormous amount of noise with his tongue and mouth in eating. His daughter Aimée always sat at his right. Though only ten, Aimée already seemed faded.

Something lifeless, an incurable greyness blunted our image of Aimée, as though unhealthy little clouds were always passing over her face.

There were moments of friction between Parapine and Baryton. But Baryton never bore anyone a grudge, as long as they laid no claim to the profits of his establishment. For many years his accounts had been the only element of the sacred in his existence.

Once, in the days when Parapine still spoke to him, he had told him bluntly at table that he was lacking in ethics. At first that remark had nettled Baryton, but then the whole thing had been smoothed over. You don't quarrel about such trifles. Listening to the story of my travels, Baryton not only relished a surge of romantic emotion but rejoiced at the money he was saving. "You're such a fine storyteller, Ferdinand, that after listening to you I don't have to visit those countries any more!" To him no prettier compliment was conceivable. Only easily managed lunatics were admitted to his institution, never vicious, out-and-out homicidal maniacs. The place wasn't absolutely sinister. Hardly any bars and only a few isolation cells. Maybe the most worrisome case was little Aimée, his own daughter. The child wasn't regarded as a patient, but the environment haunted her.

A howl or two would sometimes reach us in the dining room, but the cause of those screams was always something quite insignificant. And they never lasted long. Then occasionally a group of inmates would suddenly, for no reason at all, be shaken by a prolonged wave of frenzy in the course of their interminable wanderings between the pump, the clumps of bushes and the begonia beds. Those incidents would be handled without great alarums and protests by means of tepid baths and buckets of opium extract.

Now and then the lunatics would stand at the few dining-hall windows that opened out on the street and terrify the neighbourhood with their bellowing, but mostly they kept their horror to themselves. They took good care of their horror, defending it against our therapeutic efforts. That resistance of theirs was the spice of their lives.

When I think now of all the lunatics I knew at Baryton's, I can't help suspecting that the only true manifestations of our innermost being are war and insanity, those two absolute nightmares.

Maybe what makes life so terribly wearysome is nothing other than the enormous effort we make for twenty years, forty years and more, to be reasonable, to avoid being simply, profoundly ourselves – that is, vile, ghastly, absurd. It's the nightmare of having to represent the half-subhuman we were fobbed off with as a small-size universal ideal, a superman from morning to night.

In our nuthouse we had patients at all prices, the most opulent living in heavily padded Louis XV rooms. Baryton paid these a daily, highly priced visit. They'd be expecting him. Now and then he'd be welcomed with a titanic, truly magnificent and long-premeditated sock in the jaw, which he'd enter on the bill under "special treatment".

At table Parapine maintained an attitude of reserve. Not that he was the least bit put out by my oratorical triumphs: quite the contrary, he seemed less preoccupied than in times past, in his microbe days, and all in all, almost happy. Don't forget that he'd had a bad scare over his business with the underage girls. It had left him rather disconcerted in his dealings with the sex. In his free time, he'd wander around the grounds of our institution just like a patient. He'd smile at me when I passed, but his smiles were so vague, so pale, you'd have thought he was bidding me goodbye.

By taking us on as technical aides, Baryton had made a good bargain: in addition to our unflagging devotion, we brought him entertainment and the echoes of adventure, for which deprivation had left him with such a craving. And indeed, he often took pleasure in expressing his satisfaction with us. Yet on Parapine's score he had certain reservations.

He had never felt entirely comfortable with him. "Parapine, you see, Ferdinand..." he confided in me one day. "Parapine is a Russian!" To Baryton the fact that he was Russian was as descriptive, morphological and irreparable as "diabetic" or "nigger". Launched on a topic that had been tormenting him for months, he set his brain to work enormously in my presence and for my special benefit... You wouldn't have recognized the old Baryton. We were on our way to the local tobacconist for cigarettes.

"Parapine, you see, Ferdinand, of course he's intelligent... but really, you know, there's something dreadfully arbitrary about his intelligence! Don't you agree, Ferdinand? In the first place, he simply refuses to adapt... You can see that at a glance... And he's not at ease in his work... For that matter, he's not at ease in the world!... Admit it!... And there he's making a mistake! A big mistake!... Because it makes him unhappy!... That proves it! Take me, Ferdinand, think how adaptable I am!..." (He thumped his sternum.) "Suppose, for instance, the earth starts turning the wrong way tomorrow. What will I do? Well, Ferdinand, I'll adapt! Instantly! And do you know how, Ferdinand? I'll just sleep twelve hours more, that'll do the trick! One two three! It's as simple as that! I'll have adapted! Whereas your Parapine, you know what he'd do in such a situation? He'd ruminate projects and grudges for another hundred years!... I'm certain! I assure you!... Don't you agree?... If the earth starts going backwards, he won't be able to sleep!... He'll see some sort of special injustice in it!... Injustice, injustice! That's his bug!... He was always talking about injustice in the days when he still deigned to speak to me... And do you think he'll content himself with snivelling? Which wouldn't be so bad!... Oh no! Before you know it he'll start looking for a way to blow up the planet! To get even, Ferdinand! And the worst of it, I'll tell you the worst of it, Ferdinand!... But just between you and me... Well, the worst of it is that he will find a way!... That's right! Look here, Ferdinand, I'm going to tell you something. Try to imprint it on your mind!... There are simple lunatics and there are others, tortured by an obsession with civilization... It grieves me to think that Parapine belongs to the latter class!... Do you know what he said to me the other day?..."

"No, sir..."

"Well, here's what he said: 'Between the penis and mathematics, Monsieur Baryton, there's nothing! A vacuum!' And another thing!... Do you know what he's waiting for before starting to speak to me again?"

"No, Monsieur Baryton, I have no idea..."

"He hasn't told you?"

"No, not yet..."

"Well, he has told me... He's waiting for the dawn of the mathematical age! Neither more nor less! His mind is made up! What do you think of such impertinence? To me! His senior! His boss!..."

Of course I had to laugh a little, to join him in laughing off this extravagant fancy. But Baryton was no longer dwelling on such trifles. He had bigger and better things to get indignant about...

"Ah, Ferdinand! I see this kind of thing strikes you as innocuous... Innocent words... just one more case of idle foolishness... That's what you seem to think... Just that! Am I right?... Oh, thoughtless

Ferdinand! Let me take pains to put you on your guard against such aberrations, which only appear to be trivial! You are absolutely mistaken! Absolutely!... A thousand times mistaken!... You will believe me, I trust, when I tell you that in the course of my career I have heard, here and elsewhere, just about everything that can be heard in the way of hot-and-cold delirium! Nothing has been lacking... You'll give me credit for that, won't you Ferdinand?... And you have surely observed, Ferdinand, that I am not given to anxiety... to exaggeration... Not at all... A word or group of words carries very little weight with me! And the same goes for sentences and whole speeches!... Though a simple man by birth and nature, I am, and no one will deny it, one of those greatly inhibited persons who are not frightened by words!... Well, Ferdinand, conscientious analysis has obliged me to conclude that I must be on my guard against Parapine!... And formulate the most express reservations... His variety of extravagance resembles none of the common, inoffensive varieties... It is, I believe, one of the few dangerous forms of eccentricity, a highly contagious mania, to be precise, of the rampant social variety!... In your friend's case, we may not yet be dealing with out-and-out insanity... No... Maybe his trouble is only exaggerated conviction... But the contagious manias are well known to me!... I've known a good many sufferers from conviction mania... Of many different types!... And in the last analysis, those who talk about justice seem to be the maddest of the lot!... At first, I must confess, I took a certain interest in justice fanatics... Today those particular maniacs annoy and exasperate me more than I can tell... Don't you feel the same way?... Human beings show a strange aptitude for transmitting this mania. It terrifies me, and we find it, mind you, in all human beings!... Bear that in mind, Ferdinand, in all of them! Same as with liquor and sex... The same predisposition... The same fatality... Infinitely widespread... Are you laughing, Ferdinand? If so, you frighten me! Fragile! Vulnerable! Thoughtless! Dangerous Ferdinand! When I think that I took you for a serious-minded man!... Don't forget that I'm old, Ferdinand, I could afford the luxury of thumbing my nose at the future! I'd have every right to! But you?"

As a matter of principle, in all things and for all time, I agreed with the boss. I haven't made much practical headway in the course of my harassed existence, but I had learnt the essential principles of servile etiquette. Consequently, we had become good friends. I never opposed him, and I didn't eat much at the table. A pleasant sort of assistant, in short: economical, not the least ambitious, no threat to anyone.

* * *

Vigny-sur-Seine is situated between two sluice gates, between two hillsides stripped of vegetation, a village turning suburb. Paris will swallow it up.

It loses a garden a month. On the approaches, billboards splash it with all the colours of the Russian ballet. The town clerk's daughter has learnt to make cocktails. Only the tram seems intent on becoming historical; nothing short of a revolution will make it give up. The people are anxious, the children no longer have the same accent as their parents. It embarrasses the inhabitants to think that they're still attached to the Seine-et-Oise* Department. Miracles are under way. The last garden globe vanished when Laval came to power, the local cleaning women have just raised their prices by twenty centimes an hour. A bookmaker has been sighted. The postmistress buys pederastic novels and imagines others that are even more realistic. The priest says "shit" at the drop of a hat and gives stock-market tips to his parishioners when they are very very good. The Seine has killed its fish and is becoming Americanized between files of pusher-puller self-loading barges that look like ghastly sets of rotten-tin false teeth along both banks. Three developers have just gone to jail. Progress sweeps on.

The real-estate situation has not escaped Baryton. He bitterly regrets not having had the foresight to buy up lots in the next valley twenty years ago, when the owners were begging you to take them away, like rotten fruit, at twenty centimes a square metre. The good old days. Luckily his Psychotherapeutic Institute was holding its own very nicely. Nevertheless there were problems. Those insatiable families were always demanding, always insisting on newer and newer methods of treatment, more electrical, more mysterious, more everything.... The most recent, most impressive machines and contraptions. And he had to submit, on pain of being outdone by his competitors... those similar institutions tucked away in the neighbouring groves of Asnières, Passy, Montretout, lying in wait for the deluxe class of nuts.

Under the guidance of Parapine, Baryton did his best to modernize his establishment, as cheaply as possible to be sure, buying electrical, pneumatic, hydraulic devices, second-hand, at a discount, at clearance sales, but indefatigably, so as to seem at all times better equipped than before and so appeal to the manias of his captious, well-to-do inmates. Many a moan was wrung from him by the necessity of acquiring useless equipment... of currying favour with the very lunatics...

"I opened my institution," he confided in me one day in an outpouring of sorrow, "just before the Exposition,* the big one, Ferdinand... we alienists in those days were, or, if you will, constituted a very small group, much less curious, I can assure you, and less depraved than today!... None of us in those days tried to be as crazy as his patients... It was not yet the fashion for the healer to go off his rocker on the pretext that it furthered the cure, an obscene fashion, mind you, like almost everything that comes to us from foreign countries...

"You see, Ferdinand, in the days of my beginnings, French medical men still had self-respect. They didn't feel obliged to rave along with their patients... In the interest of harmony?... Don't ask me! To make them happy? Where will it lead us?... If we persist in being more ingenious, more morbid, more perverse than the most persecuted lunatic in our asylums, in wallowing with some sort of obscene pride in every form of dementia paraded before our eyes, what will become of us?... Do you feel able, Ferdinand, to reassure me about the future of human reason?... Or even of plain common sense?... At this rate what will be left of plain common sense in a few years? Nothing! I foresee it! Absolutely nothing! I can predict it... It's obvious...

"For one thing, Ferdinand, from the standpoint of a truly modern intelligence, haven't all differences and distinctions been effaced? No more white! No more black! Everything dissolves. That's the new approach! The fashion! If that's the case, why not go mad ourselves?... Right this minute! As a starter! And brag about it! Proclaim total psychic chaos! And advertise it with our own madness! Who's going to stop us? I ask you, Ferdinand!... What last superfluous human scruples?... What flabby misgivings? Well?... Sometimes, Ferdinand, when I listen to certain of our colleagues – and, mind you, among the most esteemed, the most sought-after by the clientele and the academies alike – I wonder where they're leading us!... It's infernal! Those madmen disconcert, terrify, diabolize and above all disgust me! Just hearing them at one of their modern congresses report on the results of their habitual researches, I'm seized with livid panic, Ferdinand! I listen and my reason deserts me! Diabolical, prurient, captious and dishonest, these minions of modern psychiatry are hurling us into the abyss with their superconscious analyses... I say it again, into the abyss! One fine morning, Ferdinand, unless you younger men do something about it, that's where we'll end up! What with stretching ourselves thin, with sublimating ourselves and torturing our minds, we'll end up on the far side of intelligence, the infernal side, that there's no coming back from!... And the fact is, what with their intellectual masturbation day and night, those ultra-super-wise men seem even now to have shut themselves up in the dungeons of the damned!

"I say day and night, because you know, Ferdinand, they fornicate themselves all night in their dreams!... Need I say more!... They dig at their minds! They dilate them! They tyrannize them!... All around them there's nothing left but a foul stew of organic debris, a marmalade of madness and symptoms that drip and ooze from every part of them... The remains of the mind are all over our hands, and there we are, sticky, grotesque, contemptuous, fetid. Everything's going to collapse, Ferdinand, everything is collapsing – I, old man Baryton – am telling you, and it won't be long now!... You'll see the end, Ferdinand, the great debacle! Because you're still young! You'll see it! Oh, you'll enjoy it, I can promise you!... You'll all end up in the nuthouse! Zoom! Just one more outburst of madness! One too many! And wham! – off you go to the loony bin! At last! You'll be liberated, as you put it. It has tempted you too much and too long! That will be the act of daring you've been clamouring for! But once you're in the nuthouse, my little friends, take it from me, you'll stay there!

"Make a note of this, Ferdinand, the beginning and end of all things is the lack of moderation! Want me to tell you how the big debacle started?... It started when men played fast and loose with their sense of proportion! With foreign exaggerations! When moderation's gone, power goes with it! It was inevitable! Is then everyone doomed? Why not? All of us? Definitely! Going to the dogs? No, running! A mad stampede! I saw the human mind, Ferdinand, losing its balance little by little and dissolving in the vast maelstrom of apocalyptic ambitions! It began about 1900... mark that date! From then on, the world in general and psychiatry in particular have been one frantic race to see who could become more perverse, more salacious, more outlandish, more revolting, more creative as they call it, than his neighbour!... A pretty mess!...

Who would be first to throw himself into the arms of the monster, the beast without heart and without restraint!... The beast will devour us all, Ferdinand, it's a certainty and a good thing too!... What is this beast?... A big head that goes where it pleases!... Even now its wars and its flaming slobber are pouring in on us from all sides!... Here and now we are in the midst of a deluge! Neither more nor less! Apparently we were bored with consciousness! Well, we won't be bored any longer! We've started buggering each other for variety's sake... And we've been going in for 'impressions' and 'intuitions' ever since... like women!...

"And come to think of it, is there any need for us to weigh ourselves down with the least bit of logic?... Of course not! Logic can only be an encumbrance to the infinitely subtle, truly progressive psychologists that our times are turning out... Don't get me wrong, I'm not saying that I look down on women, Ferdinand! Certainly not! You know that! But I don't care for their 'impressions'! I'm an animal with testicles, Ferdinand, and when I have a fact, I hang on to it for dear life... In that connection I had an interesting experience the other day... I was asked to admit a writer... He was cracked... You know what he'd been shouting for over a month? 'They're liquidating!... They're liquidating!...' That's what he was shouting all over the house! He was a case all right... He had crossed over to the far side of intelligence!... His trouble was that he simply couldn't liquidate... An old stricture was poisoning him with urine, stopping up his bladder... I had to relieve him drop by drop with a catheter... it took hours... But the family insisted that the cause of it all was his genius... I tried my level best to convince them that their writer's trouble was in his bladder – they clung to their idea... that he'd blown his top in a moment of excessive genius... In the end I had to fall in with their opinion. You know what families are like. You'll never get a family to understand that a man, related to them or not, is nothing but suspended putrefaction... No family will pay bills for suspended putrefaction."

For twenty years Baryton had been wrestling with the quarrelsome vanity of families. They gave him a hard time. Patient and well balanced as I knew him to be, he nevertheless nursed a vestige of well-fermented hatred towards families... At the time when I was living close to him, he was exasperated and trying obstinately, though in secret, to free himself, to escape once and for all, one way or another, from the tyranny of those families... Everyone has his reasons for trying to escape his private unhappiness, and each of us, to that end, coaxes some ingenious method from the circumstances. Blessed are those who can content themselves with whorehouses!

Parapine, for his part, seemed happy to have chosen the way of silence. Baryton, as I came to understand only later, doubted in his heart whether he would ever succeed in freeing himself from families, from their hold on him, from the thousand repulsive servitudes involved in alimentary psychiatry – in short, from his condition. He so longed for something new and absolutely different that he was thoroughly ripe for flight and escape. This accounted no doubt for his critical tirades.... Routine was death to his ego. Sublimation was no longer possible, he just wanted to go away, to take his body somewhere else. There was nothing of the musician in Baryton, and in the end he had to upset everything like a bear.

He, who thought himself so reasonable, set himself free by means of a scandalous and thoroughly regrettable action. Later on, at leisure, I shall try to tell what happened.

For the moment the job of assistant to Baryton struck me as quite bearable.

The therapeutic routine was far from strenuous, though now and then, as you'd expect, I'd feel pretty sick after talking too long with one of the patients, a kind of dizzy spell would come over me, as though the patients, from one commonplace little remark to another, had, without seeming to, led me away from my usual dwelling place to the heart and centre of their dementia. For a short moment I wondered how I would ever get out of there and whether I hadn't, unsuspecting, been locked up with them in their madness once and for all.

Because I was always kind to the inmates, which was my nature, I lived on the dangerous rim of madness, on the brink, so to speak. I didn't go under, but I felt in constant danger, as if they had lured me by stealth into their unknown city. A city whose streets became softer and softer as you penetrated further between its slobbery houses, with their melting, ill-closed windows and their dubious sounds. The doors and the ground are unstable, shifting... And yet something makes you want to go further, to see if you'll have the strength to retrieve your reason from the wreckage. Reason can easily become an obsession, as good humour and sleep are for neurasthenics. All you can think of is your reason. Everything's out of kilter. It's no joke.

So I was worrying along from doubt to doubt when the 4th of May came up. A big day. I was feeling wonderfully well that day. Pulse seventy-eight. Like after a good lunch. Then suddenly the world began to spin. I held tight. Everything turns to bile. People start looking weird. As if they'd gone sour like lemons and more malignant than ever before. From climbing too high, no doubt, to the very peak of health, I had fallen in front of the mirror and with passionate fascination was watching myself grow old.

On shitty days like that, mountains of fatigue and disgust accumulate between your nose and your eyes, enough in that one spot to last several men for years. Much too much for one man.

Just then, all in all, I'd have been glad to go back to the Tarapout. Especially as Parapine had also stopped talking to me. But I was in their bad books at the Tarapout. It's hard to have no source of spiritual or material comfort but your boss, especially when he's an alienist and you're not so sure of your own head. All you can do is hold tight. And not say anything. We could still talk about women together. That was a harmless subject, which gave me a chance to make him laugh now and then. In that field he gave me credit for a certain experience, for some slight and nasty competence.

It had its advantages that on the whole Baryton should consider me with a certain contempt. A boss always finds the crumminess of his staff rather reassuring. A slave must at all costs be slightly, if not superlatively, contemptible. An assortment of chronic moral and physical defects justifies the horrible treatment he is getting. Then the earth turns more smoothly, for each man occupies the place he deserves.

A person you make use of should be dull and abject, a born failure. It comes as a relief to the boss, especially since Baryton paid us very badly. An employer with his degree of acute avarice tends to be suspicious and uneasy. Failure, debauchee, black sheep, loyal!... Now there's a perfect combination that will justify anything. Baryton wouldn't have been displeased if I had been kind of wanted by the police. Those are the things that guarantee an employee's loyalty.

I had cast off all self-respect long ago. That sentiment had always struck me as far above my station, much too costly for my resources. I'd made that sacrifice once and for all and had no regrets whatever.

By then I was quite content if I could keep myself in a tolerable state of alimentary and physical balance. I had stopped worrying my head about anything else. Nevertheless, I found it hard to get through certain nights, especially when the memory of what had happened in Toulouse prevented me from sleeping.

At such times I couldn't help it, I imagined all sorts of dramatic sequels to Grandma Henrouille's fall into the mummy crypt. Fear rose up from my bowels, seized hold of my heart, and made it pound so hard that I'd jump out of bed and pace the floor, this way and that way into the depths of darkness and into the dawning light. During those attacks I despaired of ever recapturing enough peace of mind to fall asleep again. If someone tells you he's unhappy, don't take it on faith. Just ask him if he can sleep... If he can, then all's well. That's good enough.

I would never again succeed in sleeping fully. I had lost, so to speak, the habit of trust, the enormous trust you need to sleep soundly among human beings. I'd have needed at least an illness, a fever, a specific catastrophe to retrieve some small part of my old indifference, neutralize my anxiety, and recapture the divine stupidity of an easy mind. The only bearable days I remember over a period of many years were a few days of heavy feverish flu.

Baryton never asked me about my health. For that matter he chose to disregard his own. "Science and life form disastrous mixtures, Ferdinand! Always avoid taking care of your health, believe me!... Every question asked of your body becomes a breach... through which anxiety, obsession, will enter..." Such were his simplistic biological principles... He thought he was clever. "The known is good enough for me" was another of his frequent sayings. He was trying to impress me.

He never mentioned money to me, but in his secret heart he thought of it all the time.

Though I didn't exactly understand them at the time, Robinson's dealings with the Henrouille family were on my conscience, and from time to time I tried to tell Baryton bits and pieces of the story. But it didn't interest him in the least. He preferred my stories about Africa, especially the ones relating to colleagues of ours whom I'd run across here and there and to the strange and questionable medical practices of those very freakish colleagues.

At the rest home we had an alarm now and then in connection with his little girl Aimée. Suddenly at dinner time she was nowhere to be found, neither in the garden nor in her room. I fully expected to find her dismembered body in a clump of bushes one evening. She roamed all over the place with our lunatics, so there was reason to fear the worst. And indeed she had narrowly escaped being raped quite a number of times. When that happened, there'd be no end of screams and shower baths and warnings. Time and again she'd been told to avoid certain hidden paths, but the child was irresistibly attracted to nooks and crannies. On those occasions her father never failed to give her a memorable spanking. All in vain. I think she enjoyed the excitement.

We of the staff always had to be on our guard when passing the lunatics in the corridors. Madmen are more prone to murder than ordinary people. We got into the habit of turning our backs to the wall when they passed, prepared to give them a good kick in the groin at the slightest suspicious move. Watching you out of the corners of their eyes, they pass on. Madness apart, we understood each other perfectly.

Baryton deplored the fact that none of us played chess. Just to please him, I had to take it up.

During the day he distinguished himself by an active petty chicanery that made life in his entourage extremely tiresome. Every morning some new and abysmally practical idea would spring from his brain. One day he decided to replace our rolls of toilet paper with folded sheets, and we were obliged to ponder and waste a whole week with contradictory resolutions. Finally we decided to wait for the sales at the department stores. The next futile bother had to do with flannel vests: should they be worn over or under the shirt?... And what was the proper way to administer Epsom salts?... Parapine evaded these sub-intellectual controversies by stubborn silence.

In the end, inspired by boredom, I told Baryton about many more adventures than my travels had ever provided. My stock was exhausted. From then on it was up to him to fill in the conversational vacuum with his niggling pros and cons. Of which there was no end. He had defeated me by exhaustion. And I had no such defence as Parapine's total indifference. In spite of myself I had to answer him. I couldn't hold myself back from bickering with him for hours on end about the relative merits of cocoa and coffee... He was bewitching me with foolishness.

We'd start again about something or other, about elastic stockings for varicose veins, about optimum faradic currents, or the treatment of cellulitis in the region of the elbow... It got so that I'd jabber about anything under the sun in line with his tastes or recommendations, like a human talking machine. He would keep abreast or just ahead of me in those infinitely idiotic meanderings. He saturated me with conversation for all eternity. When Parapine heard us embark on quibbles as long as the noodles we were eating, he'd guffaw to himself and sputter the boss's Bordeaux all over the tablecloth.

But peace to the memory of Monsieur Baryton, the bastard! In the end I got rid of him. But what genius it took!

The frothier of the female patients entrusted to my care gave me a hell of a time... When it wasn't cold showers, it was catheters... Their little vices and perversions, their big apertures that always had to be kept clean... One of our young inmates regularly earned me a reprimand from the boss... She'd wreck the garden by pulling up flowers, that was her mania, and I didn't care for the boss's observations...

"The betrothed", they called her; she was an Argentine, physically not bad at all, but as for her head, she had only one idea, she wanted to marry her father. One by one she picked all the flowers in the garden and stuck them in the big white veil that she wore day and night, wherever she went. Her family, who were religious fanatics, were dreadfully ashamed. They hid their daughter from the world and her idea with her. According to Baryton, she had succumbed to the absurdity of too strict and rigid an upbringing. The unbending morality of her parents had exploded in her head, so to speak.

At dusk we'd read the roll call at great length and send the boarders to their quarters. Then we'd make the rounds of the rooms, mostly to stop the more agitated ones from masturbating too frantically before falling asleep. You have to watch closely and keep them in check on Saturday night, because the families come visiting on Sunday and it's bad for the reputation of the establishment if they find the patients ghost-white with masturbation.

All that reminded me of Bébert and the anti-masturbation syrup. I administered quantities of that syrup in Vigny. I had kept the formula and ended up believing in it.

The concierge at the rest home kept a little sweet shop with her husband, a big bruiser who was called in now and then when an inmate got violent.

And so life and the months went by, pleasantly enough all in all, and we'd have had nothing to complain about if Baryton hadn't suddenly conceived another of his big ideas.

349

He had no doubt been wondering for quite some time if it mightn't be possible to make more and better use of me for the same money. And he finally found the answer.

One day after lunch he came out with his idea. First he had them dish up a whole salad bowl full of my favourite dessert, strawberries and cream. Already my suspicions were aroused. And true enough, I had no sooner downed the last strawberry than he attacked.

"Ferdinand," he says. "I've been wondering if you mightn't consent to give my little girl Aimée a few English lessons... What do you say?... I know you have excellent pronunciation... And in English good pronunciation is what counts, don't you think?... You see, Ferdinand, without wishing to flatter you, I know how obliging you are."

He had caught me off balance. "Why, certainly, Monsieur Baryton," I said.

It was agreed then and there that I'd give Aimée her first English lesson the very next morning. And others followed, one after another, for weeks...

Those English lessons marked the beginning of a thoroughly murky, dubious period, during which event followed event at a rhythm quite different from that of ordinary life.

Baryton insisted on attending the lessons I gave his daughter, every one of them. In spite of my conscientious efforts, poor little Aimée made no headway in English, none at all. She had no interest whatever in discovering what all these new words might mean. In fact she wondered what we nasty men wanted of her that made us insist so on her remembering their meanings. She didn't cry, but she was very close to it. She'd have been a lot happier if we had left her alone to manage what little French she already knew, the pitfalls and joys of which were quite sufficient to keep her busy all her life.

But her father didn't see it that way, not at all. "You must grow up to be a modern young woman, my dear!" he kept insisting. That was supposed to comfort her. "I, your father, have lost a good deal by not knowing enough English to handle my foreign patients... Come come, don't cry, my darling!... You'd do better to listen to Monsieur Bardamu, who's so patient, so kind, and when you're able to say 'the' with your tongue the way he has shown you, I'll buy you a beautiful nickel-plated bicycle..."

But Aimée had no desire to say "the" or "enough", none whatever... It was the boss who said "the" and "rough" in her place, and that wasn't all he learnt in spite of his Bordeaux accent and his mania for logic, which is really no help in English. This went on for a month, two months. As the father's passion for learning English developed, Aimée had less and less need to struggle with the vowels. Baryton monopolized me. In fact he took up all my time, he never let me go, pumped all my English out of me. Since his room was next to mine, I could hear him first thing in the morning, translating his whole private life into English as he dressed. "*The coffee is black... My shirt is white... The garden is green... How are you today, Bardamu?*" he would shout through the partition. He soon acquired a taste for the most elliptical forms of the language.

With that perversion he took us a long way... Once he had made contact with great literature, there was no stopping him... After eight months of such abnormal progress, he had refashioned himself almost completely along Anglo-Saxon lines. In this way he managed to get me completely disgusted with him. Twice in a row.

Little by little we had come to leave little Aimée out of the conversation almost entirely – in other words, in peace. She was quite content to go back to her clouds. She'd never learn English, and that was that! Baryton would learn it all!

Winter returned, and with it Christmas. The travel agencies were advertising return trips to England at bargain prices... While walking on the boulevards, accompanying Parapine to the movies, I'd notice those advertisements... I even went in and asked about the prices.

Then at table, in the course of the conversation, I dropped a word or two to Baryton. At first my bit of information didn't seem to interest him. He let it pass. I thought he'd forgotten all about it, but then one evening he himself brought it up and asked me to bring him a folder when I had a chance.

Between two English literature sessions, we often played Japanese billiards or *bouchon** in one of the isolation rooms situated just above the concierge's lodge and equipped with good iron bars.

Baryton excelled in games of skill. Parapine regularly challenged him to play for drinks and as regularly lost. We spent whole evenings in that improvised little games room, especially in the winter when it was raining, so as not to mess up the chief's big drawing rooms.

Sometimes an excitable patient would be put in the same little room for observation, but not very often.

While Parapine and the boss were matching their skills at *bouchon* on the carpet or on the floor, I would amuse myself, if you want to call it that, trying to experience the same sensations as a prisoner in his cell. That was one sensation I had never known. If you really want to, you can work up friendly feelings towards the few people who pass through those suburban streets. At the end of the day, your heart goes out to the bit of movement created by the trams, bringing back docile clusters of office workers from Paris. Their debacle ends at the first bend in the street, right after the grocery store. Then they flow quietly into the darkness. You've barely had time to count them. But Baryton seldom let me daydream at my leisure. In the middle of his game of *bouchon*, he'd come to life with some ridiculous question.

"*How do you say* 'impossible' *in English, Ferdinand?*"

When it came to improving his English, he was insatiable. With every ounce of his native imbecility he aspired to perfection. No approximations or concessions for him. But then luckily events took a turn which brought me deliverance. Here they are in a nutshell.

In the course of our readings in the history of England, I saw that he was losing some of his assurance and even the greater part of his optimism. As we were feeling our way into the Elizabethan poets, his mind and personality underwent great though imponderable changes. At first I found it hard to believe, but in the end I, like everyone else, was obliged to see Baryton as he had become, in truth a pitiful spectacle. His mind, formerly razor-sharp and rigorous, had begun to wander, leading him into incredible, interminable digressions. Little by little, he developed the habit of daydreaming for hours on end, he'd be right there in his Institute, before our very eyes, and his thoughts would be off in the distance… Though he had long and totally repelled me, I felt a certain remorse at seeing him go to pieces like that. I felt partly responsible for his decline… I felt that his spiritual confusion had something to do with me… So much so that one day I suggested interrupting our study of literature, on the pretext that a break would give us time and leisure to renew our documentary sources… He wasn't fooled by my feeble ruse. His response was a friendly but categorical refusal… He was determined to carry on with the discovery of spiritual England under my guidance… Just as he had begun… What could I say?… I acquiesced. He was afraid the hours of life remaining to him might not suffice for complete success... In short, though I feared the worst, I was obliged to pursue our dismal academic peregrination to the best of my ability.

The fact is that Baryton was no longer himself. The persons and things around us became phantasmagoric and slow, losing their importance and even the colours they had formerly worn for us, and taking on a dreamlike, ambivalent softness...

Baryton had come to concern himself only occasionally and more and more languidly with the administrative details of his own establishment, though it was his life work and for over thirty years the object of his literally passionate interest. He now relied entirely on Parapine to manage the administrative end. The increasing confusion of his mind, which he still tried to conceal in public, soon became obvious to us, a physical reality.

One day Gustave Mandamour, a policeman we knew in Vigny because we sometimes employed him for certain heavy work, and undoubtedly the least discerning person I have ever come across, though I've known many of his kind, asked me if the boss hadn't received some terrible news... I did my best to reassure him, but without conviction.

Baryton had lost his interest in gossip and chit-chat. All he wanted was not to be disturbed on any pretext whatsoever... At the very beginning of our studies we had perused, too quickly to his way of thinking, Macaulay's compendious *History of England*, a seminal work in sixteen volumes. At his command and under quite alarming conditions, we went back to it. Chapter by chapter.

It seemed to me that Baryton was more and more dangerously contaminated by meditation. When we came to that merciless passage where the Pretender Monmouth disembarks on the hazy shores of Kent... where his venture starts revolving around itself... where Monmouth the Pretender no longer knows exactly what he's pretending to... or what he wants to do... or what he has come here for... Where he starts telling himself that he'd be glad to beat it... but he doesn't know where to or how... when defeat rises up before him... in the pale dawn... when the sea carries his last ships away... when for the first time Monmouth starts thinking... then likewise the lowly Baryton couldn't get to the end of his own decisions... He read and reread that passage and mumbled it over again... Overwhelmed, he closed the book and came over and lay down beside us.

For a long time, with half-closed eyes, he ran through the whole text from memory, and then in his English accent, the best among the Bordeaux accents I had given him to choose from, he recited it again...

Face to face with Monmouth's adventure, where all the pitiful absurdity of our puerile and tragic nature discloses itself in the mirror of eternity, Baryton was seized with vertigo. Only the merest thread had attached him to our common lot, and now that thread snapped... From that moment on, I can say without exaggerating, he ceased to be one of us... He'd had it...

Late that night he asked me to join him in his directorial office... At that point I expected him to communicate some monumental decision, my immediate dismissal, for instance... Not at all... On the contrary, the decision he had arrived at was entirely favourable to me! Believe it or not, I was so unaccustomed to being surprised by good news that a tear or two escaped me... Baryton chose to interpret my emotion as sadness. That reversed the roles, and he began to comfort me...

"Will you doubt my word, Ferdinand, if I assure you that it took far more than courage on my part to resolve to leave this Institute?... I, whose sedentary habits are known to you – I, a man on the brink of old age, whose whole career has consisted of long, tenacious, scrupulous verification of innumerable slow or sudden inspirations?... In the space of a very few months, I have come to abjure all that... It seems hardly believable... Yet here I am, body and soul, in such a state of detachment, of exultation... Ferdinand! *Hurrah*, as you say in English! My past has ceased to exist! I shall be reborn, Ferdinand! Neither more nor less! I am going away! Oh, kind friend, your tears are powerless to attenuate the total disgust I feel for everything that has kept me here for so many lacklustre years!... Enough! I can bear it no longer! I repeat, I am going away! Fleeing! Escaping! True, I am torn! I know it! I bleed! I can see it! And yet, Ferdinand, not for anything in the world, do you hear me, Ferdinand? Not for anything would I turn back!... Even if I had dropped an eye somewhere in this muck, I would not come back to pick it up! That's the long and the short of it! Do you doubt my sincerity now?"

I doubted nothing whatsoever. Baryton was unquestionably capable of anything. Besides, I am sure that in the state he had worked himself up into, any contradiction on my part would have been fatal to his reason.

I left him alone for a little while. But then, on second thought, I tried to influence him just a little, risked a last attempt to bring him back to us... by means of a slightly transposed, amiably oblique... argument...

"I beg you, Ferdinand, abandon all hope of my going back on my decision! It is irrevocable, I tell you! You will give me no end of pleasure by never speaking of it again... For the last time, Ferdinand, do you wish to please me? At my age, I know, a sense of mission is most unusual... That's a fact... But when it comes, it's irremediable..."

Those were his very words, almost the last he uttered. I cite them verbatim.

"Perhaps, my dear Monsieur Baryton," I nevertheless ventured to break in, "perhaps in the end this sort of impromptu holiday you are preparing to take will be nothing more than a rather romantic episode, a welcome diversion, a happy intermezzo in the course of your undoubtedly somewhat austere professional activity.... Perhaps after tasting a different life... more varied, less banally methodical than the life we lead here, then perhaps you will simply come back to us, pleased with your journey, surfeited with the unforeseen... And then, quite naturally, you will resume your place at our head... proud of your recent acquisitions... refreshed, in a word, and henceforth, no doubt, prepared to accept, to look with indulgence upon the daily monotony of our laborious routine... An older and a wiser man! If you'll forgive me, Monsieur Baryton, for putting it that way..."

"Oh Ferdinand, you flatterer!... Somehow you still manage to touch my masculine pride – which, I discover, remains sensitive, exigent in fact, despite all my weariness and past trials... No, Ferdinand! With all your ingenuity you cannot in one moment make the abominably hostile and painful essence of our whole striving look benign to me. And moreover, Ferdinand, the time for hesitation is past, it is too late to turn back!... I have been drained, I admit it, I shout it from the rooftops, Ferdinand: drained! Stultified! Defeated! By forty years of prudent paltriness!... That is far too much!... What I aim to do? You want to know?... No reason why I shouldn't tell you, you, my last friend, you who have been willing to take a disinterested part in the sufferings of a defeated old man... What I want, Ferdinand, is to try and lose my soul, as you might try to lose a mangy dog, your stinking dog, the companion who disgusts you, and to get far away from him before you die... To be alone at last... At peace... Myself..."

355

"But, my dear Monsieur Baryton, I have never, in any of your words, caught an inkling of the violent despair whose uncompromising demands you have suddenly revealed to me! I am amazed! On the contrary, your daily remarks still strike me as perfectly pertinent... All your spirited, fruitful suggestions... your splendidly judicious and methodical medical treatments... I would search your daily actions in vain for any sign of depression, of defeat... Really and truly, I discern nothing of the kind..."

But for the first time since I'd known him, Baryton derived no pleasure from my compliments. He went so far as to dissuade me, quite amiably, from pursuing the conversation in a laudatory vein.

"No, my dear Ferdinand, I assure you... True, your last professions of friendship have given my last moments here an unhoped-for sweetness, and yet with all your kindness you cannot reconcile me to the memory of a past which overwhelms me and which this place stinks of... At any cost and – do you hear? – under any conditions, I am determined to go away..."

"But Monsieur Baryton, this institution, what will we do with it? Have you thought of that?"

"Yes, of course I've thought of it, Ferdinand... You will take over the management for as long as I'm away, that's all!... Haven't you always had excellent relations with our clientele? They will gladly accept you as director... Everything will be splendid, you'll see, Ferdinand... Parapine, since he can't abide conversation, will take care of the mechanical end, the apparatus, the laboratory... He has a way with those things... So everything's in the best of order... And you know, I've stopped believing that anyone's presence is indispensable... Even on that score, you see, my friend, I've changed considerably..."

True enough, he was unrecognizable.

"But aren't you afraid, Monsieur Baryton, that your departure will provoke malicious comments on the part of your competitors in the region?... In Passy, for instance? In Montretout?... In Gargan-Livry? All those people around us... Always keeping an eye on us!... Those indefatigably treacherous colleagues!... What construction will they put on your noble voluntary exile?... What will they call it? An escapade? How do I know? Mischief? Flight? Bankruptcy?..."

That eventuality had no doubt given him occasion for long and painful reflections. It still troubled him, and he turned pale before my eyes at the thought of it...

His daughter, Aimée, our little halfwit, was in for a pretty rough time. He was entrusting her to the care of an aunt in the provinces, a total stranger if the truth be known. So, once his private affairs had been settled, Parapine and I would only have to look after his interests and property as best we could. Adrift in a ship without a captain!

After all he had told me, I thought it permissible to ask him which way he was heading in his quest for adventure...

"To England, Ferdinand!" he replied, without batting an eyelash.

So much had happened to us in such a short time, I thought we'd have trouble digesting it, but it was clear that we'd have to adapt quickly to our new mode of life.

The very next day Parapine and I helped him with his luggage. The passport with all its little pages and visas startled him somewhat. He had never seen a passport before. But while he was at it, he'd have liked to apply for a few spares. We managed to convince him that this was impossible.

One last time he stumbled over the question: should he take hard collars or soft collars away with him and how many of each? This problem, still undecided, brought us almost to train time. All three of us jumped into the last tram for Paris. Baryton took only a small suitcase, intending to travel light and preserve his mobility wherever he went.

On the platform he was impressed by the noble elevation of the car steps on the international trains. Hesitating to mount those majestic structures, he contemplated the car as though gazing at a monument. We helped him a little. Having taken a second-class ticket, he made a comparative, practical and cheerful observation: "First is no better," he said.

We shook hands with him. The time was at hand. The whistle blew, and the train pulled out on the dot with an enormous jolt and crashing of steel, abominably curtailing our farewells. He had barely time to say: "Goodbye, boys!" and his hand broke loose, carried away from ours...

Then his hand was waving in the smoke, rushing through the noise, already in darkness, farther and farther down the rails, white...

* * *

357

In a way we weren't sorry to see him go, but all the same the house seemed very empty without him.

In the first place, the way he'd gone made us sad, in spite of ourselves so to speak. It wasn't natural. After such a blow we wondered what might happen to us.

But we didn't have time to wonder very long. Only a few days after we'd taken Baryton to the station, I'm informed that there's someone asking to see me personally in the office. Abbé Protiste.

So I tell him the news, and what news! Especially the way Baryton had run out on us to go gallivanting around in the Septentrional regions... When Protiste heard that, he couldn't get over it, and when it finally sank in, the altered situation meant only one thing to him, namely, the advantage I could derive from it. "Such trust on the part of your director," he kept saying over and over, "strikes me as the most flattering sort of promotion, my dear Doctor!"

I tried to calm him down, but once launched he persisted in his view of the matter and predicted that the most glorious of futures lay in wait for me, a magnificent medical career, as he put it. I couldn't stop him.

Nevertheless, though with considerable difficulty, we finally got back to serious matters – that is, to the city of Toulouse, whence he had arrived only the day before. Of course I gave him his turn to speak and tell me all he knew. I even pretended to be astonished – nay, stupefied – when he told me about the old woman's accident.

"What? What's that?" I interrupted. "Dead? Heavens above! When did this happen?"

Little by little, he had to come clean.

Without telling me in so many words who had pushed the old woman down her little staircase, he said nothing to deter me from guessing... It seems she hadn't had time to say boo. We understood each other... It was a good job, handled with care... This time he had done for her, he hadn't botched his second try.

Luckily everyone in the neighbourhood had thought Robinson was still stone-blind. So they hadn't suspected anything more than an accident, a very tragic one to be sure, but quite understandable when you thought it over, given the circumstances, the old woman's age and the time of day, the late afternoon when she must have been tired... Just then I had no desire to hear more. He had told me plenty.

But it wasn't so easy getting the Abbé to change the subject. The thing was on his mind. He kept coming back to it, apparently in the hope that I'd make some kind of slip and give myself away... Nothing doing!... He could keep trying... So after a while he gave up and contented himself with talking about Robinson and his health... His eyes... In that department he was much better... But his morale was still low. In fact his morale was terrible! In spite of the kindness and affection the two women never stopped showing him... he never stopped complaining about his own hard lot and life in general.

It didn't surprise me to hear Protiste telling me all that. I knew Robinson. He had a low-down, ungrateful nature. But I distrusted the Abbé even more... I didn't say a word while he was talking to me. All his confiding didn't get him anywhere.

"I must admit, Doctor, that your friend, in spite of a material life that has become pleasant and easy and the prospect of a happy marriage, has dashed all our hopes... Once again he is succumbing to the same fatal penchant for escapades, the perverse impulses you detected in the past... What do you think of those tendencies of his, my dear doctor?"

In short, if I got the drift, Robinson's only thought was to drop everything. At first his fiancée and her mother were angry, then they were stricken with grief. That's what Abbé Protiste had come to tell me. All this was rather upsetting, and for my part I made up my mind to hold my tongue and steer clear of these people's little family affairs at all costs... After an abortive conversation we parted at the tram stop, rather coolly to tell the truth. Not at all easy in my mind, I went back to the rest home.

Only a short time after this visit, we had our first news of Baryton. From England. A few postcards. He wished us all "good health and good luck". After that a few vapid lines from one place and another. A card with no message on it informed us that he had gone to Norway, and a few weeks later there was a somewhat reassuring telegram: "Good crossing!" From Copenhagen...

As we had foreseen, the chief's absence provoked the most vicious comment in Vigny and environs. It seemed best for the future of the Institute that we should provide the patients and our colleagues round about with only the barest minimum of information regarding the reasons for this absence.

Months passed, months of extreme caution, dull and silent. Among ourselves we stopped mentioning Baryton altogether. To tell the truth, thinking about him made us feel rather ashamed.

And then it was summer again. We couldn't spend all our time in the garden supervising the patients. To prove to ourselves that we had some freedom in spite of it all, we ventured as far as the banks of the Seine, just to get out.

After the embankment on the far shore, the great plain of Gennevilliers begins, a beautiful expanse of grey and white, with chimneys softly outlined in the dust and mist. Right beside the towpath you'll see the bargemen's bistro. It guards the entrance to the canal. The yellow current comes pushing against the lock.

For hours on end we'd look down at all that, and off to the side at the long swamp, the insidious smell of which reaches as far as the motor road. You get used to it. That muck was so old, so worn out by the river floods that it had no colour left. Sometimes on summer evenings when the sky went pink and sentimental the mud would take on a kind of gentle look. It was there on the bridge that we'd listen to the accordion music they'd play on the barges while waiting at the lock gates for the night to be over so they could pass through to the river. The ones coming down from Belgium are especially musical, they have colour all over, green and yellow, and clothes lines full of shirts and drawers and raspberry-coloured slips, puffed up by the wind as it leaps and gusts into them.

I'd often go to the bargemen's bar at the slack hour after lunch, when the owner's cat is blissfully at peace within four walls, shut up in a little blue-enamel heaven that belongs to him alone.

There I too sat drowsing in the early afternoon, forgotten, I thought, by all the world, waiting for the time to pass.

I saw someone coming in the distance, coming up the road. I wasn't long in doubt. He had hardly set foot on the bridge when I recognized him. It was Robinson, his very own self. No possible doubt! "He's come looking for me…" I said to myself. "The priest must have given him my address!… I'll have to get rid of him quick!"

At that particular moment I thought it was foul of him to come around bothering me just as I was starting to build up a cosy bit of self-indulgence. We're always suspicious of things approaching on a road, and we're right. By then he had almost reached the bistro. I went outside. He seemed surprised to see me. "Where in hell have you come from?" I ask him, not at all friendly. "From La Garenne…" he says. "OK! Have you eaten?" He didn't look as if he'd eaten, but he didn't want to seem to be starving the moment he got there. "So you're on the loose again?" I ask him. Because, believe me, I wasn't at all glad to be seeing him again. It didn't suit me one bit.

Just then Parapine came up from the canal, looking for me. That was a good thing. Parapine was tired from being on duty so often at the asylum. It was true that I'd been taking my responsibilities rather lightly. Be that as it may, we'd both have given a good deal to know exactly when Baryton would be coming back. We hoped he'd stop gadding about pretty soon so he could relieve us of the business and start looking after it himself. It was too much for us. Neither of us was ambitious, and we didn't give a good goddamn about the prospects for the future. Which was wrong of us, I admit.

I have to give Parapine credit, he never asked questions about the financial management of the institution or my dealings with the clientele, but I filled him in just the same, in spite of him so to speak, and when that happened it was like talking to myself. About Robinson now, it was important to put him in the picture.

"I told you about Robinson, remember?" I asked him by way of introduction. "You know. My war buddy?… Ring a bell?…"

He'd heard me tell my war stories and stories about Africa a hundred times and in a hundred different ways. That was my style.

"Well," I went on, "this is Robinson in the flesh, come all the way from Toulouse to see us… We're all having dinner together at the house." To tell the truth, I felt kind of uneasy about inviting him in the name of the Institute. It was a sort of indiscretion. The situation called for a winning, ingratiating air of authority, something I didn't have at all. Besides, Robinson wasn't making things any easier for me. On our way back to the village he seemed curious and anxious, especially in regard to Parapine, whose long, pale face intrigued him. At first he thought Parapine was one of the lunatics. As soon as he found out where we were staying in Vigny, he began to see lunatics everywhere. I reassured him.

"What about you?" I asked him. "Have you found some sort of work at least, now that you're back?"

"I'm going to start looking…" was all the answer I got.

"How about your eyes? Cured? You can see now?"

"Yes, I can see. Almost as good as before…"

"Then you must be happy," I said.

No, he wasn't happy. He had other things to do besides being happy. I was careful not to mention Madelon right away. That was still a ticklish subject between us. We spent quite some time over our aperitifs, and I took the opportunity to tell him a good deal about the rest home and various other things. I've never been able to stop shooting my mouth off right and left, pretty much like Baryton, come to think of it. Our dinner went off cordially. And when it was over I couldn't very well put Robinson out in the street. I decided that for the present we'd set up a folding bed for him in the dining room. Parapine as usual expressed no opinion. "All right, Léon," I said. "You can stay here until you find a job…" "Thanks," he said simply. And every morning from then on he took the tram into Paris, to look for a job as a salesman.

He was sick of factories, he said, he wanted to be a salesman. I've got to be fair, he may have knocked himself out looking for a salesman's job, but he certainly didn't find one.

One day he came back from Paris earlier than usual. I was still in the garden, supervising my charges near the big pond. He came out and joined me. There was something on his mind.

"Listen!" he began.

"I'm listening," I answered.

"Couldn't you give me some little job right here?… I can't find one anywhere else…"

"Have you really tried?"

"Yes, I've really tried…"

"You want a job here in the nuthouse? Doing what? Can't you find some little thing in Paris? Would you like Parapine and me to ask some people we know?"

My offer to help him find a job wasn't to his liking.

"It's not that there's absolutely no jobs to be had," he said. "Maybe I'd find one… some little job… Sure… But don't you see… I absolutely have to make it look like I'm off my rocker… It's urgent, it's indispensable! It's gotta look like I'm off my rocker…"

"All right," I said. "Say no more!…"

"Don't try to shut me up, Ferdinand. I've got to say more," he insisted, "because I want you to understand… And as I know you, it takes you a long time to understand anything and decide to do something about it…"

"In that case, shoot," I said. "Tell me all about it…" I was resigned.

"If I don't make it look like I'm nuts, I'll be out of luck, I assure you… Big trouble!… She's perfectly capable of having me arrested… Now do you get the drift?"

"Madelon, you mean?"

"Madelon! Who else?"

"That's great!"

"You can say that again…"

"So you're really on the outs?"

"As you see…"

"Come this way if you want to tell me more!" I interrupted, and led him off to one side. "It's safer because of the nuts… Mad as they are, they understand certain things that'll sound even wilder when they repeat them…"

We went up to one of the isolation rooms, and once there it didn't take him long to explain the whole machination, especially as I already knew that he'd stop at nothing, and Abbé Protiste had hinted at the rest…

He hadn't bungled his second try. No one could accuse him of goofing again! Oh no! Not by a long shot!

"You see, the old bag was getting on my nerves more and more… Especially after my eyes got a little better and I could go out in the street by myself… After that I could see things… I could see the old bag too… I could see her all right, in fact I never saw anything else!… All day long I had her there in front of me!… She was poisoning my life!… I honestly think she hung around on purpose… to bug me… I can't explain it any other way!… And that house we were all living in, you know the house, it's a hard place to keep from fighting in… You saw how small it is!… We were all on top of each other! You can't say different!…"

"And the cellar stairs weren't very solid, were they?"

I myself had noticed how dangerous those stairs were, when I visited the crypt for the first time with Madelon. They'd been shaky even then.

"Yes, it was practically a set-up," he admitted very frankly.

"And what about the people down there?" I asked him. "The neighbours, the priests, the reporters… Didn't their tongues wag some when it happened?…"

"No, it seems they didn't… Besides, they didn't think I was up to it… They thought I was a washout… Blind… You understand…"

"Well, you can thank your stars for that, because otherwise… But what about Madelon? Was she in it with you?"

"Not exactly… But just a little, yes, of course, because we were supposed to inherit the whole crypt once the old bag passed on… Things had been settled that way… The two of us were going to take over…"

"So what went wrong between you?"

"Well, that's hard to explain…"

"Was she sick of you?"

"Not at all, she was crazy about me and still dead set on getting married… Her mother was all for it too, more than ever. She wanted us to do it quick, because we had come into the old bag's mummies and there'd be enough for the three of us to live on and then some…"

"So what went wrong between you?"

"Well, I just wanted them to leave me in peace! It's as simple as that… The mother, the daughter, both of them…"

"Look here, Léon!…" I stopped him when I heard that. "Listen to me!… Your story doesn't make sense!… Think of Madelon and her mother, put yourself in their shoes… How would you feel in their place?… I ask you… When you got there, you hardly had a pair of shoes to your name, no job, nothing, all day long you complained, about the old woman keeping all the money, and so forth and so on… She passes on, or rather, you pass her on… And right away you start making faces again and putting on airs… Put yourself in the shoes of those two women, stop and think!… It's unbearable!… Boy, would I have told you what you could do!… They should have sent you to jail, that's what you really deserved, I don't mind telling you!"

That's what I said to Robinson.

"Maybe so," Robinson answered back. "But even if you're a doctor and educated and all that, you'll never understand my nature…"

"You shut up!" I finally told him. "You poor jerk, don't talk to me about your nature! You talk like a nut!… I'm sorry Baryton has gone away God knows where, or he'd have taken you in! Best thing that could happen to you! Lock you up! See what I mean? Baryton would have known how to handle your nature!"

"If you'd had what I had and been through what I've been through," he came back at me, "you'd have been nuts yourself, I assure you!

Maybe worse than me! A softie like you!…" And he began to bawl me out as windily as if he'd had a right to.

I watched him closely while he was gassing. I'd often been abused that way by the patients. It didn't bother me any more.

He'd got a good deal thinner since Toulouse, and something had happened to his face, something I'd never seen before, a kind of portrait had settled on his features, with forgetfulness and silence all around it.

In all this Toulouse business there was something else that bothered him, it was only a minor part of the story, but it had gone against his grain, and when he thought about it now it came back at him like bile. It was having to grease the palms of a whole bunch of operators for nothing. When they'd taken over the crypt, he'd had to dish out commissions right and left, to the priest, the chair-hire woman, the town hall, the vicars, and God knows who else, all to no end, and that had stuck in his craw. Just talking about it threw him into a fit. Thieving he called it.

"And now tell me, did you finally get married?" I asked him.

"I've told you already, no! I didn't want to any more!"

"But your little Madelon wasn't bad. You can't tell me different."

"That's not the question…"

"Oh yes it is. You said you were free, didn't you?… If you were dead set on leaving Toulouse, you could have left her mother in charge of the crypt for a while… you'd have come back later…"

"Physically yes, you're right," he went on. "I admit it, she was first-class. You told me the truth. Especially because it so happened that when I got my sight back, the first thing I saw was her, in a mirror… Can you imagine?… In the light!… About two months after the old woman fell… I was trying to look at Madelon's face, and then suddenly my sight came back… Like a flash of light… You get the picture?"

"Wasn't it nice?"

"Sure, it was nice… But that's not everything…"

"And you cleared out all the same?…"

"Yes, but let me explain, seeing you want to understand… She started it… she started thinking I was acting funny… that I'd lost my zip… that I wasn't nice to her any more… that kind of crap…"

"Maybe your conscience was troubling you…"

"Conscience?"

"Sure, why not?..."

"Call it anything you want, I was feeling rotten, that's all... But I don't think it was conscience..."

"Were you sick?"

"Yeah, sick, that's what it probably was... For the last hour I've been trying to make you say I'm sick... Admit you're pretty slow..."

"OK, OK!" I tell him. "Let's say you're sick if you think it's the safest way..."

"It would make sense," he assured me. "Because I wouldn't put anything past her... She could start singing to the cops any day now..."

He sounded like he was giving me advice, and I didn't want his advice. That kind of thing didn't appeal to me at all, because of the complications it would lead to.

"Do you really think she'd talk?" I asked him, just to make sure... "After all, she was your accomplice in a way... That ought to make her think twice before shooting her mouth off."

"Think twice!" Those words made him jump sky-high. "I can see you don't know her..." I handed him a laugh. "Hell, she wouldn't hesitate for one second!... Like I'm telling you! If you knew her as well as I do, you wouldn't doubt it! She's in love, I tell you!... Haven't you ever known a woman in love? When she's in love, she's crazy! Crazy, I tell you! And it's me she's in love with and crazy about!... Do you know what that means? It means that anything crazy excites her! Craziness won't stop her! Hell no!"

I couldn't tell him it rather surprised me to hear that Madelon had reached such a pitch of frenzy in a few months, because after all I'd known her slightly myself... I had my own ideas on the subject, but I couldn't tell him that.

From the way she had handled herself in Toulouse and the things I'd heard her say when I was hidden behind the poplar tree on the day of the houseboat, it was hard for me to imagine that she could have changed so completely in such a short time... She had struck me as more shrewd than tragic, a smooth article, only too glad to get what attention she could with her fantasies and pretensions, wherever they seemed to wash... But in that particular situation there was nothing I could say, I had to let it ride. "All right! All right!" I said. "And how about her mother? She must have let out a squawk when she realized you were clearing out for good?..."

"I'll say! All day long she went on about my rotten character and, mind you, just when I'd have needed to be treated kindly!... You should have heard her!... Anyway, on account of the mother too, it couldn't go on, so that's when I suggested to Madelon that I'd leave them in the crypt while I went off by myself for a while to travel around and see the country...

"'Then you'll take me with you,' she protested... 'I'm your fiancée, aren't I?... You'll take me with you or you won't go at all!... And besides, you're not well enough yet...'

"'I'm all well,' I said, 'and I'm going by myself!' It dragged on and on.

"'A wife always goes with her husband!' said the mother. 'Why don't you just get married?' She backed her up just to bug me.

"Listening to that drivel made me miserable. You know me! As if I needed a woman when I went to war! Or to run out on the war! Did I have women in Africa? Did I have a wife in America?... Hearing them go on like that for hours gave me a pain in the gut! A bellyache! I know what women are good for! And so do you! For nothing! I've travelled and I know! So one evening when they'd been driving me up the wall, I couldn't stand it any more and I told the mother what I thought of her! 'You're an old fool,' I told her... 'You're even more dimwitted than Grandma Henrouille!... If you'd travelled a little more and known a few more people like I have, you wouldn't be in such a hurry to give people advice, and it's not by picking up little pieces of tallow in the corner of your stinking church that you'll learn about life! You ought to get out of there yourself, it would do you good! Why don't you take a walk once in a while, you old bag? A little fresh air would do you good! You'd have less time for your prayers and you wouldn't smell so much like a cow!...'

"That's what I said to her mother! I can assure you, I'd been aching a long time to tell her off, and what's more she needed it bad... But all in all, it's me that got the most out of it... It sort of helped me out of the situation... It looked as if the old battleaxe had just been waiting for me to fly off the handle so she could call me all the names for son of a bitch she knew! So she let loose and said a lot more than she needed to. 'Thief! Layabout!' she yelled... 'You haven't even got a trade!... It's going on a year that I've been supporting you and my daughter!... Pimp!...' Get the idea? A regular family scene... She seemed to be thinking it over for a while, and then she blurted out, she really put her heart in it: 'Murderer!... Murderer!' That kind of gave me the shivers.

"When her daughter heard that, she was afraid I'd kill her mother on the spot. She flung herself between us and closed her mother's mouth with her own hand. Which was just as well. So the two of them are in cahoots, I said to myself! It was obvious. Well, I let it go... The time for violence was past... And anyway, what did I care if they were in cahoots?... Maybe you think that after letting off all that steam they'd leave me alone... Not at all! If that's what you think, you don't know them... The daughter started up again. Her head was on fire and so was her cunt... She started up worse than ever...

"'I love you, Léon... Can't you see that I love you?'

"That's all she knew, her 'I love you' jazz. As if that was the answer to everything.

"'What! You still love him?' her mother put in. 'Can't you see that he's nothing but a thug? The lowest of the low! Now that he's got his eyesight back, thanks to our care, he'll bring you nothing but misery. Just take it from me, your mother!...'

"To finish up the scene, we all cried, even me, because whatever happened I didn't want to get in too bad with those bitches, I didn't want us to fall out entirely.

"So I went out for a walk. We'd said too much, and staying in the same room we couldn't have controlled ourselves for long. Even so we kept wrangling off and on for weeks, and keeping an eye on each other, especially at night.

"We couldn't make up our minds to break up, but our hearts weren't in it any more. It was mostly fear that kept us together.

"'You must love somebody else!' Madelon would say now and then.

"I'd try to reassure her: 'Not at all! Of course not!' But it was obvious that she didn't believe me. The way she saw it, you had to love somebody, there was no getting around it.

"'Just tell me this,' I'd say. 'What would I do with another woman?' But she had love on the brain. There was nothing I could say to calm her. She dreamt up stuff I'd never heard before. I'd never have suspected she was hiding such rubbish in her head.

"'You took my heart, Léon!' she'd fire at me in all seriousness. 'You want to go?' she blustered. 'All right, go! But I warn you, Léon, I'll die of grief!...' Die of grief on my account? Where's the sense in that, I ask you? 'No, no,' I'd say. 'You won't die! And in the first place I never took anything at all. I haven't even knocked you up! Think it over. I haven't given you any diseases either! Or have I? Well then! All I want is to go away, that's all! A kind of holiday. What's wrong with that?... Try to be reasonable...' But the more I tried to make her understand my point of view, the less she thought of my point of view. In fact we didn't understand each other at all any more... It drove her crazy to think that I might really feel the way I said I did, that everything I said was true, simple and sincere.

"Besides, she thought it was you who was trying to get me to beat it... And seeing that she couldn't hold me by making me ashamed of my feelings, she tried a different way of holding me.

"'Don't go thinking I want you because of the crypt and the business!...' she'd say. 'You know I don't really care about money... What I want, Léon, is to stay with you... And to be happy... That's all... It's perfectly natural... I don't want you to leave me... It's too cruel for people to separate when they've loved each other like we have... Swear to me at least that you won't be gone for long...'

"It went on like that for weeks. She was in love all right, a real pest... Every evening she came back to her love jazz. In the end she was willing to leave her mother in charge of the crypt, on condition that the two of us went to Paris together to look for work... Always together!... A nutcase! She was willing to put up with anything you could think of except that we should go our separate ways... On that subject the answer was strictly no... So naturally the harder she dug in the sicker I got of the whole business!

"It was no use trying to put any sense into her. I knew I was wasting my time and only getting her more stirred up. So I had to start thinking up ways to get rid of her 'love', as she called it... That was what made me think of telling her that I kind of went out of my mind now and then... That fits would come on... without warning... She gave me a funny look... She didn't rightly know if this was another fib or not. But anyway, considering the adventures I'd told her about and what the war had done to me and my latest exploit with Grandma Henrouille and the funny way I was acting with her, it gave her food for thought...

"She thought for more than a week and didn't bother me all that time... She must have said a word or two to her mother about my fits... Anyway, they didn't seem so eager to hang on to me any more... 'Good deal!' I said to myself. 'It's going to be all right! Free at last...' I could already see myself slipping quietly away in the direction of Paris without any breakage!... But not so fast! I started overdoing it... Frills... I thought I'd hit on a smart way of proving to her once and for all that I'd been telling the truth... That I really went nuts when the spirit moved me... 'Feel!' I said to Madelon one evening. 'Feel the bump on the back of my head! And the scar on top of it! Some bump, eh?...'

"When she'd had a good feel of the bump on the back of my head, it really started her off, I can tell you... But imagine, it didn't disgust her at all, far from it, it made her more excited than ever!... 'That's where I was wounded in Flanders,' I said. 'That's where I was trepanned...'

"'Oh, Léon!' she cried out, still feeling the bump. 'Can you ever forgive me, Léon?... I doubted you up to now, but now I beg your forgiveness with all my heart! I see it all now! I've been beastly to you! Oh yes, I have! I've been awful!... I'll never be mean to you again! I swear it! I want to make it up to you, Léon! Right away! You'll let me make it up to you, won't you?... I'll make you happy again! Oh, how I'll take care of you! Starting today! I'll be ever so patient with you! So gentle! You'll see, Léon! I'll be so good to you you won't be able to get along without me! I'll give you back all my heart, I belong to you!... Every bit of me! I'll give you my whole life, Léon! Only tell me you forgive me, tell me, Léon!...'

"I hadn't said any of that, she'd said it all herself, so naturally she had no trouble answering herself... How in God's name was I to stop her?

"It looked like feeling my scar and my bump had made her drunk with love all of a sudden! She wanted to take my head in both hands and never let it go and make me happy from then to eternity, whether I liked it or not! After that scene her mother wasn't allowed to bawl me out any more. Madelon didn't even let her mother talk. You wouldn't have known her, she wanted to protect me to the bitter end!

"It couldn't go on! Naturally I'd rather we parted friends... But it was no use... She was bursting with love, and she was stubborn. One morning when she and her mother were out shopping, I did the same as you, I made up a little bundle and beat it on the quiet... After all I've told you, you won't try to tell me I wasn't patient enough... Believe me, there was nothing I hadn't tried... Now you know the whole story... When I tell you that girl would stop at nothing and that she's likely to come here looking for me any minute, don't try and tell me I'm seeing things! I know what I'm talking about! I know her! And we'd be a lot safer in my opinion if she found me locked up with the nuts... That way I could pretend not to understand... With her that's the only way... Just let on that you don't know what she's talking about..."

Two or three months before, I'd have been interested in what Robinson was telling me, but I seemed to have aged all of a sudden.

I guess I'd been getting more and more like Baryton, I didn't give a damn. What Robinson had been telling me about his adventure in Toulouse didn't strike me as a very real danger any more. I tried in vain to get excited about his situation, but his situation had a musty smell about it. Maybe we like to think different, but the world leaves us long before we leave it for good.

One fine day you decide to talk less and less about the things you care most about, and when you have to say something, it costs you an effort... You're totally sick of hearing yourself talk... you abridge... You give up... For thirty years you've been talking... You don't care about being right any more. You even lose your desire to keep hold of the small place you'd reserved yourself among the pleasures of life... You're fed up... From that time on you're content to eat a little something, cadge a little warmth, and sleep as much as possible on the road to nowhere. To rekindle your interest, you'd have to think up some new grimaces to put on in the presence of others... But you no longer have the strength to renew your repertory. You stammer. Sure, you still look for excuses for hanging around with the boys, but death is there too, stinking, right beside you, it's there the whole time, less mysterious than a game of poker. The only thing you continue to value is petty regrets, like not finding time to run out to Bois-Colombes to see your uncle while he was still alive, the one whose little song died for ever one afternoon in February. That horrible little regret is all we have left of life, we've vomited up the rest along the way, with a good deal of effort and misery. We're nothing now but an old lamp-post with memories on a street where hardly anyone passes any more.

If you've got to be unhappy, you may as well keep regular habits. I insisted on everybody in the house being in bed by ten o'clock. I was the one who turned out the lights. The business took care of itself.

We didn't overtax our imaginations. The Baryton system of taking cretins to the movies kept us busy enough. Under our management

371

the institution wasn't run as economically as it had been. Wanton waste, we figured, might bring the boss back, since it gave him such nightmares.

We had bought an accordion, so Robinson could play music for the patients to dance to in the garden during the summer months. It was hard to keep the inmates busy day and night. We couldn't send them to church all the time, they got too bored.

We received no further reports from Toulouse. Abbé Protiste never came back to see us. The asylum settled down to a life of furtive monotony. We weren't easy in our minds. Too many ghosts around.

Months passed. Robinson was looking better. At Easter time our patients became rather agitated, women in light-coloured dresses had taken to strolling back and forth outside the garden. Harbingers of spring. I gave them bromides.

At the Tarapout the cast had been changed several times since the days when I'd worked there. The little English girls were far away, I was told. In Australia. We'd never see them again...

I wasn't allowed backstage since the business with Tania. I didn't press the point.

We started writing letters all over the place, especially to the con-sulates of the northern countries, to try and get some news of Baryton's movements. There were no answers of any interest.

Meanwhile Parapine performed his technical duties in dignified silence. I doubt if in twenty-four months he had uttered more than twenty sentences in all. I was obliged to attend to the daily material and administrative details practically unaided. I made a few mistakes. Parapine never held them up to me. We got along fine together by dint of sheer indifference. An adequate turnover of patients kept the institution going nicely. After paying for supplies and rent, we still had more than enough to live on, and it goes without saying that Aimée's aunt was paid regularly for the child's board.

Robinson, I had the impression, was suffering much less from anxiety than when he got there. He was looking better and had gained three kilos. On the whole it seemed that as long as families had little lunatics in their midst, they would keep coming to us, conveniently situated as we were, a stone's throw from the capital. Our garden alone was worth the trip. On fine summer days people would come from Paris just to admire our flower beds and our clumps of roses.

It was on one of those Sundays in June that I thought I recognized Madelon for the first time, in the middle of a group of strollers. For a moment she stood there, just outside our gate.

At first I didn't want to mention this apparition to Robinson, for fear of frightening him, but then, thinking it over, I advised him, for a time at least, to give up the aimless strolls in the neighbourhood that he'd got in the habit of taking. My advice had him worried. But he didn't ask to know more.

Towards the end of July we received a few postcards from Baryton, this time from Finland. We were glad to hear from him, but he didn't say one word about coming back, he only wished us good luck and sent us friendly greetings.

Two months passed and then more... Again the roads were covered with summer dust. Around All Saints' Day one of our lunatics caused something of a stir outside our Institute. This patient had always been quiet and well behaved, but the mortuary excitement of All Saints was too much for him. We weren't quick enough to stop him from standing at the window and shouting that he didn't ever want to die... The passers-by thought he was too funny for words... In the midst of this ruckus I again had the unpleasant impression, but much more definitely than the first time, of having recognized Madelon in the front row of a group at the exact same place outside the gate.

In the night that followed I was awakened by a feeling of distress. I tried in vain to forget what I had seen. There was no point in trying to get back to sleep.

I hadn't been back to Rancy in a long time. As long as I was being pursued by a nightmare, I wondered if it mightn't be a good idea to take a look out there, where all misfortunes came from sooner or later... I'd left plenty of nightmares behind me out there... In a pinch you might think of going to meet them halfway as a kind of precaution... Coming from Vigny, the shortest way to Rancy is along the Seine as far as the Gennevilliers Bridge, the low flat one. The slow river mists break up just over the water, rise, drift, race, stagger and fall on the other side of the parapet, around the little dim lamps. The big tractor factory on the left is hiding in a great chunk of darkness. The windows have been opened by a dismal conflagration that is burning it away from inside and goes on and on. After the factory you're alone on the river bank... But you can't lose your way... Your degree of fatigue gives you a pretty good idea that you've reached your destination.

At that point you just have to turn left into the Rue des Bournaires, and then it's not far. It's easy to get your bearings, because of the green and red signal lights at the grade crossing, which are always lit.

Even in the middle of the night I could have found the Henrouilles' house with my eyes closed. I'd gone there often enough in the old days...

But that night, just outside their door, I started to think instead of going ahead...

Madame Henrouille, it came to me, was living there alone now. They were all dead, all of them... She must have known, or at least suspected, how the old woman had died in Toulouse... I wondered how she had felt about it...

The street lamp whitened the glass top of the little portico over the doorstep like a snowfall. I stood on the street corner for a long time, just looking. I could have gone and rung the bell. I'm sure she'd have let me in. We hadn't quarrelled after all. It was freezing cold where I was standing...

The street still ended in a bog, same as in my time. They'd promised to send workmen, but they never had. No one passed that way any more.

It wasn't that I was afraid of Madame Henrouille. No. But all of a sudden I had lost all desire to see her. Wanting to see her had been a mistake. There, outside her house, I suddenly realized that there was nothing more she could tell me... Listening to her would have bored me, it was as simple as that... We were nothing to each other any more.

By then I'd gone further into the night than she had, further even than Grandma Henrouille, who was dead. We weren't all together any more... We had left each other for good... Death had come between us and so had life... Inevitably... Each man for himself, I mumbled... and started back to Vigny.

Madame Henrouille hadn't had enough education to follow me any further... Character, yes, she had plenty of that... But no education! That was the rub. No education! Education is indispensable! That's why she couldn't understand me any more, or understand what was going on around us, vicious and stubborn as she was... That's not enough... You need a heart and a certain amount of knowledge to go further than other people... To get back to the Seine I took the Rue des Sanzillons and then the Impasse Vasson. My worry was all straightened out. I was pleased, almost happy, because now I knew that there was no point in batting my brains out over the Henrouille woman, I'd finally dropped her by the wayside, the bitch!... What a number! We'd been pretty good friends in our own way... We had understood each other for quite some time... But now she wasn't low enough for me, and she couldn't go down any further... To catch up with me... She had neither the education nor the strength. You don't go up in life, you go down. And she couldn't get down to where I was... There was too much night around me.

Passing the house where Bébert's aunt had been the concierge, I'd have liked to go in and see who was living now in the lodge where I'd taken care of Bébert and where he had died. Maybe his schoolboy picture was still hanging over the bed... But it was too late to be waking people up. I went on without showing myself...

A little further on, on the Faubourg de la Liberté, I saw the light still burning in Bézin's junk shop... I hadn't expected that... But it was only a gas jet in the middle of the window. Bézin knew all the news and gossip of the neighbourhood from hanging around the cafés... He was known all the way from the Flea Market to the Porte Maillot.

He could have told me some good ones if he'd been awake. I pushed his door. The bell rang, but no one answered. I knew that he slept in the back room, his dining room actually... And there he was in the dark with his head between his arms on the table, sitting twisted beside his cold dinner that was still waiting, lentils. He had begun to eat. Sleep had grabbed hold of him the moment he started. He was snoring loudly. True, he'd been drinking. I well remember what day it was, a Thursday, the day of the market at Les Lilas... He had a green cloth full of his acquisitions spread out at his feet.

I had always liked Bézin, he was no crummier than most. Obliging, easy-going... I wasn't going to wake him up just out of curiosity, just to get answers to my few little questions... So I turned off the gas and left.

I'm sure he had a hard time making ends meet in that business of his. But at least he found no difficulty in falling asleep.

I can't deny that I felt sad as I started back to Vigny at the thought that all those people, those houses, those dirty, dingy, dismal things no longer spoke to me at all, no longer spoke straight to my heart as they had in the old days, and that, chipper as I might seem, I quite possibly didn't have the strength to go on much further like that alone.

* * *

About meals at Vigny, we had stuck to the same arrangements as in Baryton's day – that is, we all got together at table, except that now we usually ate in the billiard room above the concierge's lodge. It was cosier than the regular dining room, where unpleasant memories of English conversations still hung in the air. And besides, the furniture in the dining room was too good for us – genuine "1900" pieces with opaline stained-glass windows.

From the billiard room you could see everything that was going on in the street. That could come in handy. We'd spend whole Sundays in that room. Now and then we'd invite a doctor from the neighbourhood to dinner, but our usual guest was Gustave, the traffic cop. He was regular. I can vouch for that. We'd got acquainted out of the window one Sunday, watching him on duty at the crossroads coming into town. The cars were giving him trouble. First we just exchanged a few words, and then from Sunday to Sunday we really got acquainted. It so happened that I'd treated his two sons in Paris, one with measles, the other with mumps. Gustave Mandamour – that was his name, from Cantal – was our faithful friend. Conversation with him could be kind of trying, because he had trouble with his words. He could find them all right, but he couldn't get them out, they'd stay in his mouth making noises.

One evening Robinson invited him into the billiard room, as a joke I think. But it was Gustave's nature to keep on with anything he had started, so after that he came every evening at the same time, eight o'clock. He felt at ease with us, better than at the café, as he himself told us, because of the political discussions at the café that often got out of hand. We, on the other hand, never talked politics. In Gustave's case politics was a ticklish subject. It had got him into trouble at the café. The fact is, he should always have steered clear of politics, especially after he had a few drinks under his belt, which happened sometimes. In fact he had a reputation for drinking, that was his weakness. While with us he felt safe in every respect. He admitted it. We didn't drink. At our place he could let himself go and no harm would come of it. He knew he could trust us.

When Parapine and I thought of the situation we had escaped from and the one that had fallen into our laps at Baryton's, we didn't complain, there was no call to, because all things considered we'd had a miraculous stroke of luck, and we had all the social standing and material comfort we needed.

Still, for my part, I had never imagined that the miracle would last. I had a crummy past behind me, and already it was coming back at me like the belchings of fate. At the very start in Vigny I had received three anonymous letters that had seemed as suspicious and as menacing as could be. And then scads of other equally vicious letters. It's true that we often received anonymous letters at Vigny, and didn't pay much attention to them as a rule. Usually they came from former patients, whose persecution mania had followed them home.

But these letters and their turns of phrase had me worried, they weren't like the others, their accusations were precise, and they were all about me and Robinson. To come right out with it, they accused us of shacking up together. A crummy insinuation. At first I was reluctant to mention them to Robinson, but I finally decided to when I kept receiving more and more letters of the same kind. So then the two of us tried to figure out who could have sent them. We drew up a list of all the possible people we both knew. That didn't get us anywhere. Anyway, this accusation didn't make sense. Homosexuality wasn't my line, and Robinson didn't give a damn about sex one way or the other. If anything was bugging him, it certainly wasn't sex. Only a jealous woman could have dreamt up such rotten calumnies.

In short, of all the people we knew, only Madelon seemed capable of pursuing us all the way to Vigny with such foul fabrications. She could go on writing her poisoned letters for all I cared… What I feared was that, exasperated at getting no answer, she'd come around in person one of these days and kick up a ruckus at the Institute. You had to expect the worst.

For several weeks we jumped every time the bell rang. I was expecting a visit from Madelon, or still worse, from the police.

Every time Gustave Mandamour came around for his game a little earlier than usual, I wondered if he didn't have a summons tucked in his belt, but in those days Mandamour was still as friendly and easy-going as could be. It wasn't until later that he too underwent a striking change. At that time he came almost every day and lost every game he played with perfect equanimity. If his disposition changed, it was definitely our fault.

One evening, just out of curiosity, I asked Mandamour why he never won at cards. I had no serious reason for asking him, only my mania for knowing the whys and the wherefores... Especially seeing that we didn't play for money. While we were talking about his bad luck, I stepped up to him, studied him closely, and saw that he was extremely far-sighted. The fact is that with the lighting we had there he could barely distinguish clubs from diamonds. Something was bound to happen.

I corrected his impairment by giving him a nice pair of glasses. At first he was delighted with them, but not for long. Since he played better with his glasses, he didn't lose as often as before, and then he took it into his head to stop losing altogether. That was impossible, so he cheated. And when, as sometimes happened, he lost in spite of his cheating, he sulked for hours. In short, he became impossible.

I was aghast, he'd get sore for no reason at all, and to make matters worse he'd try to upset us, to give us things to worry about. When he lost, he'd get even, in his own way... And yet, I repeat, we weren't playing for money, only for fun and glory... But he was furious all the same.

One evening when his luck had been bad, he harangued us before leaving: "Gentlemen, I'm warning you to watch your step!... Considering the people you associate with, if I were you, I'd be careful!... Among others, there's a dark-haired woman who's been passing your house for days!... A lot too often, if you ask me!... She must have her reasons!... I wouldn't be surprised if she had a bone to pick with one of you gentlemen!..."

That's the pernicious way Mandamour threw this thing in our faces before leaving the room. That got a rise out of us all right!... Nevertheless, I pulled myself together in an instant. "Oh, thank you Gustave," I answered calmly. "I don't see who this dark-haired woman you refer to can be... None of our former female patients, as far as I know, has had reason to complain of our care... It must be some poor deranged creature... We'll find out... Anyway, you're right, it's always best to know... Thanks again for telling us, Gustave... And good evening."

Robinson's consternation was such that he couldn't get up from his chair. When the policeman had gone, we examined the information he'd given us from every angle. After all, it could be another woman, it didn't have to be Madelon... There were others who used to hang around under the windows of our nuthouse... Still, there was good reason to believe it was she, and the mere possibility scared us out of our wits. If it was Madelon, what was she up to now? And what could she have been living on all these months in Paris? And supposing she was going to turn up in person, we'd better talk it over right away and decide what to do.

"Look here, Robinson," I said. "Make up your mind, it's high time, and don't change it... What do you want to do? Do you want to go back to Toulouse with her?"

"No, I tell you. No no no!" That was his answer. Plain enough.

"OK," I said. "But in that case, if you really don't want to go back with her, the best thing, in my opinion, would be for you to leave the country for a while and try and make a living somewhere else. That's the surest way to get rid of her... She wouldn't follow you out of the country, would she?... You're still young... You've recovered your health... You're rested... We'll give you a little money, take it and shove off... That's my advice... Besides, you must be aware that this is no job for you... You can't go on like this for ever..."

If he had listened to me, if he had cleared out then and there, it would have suited me, I'd have been really glad. But he wouldn't buy it.

"Why are you so mean to me, Ferdinand?" he said. "It's not nice of you at my age... Just look at me!..." He didn't want to shove off. He was sick of moving around.

"This is as far as I'll go," he said. "Say what you please... do what you please... I won't go..."

That was how he requited my friendship. Still, I kept trying.

"But what if Madelon were to turn you in, just supposing, in connection with old Madame Henrouille?... You told me yourself that you wouldn't put it past her."

"That would be just too bad," he said. "She can do as she pleases..."

That kind of talk was something new, coming from Robinson. Up until then he had never been a fatalist...

"At least go find yourself some little job nearby, in a factory, then you won't have to be here with us all the time... If somebody comes looking for you, we'll have time to warn you."

Parapine was in complete agreement with me. The matter must have struck him as really grave and urgent because he even went so far as to say a few words to us. We'd have to figure out some place to put Robinson, where he wouldn't be noticed... One of our business connections was a carriage-maker not far away who owed us a small favour for certain little services we'd done him in awkward situations. He agreed to give Robinson a trial at hand-painting. It was delicate work, not hard and nicely paid.

"Léon," we told him the morning he started. "Don't make a fool of yourself in your new job, don't attract attention with your screwed-up ideas... Arrive on time... Don't leave before the others... Say good morning to everybody... In other words, behave. It's a decent shop, and you've been well recommended..."

But right away he got himself spotted, though you can't say it was his fault. A stool pigeon, who worked in one of the other workshops, saw him going into the boss's private office. That did it. Reported. Undesirable element. Fired.

So a few days later Robinson came back to us, jobless. It was bound to happen.

Then, just about the same day, he started coughing again. We auscultated him and found a whole collection of rales all up and down his right lung. Calling for bed rest.

One Saturday evening just before dinner someone asked for me personally in the reception room.

A woman, they tell me.

It was her all right, wearing a little three-cornered hat and gloves. I remember well. No need of preliminaries. She couldn't have picked a worse moment. I give it to her straight before she can say a word.

"Madelon," I said, "if you've come to see Léon, I can tell you right away to forget it... Just turn around and go home... His lungs are affected and so is his head... Quite seriously, I might add... You can't see him... Anyway, he has nothing to say to you..."

"Not even to me?"

"No, not even to you... Especially not to you," I added. I expected her to flare up. No, she only stood there in front of me, shaking her head from side to side and pursing her lips. With her eyes she tried to find me where she had left me in her memory. I wasn't there any more. I, too, had moved in her memory. In that situation I'd have been afraid of a husky man, but from her I had nothing to fear. She was only a weak woman, so to speak. I had always wanted to slap a face consumed with anger, to see what a face consumed with anger would do under the circumstances. A slap or a fat cheque is what it takes if you want to see all the passions that go beating about behind a face take a sudden tack. It's as beautiful as watching a sailing ship manoeuvring in a stormy sea. The whole person keels over in the changed wind. That's what I wanted to see.

For at least twenty years that desire had been goading me. On the street, in cafés, wherever aggressive, touchy, boastful people quarrel. I'd never have dared for fear of getting hit back and even more of the shame that comes of getting hit. But here for once I had a golden opportunity.

"Get out!" I said, just to raise her fury to white heat.

She couldn't get over my talking to her like that. She started to smile, hideously, repulsively, as if she thought me ridiculous and really contemptible... Smack! Smack! I slapped her face twice, hard enough to stun a mule.

She slumped down on the big sofa on the other side of the room, against the wall, with her head between her hands. Her breath came in short gasps and she moaned like a puppy that's been beaten too much. Then, as if she'd thought it over, she jumped up, light and bouncy, and went out the door without even turning her head. I hadn't seen a thing. I'd have to try again.

* * *

But regardless of what we did, she was smarter than all of us together. She saw her Robinson again, she saw him as often as she pleased... It was Parapine who first spotted them together. They were on the terrace of a café across from the Gare de l'Est.

I'd suspected they were seeing each other, but I didn't want to seem to be taking the slightest interest in their relations. After all, it was none of my business. He was doing his work at the rest home, and not at all badly, taking care of the paralytics, a nasty job if ever there was one, wiping them, sponging them, changing their underwear, helping them slobber. We couldn't expect any more of him.

If he chose to see his Madelon on the afternoons when I sent him to Paris on errands, that was his business. We definitely hadn't seen her at

Vigny-sur-Seine since those slaps in the face. But I was pretty sure that since then she must have told him some rotten things about me.

I stopped talking to Robinson about Toulouse, as if none of all that had ever happened.

Six months passed one way or another, and then there was a vacancy on our staff, and we suddenly needed a nurse, skilled in massage. The old one had gone off to get married without giving notice.

Quite a few fine-looking girls applied for the job. In fact, so many strapping young women of all nationalities flocked to Vigny as soon as our ad appeared that we were hard put to choose among them. In the end we picked a Slovak by the name of Sophie, whose complexion, energetic yet gentle bearing, and divine good health struck us, I have to admit, as irresistible.

This Sophie knew only a few words of French, but I undertook without delay, the least I could do, to give her lessons. And lo and behold, in contact with her youth and freshness I felt my interest in teaching revive, though Baryton had done everything in his power to disgust me with it. Impenitent! But what youth! What vigour! What muscles! What an excuse! Supple! Springy! Amazing! Her beauty was diminished by none of that false or true reticence that impedes all-too occidental converse. Frankly, I couldn't admire her enough. From muscle to muscle, I proceeded by anatomical groups... By muscular slopes, by regions... I never wearied of pursuing that concentrated yet relaxed vigour, distributed in bundles which by turns evaded and consented to the touch... Beneath her satin, taut or relaxed, miraculous skin!...

The era of these living joys, of great undeniable physiological and comparative harmonies is yet to come... The body, a godhead mauled by my shameful hands... The hands of an honest man, that unknown priest... Death and Words must give their permission first... What foul affectations! A cultivated man needs to be rolled in a dense layer of symbols, caked to the arsehole with artistic excrement, before he can tear off a piece... Then anything can happen! A bargain! Think of the saving, getting all your thrills from reminiscences... Reminiscences are something we've got plenty of, one can buy beauties, enough to last us a lifetime... Life is more complicated, especially the life of human forms... A hard adventure. None more desperate. Compared with the addiction to perfect forms, cocaine is a pastime for stationmasters.

But let's get back to our Sophie! Her mere presence seemed a feat of daring in our sulking, fearful, unsavoury household.

After she had been with us for some time, we were still glad to number her among our nurses, yet we could not help fearing that she might one day disturb the fabric of our infinite precautions or suddenly, one fine morning, wake up to our sleazy reality.

Sophie still failed to suspect the depth of our fetid resignation! A gang of failures! We admired her, so alive in our midst... just her way of getting up from a chair, coming to our table, leaving it again... She charmed us...

And every time she performed those simple gestures, we experienced surprise and joy. We made strides in poetry, so to speak, just marvelling at her being so beautiful and so much more obviously free than we were. The rhythm of her life sprang from other wellsprings than ours... Our wellsprings were forever slow and slimy.

The joyful strength, precise yet gentle, which animated her from her hair to her ankles troubled us, alarmed us in a charming sort of way, but definitely alarmed us, yes, that's the word.

Though our instinct revelled in her innate joy, our peevish knowledge of the things of this world rather frowned on it – that essentially frightened, ever-present knowledge which cowers in the cellars of existence, accustomed to the worst by habit, by experience.

Sophie had the winged, elastic, precise gait that is so frequent, almost habitual, among the women of America, the gait of heroic creatures of the future, whom life and ambition carry lightly towards new kinds of adventure... Three-masters of joyful warmth, bound for the Infinite...

Parapine, who was hardly given to lyricism on the subject of attractive women, would smile to himself when she left the room. Just to look at her did your soul good. Especially mine, I must say, which had lost none of its aptitude for desire.

Wishing to take her by surprise, to ravish a little of her pride, of the prestige and power she had acquired over me, to diminish her, in short to humanize her a little and reduce her to our paltry proportions, I would go into her room when she was sleeping.

At such times, Sophie offered a very different sight – more commonplace, yet surprising and reassuring as well. Without ostentation, almost uncovered, lying crosswise on the bed, legs every which way, skin moist and relaxed, she was battling with fatigue.

In the depths of her body she dug into sleep, so hard that it made her snore. That was the only time when I found her within my reach. No more enchantment. No joking. This was serious. She toiled as though to pump more life out of existence... At such times she was greedy, drunk with wanting more and more. You should have seen her after those sleeping bouts, still swollen, her organs exultant, ecstatic under her rosy skin. At such times she was funny, as laughable as other people. For some minutes she'd reel with happiness, then the full light of day would come to her and delivered, as if too heavy a cloud had just passed, she'd resume her glorious flight...

All that was very fuckable. It's extremely pleasant to grasp this moment when matter becomes life. You rise up to the endless plateau that spreads out before men. "Whew!" you go. And again "Whew!" You come the limit up there, and then it's like an enormous desert...

Among us, her friends rather than employers, I, I believe, was the most intimate. True, she was regularly unfaithful to me with the orderly in charge of the violent ward, an ex-fireman. For my own good, she told me, so as not to put too great a strain on me, considering all the brain work I had under way, which wasn't exactly compatible with the demands of her fiery temperament. Entirely for my own good. She cuckolded me in the interest of hygiene. What could I say?

All this, when I think of it, could have given me nothing but pleasure if the Madelon business hadn't been weighing on my mind. One fine day I told Sophie the whole story to see what she'd say. Telling her my troubles made me feel a little better. I was sick of the endless quarrels and resentments growing out of that wretched passion, and Sophie thought I was perfectly right.

Seeing that Robinson and I had been such good friends, she thought we should all have one big reconciliation, just patch the whole thing up as quickly as possible. Her advice came from a good heart. Central Europe is full of good hearts. The only trouble was that she didn't know much about the characters and reactions of the people around here. With the best intentions in the world she gave me the worst possible advice. I came to realize that she'd been wrong, but too late.

"You should see Madelon," she advised me. "From what you've told me, I'm sure she's a good girl deep down... It's just that you provoked her, and you were really brutal and mean to her... You owe her an apology and a nice present too, to make her forget..." That's the way things were done in her country. Everything she advised me to do was exquisitely polite but not at all practical.

I took her advice, mostly because behind all the frills and foolishness, behind the diplomatic manoeuvres, I envisaged the possibility of a little foursome that would have been most entertaining, in fact it would have made a new man of me. Under the pressure of age and circumstances, I note to my sorrow, my friendly feelings were taking an insidiously erotic turn. Betrayal. And Sophie, without meaning to, was abetting me in this betrayal. There was so much curiosity in Sophie she couldn't help being attracted by danger. An excellent nature, nothing Protestant about her, she never tried to belittle the opportunities life offered and was never suspicious of them. Just my type. She went further. She understood the need for variety in the distractions of the rear end. An adventurous disposition of that sort, you'll have to agree, is most unusual in women. We had definitely picked the right one.

She wanted me, and I thought it perfectly natural, to give her some idea of Madelon's physique. She was afraid of seeming awkward in an intimate situation with a Frenchwoman, in view of the stupendous reputation in this line that has been pinned on Frenchwomen in foreign parts. As for enduring Robinson's attentions at the same time, it was only to give me pleasure that she consented. Robinson didn't send her at all, so she said, but on the whole we were in agreement. That was the main thing. OK.

I waited a while for a good opportunity to approach Robinson with my plan for a general reconciliation. One morning when he was in the office copying medical reports into the big book, the moment struck me as propitious, and I interrupted him to ask him very simply whether he thought it would be a good idea for me to see Madelon and suggest that we let our violent bygones be bygones… Whether on the same occasion I might introduce her to Sophie, my new friend? And lastly, if he didn't think it was time we all got together and patched up our quarrels.

At first, I could see, he hesitated, then he replied, but without enthusiasm, that he saw no objection… I suspect Madelon had told him that I'd try to see her soon on one pretext or another. About the slap in the face I'd given her the day she came to Vigny, I didn't breathe a word.

I couldn't run the risk of his yelling at me there and calling me a brute in public, because after all, though we'd been friends a long time, there in the institution he was under my orders. Authority first.

January was a funny time for that sort of operation. Because it was most convenient, we decided to meet in Paris one Sunday and go to the movies together. We thought maybe we'd drop in at the Batignolles carnival for a while first if it wasn't too cold out. Robinson had promised to take her to the Batignolles carnival. Madelon, he told me, was wild about carnivals. That was a lucky thing. Meeting again for the first time, a carnival was the best possible place.

* * *

We sure got an eyeful of that carnival! And a headful too! Bim bam! And bam again! We whirl around! And we're carried away! And we scream and we yell! There we were, in the crowd with lights and noise and all the rest of it! Step up, step up! Show your skill, show your daring, and laugh laugh laugh! Whee! Everyone tried in his overcoat to appear to his best advantage, sharp and just a little aloof, to show that he usually went elsewhere for his entertainment, to more "expensive" places, as they say in English.

You tried to make the impression of knowing, light-hearted young blades in spite of the icy wind, just one more humiliation, and the depressing fear that you were spending too much money on these amusements and might have occasion to regret it for a whole week.

The merry-go-round sends up a big belch of music. It can't quite deliver itself of the waltz from *Faust*, but it tries hard. The waltz plumps down and shoots up again and swirls around the circular ceiling, which spins with its thousands of pastry light bulbs. The steam calliope's having a bad time. The music is giving it a pain in its pipe, its stomach. Would you care for a piece of nougat? Or would you rather try another target? Take your choice.

In our group at the shooting gallery it was Madelon, with the brim of her hat turned up over her forehead, who showed the most skill. "Look," she says to Robinson. "My hand isn't shaking. And we had plenty to drink, didn't we?"... Just to show you the kind of things we were saying. We'd just come out of a restaurant. "One more try!" And Madelon won the bottle of champagne. Bing bang! Bull's eye! Then I bet her she can't catch me on the dodgem cars. "I'll take you up on that," she says as chipper as you please. "We'll take separate cars!" And there we go! I was glad she'd accepted. It

386

was a way of making up to her. Sophie wasn't jealous. She had her reasons.

So Robinson climbs into the back car with Madelon and I get into another up front with Sophie. Man, do we collide! And it's crash! And hold tight! But I see right away that Madelon doesn't enjoy being shaken up. Neither does Léon for that matter, he used to like it, but no more. It's plain that he doesn't feel comfortable with us. While we're clutching at the rail, some sailor boys come along and start feeling us up, men and women alike, and making propositions. We're freezing. We shake them off. We laugh. More and more gropers come from all directions with music and rhythm and excitement. You get such jolts on these barrels on wheels that your eyes pop out of your head every time you clash. Great fun! Violence and joy! The whole accordion of pleasures! I want to make up with Madelon before we leave the carnival. I want to very much, but she doesn't respond to my overtures any more. It's no soap. She's snubbing me. Keeping me at a distance. I can't make her out. These moods that come over her. I'd had hopes of something better. Physically, come to think of it, she has changed completely.

She can't bear comparison with Sophie, no sparkle, no lustre. Good humour was more becoming to her, but now she has an air of superiority. That irritates me. I'd gladly give her another slap in the face, maybe that would bring her around or maybe then she'd tell me what she knows that's so superior. Come on, smile! This is a place of merriment, we haven't come here to weep! Let's whoop it up!

She's found work with an aunt of hers, so she tells Sophie while we're strolling later on. On the Rue du Rocher. Her aunt is a corset-maker. May as well believe her.

It wasn't hard to see that if reconciliation was the idea, this meeting was a failure. My little scheme was a washout too. In fact, a gigantic disaster.

Seeing each other again had been a mistake. Sophie hadn't really grasped the situation. She hadn't realized that this get-together would just make everything more complicated... Robinson should have warned me, told me how stubborn she was... Too bad! Oh well! Bam! Bam! The carnival goes on! Let's try the "Caterpillar", as they call it. My idea and my treat! One more attempt to make up with Madelon. But she keeps slipping away from me, avoiding me. Taking advantage of the crush, she climbs into another seat up front with Robinson, I'm flummoxed again. We're dazed by waves and whirls of darkness. I mutter under my breath that it's hopeless. Sophie finally agrees with me. She realizes that in this whole affair I had been led away by my lecherous fantasies. "You see how it is? She's sore. I think we'd better leave them alone now… You and I could drop in at the Chabanais before we go home…" That suggestion appealed to Sophie, because while still in Prague she had often heard people talking about the Chabanais, and she was delighted at the thought of trying the Chabanais and judging for herself. But then we figured that considering the amount of money we had brought with us, the Chabanais would be too expensive. We'd just have to try and revive our interest in the carnival.

While we were in the Caterpillar, Robinson must have had a scene with Madelon. They were both in a foul humour when they got out. You really couldn't have touched her with a ten-foot pole that evening. To smooth things over I suggested an absorbing amusement – fishing for bottlenecks. Madelon accepted sulkily. Even so she beat us all hollow. She got her ring just over the cork and slipped it on just before the bell rang. Click! And that was that. The stand owner couldn't get over it. He gave her a half-bottle of Grand-Duc de Malvoison.* Just to give you an idea of how skilful she was. But it didn't make her happy. Right away she announced that she wouldn't drink it. "It's no good," she said. So Robinson uncorked the bottle and drank it. Down the hatch! At one gulp. A funny thing for him to do, because he practically never drank.

Then we came to the tin wedding. Biff! Bang! We all had a try with hard balls. It's depressing how clumsy I am at these things… I congratulate Robinson. He beats me at any game. But not even his skill could make him smile. They both looked as if we were leading them off to slaughter. We tried hard, but nothing could put any life into them. "This is a carnival!" I yelled at them. For once I was completely out of ideas.

My shouting things in their ears and trying to cheer them up didn't mean a thing to them. They didn't even hear me. "What about youth?" I asked them. "What are we going to do about it?… Has youth stopped making merry? Look at me, ten years older than the rest of you! All right, sweetheart, what do you say?" He and Madelon looked at me as if I were drunk, gassed, nuts, and there was no point in even answering me... no point in trying to speak to me, because I'd certainly be incapable of understanding anything they could say... I wouldn't understand a thing... maybe they're right, I said to myself, looking anxiously at the people around us.

But all those people were doing the things you do to have fun, they weren't nursing their little troubles like us. Far from it. They were getting something out of the carnival. A franc's worth here!... Fifty centimes' worth there!... Lights! Music, banter and candy... They were buzzing around like flies, scads of them, with their little grubs in their arms, livid, pasty-faced babies, so pale in the glaring light that you could hardly see them. Just around their noses those babies had a bit of pink, in the area for colds and getting kissed.

Among all the stands I immediately recognized the Gallery of the Nations... A memory, I didn't mention it to the others. That makes fifteen years that have gone by... A long time... And what a lot of friends I've lost along the way! I'd never have thought the Gallery of the Nations could drag itself out of the mud it was sunk in out there in Saint-Cloud... But now it was all refurbished, as good as new, with music and everything. You gotta hand it to them. And all these people shooting. A shooting gallery always does business. And the egg was back again like me, there in the middle, supported by practically nothing, bobbing up and down. It cost two francs. We passed it by, we were too cold to try, it was best to keep moving. But not because we were short of change, our pockets were still full of change, our little pocket music.

I'd have tried anything just then to put some life into us, but no one was doing a thing to help. If Parapine had been with us, it would probably have been worse, seeing how gloomy he was with people. Luckily he'd stayed home to look after the loonies. I was sorry I'd come. Then Madelon started laughing after all, but there was nothing funny about her laugh. Robinson, who was beside her, sniggered so as not to be different. Then Sophie started making jokes. That was all we needed.

As we were passing the photographer's booth, he noticed our hesitation. We had no great desire to go in, except Sophie maybe. But a moment later, thanks to our hesitation, we were at the mercy of his camera. He drawled out his commands, and we submitted on the cardboard bridge – he must have built it himself – of a purported ship, *La Belle France*. The name was written on imitation lifebelts. We stood there for quite some time, staring straight ahead, challenging the future. Other customers were waiting impatiently for us to come down off the bridge, and already they were avenging themselves for having to wait by not only finding us too ugly for words, but telling us so out loud.

They thought they could take advantage of our not being able to move. But they couldn't faze Madelon, she slanged them back with the full force of her southern accent. She could be heard for miles around. She told them where to get off!

A magnesium flash. We all flinch. We each get a picture. We're even uglier than before. The rain comes through the canvas roof. Our feet are sore and frozen stiff. The wind had found holes all over us while we were posing, so much so that there's hardly anything left of my overcoat.

All we can do is keep walking among the booths. I didn't dare suggest going back to Vigny. It was too early. Our teeth were already chattering with the cold and the heart-throb organ of the merry-go-round jangled our nerves till we were shivering even more. The end of the whole world – that's what the damned organ is laughing about. It bellows its message of disaster through its silver-plated kazoos, and the tune goes out to die in the surrounding darkness, along the pissy streets that come down from Montmartre.

The little housemaids from Brittany are definitely coughing a lot more than they did last winter, when they'd just arrived in Paris. Their green-and-blue mottled thighs do their best to decorate the flanks of the wooden horses. The boys from Auvergne, who treat them to their rides, are cautious post-office clerks and, as everyone knows, never lay them without a rubber. They have no desire to catch it a second time. In expectation of love, the housemaids squirm and wiggle in the disgustingly melodious din of the merry-go-round. They're kind of sick to their stomachs, but that doesn't stop them from posing in the freezing cold, because this is the great moment, the time to try their youthful charms on the definitive lover, who may be there, already smitten, tucked away among the yokels in this frozen crowd. Love is still hanging back... but it'll come, same as it does in the movies, and happiness with it. If the rich man's son loves you for just one evening, he'll never leave you... It's been known to happen, and it's good enough. Naturally he's sweet, and naturally he's handsome, and naturally he's rich.

The old woman who keeps the news-stand over by the Métro doesn't give a damn about the future, she scratches her old conjunctivitis and slowly festers her eyes with her fingernails. An obscure pleasure that costs nothing. It's been going on for six years now, and her itching gets worse and worse.

Strollers, driven into groups by the bitter cold, gather around the lottery booth. A brazier of rear ends. They can't get in. So quickly, to warm themselves, they run, they bound into the knot of people across the way, waiting to get in to see the two-headed calf.

Under cover of the urinal, a young candidate for unemployment quotes his price to a provincial couple flushed with excitement. The cop from the vice squad knows what's going on, but he doesn't care, his assignment at the moment is the entrance to the Café Miseux.* He's been watching the Café Miseux for a week. The instigator must operate in the tobacco shop or in the backroom of the filthy bookshop next door. Anyway it was reported long ago. Either one or the other of them, it seems, procures under-age girls, who appear to be selling flowers. Anonymous letters again. The chestnut vendor on the corner does a bit of informing too. He has to. Everything that's on the pavement belongs to the police.

That kind of machine gun that you hear over there, shooting in crazy short bursts, is only the guy who runs the "Wheel of Death" on his motorcycle. An escaped convict, so they say, but I'm not sure. Anyway, he has crashed through his tent twice in this same spot, and once a couple of years ago in Toulouse. Why can't he and his contraption smash up for good! Why can't he break his neck and spine once and for all! That noise would put anybody in a temper! The same goes for the streetcar with its bell, in less than a month it's killed two old folks in Bicêtre, hugging the walls of the shanties. The bus on the other hand is quiet, it pulls up slowly on the Place Pigalle, taking every possible precaution, staggering a little, blowing its horn, all out of breath, with its four passengers who get off as slowly and carefully as choir boys.

Strolling from booth to booth, from clump to clump of humanity, from merry-go-rounds to lotteries, we'd come to the end of the carnival, to the big dark vacant lot where the families go to pee...

Nothing to do but turn back. Retracing our steps, we ate chestnuts to work up a thirst. We got sore mouths but no thirst. There was a worm in the chestnuts, a cute little fellow. Naturally it was Madelon who got it. That was exactly when things started going really badly between us. Up until then we had kept ourselves more or less under control, but that worm really made her furious.

As she was going over to the gutter to spit out the worm, Léon said something to stop her, I don't remember what he said or what had got into him, but all of a sudden her going over to spit went against Robinson's grain. Like a damn fool he asked her if she'd found a seed in it... Honestly, that was no question to ask her... And then Sophie sees fit to join in their argument... She couldn't see what they were fighting about... She wanted to know.

Being interrupted by Sophie, a foreigner, exasperated them even more, what would you expect? Just then a bunch of hoodlums come between us, and we're separated. Actually they were young fellows trying to pick up customers, but with mimicry, kazoos and assorted cries of terror. When we managed to get back together, she and Robinson were still fighting.

"It looks like time to go home," I thought... "If we leave them here together for another few minutes, they'll embarrass us right here in the middle of the carnival... Better call it a day..." The whole thing had been a failure, you couldn't deny it. "Let's go home," I suggested to Robinson. He gave me a look of surprise, but it still struck me as the wisest, most sensible course. "Haven't you had enough?" I added. He made a sign meaning that I should ask Madelon how she felt about it. I had no objection to asking Madelon, but I didn't think it was a very bright thing to do.

"We'll take Madelon with us," I finally said.

"Take her?" he asked. "Where do you want to take her?"

"To Vigny, of course," I said.

That was a big mistake. I'd done it again. But once I'd said it, I couldn't take it back.

"We have an empty room for her in Vigny," I went on. "There's no shortage of rooms out there!... We could all have a bite to eat before going to bed... At least it'll be more cheerful than freezing around here, like we've been doing for the last two hours... No trouble at all..." Madelon made no answer to my suggestions. She didn't even look at me while I was speaking, but I know she hadn't missed a word of what I'd said. Anyway, I'd said it and it couldn't be helped.

Then when I'd wandered a few steps away from the group, she came over to me quietly and asked if I wasn't trying to put something over on her, inviting her out to Vigny. I didn't answer her. No sense trying to reason with a jealous woman. Anything I could say would only be a pretext for another endless scene. Besides I didn't even know whom or what she was jealous of. It's often hard to localize feelings of jealousy. Come to think of it, she was probably jealous of everything, same as everyone else.

By that time Sophie didn't know where she was at, but she went on trying to be agreeable. She even took Madelon's arm, but Madelon was much too furious and much too glad to be furious to let herself be distracted by friendly gestures. We fought our way through the crowd to the streetcar stop on the Place Clichy. Just as we were about to board a car, a cloud burst right over the square, and the rain came down in cascades. The heavens emptied.

In half a second every taxi in sight had been grabbed. I heard Madelon right near me asking Robinson in an undertone: "You're not going to humiliate me in front of all these people?... Are you, Léon?" She was in bad shape. "You're sick of me, aren't you? Why don't you say so?" she went on. "Say you've had enough of me... That you'd rather be alone with these two... You all go to bed together, I bet, when I'm not there, don't you?... Say you like it better with them than with me... Go on, say it so I can hear you..." After that she stood silent, her face contracted into a grimace around her nose, which pointed upwards and tugged at her mouth. We were waiting on the pavement. "You see how your friends treat me?" she started again. "You see, Léon?"

Léon, I have to give him credit, didn't answer back, he didn't do anything to provoke her, he could be very violent at times, but he just looked the other way at the house fronts and the boulevard and the cars.

And yet Léon had his violent moments. When she saw she wasn't getting anywhere with threats, she came back at him in a different way, with love talk, while we were all waiting. "I love you, Léon, hear, I love you... Do you realize at least what I've done for you?... Maybe I shouldn't have come today... but you do love me just a little, don't you? You must love me just a little... You have a heart, haven't you, tell me,

Léon, tell me you have a heart... Then why do you despise my love?... We had a beautiful dream, the two of us together... And now you're so cruel to me!... You've trampled my dream, Léon!... You've soiled it!... You've destroyed my ideal, you can't say different... I suppose you don't want me to believe in love any more... Is that it? And now you want me to go away for good... Is that what you want?..." All these questions while the rain was dripping through the awning of the café.

It was coming down on us all. He had warned me all right, she was exactly the way he had said. He hadn't made anything up. I'd never have thought them capable of rising to such an emotional paroxysm in so little time.

Seeing the cars and all were making so much noise, I was able to whisper a few words in Robinson's ear. I suggested that we try to run out on her and get this shindig over with as quickly as possible, because it was a disaster and we'd better break up quietly before the situation soured in earnest and people got really angry as there was good reason to fear. "You want me to find you a pretext?" I whispered. "Then we'll all beat it separately?" "No!" he answered. "Don't do that! Don't! She's capable of throwing a fit right here, and we'd never be able to stop her!" I let it go at that.

Come to think of it, maybe Robinson enjoyed being yelled at in public, and besides he knew her better than I did. As the shower was letting up, we found a taxi. We jumped in, and there we were all squeezed together inside. First we didn't say a word to each other. The air was too heavy between us and I felt I'd put my foot in it enough. I thought I'd better wait a while before doing it again.

Léon and I took the folding seats, the two women sat in the back. On weekend nights the road to Argenteuil is badly congested, especially as far as the Porte. After that you have to count a good hour before you get to Vigny, on account of the traffic. It's no fun sitting face to face and eye to eye without saying a word, especially when it's dark and everyone's kind of suspicious of everyone else.

Even so, if we had stayed like that, nettled, but keeping each to himself, nothing would have happened. That's still my opinion when I think of it today.

It was my doing, I have to admit, that we started talking again and the quarrel resumed, worse than ever. We're never suspicious enough of words, they look like nothing much, not at all dangerous, just little puffs of air, little sounds the mouth makes, neither hot nor cold and easily absorbed, once they reach the ear, by the vast grey boredom of the brain. We're not suspicious enough of words, and calamity strikes.

Certain words are hidden in with the rest, like stones. They're not very noticeable, but before long they make all the life that's in us tremble, every bit of it in its weakness and its strength... The outcome is panic... An avalanche... You're left dangling like a hanged man, over a sea of emotion... A tempest comes and goes, much too powerful for you, so violent you'd never have thought mere emotions could lead to anything like it... I therefore conclude that we're never suspicious enough of words. But now let me tell you what happened: the taxi was slowly following a streetcar, because the road was being repaired... "Hum... hum" went the engine. A pothole every hundred yards... But the streetcar up ahead of us wasn't enough for me. Always childish and talkative, I was impatient. The snail's pace and the indecision all around me were more than I could bear... So, quick, I shattered the silence like a piggy bank to see what might be inside. I watched, or rather, since by then you could hardly see, I tried to watch Madelon in the left-hand corner of the cab. She kept her face turned towards the outside, towards the landscape, towards the darkness would be more like it. I noted with annoyance that she was as stubborn as ever. I, on the other hand, acted like a regular pest. Just to make her turn her head my way, I spoke to her.

"Look, Madelon. Maybe you've got some idea how we could amuse ourselves, but you're afraid to tell us? Would you like us to stop somewhere before we go home? Come on, tell us!..."

"Amuse ourselves! Amuse ourselves!" she said, as if I'd insulted her. "All you people think of is amusing yourselves..." Then she let out a whole barrage of sighs, deep and so touching that I've seldom heard the like.

"I'm doing my best," I said. "It's Sunday."

"How about you, Léon?" she asked him. "Are you doing your best too?" Straight from the shoulder.

"Are you kidding!" was his comeback.

I looked at them both when we passed a street lamp. What I saw was anger. Madelon leant forward as if to kiss him. It was written that no one would miss a chance to put his foot in it that night.

The taxi had slowed down again because of the trucks that were strung out all along the road. It annoyed him to be kissed, and he pushed her away, rather roughly, I must say. Of course that wasn't a nice thing to do, especially in front of us.

When we came to the end of the Avenue Clichy, to the Porte, night had fallen, the lights were going on in the shops. Under the railway bridge, in spite of the echo that's always so loud, I could still hear her asking: "Don't you want to kiss me, Léon?" She kept at him. He still didn't answer. So then she turned to me and harangued me directly. The affront was too much for her.

"What have you done to Léon to make him so mean? Tell me this minute!... What kind of stories have you been telling him?" That's the way she lit into me.

"Nothing at all," I told her. "I haven't told him anything!... Your quarrels are no concern of mine!"

The worst of it was that it was true, I hadn't said anything to Léon about her. He was free, it was up to him whether he stayed with her or left her. It was none of my business, but it was no use trying to tell her that, she had stopped listening to reason. Again we fell silent, sitting face to face in the cab, but the air was so charged with fury that it couldn't go on for long. She had spoken to me in a thin sort of voice I'd never heard her use before, the monotonous voice of a person whose mind is fully made up. Scrunched up as she was in the corner of the cab, I couldn't see her movements any more, and that troubled me.

All that time Sophie had been holding my hand. With these goings on the poor kid didn't know what to do with herself.

Right after Saint-Ouen Madelon resumed her catalogue of grievances against Léon. In long-winded frenzy she asked him questions and more questions, now at the top of her lungs: did he love her, had he been faithful, and so on. For the two of us, Sophie and me, it was hopelessly embarrassing. But she was so excited she didn't care at all whether we were listening or not. If anything she welcomed it. On the other hand, it hadn't been very bright of me to shut her up with us in that box... every word resounded and, with her character, that made her want to put on a big act for our benefit. The taxi had been another of my brainstorms.

Léon had stopped reacting. He was tired after the evening we'd spent together, and he was always a little short of sleep, he'd always had that trouble.

"For God's sake, calm down," I managed to shout at Madelon. "The two of you can have it out when we get there... You'll have plenty of time!"

"Get there! Get there!" she said in a tone that would make your hair stand on end. "We'll never get there, I tell you!... And anyway," she went on, "I'm sick of your dirty nasty ways... I'm a decent girl... I'm better than the whole lot of you together!... Pigs!... You can't make a fool out of me!... You can't understand a girl like me, you're not good enough... You're too rotten the whole lot of you to understand someone like me!... You'll never understand anything that's clean and beautiful!"

In short, she attacked us in our self-esteem. She went on and on. I kept strictly quiet on my folding seat, I didn't so much as let out a murmur. But it did no good, every time the driver shifted gears she'd start yapping again. At times like that the least little thing can provoke disaster. Just making us miserable seemed to be giving her a big kick, she followed out her nature to the bitter end, she couldn't help it.

"Don't imagine you're going to get off so easy!" she threatened us. "That you're going to get rid of me on the quiet! Oh no! I may as well tell you right away! No, you won't get away with it! You no-good scum!... You've ruined my life! I'll wake you up, you bastards!"

Suddenly she bent over towards Robinson, grabbed him by the lapels of his overcoat, and started shaking him. He made no attempt to break loose. You wouldn't catch me interfering. It almost looked as if Robinson enjoyed seeing her getting more and more excited on account of him. He was grinning, it wasn't natural. She was yelling at him, and he was jerking back and forth on his seat like a marionette, nose down, all the starch gone out of his neck.

Just as I was going to attempt some little gesture of remonstrance to stop the rough stuff, she bristled and started giving me a piece of her mind... Unloading things she'd been storing up for a long time... I was in for it all right. And there in front of everybody. "You shut up, you lecher!" she screams at me. "This is between Léon and me, and it's none of your business! I'm not having any more of your brutality! If you ever again lift a finger against me, Madelon will teach you how to behave!... First you cuckold your friends, then you beat their women!... Of all the blasted nerve! Aren't you ashamed of yourself?"

Hearing these truths, Léon kind of woke up a bit. He wasn't grinning any more. For a second I even wondered if he and I weren't going to bash each other to kingdom come, but for one thing, with four of us packed into that cab, there wasn't room enough for a fight. That reassured me. Too cramped.

Especially since we were making pretty good time over the cobblestones of the boulevards along the Seine. The taxi was jolting so bad you couldn't even move.

"Come, Léon," she commanded him. "I'm asking you for the last time, come! Drop these people! Do you hear what I'm saying?" A riot!

"Make him stop, Léon! Stop the car, or I'll stop it myself!"

But Léon didn't stir from his seat. He was screwed on tight.

"So you won't come?" she said again. "You won't come?"

She'd warned me that I'd better lie low. I'd had enough. "Are you coming?" she repeated. The cab was still going fast, the road was clear in front of us, and the jolting was worse than ever. We were bouncing around like crates in a truck.

"All right!" she concluded when he didn't answer. "All right, that does it! You asked for it! Tomorrow! You hear, no later than tomorrow, I'm going to the police and telling them exactly how Madame Henrouille fell down the stairs! Do you hear me now, Léon?... You happy now?... Not playing deaf any more? Either you come with me right away or I go to the police tomorrow morning!... So are you coming or aren't you? Speak up!" She couldn't have made her threat any plainer.

So then he decided to say something after all.

"You were involved in it yourself," he said. "You can't say a thing..."

That didn't quiet her in the least, far from it. "I don't care!" she said. "What if I was? You mean we'll both go to jail?... That I was your accomplice?... Is that what you mean?... Well, that suits me fine!..."

And she started laughing hysterically, as if nothing could have been funnier...

"That would suit me to a T, I tell you! I'm crazy about jail, I tell you!... Don't go expecting me to back down because of your jail talk!... I'll go to jail any time you say!... But you'll go too, you bastard!... At least you won't be able to give me the run-around any longer!... I belong to you, OK! But you belong to me too! You should just have stayed with me down there! I can only love once, Monsieur! I'm no tart!"

In saying that she was defying me and Sophie too. Making a point of fidelity and respectability.

In spite of it all the taxi was driving on, and he still made no move to stop the driver.

"Then you're not coming? You'd rather go to the pen? OK!... You don't care if I turn you in?... You don't care if I love you or not?... You don't care about my future? You don't care about anything, do you?..."

"No," he says. "In a way you're right... But it's not just you... I don't care about anyone else either... Christ, don't take it as an insult!... I know you're a sweet kid... But I don't want to be loved any more... It disgusts me!..."

She didn't expect to have that kind of thing thrown in her face... She was so surprised that she didn't know how to pick up the tirade she'd already begun. She'd been thrown off balance, but she recovered quick enough. "Oh! It disgusts you, does it?... What do you mean by that?... Tell me a little more, you ungrateful weasel!"

"No!" he said. "It's not you that disgusts me, it's everything. I don't want anything... You can't hold that against me..."

"What's that you say? Say it again! Me... everything?" She was trying to understand. "Me, everything? Don't talk Chinese!... Tell me in French, in front of these people. Why do I disgust you now? Don't you get a hard-on like everybody else, you big pig, when you make love? Oh, so you don't get a hard-on, is that it?... Out with it!... In front of these people... Tell us you don't get a hard-on!"

In spite of her fury, her way of arguing her case made you want to laugh. But I didn't have time to laugh very long, because she started up again. "And him there! I suppose he doesn't squirt every time he catches me in a corner! The beast! The sex fiend! I dare him to say it's not true!... You're all looking for something new!... Admit it!... Variety, novelty! That's what you want! A daisy chain! Why not a virgin! You degenerate pigs! Why look for pretexts?... You're jaded, that's all. You haven't even got the courage of your vices! You're scared of your vices!"

At that point Robinson took it on himself to answer. By that time he, too, had lost his temper, and he shouted as loud as she had.

"Wrong!" he shouted. "I've got plenty of courage, as much as you!... Only, if you want the whole truth... everything – absolutely everything! – disgusts me and turns my stomach! Not just you!... Everything!... And love most of all!... Yours as much as anyone else's!... The sentimental tripe you dish out... Want me to tell you what I think of it? I think it's like making love in the crapper! Do you get me now?... All the sentiment you trot out to make me stick with you hits me like an insult, if you want to know... And to make it worse, you don't even realize it, you're the one that's rotten, because you don't understand!... You're satisfied repeating the rubbish other people say... You think it makes sense... People have told you there's nothing better than love, they've told you it'll go down with everybody, everywhere and always, and that's good enough for you... Well, I say fuck their love!... You hear?... Their putrid love doesn't go down with me... not any more!... You've missed the train! You're too late! It won't go down any more, and that's that!... What a stupid thing to get steamed up about!... Why do you have to make love, considering all the things that are happening?... All the things we see around us!... Or are you blind?... More likely you just don't give a damn! You wallow in sentiment when you're a worse brute than anybody... You want to eat rotten meat?... With love sauce?... Does that help it down?... Not with me!... If you don't smell anything, it's your hard luck! Maybe your nose is stuffed up! If it doesn't disgust you, it's because you're stupid, the whole lot of you... You want to know what it is that comes between you and me?... All right, I'll tell you! A whole life is what comes between you and me... Isn't that enough for you?"

"My house is clean!" she comes back at him. "A person can be poor but clean, can't they? When did you ever see that my house wasn't clean? Is that what you're insinuating with your nasty remarks?... My rear end is clean, Monsieur!... Maybe you can't say as much for yourself!... Nor your feet neither!"

"I never said that, Madelon! I never said anything like that!... About your house not being clean!... You see that you don't understand a thing!" That was all he could think of saying to calm her down.

"So now you say you haven't said anything? You haven't said anything, have you? Would you listen to him! He insults me worse than garbage and then he claims he hasn't said anything! You'd have to kill him to make him stop lying! Jail isn't bad enough for a skunk like him! A lousy rotten pimp!... It's not enough! What he needs is the guillotine!"

Nothing could stop her. I couldn't make anything of what they were saying in that taxi. All I could hear was curses and insults amid the roar of the motor and the sloshing of the wheels in the wind and rain that came beating against our door in ferocious gusts. The air between us was charged with threats. "It's vile!..." she said several times. She couldn't say anything else. "It's vile!" And then she raised the stakes, double or quits. "You coming?" she said. "You coming, Léon? One... You coming? Two..." She waited. "Three?... So you're not coming?..." "No," he said, without moving an inch. He even added: "Do what you like!" That was an answer of sorts.

She must have moved back a little on the seat, as far as she could go. I guess she was holding the revolver in both hands, because when the shot went off it seemed to go straight into his belly. Then, almost at the same time, there were two more shots, one after the other... and then the car was full of acrid smoke.

But we kept right on going. Robinson slumped down on me, sideways, jerking and gasping: "Hep! Hep!" And more of the same: "Hep! Hep!" The driver must have heard.

First he slowed down a little to see what had happened. Then finally he stopped right under a gas lamp.

The moment he opened the door, Madelon gave him a violent push and jumped out. She scrambled down the embankment and beat it across the fields in the darkness, right through the mud. I tried to call her back, but she was already far away.

I didn't quite know what to do with my wounded man... In a way it might have been wisest to take him back to Paris... But by then we weren't far from our place... The townspeople wouldn't know what was going on... So Sophie and I bundled him up in overcoats and settled him in the corner where Madelon had fired her shots. "Take it easy!" I said to the driver. But he kept driving much too fast. He was in a hurry. The bumps made Robinson groan still worse.

When we pulled up in front of the rest home, the driver didn't even want to give us his name, he was worried about trouble with the police, having to testify and all that... He also said there were sure to be bloodstains on the cushions. He wanted to beat it right away without waiting. But I'd taken his number.

Two bullets had gone into Robinson's gut, maybe three, I wasn't quite sure yet how many.

She had fired straight in front of her, I'd seen that. The wounds weren't bleeding. Though Sophie and I were holding him up between us, he got a bad shaking and his head was wobbling. He spoke, but it was hard to understand him. He was already delirious. "Hep! Hep!" he kept chanting. He'd have time enough to die before we got there.

The street had been freshly paved. As soon as we came to our gate, I sent the concierge to get Parapine from his room in a hurry. He came down right away, and he and a male nurse helped us carry Robinson to his bed. Once we'd undressed him we were able to examine him and palpate the wall of his abdomen. It was already distended, and soft in places. I found two holes practically on top of each other, but no third; one of the bullets must have gone astray.

If I had been in Léon's place, I'd have preferred an internal haemorrhage, it floods the abdomen and doesn't take long. The peritoneum fills up, and that's the end. With peritonitis on the other hand an infection sets in, and it takes for ever.

It was still too soon to tell how he'd go about dying. His belly was swelling up, he was staring at us, his eyes were already set, he was groaning, but not very much. He was having a sort of calm spell. I'd already seen him very sick in a lot of different places, but this time everything was different, his moans and his eyes and everything. It looked as if we couldn't hold him much longer, he was slipping away from minute to minute. He was sweating big drops that made it look as if his whole face were crying. At times like that you're sorry you've become as poor and as hard as you have. We're short of practically everything we'd need to help someone die. All we have left inside is the things that are useful in our everyday life, a life of comfort, a life all for ourselves, a life of viciousness. We've lost our confidence along the way. We've harried and goaded what pity we had left, driven it to the bottom of our body like some nasty pill. We've pushed pity to the bottom of our bowels along with our shit. That's a good place for it, we say to ourselves.

I stayed with Léon to commiserate, I had never felt so embarrassed. I couldn't manage it… He couldn't find me… it was driving him wild… He must have been looking for another Ferdinand, somebody much bigger than me, to help him die more easily. He was straining to figure out if there'd been any progress in the world... Poor fellow... Drawing up an inventory in his mind... Wondering if people hadn't changed just a little for the better during his lifetime, if maybe he had been unfair to them without meaning to... But there was only me, just me, me all alone, beside him, the genuine Ferdinand, who was short of everything that would make a man bigger than his own bare life, short of love for other people's lives. Of that I had none, or so little there was no use showing it. I wasn't as big as death. I was a lot smaller. I had no great opinion of humanity. I think I'd have found it easier to grieve for a dying dog than for Robinson, because a dog isn't tricky, and Robinson, in spite of everything, was tricky in a way. I was tricky myself, we were all tricksters... Our other qualities had left us along the way, I'd even lost the grimaces that can come in handy over deathbeds, I'd lost everything along the way, I couldn't find any of what we need to help a man die, all I could find was cunning. My feelings were like a house where you only go on holidays. Scarcely inhabitable. Besides, a dying man is demanding. Dying isn't enough for him. He has to get a kick out of it... At the very bottom of life, with his arteries already full of urea, he has to get a kick out of his last gasps.

And the dying snivel, because they're not having as much fun as before... They make demands... they protest. The dramatics of misery wants to carry over from life into death.

He came partly to his senses when Parapine gave him his injection of morphine. He even talked a little about what had happened. "It's best to have it end like this," he said. And later: "It doesn't hurt as much as I'd have thought." When Parapine asked him exactly where the pain was, you could see he wasn't all there any more, but even so there were still things he wanted to tell us... He hadn't the strength, his head wasn't clear enough... He wept, he gagged, and a moment later he laughed. He wasn't like the usual sick man, we didn't know how to act in front of him.

It looked as if he were trying to help us live. As if he'd been trying to find us pleasures to go on living for. He held us by the hands. One hand each. I kissed him. That's all you can do in a case like that without going wrong. We waited. He didn't say anything more after that. A little later, maybe an hour, the haemorrhage came, internal and profuse. It carried him off.

His heart started beating faster and faster, and then very very fast. His heart was running after his exhausted, diminished blood, chasing it to the ends of his blood vessels, throbbing in his fingertips. The pallor rose up from his neck and took hold of his whole face. He died in a choking fit. He went as if he had taken a running start, squeezing the two of us in his arms.

Then, almost immediately, he was back again in front of us, already taking on the weight of a dead man.

We stood up. We disengaged ourselves from his hands. They stopped in mid-air, stiff, yellow, and blue in the light of the lamp.

Then Robinson was like a stranger in the room, someone who had come from a horrible country and you wouldn't have dared speak to.

* * *

Parapine kept his wits about him. He managed to send someone to the police station for a cop. The cop just happened to be Gustave, our Gustave, who was on standby after his traffic duty.

"Oh my God!" said Gustave when he entered the room and saw Robinson.

Then he sat down at the nurses' table, which hadn't been cleared yet, to get his breath and take a little drink. "Seeing it's a crime," he said, "we'd better take him to headquarters." Then he remarked: "Robinson was all right, he wouldn't have hurt a fly. I wonder why she killed him…" Then he drank some more. He shouldn't have. Drink didn't agree with him. But he liked the bottle. It was his weakness.

We went up to the storeroom to get a stretcher. By then it was too late to disturb the staff, so we decided to carry the body to the police station ourselves. It was far away, at the other end of town, after the grade crossing, the last house.

We started out. Parapine held the front of the stretcher, Gustave Mandamour the other end. But neither of them walked very straight. Going down the little stairway, Sophie had to steady them a bit. It was then I noticed that she didn't seem terribly upset. Yet it had happened right beside her, so close that one of that madwoman's bullets could have gone right into her. But Sophie, as I'd noticed on other occasions, needed time to get her emotions started. Not that she was cold. When it hit her, it was like a ton of bricks, but she needed time.

I wanted to follow the body a little way to make sure it was really over. But instead of actually following as I should have, I veered from side to side of the road and finally, after passing the big school building near the grade crossing, I slipped into a side street that leads down to the Seine, first sloping gently between hedges and then taking a steep plunge.

Over the fences I saw them moving off with their stretcher.

They looked as if they'd suffocate in the sheets of mist that slowly closed behind them. Along the river bank the current was driving hard against the barges, which had been wedged tight as a precaution against the flood water. More cold came from the Gennevilliers plain, in puffs of mist that spread over the swirling river and made the water glisten under the arches.

Down there in the distance lay the sea. But there was no more room in me for imaginings about the sea. I had other things to do. I had tried to lose myself, I hadn't wanted to be face to face with my own life any more, but everywhere I kept finding it. I was always coming back to myself. My wanderings were over. No more knocking about for me... The world had closed in... We had come to the end! Like at the carnival! It's not enough to be sad; there ought to be some way to start the music up again and go looking for more sadness... But not for me... We may not admit it, but what we really want is to have our youth back again... We ought to be ashamed... Anyway, I wasn't prepared to endure any more!... Yet I hadn't gone as far in life as Robinson!... All in all, I hadn't succeeded... I hadn't conceived even one good, sound idea, like his idea of getting himself bumped off... That idea was bigger than my big head, bigger than all the fear that was in it, a fine, a magnificent idea to die with... How many lives would I need to make myself an idea more powerful than anything in the world? No saying. A flop! My ideas went rattling around in my head with lots of space between them. They were like faint, flickering little candles, trembling throughout a lifetime in the middle of a ghostly, abominable universe.

Maybe things were a little better than twenty years ago, nobody could say that I hadn't made a wee beginning of progress, but there seemed no possibility of my ever managing, like Robinson, to fill my head with one single idea, just one superb one, a thought far stronger than death, and of my succeeding, just with my idea, of exuding joy, carefreeness, and courage wherever I went. A scrumptious hero!

I'd be brimful of courage then. I'd be dripping with courage, and life itself would be just one big idea of courage, that would be the driving force behind everything, behind all men and things from earth to heaven. And by the same token there would be so much love that Death would be shut up inside it with tenderness, and Death would be so cosy-comfortable in there, the bitch, that she'd finally start enjoying herself, she'd get pleasure out of love along with everyone else. How wonderful that would be! What a production! I was laughing to myself all alone on the river bank, when I thought of all the things I'd have to do if I wanted to inflate myself like that with infinite resolutions... An idealistic toad! Fever, you know.

My friends had been looking for me for at least an hour. Especially because they'd noticed that I wasn't in very good shape when I left them... Gustave Mandamour was the first to sight me under my gas lamp. "Hey, Doctor!" he shouted. Mandamour, I can assure you, had some voice! "This way! They want you at the police station. They want your deposition. You know, Doctor," he added, but now he was whispering in my ear, "you're not looking well." He walked beside me, in fact he held me up. Gustave was fond of me. I never found fault with him for his drinking. I was full of understanding. Whereas Parapine was rather severe and sometimes made him feel ashamed of himself for drinking so much. Gustave would have done practically anything for me. He admired me in fact. He told me so. He didn't know why. Neither did I. But he admired me. He was the only one.

We went down two or three streets together until we saw the lantern outside the police station. After that you couldn't go wrong. Gustave was worrying about the report he'd have to write. He didn't dare tell me so. He'd already made everyone sign at the bottom, but a lot of things were still missing from his report.

Gustave had a big head. Like me. I could actually wear his kepi, which goes to show, but he tended to forget details. Ideas didn't come easy to him, it cost him a struggle to speak and even more to write. Parapine would have been glad to help him write his report, but he hadn't seen the crime, he didn't know the circumstances. He'd have had to invent, and the inspector didn't want any inventions in his reports, he wanted nothing but the truth, so he said.

Climbing the stairway at the police station, I was shivering. I couldn't tell the inspector much either. I really wasn't feeling so good.

They'd put Robinson's body down beside the rows of big filing cabinets.

All around the benches the floor was littered with printed matter and cigarette butts. On the wall the inscription "Fuck the Fuzz" was only partly erased.

"Did you get lost, Doctor?" the secretary asked me, quite amiably I must say, when I finally got there. We were all so tired we couldn't really talk straight.

In the end we were agreed about the phrasing and the trajectory of the bullets, one of which was still embedded in the spine. It hadn't been found. He'd be buried with it. They looked for the other bullets. The other bullets were embedded in the wall of the taxi. It was a powerful revolver.

Sophie came and joined us. She'd gone back for my overcoat. She kissed me and pressed me close to her, as if I were going to die too or fly away. "I'm not going away," I kept saying. "Be reasonable, Sophie, I'm not going away." Nothing I said could set her mind at rest.

Standing around the stretcher, we chewed the fat with the inspector's secretary, who'd seen worse in his time, crimes and non-crimes and disasters, and he wanted to tell us about all his experiences in one breath. We didn't dare leave for fear of offending him. He was so affable. It gave him pleasure to be talking with educated people, for a change, instead of thugs. We didn't want to hurt his feelings, so we stuck around.

Parapine had no raincoat. Listening to us lulled Gustave's mind. His mouth hung open, and his thick neck was thrust out as if he was pulling a handcart. I hadn't heard Parapine pour out so many words for many years, not since my student days, to tell the truth. All the things that had happened that day went to his head. But we decided to go home all the same.

We took Mandamour with us, and Sophie too. Now and then she gave me a hug, her body was filled with the strength of worry and tenderness, and so was her heart. Her strength was all over her, it was wonderful. I, too, was full of her strength. That bothered me... it wasn't mine, and it was my own I'd need if I were to go and die magnificently one day, like Léon. I had no time to waste on grimaces. To work! I said to myself. But nothing came of it.

She even wanted me to go back and look at the corpse again. So I left without turning around. A sign said: "Close the door". Parapine was thirsty. From talking, no doubt. From talking too much for him. Passing the bistro by the canal, we knocked on the shutters for a while. It made me think of the road to Noirceur during the war. The same little light over the door, on the point of going out. Finally the owner in person came and opened. He hadn't heard anything. We told him all the news, ending up with the murder. "A crime of passion!" Gustave called it.

The bar opened just before dawn for the benefit of the bargemen. As the night draws to an end, the locks open slowly. And then the whole countryside comes to life and starts to work. Slowly the banks break away from the river and rise up on both sides. Work emerges from the darkness. You begin to see it again, all very simple and hard. Over here the winches, over there the fences around the work sites, and far away on the road men are coming from still farther away. In small chilled groups they move into the murky light. For a starter they splatter their faces with daylight as they walk past the dawn. All you can see of them is their pale, simple faces... the rest still belongs to the night. They too will all have to die some day. How will they go about it?

They move towards the bridge. Then little by little they vanish across the plain, and other men come along, paler and paler as the light rises all around them. What are they thinking about?

The owner of the bar wanted to know all about the tragedy. He wanted us to tell him everything.

Vaudescal was the owner's name; he was from the north and very clean.

Gustave gave him an earful.

Gustave kept chewing over the details. But that wasn't the essential, again we were losing ourselves in words. Besides, he was drunk and kept starting all over from the beginning. But there really wasn't any more to say, nothing at all. Even so, I'd have listened to him for a while yet, quietly half asleep, but the others started contradicting him and that made him mad.

In his rage he clouted the little stove. The whole thing collapsed and turned over: the stovepipe, the grate, the glowing coals. Mandamour was as strong as an ox.

To make matters worse he wanted to show us the genuine Fire Dance. He wanted to take off his shoes and prance around on the coals.

There had been some bad blood between Gustave and the bar owner about a slot machine that hadn't been licensed... Vaudescal was a snake in the grass. You couldn't trust him. His shirts were too clean for him to be really honest. He was vindictive and he was a stool pigeon. The river banks are full of that kind.

Parapine suspected that he was laying for Mandamour, hoping to take advantage of his drunkenness and get him fired.

Parapine had stopped him from doing his Fire Dance and made him feel ashamed. We pushed Mandamour to the end of the table. There he finally collapsed, as quiet as a mouse, amid gargantuan sighs and smells. And fell asleep.

Far in the distance the tugboat whistled; its call passed the bridge, one more arch, then another, the lock, another bridge, farther and farther... It was summoning all the barges on the river, every last one, and the whole city and the sky and the countryside, and ourselves, to carry us all away, the Seine too – and that would be the end of us.

Notes

p. XII, *Sarabbath*: A combination of witches' sabbath and saraband.

p. 5, *Littré*: Émile Littré (1801–81), French lexicographer. His *Dictionnaire de la langue française* enjoys the prestige of Webster in the United States and of the *Oxford English Dictionary* in Great Britain.

p. 7, *Ganate*: Perhaps derived from *ganache*, meaning "blockhead".

p. 7, *Poincaré*: Raymond Poincaré (1860–1934), then President of France, a largely ceremonial office at the time.

p. 7, *Le Temps*: A daily newspaper, regarded as the semi-official organ of the Third Republic. It was liberal in tendency, but became rightist after the First World War.

p. 11, *Déroulède*: Paul Déroulède (1847–1914), writer and politician. He was an extreme nationalist and a supporter of General Boulanger and founder of the League of Patriots.

p. 12, *General des Entrayes*: *Entrayes* seemingly derives from *entrailles* ("entrails"). As will be seen later on, his first name is Céladon, which suggests a languishing lover.

p. 14, *Belisarius*: Byzantine general (500–65). According to the legend, he was blinded by order of Emperor Justinian. Numerous paintings show him as a beggar, holding out his reversed helmet for alms.

p. 17, *Fragson*: Harry Fragson (1869–1913), a popular cabaret singer early in the century.

p. 19, *Barbagny*: Connected no doubt with *barbant*, *barbe*, meaning "boring", "annoying".

p. 26, *Lieutenant de Sainte-Engence*: "*La sainte engeance*" means roughly "the holy rabble".

p. 30, *Noirceur-sur-la-Lys*: The Lys River is partly in Belgium and partly in northern France. The word *lys* also means "lily". In French as in English lilies are proverbially white, whereas *Noirceur* means "blackness".

p. 42, *Hôtel Paritz*: A combination of Paris and Ritz.

p. 43, *Boston in 1677*: This is typical of Céline's cavalier treatment of history. He was well aware that the *Mayflower* landed neither in Boston nor in 1677.

p. 46, *On les aura… Madelon, viens*: "We'll get them… Madelon, come" (French). The latter is an allusion to the words "*Quand Madelon vient nous servir à boire…*" ("When Madelon comes and serves us drinks…"), from the popular First World War song.

p. 57, *Carnot*: Lazare Carnot (1753–1823), statesman and general. He was a member of the Convention and of the Committee of Public Safety under the French Revolution. He was given the epithet "Organizer of Victory" for his work in organizing and directing the Revolutionary armies.

p. 58, *Dumouriez*: Charles-François Dumouriez (1739–1823) was a French general who went over to the Revolution and in collaboration with Kellermann won the battle of Valmy against the Prussians in 1792. In the following year he was defeated at Neerwinden and denounced to the National Assembly as a traitor, whereupon he defected to the Austrians.

p. 58, *Goethe*: Goethe was indeed present at the battle of Valmy, and Céline's quotation is reasonably accurate.

p. 58, *Barrès*: Maurice Barrès (1862–1923), writer and politician. An extreme French nationalist, he was obsessed by the threat of Germany.

p. 58, *Elsa the Horsewoman*: *Elsa la Cavalière* is the title of a novel by Pierre Mac Orlan (1882–1970). This is a slight anachronism because the novel did not appear until 1921.

p. 60, *Madame Herote*: The name presumably derives from *érotique* ("erotic").

p. 60, *Impasse des Bérésinas*: This street figures prominently in *Death on Credit* and is no doubt the Passage Choiseul, where Céline grew up.

p. 62, *a wedge… Porte des Ternes*: Céline's geography is as free and easy as his history, though he knew Paris like the back of his hand. Both extremities of the wide end of the wedge are slightly displaced, the one linguistically, the other geographically. Pont d'Auteuil should be Porte d'Auteuil, which is far away, and Porte des Ternes should be Porte Maillot, which is not far at all. Then you get the eastern edge of the Bois de Boulogne, hence the trees.

p. 63, *Pétain*: Philippe Pétain (1856–1961) was a French general who took part in the battle of the Marne and commanded victorious French troops at Verdun. He was made commander-in-chief of the French armies in 1916 and created a marshal of France in 1918. After French defeat in the Second World War he became premier of Vichy France. He was tried and sentenced to death in 1945, but his sentence was commuted to life imprisonment by de Gaulle.

p. 64, *Variétés*: Théâtre des Variétés, a theatre in Montmartre devoted chiefly to operettas and light comedies. Several of Offenbach's operas were performed there.

p. 66, *Pont de Grenelle*: The bridge with the Métro on it is not the Pont de Grenelle but the next one in a north-westerly direction, the Pont de Bir-Hakeim, then called the Pont de Passy.

p. 67, *Claude Lorrain*: Claude Gellée, known as le Lorrain (1600–82), a French landscape painter who spent most of his life in Rome.

p. 71, *Val-de-Grâce*: A former abbey, converted into a military hospital in 1795.

p. 75, *Old Man Birouette*: From *biroute*, a familiar term for the male sex organ.

p. 76, *Sergeant Branledore*: From *se branler* ("to masturbate").

p. 77, *Vaudesquin*: Probably fictitious.

p. 77, *Dupré*: Ernest Dupré (1862–1921) was an eminent specialist in neurology and psychiatry.

p. 78, *Margeton*: Probably fictitious.

p. 85, *Puta*: From *pute*, *putain*, meaning "whore".

p. 87, *Voireuse*: Probably from *foireux*, argot for "coward".

p. 93, *Bragueton:* Probably from *braguette*, meaning "fly" (of trousers).

p. 93, *Pilett*: Transformation of Gillette.

p. 99, *Frémizon*: From *frémir*, meaning "to quiver, quake, shake".

p. 100, *The Mangins! The Faidherbes! The Gallienis!*: General Charles Mangin (1866–1925) owes his fame largely to his prowess in the First World War, but he began his career in Africa and Indochina. Louis Léon César Faidherbe (1818–89) was a general and colonizer who began his career in Algeria and Guadeloupe. Joseph Gallieni (1849–1916) was a general and administrator who had a distinguished career in the colonies. It was he who requisitioned the Paris taxicabs to carry reinforcements to the battle of the Marne.

p. 104, *Bambola-Fort-Gono*: From *bamboula*, offensive slang for a black man, and "gonorrhoea".

p. 106, *Bugeaud*: Thomas Robert Bugeaud, Marquis de la Piconnerie (1784–1849), figured prominently in the conquest of Algeria.

p. 106, *the Marchands*: Jean-Baptiste Marchand (1863–1934) was a general and explorer who took part in various expeditions in West Africa. In the course of an expedition begun in 1897 he reached Fashoda on the Upper Nile, but the French government ordered him to evacuate when British troops arrived under Kitchener.

p. 106, *Pordurière*: A combination of *port* ("seaport") and *ordures* ("rubbish").

p. 117, *Tombat*: A combination of *tomber* ("to fall") and *combat*.

p. 118, *Charleroi*: A city in Belgium, the scene of a battle in 1914, ending in a French withdrawal.

p. 118, *Verdun*: A city in eastern France, the scene of a long-drawn-out and extremely bloody battle in which the French withstood a powerful German offensive and were finally victorious in 1917.

p. 120, *Avenue Fachoda*: See second note to p. 108 above. This is a bit of a joke: since Fashoda represented a French humiliation, an Avenue Fachoda in France or the French colonies was obviously unthinkable.

p. 144, *Nord-Sud Métro*: One of the earliest Métro lines, crossing Paris from north to south. Since unification of the Métro lines, known as Line 12.

p. 149, *San Tapeta*: From *tapette*, argot for "homosexual".

p. 151, *Combitta*: Probably from *con*, the female sex organ, and *bite*, the male sex organ.

p. 164, *Laugh Calvin*: The reason for this odd name is that Calvin Coolidge, President of the United States from 1923 to 1929, was never known to smile, much less laugh.

p. 176, *Chabanais... Invalides*: Le Chabanais on the Rue Chabanais was one of the most celebrated and luxurious of Paris brothels. The Invalides were a group of buildings put up in 1670 by Louis XIV as a home for wounded soldiers. The tomb of Napoleon is situated in the church of Saint-Louis-des-Invalides, the most prominent building in the compound.

p. 183, *Coué method*: A popular method of self-healing devised by Émile Coué (1857–1926), pharmacist and psychotherapist. It consisted in repeating to oneself several times a day: "Every day in every way I'm getting better and better."

p. 196, *La Garenne-Rancy*: There actually is a La Garenne (La Garenne-Colombes) in the Paris suburbs, not far from where this imaginary town seems to be. The word *garenne* means "rabbit warren", and Rancy suggests *rance*, meaning "rancid".

p. 196, *Porte Brancion*: All other indications are that La Garenne-Rancy was situated north-north-west of Paris. The Porte Brancion is on the southern rim of the city.

p. 197, *fortifications*: These fortifications were built between 1841 and 1844, in the reign of Louis-Philippe, to protect Paris from foreign invasion. They consisted of a circular wall thirty-nine kilometres long with ninety-four bastions. Used during the siege of Paris by the Prussians in the war of 1870, they were destroyed after the First World War.

p. 198, *Fortified Zone*: Properly "*la Zone Militaire de Paris*", commonly referred to simply as *la Zone* ("the Zone"): the strip of land between the fortifications and the suburbs, where for military reasons construction was prohibited. In late popular usage the more depressing suburbs on the outskirts of Paris.

p. 198, *tollhouse*: Up to the late Twenties a tax was levied on certain foodstuffs entering Paris. There were toll stations at all the city gates.

p. 200, *Dr Frolichon*: From *folichon* ("frolicsome").

p. 201, *Gagat*: From *gaga* ("feeble-minded").

p. 216, *the Tower*: The Eiffel Tower.

p. 228, *Joseph Bioduret Institute*: Bioduret seems to suggest the prolongation of life. The institute is clearly the Pasteur Institute. Although the Pasteur Institute is at the opposite end of Paris from La Villette, this is just Célinian mystification. The institute is accurately located off the Rue de Vaugirard a few pages further on.

p. 229, *Jaunisset*: From *jaunisse* ("jaundice").

p. 236, *the chateau*: The Louvre, which is never referred to as a chateau.

p. 238, *Caulaincourt Bridge*: From this point one would look out over the Montmartre cemetery and the "great lake of night". But only in a dream is one anywhere near the fortifications or the suburbs.

p. 242, *diabolo*: A mixture of *limonade* (fizzy water with synthetic lemon flavouring) and some sort of syrup, usually mint or grenadine.

p. 284, *campaign of 1816*: In 1814, and not in 1816 as Céline whimsically says, Marshal Moncey (Adrien Jeannot de Moncey, Duc de Conegliano) defended the Clichy Barrier against the invading troops of the anti-Napoleonic coalition. There is a monument commemorating the event in the middle of the Place Clichy. The invading troops included Cossacks, who were long remembered with horror.

p. 285, *Tarapout*: The Paramount Theatre.

p. 287, *emberezina'd*: A reference to the crossing of the Berezina River by Napoleon in 1812, in the course of his retreat from Moscow. More than twenty thousand French troops were lost.

p. 288, *Porte Saint-Martin*: The Théâtre de la Porte Saint-Martin, situated on the Boulevard Saint-Martin. One of the holy places of the Romantic drama, it burned down under the Commune in 1871, before being rebuilt in 1873.

p. 292, *Pomone*: From Pomona, goddess of fruit trees.

p. 293, *Balthazar*: The wicked king of Babylon, who saw the handwriting on the wall (Daniel 5:25).

p. 297, *Bourse*: The Stock Exchange.

p. 297, *Galeries Dufayel*: A large furniture store in Montmartre, its name was regarded as synonymous with cheap luxury.

p. 298, *La Pérouse*: Jean-François de Galaup, Comte de la Pérouse (1741–88), a French navigator who died in the course of a voyage around the world, probably massacred by the inhabitants of the island of Vanikoro. He did not have a wooden leg; this attribute seems to have been borrowed from Nelson.

p. 299, *the Moulin*: Le Moulin de Galette was a famous dance hall built in the nineteenth century beside a windmill, and was immortalized in a painting by Renoir.

p. 301, *"the Cid"*: The leading character in Corneille's tragedy *Le Cid* (1636), inspired by the life of the Cid Campeador, an eleventh-century Spanish hero.

p. 314, *Madelon*: See note to p. 48 above.

p. 316, *Cayenne*: Capital of French Guyana, a penal colony up to 1942.

p. 321, *La Bruyère*: Jean de La Bruyère (1645–96) was the moralist author of *Les Caractères*, a book of maxims and portraits of contemporary figures, which gained great popularity.

p. 341, *Seine-et-Oise*: At that time the immediate suburbs of Paris belonged to the Seine Department, which in turn was surrounded by a wider belt, also regarded as suburban – the Seine-et-Oise Department.

p. 342, *the Exposition*: The Exposition Universelle (World Exhibition) held in Paris in 1900.

p. 351, *bouchon*: A game once especially popular among Breton fishermen, in which coins or other valuables are placed on top of a large cork. Standing at some distance from it, the contestants toss disks; the player who first overturns the cork takes the coins.

p. 388, *Grand-Duc de Malvoison*: This is a take-off on the fancy names often given to poor-quality wines.

p. 391, *Café Miseux*: Suggests *miséreux*, meaning "seedy".